The Skaket Creek Inn
August 18th, 1968
7:52 a.m.

Bridget picked up the oddly shaped pieces one by one and turned them over in her hands. She held one up to the filtered morning light streaming in through the small semicircular window set high up in the basement wall. She shook her head and blew a stray wisp of jet-black hair from her eyes. Finally she turned back to Kathy Dawes standing in the doorway, leaning against the heavy oak door. An old fashioned brass key dangling from a faded, red velvet ribbon hung from her right hand.

"All right." Bridget sighed. "I give up. What are they?"

Before Kathy could answer, Mick asked quietly, "Do you remember what you asked me the first time we walked into the pub upstairs?"

Bridget glanced up at the heavy beams overhead that supported the pub's wooden floor. Yes, she remembered, the night before last. Had it really been so short a time? Time enough for their lives to be horribly changed. She gave a tiny, involuntary shudder and said, "Yes, I think so."

She frowned and tried to recall the exact words. "We'd just come in, and I was looking over at the bar, and there was a sign above it and... yes—the sign. I asked you what that word meant. Scrimshaw."

Mick nodded and pointed his right index finger to the yellowed, cream-colored object in Bridget's left hand. "There's your answer, babe," he said softly.

She stared at the object for a moment and then stepped back from one of a dozen heavy dark walnut cabinets that completely lined the cellar. She swept her gaze around the octagon-shaped room again. Cabinet after cabinet, and each one filled with dozens and dozens of the fantastically carved yellow, brown, and dusky-white ivory objects—a room directly under the bar, a locked room with but one small window. A room dedicated to and filled with hundreds of objects that gave the name to the pub above. Scrimshaw.

Bridget held the curved tooth of a long-dead sperm whale up to the dappled light let in by the basement room's single window and studied the thin black lines and the odd patterns that had been etched into the old ivory. She turned it over in her hands until she finally saw one recognizable shape in the intricate and vaguely disturbing patterns. A three-mast ship under full sail. It appeared to be running from a pursuing storm or a giant wave or a....

The room began to spin, and the yellowed piece of ivory fell from her fingers.

Reviews for *The Scrimshaw*

"a web of intrigue that ensnared me to read The Scrimshaw in one sitting... A wonderful tale of suspense and intricate sub-plots that at times had me on the edge of my seat..."

5 Flutes from Nutty Nana, Cocktail Reviews

Other books in print available at Wild Child Publishing:

Fade to Pale by James Cheetham
Iron Horse Rider by Adelle Laudan
Pervalism by M. E. Ellis
Quits by M. E. Ellis
The Thorazine Mirrorball by Jack Maeby
Weirdly: A Collection of Strange Tales by Various

Other McCarthy Family Mysteries by Ric Wasley:

Acid Test – 2004
Shadow of Innocence - 2007

The Scrimshaw

by

Ric Wasley

Wild Child Publishing.com
Culver City, California

The Scrimshaw
Copyright © 2008
By Ric Wasley
Cover illustration by Wild Child Publishing © 2008
For information on the cover art, please contact covervan@aol.com

This book is a work of fiction and any resemblance to any person, living or dead, any place, events or occurrences, is purely coincidental. The characters and story lines are created from the author's imagination or are used fictitiously.

Editor: M.E. Ellis

ISBN: 978-1-935013-37-2 – ebook, 978-1-935013-38-9 – paperback

Wild Child Publishing.com
P.O. Box 4897
Culver City, CA 90231-4897

Printed in The United States of America

Dedication

I would like to thank my family and friends, such as Joylene, Suzi and our "summer buddies", for their support and enthusiasm as well as many helpful suggestions while writing this book.

Would also like to thank my Editor-in-Chief, Marci, and my editor, Emmy, for all of their tireless work and expertise.

But most of all, I want to give my special thanks to my wife, Barbara, for her love and support for me and my writing each and every day.

The Scrimshaw

Scrimshaw – A carved artistic etching on whale teeth or bones.

Practiced for centuries by the native peoples along the Northwest Coast of North America, the art form was adopted by the Yankee whalers and sailors of the 1800s.

As a way to pass the time on long voyages, seamen and whalers turned to working with whale teeth and jawbones, all of which were in abundant supply.

The resulting curiosities and minor works of art were often traded to shopkeepers in port for goods or services.

The origin of the word is the subject of conjecture. One popular theory holds that the term originates from a Dutch phrase meaning "to waste one's time!"

Whatever the origin, until the practice died out with the decline of whaling in the 20th century, the hand carved and often amazingly intricately etched scrimshaws still retain the power even today, to give us a glimpse into a forgotten world.

There are others, however, who maintain that they retain the power to do more than that...much more.

* * * *

"Cape Cod girls they have no combs...heave away, haul away. They comb their hair with a whipperback bone; we are bound for Australia. Heave away, me bully, bully, boys...heave away, haul away. Heave away and don't you make a noise.... We are bound for Australia" (*)

* Nineteenth century whaling song

Prologue

Nantucket Harbor
April 14th, 1858

The sound of a thick-knotted piece of rope striking flesh cut through the ordinary shipboard noises of creaking timbers and flapping sails. Jeptha Dawes winced but instinctively turned towards the sound.

"Mr. Dawes!" a hoarse voice barked from the foredeck.

"Aye, Mr. Foster?" Jeptha turned and looked up at the red, salt-wind scoured face staring down at him.

"Tell those ham-fisted goat droppings from the starboard watch to haul in smart on the main brace before I come down there and lay about 'em with the rope's end."

Jeptha stared at the compact but brutal figure standing on the foredeck, smacking the knotted end of a flogging rope into the palm of his calloused hand.

"Aye, aye, Mr. Foster." The second mate of the *Elizabeth James* nodded, bringing the first knuckle of his right forefinger to the middle of his forehead. "I'll have 'em run out the jib while we warp up to the quay."

The first mate's lips curled up in a parody of a grin. "Mr. Dawes, you misunderstand me. They're to haul in and make fast all canvas in preparation to drop anchor."

Jeptha froze in mid-turn and looked back at the first mate. Though not quite as tall as Jeptha, the first mate out-weighed him by a good fifty pounds, and Jeptha had personally witnessed the brutal strength in those powerful hands when First Mate Ezra Foster had nearly beaten a man to death in a Shanghai bar. But on this last leg of the voyage home, the mate's explosive temper and the vindictive power of those hands had most often been used against the terrified crew of the *Elizabeth James*.

The snap of the rope made Jeptha jump.

"Have you gone deaf, Mr. Dawes?" Ezra Foster moved towards the steps leading down to the main deck. "I believe I gave you an order."

"But Mr. Foster—sir. Surely you don't mean to drop anchor here—at the harbor mouth and with the welcome lights of Nantucket Town not a half mile off."

"Aye, Mr. Dawes, that's exactly what I mean to do and I suggest you snap to it right smartly or I may have to use the rope's end on the starboard watch *and* the second mate of the *Elizabeth James*."

"Have a care, Mr. Foster, of how you use the name of my ship and my wife," a phlegmy voice spoke quietly but forcefully from the doorway of the captain's cabin.

The first mate slowly turned and looked at the pale, white face of the man dressed in a black frock coat and black silk neck stock leaning against the doorjamb of the cabin doorway for support.

"Beg your pardon, sir," the first mate replied with barely masked contempt, "I meant no disrespect."

The captain stared at the first mate; his eyes seemed to burn with a fire that consumed him from the inside out.

The east wind whipped lines that had suddenly gone slack as the crew paused in their duties to stare at the scene unfolding on the foredeck.

Finally, the first mate dropped his gaze to the holly-stoned deck planking and slowly touched his fingers to the brim of his salt-stained cap. "Beg your pardon—Captain."

Captain Palmer James, of the ship with the same last name, continued to stare at his second-in-command for a few more moments and leaned back heavily against the cabin doorframe. The fire in his eyes seemed to dim and then gradually flicker out like an old oil lamp fluttering out its last few flames.

The thin, deathly pale man dressed in the somber black of his long ago Puritan ancestors, staggered and gripped the doorframe for support.

"Stebbins!" the first mate yelled to the starboard watch.

One of the gang handling the ropes to the mainsail darted up to the foredeck and knuckled his forehead. "Aye, Mr. Foster, sir."

The first mate jerked his head in the captain's direction and said, "Help Captain James back to his cabin."

The forecastle hand stooped to brace the captain's arm with his shoulders, but the captain held up his hand. "Mr. Foster."

"Sir?"

"Why are we dropping anchor outside of the harbor entrance?"

The first mate raised his eyes to where the sun sunk into the slate-gray water and cast purple and blood-red streaks across the darkening sky.

"By the time we could warp up to the quay, sir, it would be pitch black and dangerous going on a moon-dark night."

Silence ensued, broken only by the sound of the waves lapping against the hull.

The first mate continued in a tightly controlled voice that almost, but not quite, masked the underlying condescension. "So I thought it best to wait until morning, sir, and—"

"And what, Mr. Foster?"

The shadow of a smirk hovered around the first mate's lips.

"And, well, I hoped that in the morning you might be feeling well enough to take her in yourself.... Sir."

The captain drew in a ragged breath and stared at the first mate again. "Yes," he said softly, "these past weeks you've made yourself virtual master of the *Elizabeth James*, haven't you?"

"It's only that you been feeling so poorly, sir," the first mate said, his face expressionless as he clasped his hands behind his back and stared at the darkening horizon.

"Yes—poorly!" the captain hissed; his remaining strength seemed to leak out of him with the words.

"Stebbins!" the first mate growled, "help the captain back to his bunk...now!"

Stebbins grabbed the captain's arm again, but Captain James pushed him away.

"No, Mr. Dawes will help me." The captain's hollow eyes locked on to Jeptha's, and he motioned him to come.

Jeptha skirted the first mate and stepped up next to the captain. "Here, Captain James, sir, lean on me."

Jeptha staggered as the captain's knees buckled and his entire weight fell on Jeptha's shoulders.

"Help me to my cabin, Mr. Dawes, but stay a bit. I need to have words with you."

Jeptha carefully helped the captain down the narrow passageway. This close to him, he felt the heat of fever sickness radiating off him like a coal stove. But even the heat of the captain's fever was nothing compared to the heat of the first mate's glare as his burning eyes followed him all the way down the dark corridor.

* * * *

"Close the door, Mr. Dawes."

Jeptha gently lowered the captain to the edge of his narrow, oak-carved bed frame and closed the door. He stood there, uncertain.

"Now bolt it," the captain rasped and sank down on the lumpy mattress letting his head fall back onto the pillow.

Jeptha threw the brass bolt. Uneasy, he shifted from one foot to the other and watched the captain painfully pull himself into a sitting position on the bed. He moved forward to help, but the captain held up a hand and shook his head. He pointed instead to a locked cabinet built into the framing timbers of the cabin's bulkhead. It had small, carved mahogany doors inset with colored glass and brass wire. It was also locked.

"In the top right hand cubby of my desk, you'll find a key on a red ribbon. The ribbon my wife took from her hair so I could attach it to the key." The captain paused and stared through the large stained-glass windows in his cabin at the twinkling lights of Nantucket Town winking across the harbor. "That last time she was here in my cabin, the evening before we sailed...nearly two years ago." The rasp in his voice became a whisper and trailed off.

Then silence as the captain appeared to grow mesmerized by the rhythmic creak of the ship's timbers while she slowly swung back and forth on her anchor cable.

Finally, Jeptha cleared his throat and, nervous, asked, "Captain—you said you wanted words with me, sir?"

The captain shifted his faraway gaze back to Jeptha and looked confused for a moment. Jeptha reached into the desk cubby and pulled out a bright red silk ribbon attached to a small brass key.

The captain seemed to gather strength and sat up straighter. "Yes," he snapped out with his old force of command. "Open the cabinet and bring me the log book."

Jeptha opened the cabinet and saw a thin book bound in green Moroccan leather with gold lettering. The letters read: *Log and Sea Journal of Capt. Palmer James, Master of the vessel Elizabeth James of Nantucket Town.*

"Bring it to me," the captain repeated.

Jeptha started to close the cabinet door.

"Wait." The captain motioned with his hand. "There's a bottle of brandy-wine on the first shelf. Bring that too."

Jeptha tucked the book under his arm, picked up the bottle, and crossed the room to the captain.

"Bring that chair and two glasses." The captain gestured at the shelf.

Jeptha pulled the chair up close to the captain's bed and handed him the logbook. He picked up one of the glasses and poured it half full of the amber liquor. "Sir," he said, handing it to the captain.

"Pour yourself one too, Mr. Dawes." Captain James took the glass and opened the logbook. "My upbringing was not one that countenanced strong spirits, but I think we will both have need of this with what I am about to tell you."

Jeptha nodded and lifted the glass of brandy to his lips but it went un-tasted. Captain James's eyes bored into his, and he said, "Second Mate Jeptha Dawes of the ship *Elizabeth James*. Pay close heed to what I'm about to tell you, and mark you this...that as your captain and lawful commander, I do charge you with a solemn and heavy burden." His eyes shone fever-bright again as they searched Jeptha's face. "Are you a good and true Christian man and do you love your neighbor and fear God's judgment?"

Jeptha swallowed hard and breathed out. "Aye, sir."

"Then heed me well, Mr. Dawes. That man on the foredeck, who calls himself First Mate Ezra Foster, must not be allowed to set foot in Nantucket Town."

"I-I don't understand, sir?"

Captain James reached out and grabbed onto Jeptha's right arm with surprising force and hissed, "He has taken control of the ship and is dropping anchor here, outside of the harbor, because he means this night to murder me, Mr. Dawes. In that, he may well succeed."

The captain slumped back onto his bunk for a moment, but appeared to gather strength and leaned his face close to Jeptha's. "That devil may end my life before the sun rises, but mark me well and heed my words, Mr. Dawes. If you fear for your immortal soul, he must never set foot off of this ship!"

Jeptha's hands trembled so violently that the liquid splashed out of his glass and onto the captain's Oriental rug.

"Here, Mr. Dawes," the captain said with the barest hint of a smile, "drink some of that before you ruin the rest of Mrs. James's good Turkey carpet that she gave me for this voyage and then listen and pay close heed to what I'm about to read to you."

He paused and looked at Jeptha. "Do you recall, Mr. Dawes, that day and some thirteen months ago when we first raised that island south by sou'west off of the Fiji chain?"

"Aye, sir." Jeptha nodded.

"Aye indeed," the captain muttered. "So that's where it all began."

The captain opened the thick, stiff paper of the leather bound logbook and began to read:

"*The third of March, 1857—eleven months and six days since we left Nantucket harbor in search of 'right' whales along with forty chests of trade goods to exchange for copra and spices amongst the natives of these islands.*

"*This morning, lookout spotted a small island three points off the larboard bow. The water casks showed signs of going foul, so we put in for fresh water and fruit and such other provisions as we could barter with the natives of this place.*

"*I took a small landing party ashore, accompanied by First Mate Foster, leaving Second Mate Dawes in charge of the ship. Once ashore, Mr. Foster suggested we split up—one half of us to go for water and the other to trade for food. While normally the captain would take charge of all negotiations, Mr. Foster told me he'd sailed through these islands three years ago and knew the lingo. So with some misgivings, I let him take the party up to the village. It was a grave error in judgment for which I have come to pay—dearly.*

"*When he returned to the longboat some hours later, his clothes*

13

were torn and bloody, and two of his men were missing. I immediately started towards the village to find them when a group, upwards of a hundred savages, came rushing upon us from out of the jungle. We had only one musket and two pistols among us, so to my shame and bitter regret, we were forced to take to the longboat and pull for the ship.

"Once on board, we saw that the natives were disinclined to abandon their pursuit and commenced to launch out-rigger canoes to take after us. Having no cannon and being greatly outnumbered, we had no choice but to weigh anchor and flee. In my anger, I called the first mate to my cabin and proceeded to question him sharply as to what transpired in that village."

The captain paused and looked up at Jeptha. "Do you know what transpired in that village, Mr. Dawes?"

Jeptha shrugged and said, "Only what I heard from Hancock and Morley, sir—two of the men who were with him. They said he got into an altercation with an old medicine man or village shaman."

The captain shook his head. "He took something from that village, Mr. Dawes. Something he had no right to. Something wicked, un-Christian, and unclean that he wears secreted upon his person day and night—a heathen talisman that hangs upon a chain about his neck."

The captain reached out and grabbed Jeptha by the arm again. His fever-bright eyes burned so fiercely that they looked as though they would ignite his face. He pulled Jeptha toward him and whispered, "Mr. Foster, and that thing he bears around his neck—an object I have come to realize is of great and terrible evil—a foul focus for...."

The captain suddenly gasped for breath and coughed violently into a white linen handkerchief he clutched in his left hand. He stared down at the handkerchief for a moment and slowly opened his hand. Bright red spots covered the white linen square of cloth.

The hot, shaking hand that still clenched Jeptha's arm became deathly still, and the captain stared at Jeptha with a gaze that would haunt him for many sleepless nights.

"Forgive me, Mr. Dawes." The captain closed his fist around the handkerchief and continued. "I must also confess that in my haste to secure the necessary supplies in the quickest way possible, so as to see my dear wife and home all the sooner, I was guilty of a shameful lack of judgment. I should have known that Foster had heard the rumors of the island and its legend of wealth and dark power."

Captain James looked through Jeptha, staring as if at some purgatory of his own making. He shook his head once more and looked back to Jeptha. "For that selfish error I am now reaping punishment in full measure." His body trembled as another spasm wracked him. "But it is not enough that I suffer. I must somehow endeavor to set things right. I must prevent this pestilence from reaching into the wide world." He raised a bloodstained finger and pointed towards the town nestled snugly against the edge of the harbor. "Do you see the lights of Nantucket town, Mr. Dawes?"

"Yes, sir."

"Do you see how they welcome and beckon?"

"Aye, Captain James."

The captain struggled to draw a breath. "My own dear wife Elizabeth lies sleeping in that town. And I cannot and will not allow any harm to come to her—nay, or anyone else due to the consequences of my own negligence." The captain clutched Jeptha's hand again. "Know that I care not for my own self or even what torment my soul must face. But I must not go to my grave before I have set things right—thus my need of you, Mr. Dawes, as my last and only hope!"

Jeptha swallowed and after a moment nodded. "Aye, Captain James, you've been like a second father to me, sir. Ask what you will, and I will do all in my power to help."

The captain stared at Jeptha with eyes like burning coals. "The First Mate, Ezra Foster, must never be allowed to leave this ship with that heathen abomination...alive."

Chapter One

Skaket Harbor
MA. Cape Cod
August 16th, 1968
5:37 p.m.

Mick smelled the salt air now. It rushed past his face at more than sixty mph as he wound the big metallic blue motorcycle down the center line of the Mid-Cape highway. Occasionally a driver coming from the other direction on the two lane blacktop road beeped or blinked his lights, and Mick leaned the bike an inch or two to the right and then slowly glided back into the center of the road. No sweat. The bike was like an extension of himself. He felt the road as the two knobby tires rolled over it.

Michael Prescott McCarthy drew in a deep breath. Yeah, there it was again, the smell of salt, sand, and scrub pine swirling all around him. A familiar shape behind him shifted her weight slightly and leaned forward, pressing her face against his right shoulder.

Not far now. The next exit up ahead, if he recalled correctly. A tap on his shoulder confirmed it. He shot a quick glance back at his girlfriend, Bridge—Bridget Connolly. She pointed to a green-and-white sign poking through the dusty late summer oak leaves.

SKAKET HARBOR – 2 MILES.

Mick nodded to her and smiled. He had to admit that he was really looking forward to kicking back with Bridge and just spending the next week chilling on the beach. He pictured the two of them lazing around the beach all day and sitting up on the long porch of that little inn they'd spotted the last time they were down here. Yeah, popping the tops on a couple of cold Schlitz and watching the sun go down over Cape Cod Bay.

He looked at the road up ahead and thought of how Bridget had forced the issue last night. Mick had made a promise to her the day after they'd barely escaped with their lives from a four-day nightmare, two weeks ago—the final violent exclamation point in an attempt to clear a friend of murder.

It had ended with a bloody confrontation and near fatal explosion, in a terror-filled cellar in Newport, RI. He had promised her that night as he lay bleeding in the ambulance that he—they—were getting out of the "detective" business for a while (even though they were only supposed to be doing it part time) and taking a break down by the warm waters of Cape Cod. And last night she had reminded him of that promise.

He smiled as he remembered how she'd stood there in the third floor walk-up they shared in Cambridge's Inman Sq., both hands planted on her hips. "You promised me, Michael Prescott McCarthy, that there would be no cases, no crime solvin', no corpses, and no crooks! No nothing but blessed peace and quiet—just you and me and the sea."

Well, she was right. That's what he'd promised his lover and best friend—and that's exactly what he intended to do. Besides—he grinned—a week or two lounging around a beach with the cutest little chick on either side of the Atlantic wasn't exactly what they'd have called 'tough duty' back in 'Nam.

Another tap on his shoulder snapped him out of his daydream. Yup, there it was. He clicked the foot-shift down into third as the exit sign loomed up ahead.

A loud whining roar ripped through the late afternoon heat haze, and the big blue motorcycle tilted right towards the exit. Bridget instinctively leaned slightly to counterbalance the bike's centrifugal force. A patch of wind-blown sand covering a three foot section of the exit road lay directly in front of them. But rather than brake for it, Mick goosed the throttle and slid the back tire through the sand in a showy, although controlled, skid. The bike inclined slightly left again, the back tire bit down on the hot asphalt, and the bike straightened out. He wound the bike down into first gear and gradually coasted past a sign that read: ENTERING TOWN OF SKAKET HARBOR.

The bike glided up to a blinking red stoplight, and he maintained just enough forward speed to keep it upright as they rolled slowly up to the light.

"Nice driving, McCarthy," Bridget said with a tone that was somewhere between admiration and exasperation.

Mick turned to look back at her. Her tone may have been a tad sarcastic, but her sea-green eyes shone with excitement. And despite her half-hearted denials, Mick knew that she was secretly somewhat of an adrenaline junkie.

"We aim to please, ma'am, and hey—I gottcha here in one piece, right?"

"I don't know, McCarthy, I haven't checked all the 'pieces' yet."

"Can I help?" Mick asked, matching her teasing smile.

"Stop playing games, McCarthy." Bridget lightly punched his back. "I'm tired, hot, and dirty, and I just want to get into a nice cool bath or have a lovely dip in the sea or maybe both."

"Well keep your mind on those last two items, and I'll take you anywhere you want to go." Mick grinned as he feathered the handgrip throttle, sending a ripple of vibration through the frame of the 650cc machine.

"What?" Bridget asked distractedly, bending forward again. "You mean that you want a cool bath and a swim in the ocean too?"

"Ah...no." He turned his head until his lips brushed hers. "I meant the part about you being 'hot and dirty'."

Bridget pulled her head back. "Michael Prescott McCarthy! I swear fer a lad not yet gone twenty-three, you've the makings of a nasty, dirty old man!"

"Guess you just bring out the old goat in me, babe." He grinned back over his shoulder. "What...?" he asked, still grinning.

She edged forward again and startled him by darting her hummingbird-quick little tongue between his lips.

His grin became even wider, and he tilted his head backwards, but she moved away and settled back on to the bike's rear seat. She took a tiny compact from the pocket of her suede jacket and reapplied her pale pink lipstick. Then she looked up at him with a small, teasing hint of unspoken possibility.

"Well, you find me that seaside inn with the cool bath and lovely ocean, McCarthy, and you just may find out...'what'."

Mick's smile widened from amusement to an ear-to-ear grin that hid a whole host of "hot-and-bothered" possibilities. Maybe that's why he wasn't really paying much attention when he gunned the BSA, snapped the footgear into first, and leaned the bike left with a partial wheelie through the blinking red light. So when he heard the sound of a siren ten seconds later, he wasn't really surprised and all he could say was: "Shit!"

"Hush up, Mickey," Bridget hissed in his ear. "Maybe you better let me do the talking."

"Suit yourself, babe," Mick shrugged, "but you know some of these smalltown cops down here can get real pissy."

"I'll just give him me County Cork smile," Bridget whispered back.

Mick shrugged again as the driver's side door of the black-and-white squad car opened and a skinny young cop got out and walked towards them. The cop, who looked no older than Mick, strolled up to them, hooked his thumbs in his belt, and stared at them over the top of his silver-tinted sunglasses.

There was something about this guy that gave Mick that little "crawling feeling"—the one he used to get on recon missions in 'Nam. That sense of "wrongness"—bad news on two legs. Something that made his internal warning lights all start flashing red. Maybe it was the way his mouth was set in a sneer. Or the way he kept pushing the silver-tinted sunglasses up and down on his nose. Like he wanted to get a better look at them but didn't want them to see him doing it. Or maybe it was the way he kept fiddling with the butt of his .38 sticking out of the holster—like he was just itching for the day that he could actually take it out of the holster and use it. But mostly, it was the way he kept staring at Bridget. Like a junkyard rat eyeing a particularly tasty morsel.

"Okay, pal, lemme see ya license and registration."

While Mick pulled his wallet out of his back pocket, the deputy continued staring at Bridget. Mick reached out to the deputy with the required papers, but he seemed more interested in staring at Bridget than in looking at what Mick held in his hand. Mick watched the deputy's face—and he didn't like what he saw. He'd seen that look in one form or another on the face of dozens of guys whenever she walked into a room. Sometimes when they were just crossing a crowded street or waiting at the Harvard Sq. T stop. Most of the time it was pretty harmless and even a little flattering—to Bridget, and to the guy who was lucky enough to be on the receiving end of *those* looks back from her. But sometimes Mick caught one of *those* looks coming from a guy who wasn't harmless and didn't mean well.

This was one of those times.

Mick's eyes narrowed, and he felt the old scar that ran the length of his jaw straighten into a thin white line.

"You wanted to see my papers," Mick said in a tone that was as tightly controlled as he could make it.

The deputy realized that Mick was studying him. Slowly, he tore his eyes away from Bridget and took the papers Mick still held out to him.

"Where ya off to in such a hurry, pal?"

Before Mick could answer, Bridget flashed her best hundred-watt smile, lowered her long black lashes, and said in an exaggeration of her lilting County Cork brogue, "I'm so sorry, Officer. I'm afraid I was just rattlin' on something awful in his ear and musta distracted the poor lad."

The deputy shifted his gun belt and looked at Bridget with that hungry rat look again.

"Hummm. Yeah—I can see how that might have an effect, missy."

Bridget's smile wavered around the edges. She looked at Mick.

Yeah, looks like that little bit of sweet talking might have not been such a good idea in this case.

The cop finally gave Mick's license and registration a quick glance.

"Cambridge, huh? Like where Ha-a-avard and all them high-class schools is. Whaddaya, some kind of college boy, then?"

"Yeah." Mick nodded. "Something like that—by way of Vietnam."

The deputy pushed his sunglasses down on his nose and stared at Mick. The cop's gaze touched his for a moment, glanced over at Bridget, and dropped back to Mick's license. "Okay, pal, I'm gonna let it slide this time, but keep a leash on this thing while you're in Skaket Harbor. Where are you staying?" His eyes focused back on Bridget.

"I-I mean, we-we're looking for an inn that we saw when we were down in Brewster two weeks ago," Bridget said. "It's got a big porch in the front and white shingles and is right on the beach."

The deputy's smile morphed into that of the junkyard rat whose tasty meal had just decided to plop itself right down in front of him. "Yeah, I know the place—the Skaket Creek Inn. Follow the beach road all the way to the end and you can't miss it."

Mick nodded once, flipped the lever down on the bike's recoil starter, and slid the sole of his boot forward until the lever rested between his boot's instep and heel.

The cop moved closer to the motorcycle, all the while staring at Bridget. The pressure of her arms tensed around Mick's waist.

"So, you two are gonna get a room, right?"

"That's the plan."

"Just one room?"

"Yeah."

The sneer became a smirk. He rubbed an old acne scar on his jaw. "Yeah, I'll bet you got some real *fun times* planned. You some of them *free love* hippies they got up in Boston at all those colleges? You know, the ones who go out protesting all day and then play on their guitars, smoke their pot, and bang all them hot hippie chicks. You one of them, Mr. Michael P. McCarthy from Cambridge?"

Bridget's hand squeezed a warning on Mick's left arm. He drew a deep breath. "No, Deputy Douglas Frost of the Skaket Harbor Police," Mick read off of the ID tag pinned to the gray uniform, "I did all of my protesting while I was in 'Nam. And it was against a nasty little guy we called Charlie. I kept protesting against him constantly trying to slip a bayonet into my guts or an AK round into my head."

"Think you're a tough guy 'cause you spent a year or two playing soldier?"

"No, Deputy. It wasn't playing. I actually learned how to use that thing on your hip that you keep fiddling with."

The deputy dropped his hand from the butt of his pistol and flushed for a moment. He looked at Mick and then at Bridget. The sneer turned nasty.

"So what about you, missy? Does your soldier boy keep you happy or does he pass you around the way they do them joints at your sex and pot *love-ins*, hum?"

"You goddamn fuc—"

Mick was off the bike and reaching for the Deputy, but Bridget grabbed onto his arm and wouldn't let go. Deputy Frost took a step backwards, scrabbling at the snap holding his .38 in its holster.

Mick had pulled Bridget half off the bike before he realized he that he hadn't put the kickstand down and the bike was about to topple over and take Bridget with it. He turned back, pushed it upright, and savagely jabbed the kickstand down. He raised his right fist, turned back to the deputy, and found himself staring down the barrel of a .38 Police Special.

"Yeah, tough guy—go ahead and try it."

"Mickey, please! Please—let's just go."

"Hold on there, missy, he's not going anywhere except maybe to jail."

"But he didn't do anything! He didn't even touch you. He...he just saw that I was going to let the motorcycle fall so...so he jumped off to catch it. That's all!"

Deputy Douglas Frost pushed the silver-tinted sunglasses back up his nose until they completely covered his eyes again. Finally he said, "That the way it was, soldier boy?"

Bridget looked up at Mick. He knew that she was as mad as he was but she was sucking it up. He wouldn't do her any good in jail, so he was going to have to suck it up too.

"Yeah, that's the way it was."

The deputy smirked and put the .38 back in his holster. "Well then, I guess I'll just let you two little flower children be on your way."

"Yeah," Mick muttered, "far away from here." He jammed his foot down on the recoil starter. The engine rumbled and caught. He clicked the foot shift into first.

"Oops. Hold on there, soldier boy. I almost forgot. You coasted through a red light." The deputy had his ticket book out and scribbled on it with a ballpoint pen. "Yeah, we can't have all you hippies coming down here on your cycles and breaking all of our traffic laws now, can we?"

He ripped off the ticket and handed it to Mick. "Traffic court is held eight a.m. to noon every Monday. Let's see...it's Thursday today, so I guess you better find some place to relax until Monday. You wouldn't want to miss court, would you? Then we'd have to issue a warrant for you, and your next vacation would be in one of our jail cells."

Bridget's fingers closed on Mick's arm again, so he clenched his teeth and kept his mouth shut.

"Well, you said you were looking for the Skaket Creek Inn, so there's a nice place to stay until Monday. You just tell 'em that Deputy Dougie sent you. They'll trot out the red carpet for you." He hooked his thumbs in his belt and laughed.

As Mick slowly let the clutch out and the bike picked up speed, he heard, "You two have a nice day now. Peace and love!"

21

The Scrimshaw

* * * *

"Stop!" Bridget yelled, half rising off of the bike's back foot rests and leaning forward until her cheek rested next to his. "This is it!"

Mick pressed down on the footbrake and eased the BSA to a stop in front of a three-story white shingle structure fronted by a long porch facing the beach across the street.

She slipped off the back of the motorcycle and walked a few paces up a red-brick walk to a white-picket gate, set between a hedge of beach plums and primroses.

Mick swung his right leg over the motorcycle's frame and eased the heavy bike down onto its kickstand. He walked up behind Bridget and put his arms around her, nestling his chin on her shoulder. Bridget turned around and rested her hand on his arm, pulling him around 180 degrees until he stood next to her. They stared out at a wide expanse of golden sand beach where low-tide puddles shimmered in the late day sun.

Bridget stood on tiptoes and stretched both of her arms over her head, inhaling the salt air. She looked out over the ocean and sighed. "Umm. Lovely, McCarthy, eh?"

Mick didn't say anything, content to just watch her and think for the thousandth time how damn lucky he was to have walked into Cambridge's Club 47 folk music cafe that night over a year ago. They'd been together ever since and now they were back on the Cape with no plan other than to let a few days of sun and surf wash away the hassles of the past three weeks. At least until they'd met up with Deputy "Dougie".

Mick shook his head. Damn it, all they wanted was to wash away the memories of the near fatal attempt to clear one of Mick's old army buddies of murder just two weeks ago. Mick tried to push that memory back down into the cobwebs of his brain along with all those other nasty images he kept locked up in his personal dark closet.

Bridget, still looking at the water, said, "Mickey, I was proud of you back there."

"Proud? How the hell could you be proud of me? Just sitting there and letting that bastard get away with what he said! I don't give a shit what he calls me, but you...I wanted to rip the bastard's throat out!"

"But you didn't. And that's why I'm proud. I'm proud because you love me enough to do something that was the hardest thing in the world for you to do—walk away. And because you did, I've got you all to myself for the next four days instead of talking to you through the bars of some jail cell."

Mick breathed out and nodded.

"And darlin'?"

"Yeah, Bridge?"

"Promise me that you're gonna forget all about it—at least until Monday. And that the only thing you're gonna think about is me and that lovely blue ocean."

"And can I maybe spare a thought or two for a big plate of fried clams?"

She smiled at him, and her eyes sparkled again. "As long as you don't forget which one you want to spend the night with."

"Zero chance of that, babe." Mick grinned back.

Bridget leaned over and kissed him, then brushed her short black hair out of her eyes and took his hand again.

She pulled Mick around until they both faced the large rambling white structure with a carved signboard that read: SKAKET CREEK INN – LODGING & MEALS – VACANCY.

"Shall we see if they have a nice room with a cool bath overlooking the ocean?" Bridget smiled again and took his hand as they started up the brick walkway.

Mick put his hand on the green painted screen door and opened it for Bridget. As he did, out of the corner of his eye he noticed a flash—a flash of silver. He turned and looked down the sandy beach road to the parking lot and town landing. There the deputy stood, with his silver fish eyes, staring at them. Mick stared back for a moment. No—he'd promised Bridget. He shook his head.

As the screen door closed, Mick took one more glance back at the parking lot. The cop leaned against the cruiser's door and raised his right hand with the first two fingers formed into a V.

Peace.

Chapter Two

Skaket Creek Inn
Skaket Harbor, MA
August 16th, 1968
6:42 p.m.

For a moment Mick felt almost blind. Stepping into the dim interior of the inn from the blaze of the sinking sun had the effect of making the entire lobby seem to be coated in thick brown gauze. Still holding on to Bridget's hand, he groped his way to what he assumed was the registration desk. He rubbed his eyes and glanced around—no one there.

"Mickey. Look, there's a bell."

Mick looked to where Bridget pointed towards the right of a large registration book lying open on the desk. A faded, hand lettered piece of cardboard lay taped under an old-fashioned bell-hop style bell.

Please ring bell once for service.

Mick shrugged and slapped his palm down on the bell. They waited. Nothing. He turned to Bridget and raised his eyebrows. She nodded, and his hand came down on the bell again.

"That was one time too many! What's the matter, are you blind or can't you read or do you think I'm deaf? Well?"

Mick took a quick step back, and Bridget gave a startled yelp.

He rubbed his eyes again, and a face finally became visible poking out from the shadows behind the registration desk. He was glad that he wasn't eight years old—the age he'd first seen *The Wizard of Oz*—'cause if he was, he'd have run screaming from the inn after seeing a dead ringer for Dorothy's munchkin-thumping nemesis materialize out of the gloom.

"Jeeze, lady. You scared the sh—ah, I mean, we didn't see you standing back there."

"Obviously," she snorted. "Well, what do you want?"

"And a gracious good afternoon to you too," Mick muttered.

"What was that?"

Mick had spent enough summers hanging out on the Cape to recognize the harsh nasal Yankee twang that had evolved over three-hundred years of living in old time Yankee independence and isolation.

"Ummm...I said we'd like a room."

As Mick waited to see what sort of reaction that request would

24

bring from the old biddy glowering at them, he thought about how for more than three centuries the farmers, sailors, and fishermen who had put down roots in the sandy soil had been content to eke out a living in sullen but self-sufficient seclusion. That is until they discovered something that was far more lucrative than corn and cod.... Tourism!

And even though the locals soon found themselves making money faster than they could count it, a lot of the Cape's original families or "First-Comers" as they called themselves, didn't like it. And from where Mick stood, it looked like the crabby old lady most definitely fell into the category of those who didn't like it. In fact, she typified the sort of love/hate relationship that many of the old-timers had with the tourists. They loved their money but they hated them.

"So you two are married, then?" the woman behind the desk of the Skaket Creek Inn snapped.

Bridget, who had been born without Mick's natural talent of bullshit at short notice, drew in a single panicked breath and opened her mouth only to shut it just as quickly as Mick smiled at the woman with his best disarming, boyish smile.

"Well, Miss...?"

"It's Mrs. Mrs. Helen Dawes," she said without answering his smile. "Although only by marriage, thank God."

"Well, Mrs. Dawes—although you must have been a child bride," Mick continued.

The frown remained fixed.

I'm selling, but she sure as hell isn't buying.... The big smile he wore started to set into his face like rigor mortis.

"Well, you see, Mrs. Dawes, it's this way," Mick said, leaning forward and lowering his voice conspiratorially, "my wife and I...."

Mick was sure the scowling Mrs. Dawes heard Bridget's gasp of astonishment, and her beady little crow's eyes seemed to fasten on Bridget's left hand as she guiltily pulled it off of the registration desk's worn countertop.

The woman's eyes bored into Bridget's for another moment before she turned back towards Mick and said, "Married—then where are your rings?"

"Well," Mick answered smoothly, though small beads of sweat formed on his upper lip, "as a matter of fact, that's exactly why we're here!"

"Oh really?" she said sarcastically and sorted through a stack of mail.

"Yeah," Mick said, putting his arm around the now thoroughly mortified Bridget. She gave Mick a look that said, "You better not if you know what's good for you!" But Mick seldom did. *And besides, I'm in too deep to back out now.*

"You see, me and my little lady here kind of eloped. And, well, it all happened so fast that we didn't even have time to get a ring. Did we, babe?"

Bridget's right foot began the all too familiar tapping that usually preceded a very frank and often quite pointed description of her boyfriend's lack of judgment.

"So," Mick continued, giving Bridget's tense shoulders a "hang-in-there" squeeze, "we were passing by your charming little inn on our way up to P-Town to get ourselves—guess what?"

"A big fat striped bass," she answered flatly.

"No," Mick went on and for the first time thought that he'd finally come up against an impervious wall to the usually irresistible McCarthy BS. "We've got this friend up there who's a dynamite jeweler. You know, does all kinds of handcrafted stuff in silver and gold. And he's gonna make us a couple of wicked cool wedding rings."

"Is he a *Nancy Boy*?" she shot back. "They all are up there."

For once, Mick was speechless. "I-ah-well...."

"Aunt Helen!"

The old woman turned her head in annoyance towards a pretty gold-and-auburn-haired girl who stood in the doorway to the inn's small back office.

"That's terrible thing to say, Aunt Helen!"

"Well, they all are, you know," she muttered.

The girl walked up to the older woman and put a hand on her shoulder. "You've been up since six a.m., Aunt Helen. Why don't you go help Mom upstairs and let me finish up here?"

The older woman still focused her accusing stare on Mick, who tried to decide if he was going to be bewildered, amused, or pissed—or possibly a combination of all three. Bridget looked like she had already made up her mind, and the verdict was: pissed.

"Aunt Helen," the soft voice said again. "Please?"

The old woman's pinched face seemed to relax for a moment but quickly snapped back into hostility as she spat, "Well, they all are queer as three dollar bills up in Provincetown, and if those two are married, then I'm one too!" She returned to sorting mail.

"Mickey.... Oh, forget it, let's just go," Bridget said with disgust and pulled at his sleeve.

Mick's forced good cheer had already begun to fray around the edges, and the old lady's last remark just about tore it as far as he was concerned. So he turned back and said, "Well, if you want to know the truth, we'd be just as happy splitting from your crummy little seaside mortuary if we hadn't had the misfortune to meet up with one of Skaket Harbor's *finest*."

The old lady stopped sorting the mail and looked up. "Who?"

"His name was Deputy Douglas Frost," Bridget said in a tone that left no doubt as to her feelings.

"Yeah." Mick put his arm around Bridget's shoulder. "And he said to tell you that Deputy Dougie sent us and you'd roll out the red carpet. And you know something? This is just about the kind of red-carpet treatment that I'd expect from anyone recommended by *Deputy Dougie.*"

The effect on the old woman was electric. She let the neat stack of bills and magazines she was sorting slip into an untidy jumble on the desk. She slowly wiped her hands on her apron and said, "Oh, well.... Well, you should have said something. Well, if Deputy Frost is vouching for you...well maybe I can find something for you up on the third floor, near the back. It's not fancy, but then again I don't suppose that you two—"

"Aunt Helen! That's where the bartenders and kitchen staff stay!"

"C'mon, Bridge, I'd rather sleep on the beach than stay here with that old bat."

Mick started to turn towards the door, but the slender girl with sunset hair came around from behind the counter and stood in front of them.

"Hey, guys, please don't go. Oh, wow, I mean, I can hardly blame you. I know that my aunt can be a real pain sometimes, but she means—"

"Means what?" Mick asked.

"I was gonna say 'she means well', but to tell you the truth, she probably doesn't. Yeah," she sighed, "she can be a real old witch sometimes."

"I was thinking about another word that rhymes with it but probably fits her better," Bridget muttered.

The girl broke into a bright easy laugh and said, "You know, you're probably right." She looked at them and winked. "Come on, how about if we trot out the Honeymoon Suite for you."

Bridget blushed, but the girl leaned towards her and gave her a quick girl-to-girl hug and whispered, "Hey, sister—after all, it is 1968!"

"Right on!" Bridget smiled weakly.

"And I tell you what," the girl continued, stepping back from behind the registration desk counter, "just to make up for my auntie's 'welcome', I want you both to be our guest tonight."

"For what?" Mick answered. "Is your aunt gonna boil us along with the lobsters and the clams?"

"No!" The girl smiled, stifling a giggle as she passed Mick the frayed old register book to sign. "It's Friday night, so we have live music in the taproom. Usually there's a three-dollar cover charge, but tonight I want you to be our guests."

"Yeah?" Mick said, still suspicious. "And what makes you think that the Wicked Witch of the West up there will go along with it?"

"Because," the girl answered, leaning forward and putting her elbows on the counter, "I just happen to be in very tight with one half of the show's starring act, Kathy and Karen."

Her smile widened, and she stuck out her hand. "Hi guys. I'm Kathy Dawes."

Chapter Three

The Skaket Creek Inn
Skaket Harbor, Cape Cod
August 16th, 1968
8:22 p.m.

"If you're looking for dinner you're too late." The grouchy old lady who had been behind the reception desk that afternoon had resumed her station. Her   sharp chin and thin, pursed lips pointed in the direction of the inn's small dining room. She hadn't bought or approved of Mick and Bridget's fabrication to explain their current cohabitation in a sunny front room on the second floor overlooking Cape Cod Bay. And the passing of a few hours had most definitely not modified her feelings.

"And it's nice to see you again too, Mrs. Dawes."

She snorted. "And you're still too late."

"Oh," Mick said, putting on his best noncommittal smile, "what time do you stop serving?"

"Eight-thirty sharp!" she snapped. "So the dining room is closed!"

"No it isn't, Auntie," a voice from the far end of the dining room called. "For Heaven's sake, we serve dinner until eight-thirty, and the kitchen doesn't even close until the bar stops serving at eleven p.m.," said Kathy, the cute girl with the auburn/blonde hair that had stood up for them earlier that afternoon. "They can sit in the pub and order, and I'll serve them personally."

"When your mother hears about this she sure as certain won't approve of—"

"But why should she hear, Auntie? She's had enough sadness and responsibility thrust on her without any more needless worries."

The older woman's eyes narrowed as she looked at her niece and sneered, "You've taken a very free hand in the operation of that pub, young missy. In my opinion, much too free a hand, and if I had my way...."

The twenty-year-old locked her eyes on those of her aunt's and answered back in a soft voice underlined with steel, "But you don't, Aunt. I do."

Her aunt opened her mouth in response but paused and clamped it shut again. She shook her head and moved out of the doorway.

"Do what you will, my smug little miss. But just you keep in mind that your mother—my sister-in-law—went tripping through these very halls thirty years ago spreading her vision of sweetness and light." She stared at her niece with a knowing glare and finished triumphantly, "and just you go upstairs and look at her now!"

The young girl paled and shot back at the older woman, "No, Aunt, I'll leave those dark dreams of hopelessness and bitterness and...curses, to you. I'm not ready or willing to bury myself in this place yet."

Kathy took Bridget by one hand and Mick by the other and pulled them through the small dark dining room towards the noisy smoke-filled pub beyond saying, "C'mon guys, we've got fried clams and fish and chips in here—and tonight they're on the house!"

As Kathy chattered away to Bridget, Mick dropped behind a step and turned to look back into the front lobby. He stood in the shadows of the dining room and watched Helen Dawes pick up the receiver of the black rotary dial phone on the desk. Mick waited while she dialed. Something about the woman bothered Mick. Oh, sure, she was a cranky old bitch. But it went beyond that. She obviously hated everything and everybody—including her niece and sister-in-law who appeared to own the place.

So why had she been so hostile to him and Bridge from the moment they'd walked in? It seemed to go beyond them being young, or maybe looking like hippies. She had acted like she wanted them to go even before she found out they weren't married. And while Mick knew that a lot of the old timers in the more remote little towns on the end of the Cape might be old fashioned, they all still needed tourist dollars to survive. So why was she trying to turn away business before they'd even spoken to her? What's more, she didn't even own the place. It didn't add up. What was it that his old man, ex-Boston cop, "Big Mike", always said about things that didn't add up and week-old-mackerel...? They all smelled fishy. *Yeah, might also want to give Pop a call and have him do a quick check on "Deputy Dougie".* And, that's right, the old witch had suddenly changed her tune big time when they'd mentioned that bastard's name.

Hmmm, I wonder who old Aunt Helen is calling.

Someone had answered on the other end, and she spoke into the phone. Mick strained to listen, but she turned around facing the wall and cupped one hand close to the mouthpiece.

Shit!

Keeping his back to the wall, Mick edged closer to the lobby. He tried to slow his breathing and focus on listening. He could just barely hear her.

She said, "Well, all I'm saying is that you better tell him that...."

A hand brushed Mick's shoulder, and he spun around, his right forearm whipping up and knocking the hand away while his left arm straightened and his hand closed around the slender neck of... Bridget?

Her eyes opened wide with fright, and she choked out, "Mickey!"

Mick's left hand immediately dropped away from her throat, but a split second later he clamped it over her mouth just as she began to scream, "What the bloody hell are you...?"

"Shsshh. Quiet, Bridge, she'll hear you and.... Ow!"

Mick pulled his hand away from Bridget's mouth and looked at the tiny circular red mark in the center of his palm, left by her small, perfect, and very sharp teeth.

"And that's what ya get, McCarthy, fer shovin' yer paw in me face like that." She hissed, "What the hell are you doing?"

Helen Dawes turned around and looked towards the dining room door.

Crap!

He pushed Bridget through the dim dining room towards the noise and smell of beer and fried food coming from the pub.

"Answer me, McCarthy!" Bridget whirled around and put her hands on her hips. Mick paused just long enough to lift her on to her tiptoes and plant a big kiss on her angry lips. Her mouth relaxed slightly, and her lips parted. "I'm waiting, McCarthy."

Mick smiled. "For what—an explanation or another kiss?"

"Well, I guess you'll just have to figure that out then, won't you, lad?"

Mick kissed her on the nose and said, "You've got yourself a deal, Miss Connolly—just as soon as we polish off a basket or two of those fried clams."

They walked through the beaded curtain that led to the pub, and the glass beads tinkled as they dropped back into place.

* * * *

From the other side of the shadowy dining room, Helen Dawes walked back to the registration desk and picked up the phone again. She cupped her hand around the mouthpiece once more and said, "Yes, it was exactly who I thought it was." She nodded to the phone unconsciously. "Yes—those two."

Chapter Four

The Scrimshaw Pub
The Skaket Creek Inn
Skaket Harbor
Cape Cod, MA
August 16th, 1968
9:36 p.m.

"So how was everything?" Kathy smiled as she cleared away the wax paper lined wicker basket, littered with just a few golden brown scraps of fried cod, clams, and French fries.

"Oh, it was grand, luv!" Bridget answered. "I don't think I've had fish and chips that good since The Boar's Head Pub in Dublin."

"Yeah, and those clams were far out too," Mick said, following up the compliment with what started out as a polite burp but ended as a huge belch.

"McCarthy!" Bridget cried out, genuinely embarrassed. Her cheeks glowed bright crimson, and she looked up at Kathy who, by now, used both of her hands to stifle her laughter.

"Hey, no sweat guys," she laughed.

"But he does know better," Bridget said and glared at Mick. "He grew up in a grand house on Brattle Street in Cambridge—went to Andover and Harvard!" She continued accusingly, "And he most certainly knows better!"

"I'm very sorry for my bad manners, Mommy," Mick replied with a mock-innocent grin and then added with equal amounts of mock piety and pedantry, "And, that expensive and exclusive education also taught me that in Arab countries a generous belch at the end of a good meal is considered to be the highest of compliments. So please take this as heartfelt appreciation of your magnificent cuisine, Miss... Dawes, right?"

"Just Kathy," she said and smiled. She gave the table a final wipe with her cloth and picked up the tray.

"Wait—can we buy you a drink to show our appreciation?"

"Maybe later," she called over her shoulder as she headed for the kitchen. "Right now, we've got to get ready for the entertainment."

"What kind of music?" Mick called back.

She paused at the kitchen doors, half turned, and said, "Folk music—lots of old sea shanties and a few original songs too. Some are kinda sad and some are almost spooky." She pushed the swinging door open and just before it closed, said softly with a shy smile, "But I hope you like them."

* * * *

"You want another beer, Bridge?"

Bridget didn't answer for a moment. Instead, she took a small sip of the last of her Papst Blue Ribbon beer and looked around the noisy pub room.

"You know, Mickey, in some ways this is similar to the pubs back home." She pointed to the dark walnut bar that ran the length of the far wall and the old, exposed oak ceiling beams. "But in other ways it's quite different. First of all, there are all of those fishing nets festooned with their cork and glass ball floats. Hurummp, no self-respecting publican would let a bunch of fisherman bring their dirty old nets into his place of business." She raised her eyes to the letters carved into a broken driftwood plank that hung above the bar. She studied the word etched into the weathered old piece of driftwood and turned back towards Mick with a puzzled frown. "Mickey, what does 'scrimshaw' mean?"

* * * *

The Scrimshaw Pub
Skaket Creek Inn
Cape Cod, Mass
August 16ᵗʰ, 1968
9:39 p.m.

Mick shook his head and leaned closer to Bridget to hear her question again over the noise of the bar. "I'm sorry, babe, what was that?"

"I said, Mickey," Bridget repeated, "what does 'scrimshaw' mean?"

"Scrimshaw?" Mick answered distractedly, his gaze focused on the pub's small stage where one of the busboys arranged two small stools around a single microphone and stand. "Why, are you thinking of opening up a whaling museum?"

Instead of responding, Bridget reached over the table and put her forefinger on the side of his jaw, gently turned his head away from the stage and back towards the long bar. "There," she said and pointed to the driftwood plank sign hanging over the bar.

"Ah," Mick said, leaning back in his chair. "Which one would you like, the dictionary version, the folk art version, or the historical version?"

"How about the 'short' version."

"Well," Mick placed his hands behind his head, his voice taking on a faintly 'professorial' tone, "It's actually an art form that has its roots in

Neolithic Europe—when Cro-Magnon man began etching pictures and symbols on pieces of bone and animal tusks...."

Bridget blew a stray strand of hair away from her left eye and sighed. "I said, the short version, McCarthy."

"Humph." Mick shook his head while letting the chair's front legs settle back to the floor. "And you're the one who's always after me to put my Harvard education to better use."

"Mickey...!" Bridget's voice took on a dangerously exasperated tone.

"Okay, okay." Mick smiled and held up his hand in mock surrender. "The most common reference to scrimshaw centers around the carvings sailors did on the teeth of the whales they killed. Although it was most commonly practiced on whaling ships, sailors on all types of ships from merchant men to naval vessels made it a hobby, an art form, a way to pay for a few drinks from the early 18th century all the way up until whaling all but died out at the turn of this century."

Bridget looked up at the signboard again and then back at Mick with another puzzled frown. "But I still don't understand," she said, shaking her head. "What does that have to do with pubs? Why is this place called the Scrimshaw Pub?"

Mick looked around and realized she was right.

"You got a point, babe," he agreed and shrugged, "nary a whale bicuspid in sight. So we'll just have to ask Kathy the next time we see her. Which, unless I miss my guess," he turned back to the small stage, "ought to be right about...now."

The bartender reached back to a small panel of switches set to the left of the bar's smoke-filmed mirror and turned a knob. The overhead lights around the stage dimmed. He flicked another switch, and a small pink spotlight lit up the two stools and the microphone stand. The level of conversation, laughter, and clinking glasses seemed to die down for a moment as the people in the crowded pub began turning towards the stage. There was a brief pause—almost like an intake of a collective breath—and two girls walked up onto the stage.

Their new friend and protector from the Wicked Witch of the Front Desk carried an autoharp which she lay across her left arm while she settled gracefully onto one of the two stools.

The other girl—Mick tried not to stare and surreptitiously checked to make sure that his jaw wasn't hanging open—was just plain drop dead gorgeous!

No, strike that. This chick must have been who Jimi Hendrix had in mind when he sang Foxy Lady. She had long, straight, almost platinum-blonde hair. Electric blue eyes, and a body that....

"Down boy!" Mick was snapped out of his momentary daydreams as Bridget added, "Pull your tongue back in, lad, you're drooling on the table."

Mick gave a guilty start and smiled. "Momentary lapse, babe. Hey, I was really just thinking that she's not bad looking—for a blonde. Why, change that blonde hair to jet-black, and she might even be almost half as cute as you!"

Bridget rolled her eyes. "It's getting deep in here, McCarthy."

"No really, I—"

"Shush, Mickey, we're about to find out if your bleached blonde *beauty* can sing—or if all that peroxide has bleached her brain as well as her hair."

Mick started to open his mouth and then remembered what his old South Boston cop father had always told him: "Once yer big mouth has dug yourself a hole, don't make it any deeper by opening it again."

So Mick shut it—tight.

And the two girls started to sing.

Mick was mesmerized—along with every other male in the room under the age of eighty. Their combined voices had a strange, hauntingly sweet quality that seemed to hark back to an earlier America, a time before records and movies and TV. A time when the songs sung had come from the villages of England, the hills and moors of Scotland, and the long-suffering, green, mist-shrouded land called Ireland.

Mick recognized the first song from his prep school nights spent hanging out in the early days of one of the East Coast's best folk music clubs, the Club 47. A song that had traveled from the stone walls of New England to the split-rail fences of Appalachia.

"Oh, I'll pawn you my gold watch and chain, love. I will pawn you my bright diamond ring. I will pawn you this heart in my bosom, only say that you'll love me again."

The song finished with a flourish of guitar and autoharp as the smoky barroom erupted into applause.

Karen nodded to the audience and leaned closer to the microphone. "Here's another song—a song with local origins, in fact. They say that more than a hundred years ago, something happened in this inn, in this very room. Love, lust, jealousy, greed, and...." She paused dramatically. "Murder."

The two girls began to play.

* * * *

The Scrimshaw Pub
Skaket Harbor
Cape Cod

The Scrimshaw

The long, sad ballad was winding to a close. The two girls lowered their voices to a whisper as they softly harmonized the last tragic line.

"Look for me by the moonlight; I'll come to thee by the moonlight, though Hell should bar the way."

The last notes of guitar and autoharp floated out into the smoky room and seemed to hang there in the haze.

The room was silent.

Mick stood up and began a slow, measured clapping. Soon, one table after another joined him, until the entire room resounded with applause and stamping feet.

Kathy smiled shyly and whispered, "Thank you," into the microphone.

Karen smiled too. A slow, sensuous smile aimed directly at Mick.

"Hey, sit down," Mick said, pulling out two heavy wooden pine chairs as Kathy and Karen approached the table. "You ladies were friggin' far out, fantastic!"

"Thanks," Kathy smiled and sat down next to Bridget. "I'm really glad you liked it."

Karen smiled as well and said in a low, husky voice, "Yeah me too," and also sat down—right next to Mick.

Chapter Five

The Scrimshaw Pub
Skaket Creek
August 16th, 1968
11:32 p.m.

"So here I am, a skinny little PFC, and this mean-ass gunny sergeant yells at me, 'McCarthy, take the point!' And I look up at the sergeant and say, 'Sarge, if I take the point, the VC are gonna blow my friggin' head off before I get ten meters down the trail.'"

Bridget looked at Mick and the two girls seated around the table now littered with empty cans of Bud, Schlitz, and half empty mugs of the pub's Papst Blue Ribbon beer on tap.

She had returned from the ladies' room to find Mick in the middle of one of his story-telling moods. But this one was about Vietnam, a subject that he rarely discussed and that quite often left him in a brooding silence—but not tonight. Tonight, for some reason, he seemed to be on a real roll.

Kathy listened to his tale of his first days in Vietnam, with equal parts of compassion, amusement, and alarm. Karen listened with amusement and what Bridget recognized as calculation going on behind her blue eyes.

Bridget sat down and listened too, her eyes focused on the platinum blonde with the big chest.

Mick finished the story with a laugh and slapped his palm on the table.

Kathy giggled, and Karen smiled, continuing to look at Mick as he leaned across the table. He set his beer mug down unsteadily and said with a bleary eyed wink in Bridget's direction, "Right, babe?"

Bridget didn't answer. Why was he drinking like this—and talking about Vietnam? She tried to reach deep within herself for some understanding. Maybe it was some left over combat reaction from their run-in with that creepy cop. Maybe he was tired. Maybe he was.... She stared at Mick, who glanced around with an increasingly befuddled grin, and then she looked at Karen's knowing, self-satisfied smile—a smile like a cat licking her whiskers.

And maybe he was going to be in a whole lot a trouble—real soon.

Kathy glanced at her friend and made a tiny, "let's go" gesture with her eyes. Karen arched one eyebrow slightly and turned back to Mick. Bridget recognized the subtle "girl code". "Message received, but no sale. Don't bother me, girlfriend—I'm working."

Bridget's gaze narrowed until she felt as if her green eyes glared sharp as broken bottle glass.

Kathy tried to make small talk. "So, Bridget, you sound like you're from England or...."

"Ireland," Bridget spat, "not bloody England!"

Kathy smiled nervously and turned to Bridget. "You must know lots of really cool old folk songs, coming from Ireland and everything."

"One or two, luv," Bridget answered dryly.

"Hey, babe," Mick spoke up as the bartender shuffled over and placed four fresh draft beers on the table. "Let's do a couple for them. You know, like we did when we sang down in Falmouth a few weeks ago."

Bridget shook her head.

"Aw, come on, Bridge, it'll be great, just like that night. We can do—"

"No!"

Mick stopped, surprised.

"I said no, Mickey." Bridget lowered her voice. "No."

"How about you, Mick?" Karen asked, licking the rim of her glass with her cat-like tongue. "You play, don't you?"

"Yeah sure," Mick said and shrugged. "I-I mean, me and Bridge, we do a few clubs here and there, but mostly parties and friends and—"

"So we're all friends, right? Then why don't you guys go up there," she gestured towards the empty stage, "and give us a few tunes?"

"Well, I don't know. Bridge, whaddaya say?"

Bridget shook her head and watched Karen. She knew she'd given the blonde girl her opening—and she was going in for the kill. Karen obviously knew it too. She smiled back at Bridget and slowly turned to Mick, who leaned back in his chair and let beer number eight join the other seven.

"Okay, Mick, then if Bridget isn't into singing tonight, how 'bout joining me and Kathy for a couple of songs at the end of our last set? Okay, Kath?" she said to her friend, but her cobalt-blue eyes never left Mick.

Kathy looked around the table. "Bridget, you join us too. Please?"

"Yeah, Bridge, c'mon. Don't poop out. Night's still young and all that crap," Mick said, slurring his words.

Usually, Bridget loved singing—especially with Mick. But there was something here—something about this place—some kind of bad vibe, negative energy that made her feel that any notes she sang would fall as flat as the thin yellow beer at the bottom of her mug. She shook her head once more and said quietly, "No, Mickey, you go on and...sing."

Mick gazed at her for a few moments through bleary eyes, shook his head, and shrugged. "Okay, what-ever. Yeah, ladies, count me in."

"Cool!" Karen smiled. "Okay, Kath, we might as well get it on now." She started to get up.

Bridget also stood up and smiled a cold smile. "You're right, I'm not up fer singin' myself tonight, but while yer gettin' ready for your last set, I'll play you a little song to help you tune up by."

She crossed over to the pub's jukebox, put some coins into the slot, and punched in two quick numbers. As Mick and the two girls walked back up to the small stage, the jukebox whirled to life, and Little Eva came on. And with tough but perfect dual track harmony, warned the world to keep your hands offa my baby. Girl, you better watch yourself, that boy is mine.

* * * *

"I got you, babe.... A one and then two strums, a C cord, and a quick change to F. A double strum, and then repeat." Bridget remembered it well.

Mick had taught her to sing Cher's part while he harmonized Sonny's and played the guitar that first magical night that they'd made love, almost two years ago.

Her eyes stung as she remembered. Now, here he was, slurring the words up on the small stage, leaning into the microphone while the girl with long, platinum-blonde hair smiled her cool, amused smile and perfectly finished the Cher part. *My part.* Bridget seethed. She drew a deep breath and struggled to push the anger and jealousy back down inside of her. She tried instead to concentrate on the often sweet, sometimes foolish—and sometimes just plain dumb!—boy she loved.

Bridget glanced over at Mick. Was she right to feel jealous? Oh, sure, the blonde was good-looking enough, and growing up with five brothers had taught her at a very early age that all men looked. Almost in the same way that she and her girlfriends had stared drooling at the trays of fudge and chocolates in the sweet shop at home. No, it wasn't the blonde hair or the curves underneath the low cut peasant blouse and wide-flowing skirt. Bridget knew she could handle that kind of competition with one hand tied behind her back.

No, it was the music. She hated to admit it, but this girl could really sing—and play. And that's what was infatuating the love of her life.

Mick told a joke to the two girls and laughed, picking up his beer from the stage floor and chugging the rest of the mug in one long gulp.

He's a lot like his father. She saw the tough, old, broken-nosed Irish face peeking out from behind Mick's own square-jawed face. But

39

the resemblance between Michael McCarthy Senior and Junior was plain as day even to the most casual observer. Right down to the same sappy sentimental look that arose sometimes when they thought no one was watching. And the best part of all, the free flowing easy laugh that crinkled up their eyes. And in the case of the younger Michael McCarthy, it usually came just after he told one of his long convoluted jokes, or preceded him grabbing her around the waist, picking her up, and kissing her with an intensity that never failed to make her knees turn to water.

Bridget smiled the first smile she'd had in the last two hours as she remembered and thought to herself. *Yes, and that was probably the answer to the question those dried up old prunes sitting in their cold, marble mansions up on Beacon Hill had asked. 'What, for Heaven's sake, had Mick's blue-blood mother, Miss Felicity Parker Prescott, descendant of 300 years of Boston Brahmin Puritan correct aloofness, ever seen in a brash, crude, Irish cop from South Boston?'*

Bridget thought back on sweet nights. Yes, that was the one thing—and probably the only thing—that Miss Felicity Parker Prescott (for a short while, McCarthy) and she, had in common. They both knew "what".

Mick looked out at the crowd in the still tightly packed pub and said, "We'd like to do an Ian and Sylvia song now, and I've got to tell you that I'm, like, one lucky dude to be able to do this song with two chicks that are not only foxy as hell, but dynamite musicians. Hey, guys, let's hear it for Miss Kathy Dawes on autoharp and Miss Karen Randolph, who's been kind enough to let me borrow her guitar, and more importantly, has agreed to accompany me on vocals!"

Mick flat-picked out the introduction and launched into the first verse, accompanied by Karen's beautiful harmony singing.

"Well, I woke up this morning, you were on my mind."

Bridget's heart contracted. She knew that was the song suggestion that Karen had whispered in Mick's ear. She squeezed her eyes shut and bit the inside of her lip. *Damn her, how did she know?* This was another of Mick and Bridget's "special" songs!

She did know, didn't she?

Bridget forced her eyes open and stared back at the stage through a film of tears. And saw Karen smiling back at her

Oh, yes, she knew.

* * * *

The Scrimshaw Pub
Skaket Harbor

Ric Wasley

Cape Cod
August 17th, 1968
1:17 a.m.

Footsteps sounded behind Bridget. They broke the moody spell she'd been under for the past half hour. She glanced up from the stale beer she stared into. The bar was empty, except for them and Dave, the bartender standing beside her.

"Ah–ha, uh, Kathy, 'scuse me, I'm sorry, but it's past closing, and we got to lock up. You remember what happened the last time Chief Frost came by and found us open after one a.m. He said the next time he was gonna pull our license." Dave looked uncomfortable and shifted from foot to foot.

"Chief Frost, that old fart," Karen snorted. "He thinks just because his family owns half of the town and can pack the town's offices with all of their idiot relations, he can do whatever he wants. The hell with him, Kath, let's do another round just to show that old fossil."

"No, Karen," Kathy said. "Dave's right, we can't afford to lose our liquor license." She turned to the bartender. "Go ahead, close up, Dave."

"Hmmmm, closing time, huh?" Mick said and leaned back in his chair. "Well, in that case, I guess we ought to have at least one more round before we gotta pack it in. Hey, uh, Dave? Yeah, Dave, ah, bring us another—"

"No." Bridget reached out her hand and pulled Mick's half-raised arm down. "We've had enough, Mickey."

Mick turned and peered at her owlishly. "Well maybe you have, but I haven't. Hell, I'm just getting started. Hey, Karen, Kathy, what about it? How 'bout another? I'm buying."

"Ah, no thanks, Mick," Kathy said, getting up. "I've got to be up by eight a.m. tomorrow, so I think I better turn in."

"Aw, no, the night's still young. How about you, Karen? Have one more with me?"

"Sure, Mick, love to."

"Mickey, I said no!" Bridget snapped. She gripped his arm tighter. Mick swayed slightly in his chair and stared back at her. Then he gently but firmly moved her hand off of his arm.

"I heard you the first time, Bridget, and I'm not three friggin' years old—and you're not my friggin' mother."

Bridget stood up, suddenly furious with Mick and his childish antics.

"Michael Prescott McCarthy, I will say this only once. I am leaving now and going up to the room. Are you coming?"

With a tone unlike any he'd ever used to her before, he shrugged and said, "Have fun, babe."

The tension that had been building in her all night flooded through her body. Her head throbbed as if someone drove a spike through it. Her stomach contracted with twisting pains. She couldn't stand it anymore—the pub, the noise, the smoke—and especially the smirking blonde sitting next to Mick. And as she watched, Karen deliberately whispered something to Mick, letting her hand fall across his shoulder. It was too much. Bridget stared at him with glistening eyes, clenched both of her tiny hands into fists. "Go to Hell!" She spun on her heel and stormed out of the room.

* * * *

"Oh, shit!" Mick muttered, watching her stiff back retreat through the fishnet curtain door. He started to get up.

"Wait." Karen touched his arm. "Where are you going?"

"I-I have to go and...I mean, Bridge, she...."

"Oh." She smiled. "I thought you wanted another drink—with me."

Mick paused.

"And besides, I want to hear more of your stories."

She reached her hand up and pulled him back down to the table. "Now, where were we, Mick?"

"Ah, crap, I should probably pack it in, Karen," Mick said and groggily pushed back his chair and got unsteadily to his feet. "If I stay up drinking all night, I'm probably gonna get us thrown out of here. Hell, the Wicked Witch of the Front Desk already looks at me like she'd like to mince me up in tomorrow's chowder. And besides, I probably oughta get up stairs and tell Bridge—or least try to tell her before she brains me with the nearest heavy object—that I've been a first class jerk—again. And that I'm sorry and...."

"Oh, chill out, man." She smiled, getting up too. "Hey, where's my Saigon Sarge? C'mon, let's go do a joint. I've got some real choice Acapulco Gold all rolled."

"Shit, I don't know, Karen. It took me a while to get my head straight after I came back from 'Nam and I promised Bridge I wouldn't do that crap anymore."

"So who says she has to know?" Karen shot back with a wink. "C'mon."

"Where?" Mick stumbled through the curtained exit and into the darkened dining room.

Karen's smile grew wider as she took his hand and led him through the dimly lit lobby towards the stairway beyond. "My room," she answered.

Chapter Six

Skaket Creek
Township of Skaket Harbor
Cape Cod
April 15ᵗʰ, 1858
Dawn

The groan of the slender mast bending before the single sail almost drowned out the hissing of the surf as it rolled onto the sand of the tidal beach that ran the length of Cape Cod Bay.

Second Mate Jeptha Dawes let the mainsheet line of the *Elizabeth James's* longboat's tattered sail run through his hand and flap slowly in the dying east wind as he listened.

Yes, off the port bow of the eighteen-foot wooden boat, the distant sound of surf breaking on sand and the hiss of the waves as they ran back to their unchanging source again.

Jeptha strained his eyes and...there! Between two windswept sand dunes—a silver-gray hued tidal creek, its brackish water turned to liquid mercury in the pre-dawn light—emptied the final ebb of the night's contents of the tidal marsh into the bay.

Jeptha pulled in on the mainsheet and pushed the tiller hard over as the changeable wind shifted once again into the north and began to propel the longboat of the *Elizabeth James* through the shallow water and into the tidal creek.

The slate-gray light of what his father had always referred to as the "false dawn" filtered through the clouds. He remembered the bitter cold mornings when they had gone out to feed the cows and chickens on the hardscrabble, dirt-poor farm that he'd grown up on in the tiny hamlet of Hancock, New Hampshire. It was the same sort of half-light that now cast a smoky pall over the shallow, muddy creek.

Jeptha let the salt-stiff rope of the mainsheet slip through his fingers and momentarily slow the longboat's progress as he looked for...something. He wasn't sure what. The captain had told him that he'd been entrusted with a charge that was more important than both of their lives. Jeptha stared at the brackish water now flowing faster and faster back into the tidal stream as it spread outwards, filling the black mud banks of the shoreline's marsh.

He looked down at the former master of the *Elizabeth James's* sea chest.

The dark wooden chest was still lashed to the bow thwart where Jeptha had placed it some five hours before. He glanced at the salt-stained gilt letters etched into the chest signifying it belonged—no, *had belonged to*—Capt. Palmer James of the clipper ship *Elizabeth*

44

James.

No again, Jeptha thought with sad resignation, *make that the "former" captain of the Elizabeth James.*

His captain had leaned over the mid-ship railing and with his last bit of strength lowered his sea chest into Jeptha's waiting hands. Jeptha had taken the chest with trembling hands and a sick heart. And, lashing it to the longboat's forward thwart, he had looked up at the fever-tortured man who'd been like a second father to him. How could he refuse him? Refuse what was most certainly the last request of that soul-shattered descendant of New England's uncompromising Puritans.

Bright red blood froth had bubbled up from the captain's wheezing lungs and stained his lips as he'd leaned over the railing and rasped, "Go, Mr. Dawes. Take my chest and its contents as far as you can before dawn. But remember—you must have it buried safely underground before the first light of tomorrow's day touches it."

He'd coughed, and the red liquid from his lungs dripped through his sopping wet crimson handkerchief. The captain stared down at his own certain death running through his clenching fingers. "Promise me," he'd whispered.

"Aye, sir," Jeptha had answered, the words catching in his throat.

Captain Palmer James had drawn himself up straight, pushed the red kerchief into his pocket, and saluted Jeptha.

"May God go with you, Mr. Dawes, along with my prayers and thanks for all those who sleep unawares, and if it pleases the Almighty, safe and secure in their beds tonight. And if the Good Lord sees fit to bless you in this endeavor, the malignant evil that Foster had planned to unleash to achieve his wicked dreams will remain forever bound and fettered.

"I must tell you the truth of it. If you do your duty and shoulder this terrible responsibility, good folk everywhere will never know what service you have done for them this night, but I will, Mr. Dawes, and in their name and for my own part, I do bless you."

The captain coughed again and leaned onto the rail. His knees began to buckle, and he clutched the railing with a death grip. "Now hoist your sail and go before the tide turns."

Jeptha pulled on the mainsheet, and the wooden rings clattered against the slender mast as the coarse sailcloth popped open and caught the outgoing tide's damp wind. The longboat pulled away from the midnight-dark hull of the ship. As the boat rounded the headland of Nantucket harbor and headed downwind for Race Point off of the tip of Cape Cod's long arm, Jeptha looked back over his shoulder one last time at the diminishing figure of his former captain leaning against the starboard rail of the *Elizabeth James.*

He thought back to the final glimpse of his captain on that horror-filled night as he'd held up a pale shaking hand in farewell. He'd seen an expression on the reserved Yankee face he'd never seen before. An incredible sadness and something strange in the captain's haunted eyes—tears.

Jeptha was suddenly dragged back to his promise...or was it his curse?

The first red light of the true dawn touched the tip of the mast. He was out of time. He needed to fulfill his oath and get that hellish chest below ground before the dawn's thickening light touched it—but where?

The longboat rounded a slight curve in the tidal river, and there just above the bank's muddy, mussel-speckled slope, was a large sand-and-seagrass-covered mound.

With only a moment's hesitation, Jeptha ran the prow of the longboat into the mud bank and scrabbled up the small hill, dragging the tarred and iron-chain-bound sea-chest behind him. As the first rays of the new dawn broke over Cape Cod Bay, he began quickly and determinedly to dig.

After burying the chest, Jeptha followed a narrow track that meandered through the seagrass-covered dunes until it eventually joined with the main road leading to Skaket Harbor town. There he sat on the steps of a gray, weathered, shingled building that displayed a faded signboard proclaiming it to be: TOWNSHIP OF SKAKET HARBOR, COUNTY OF BARNSTABLE – CLERK'S OFFICE. Finally, at four minutes past eight a.m., a sleepy-eyed clerk approached the steps with a large key ring in his hand and asked Jeptha what he was doing there.

Jeptha told him, and the clerk looked dubious until Jeptha placed a small silver coin in his hand. The clerk sighed and nodded, ushering Jeptha inside. There, he took down the enormous old ledgers that recorded every parcel of land in Skaket Harbor—and who owned them.

Jeptha placed another coin in the clerk's hand.

"Could you direct me, sir, to the home of Mr. Isaiah Frost?"

He was going to buy Skaket Creek.

Chapter Seven

Township of Skaket Harbor
Cape Cod
April 15ᵗʰ, 1858
9:02 a.m.

"Yes? And who should I say is calling, then?"

The young parlor maid, who stood in the half open door behind the white porticoes flanking the three-story clapboard home of Deacon and First Selectman Isaiah Frost, looked disapprovingly at the faded and travel-stained clothes of the grimy figure standing on the front porch, nervously twisting his sea cap in his hands.

"Well? Cat got yer tongue?" The girl in the severe black uniform that couldn't quite mask the youthful figure underneath expelled an exasperated breath and started to close the door.

"Wait!" Jeptha cried and put his hand on the heavy oak door. "Wait," he said in a softer tone. "Please."

The door halted and was slowly drawn back.

The young woman, whose hazel eyes came up no further than Jeptha's shoulders, looked up at him. "So then, do ya have business with Mr. Frost?"

"Yes.... Yes, I think I do. That is, I mean, yes, yes I do. I most certainly do, Miss...?"

"It's MacDonald. Miss Fiona MacDonald, if you must know."

"Miss...MacDonald," Jeptha breathed.

"Well?"

"Well what?" Jeptha stammered.

"Well, what is your business? What is it that yer wishin' to see Mr. Frost about?"

Jeptha tried to frame an answer, but his exhausted brain didn't seem up to it. All he could focus on was the girl with the hazel eyes who stood impatiently in front of him.

The more he looked, the more he realized how very young she was despite her severe black dress and cap. She couldn't have been more than seventeen or eighteen and she was the first woman—girl—he'd seen in almost two years. And she was...lovely. But just now, she was getting angry.

"Look then," she snapped, her patience obviously exhausted, "I've got morning duties to attend, so if yer a tinker or a peddler you'd best move along."

Suddenly her eyes softened, and she sighed. "And if you're down on your luck and hungry, well...." She reached into her apron pocket and pulled out a worn copper coin. "There then, here's a penny, and if you go round to the back door, I'll see if cook can't find some bread and maybe a scrap from last night's mutton for ya."

Jeptha's eyes grew moist. He knew how hard she had worked for that penny she held out to him with her red chapped hand.

He could guess her story: the long, uncomfortable voyage from Glasgow, Belfast or Queenstown; her parents dead or too old and sick to care for their children or make the trip from Great Britain's starving slums to a better life. She'd probably landed in one of the Massachusetts port cities and signed herself into domestic service for little more than the promise of a hot meal and a roof over her head. And now she was holding out to him a penny. And he was fair certain she didn't have ten more like it.

"Go on then." She sighed. "You look all in. You march yourself round to the back door, and we'll find something for ya." She started to close the door again.

"No! Miss MacDonald—wait. Please."

She paused.

"Look," Jeptha said softly. He pulled out the lambskin wallet pouch from his sea coat and opened it. "Look," he said again.

He opened the wallet and let some of the coins spill into her outstretched hand. They clanked into her small palm until they covered the single copper penny. They sparkled and glistened in the morning sunlight, all a rich, bright yellow. Just like the bright morning light. Golden.

* * * *

Town of Skaket Harbor
The Parlor of Isaiah Frost
April 15ᵗʰ, 1858
9:51 a.m.

"Well, sir, what is it you want? My maid tells me that you claim to have business with me."

Jeptha looked at the imposing figure of Isaiah Frost. He'd heard of this man even on Nantucket Island. He owned warehouses and dockyards as well as dozens of ships sailing out of Nantucket town itself. He also owned vast tracts of land all over Cape Cod, including ten acres on a windswept hillside bordering Skaket Creek. That's why Jeptha stood nervously in the formal parlor of one of the wealthiest men on Cape Cod.

He looked at Mr. Isaiah Frost and saw no reason not to be nervous.

The white-haired, stern-faced man was not so large as imposing.

Maybe it was the somber black suit or the gray beard that bristled like an angry hedgehog. Or maybe it was the stilted, stifling atmosphere of the dark, cherry wood-paneled parlor, where each piece of furniture, silver or pewter ornament, looked as though it just dared any common, unwashed hand to touch it.

What ever it was, it all combined to make a poor farmer's son from Hancock, New Hampshire, feel awkward and unsure. Jeptha swallowed, his throat suddenly dry. He started to speak, but the words turned into a tongue-tied cough.

Isaiah Frost looked at him contemptuously and began to turn away.

"Good day to you, sir. I have important matters to attend to. You can see yourself out."

Jeptha was still trying to find the words when a high, lilting voice spoke up from the parlor's doorway.

"Mr. Frost, sir. Beg your pardon, sir. Jeptha—I mean, Mr. Dawes—does have business with you, sir, important business." The little Scotts-Irish maid walked determinedly into the room and pulled on Jeptha's hand until it hovered over a mahogany-and-brass round pedestal table.

"Go on," she whispered, gently pushing his right hand forward. "Show him."

Jeptha slowly turned his hand over and emptied the contents of the lambskin wallet, letting coin after golden coin clank heavily on to the table until they covered it with a small mound of gold.

"I've come to buy Skaket Creek," he said.

* * * *

Skaket Creek
Town of Skaket Harbor
Cape Cod
May 1ˢᵗ, 1858

"Now what exactly is it I'm supposed to be lookin' for, then?" Fiona MacDonald asked, half rising from the rented surrey's leather seat.

"Wait," Jeptha smiled and flicked the long leather traces over the tired old horse's rump, "just over this rise."

The four-wheeled surrey slowed as the horse clopped to the top of the last low hill between the rutted sand track of the salt marsh and the sea. Jeptha pulled in on the reins, halted the horse at the top of the rise, and pointed to a low hill next to the tidal creek bisecting the dunes. "There," he said.

Fiona looked to where his finger pointed. A thin, raw pine timber skeleton poked anemic ribs of a house frame up from the crest of a low hill nestled between two shallow arms formed by the brackish salt water creek.

Yes, this was Skaket Creek. And the intense, serious young man that Fiona MacDonald had been keeping company with for the past two weeks had purchased it but a week ago from her employer, Mr. Isaiah Frost, for $200 in gold. That was $20 an acre! No one had ever known land around here to sell so dear. Fiona had tried to tell Jeptha he could have offered Mr. Frost half of that amount and still consummated the bargain. But Jeptha Dawes wouldn't listen. For some reason, he had to have this particular piece of land—at any price. And just why the sailor would pay such an outrageous amount for a patch of bleak windswept dunes, local folks couldn't imagine.

But Fiona was about to find out.

Chapter Eight

Skaket Creek
Skaket Harbor
Cape Cod
May 1st, 1858
5:02 p.m.

The shadows were just beginning to lengthen when Jeptha called to Fiona, "Miss MacDonald, the hour is growing late. I'm afraid I've kept you too long. I don't want to be the cause of trouble with your employer, Mr. Frost, if you were to return after dark."

Fiona MacDonald looked up from where she poked her way through the rough-hewn framing timbers of the house.

"Well, and so what of it, I'd like to know? It is my own day off, is it not? I've every Sunday afternoon right after service and the clearing away of the Sunday dinner dishes. So I've the whole afternoon all to my own self and do not need a by your leave as to where I go—or who I go with. It says so, right on my papers!" She finished, the jut of her jaw determined.

"Of course, Miss MacDonald," Jeptha said with a slight smile as she paced off the dimensions of each room in the house that he was building on the sandy, seagrass-covered hill next to Skaket Creek.

Suddenly she stopped at a spot where the very center of the half-framed house perched on the crest of the low hill.

"Mr. Dawes?" she called, looking down at the sand and darker soil of recently turned earth underneath her feet.

Jeptha froze and slowly answered, "Yes, Miss MacDonald?"

She dug the toe of her high-button leather boot into the loose dirt of the small mound in the center of a tiny, partially framed room.

"Mr. Dawes," she stared with puzzlement at the three-foot square spot between the timber frames, "this room...this room, well, I'm no fine architect and that's for certain, but my father was a carpenter in Belfast, and I do have a fair eye for how a finished frame will fill out." She looked around with a perplexed frown. "And unless I miss my guess, this room has no doors, no windows...." She looked Jeptha square in the eyes. "And as near as I can tell, no way in and no way out."

* * * *

Skaket Creek
Skaket Harbor

The Scrimshaw

Cape Cod
May 1ˢᵗ, 1858
5:22 p.m.

The salt wind blew a bank of gray clouds over the lowering sun. The raw pine timbers of the house took on a dark-shadowed hue, like soot-blackened bones. Fiona MacDonald still stood in the middle of the partially framed room that occupied the very center of the dark heart of the house that was to be.

She gazed back at Jeptha, to where he stood at the edge of the wooden stakes that marked off what would eventually become a wide porch leading to the main entrance's double doors. Or so Jeptha had told her shortly after he'd halted the rented surrey and helped her down. He'd excitedly pointed out one feature and room after another as he'd taken her work-roughened hand in his own calloused one and led her from room to partially finished room.

"And here, Miss MacDonald," he said, brimming with pride, "there will be a grand parlor with two fine, large windows facing the sea, so that we may gaze upon the ocean's gales in winter and open them in summer to let their refreshing breezes cool us!"

"Us, Mr. Dawes?" Fiona replied quietly.

Jeptha suddenly realized the implications of what he had been saying, and he felt a flush, surely bright, tongue-tied crimson burn his cheeks. "Forgive me, Miss MacDonald," he stammered. "I didn't mean to be so...presumptuous."

"Do not apologize, Mr. Dawes," she said softly. "I do not find you presumptuous—no, not at all."

Jeptha drew in a deep breath and said, "Miss MacDonald, then if you don't think me too forward, there is something that I would like to ask you."

The little maid from Belfast looked at him from the house's interior most room and answered, "And yes, Mr. Dawes, I think that I would like to hear your question. But first I have one of my own."

Jeptha waited with dread as she walked to the very center of the tiny room. She stopped and stood over a mound of still-raw earth covered with a large flat rock and stared deep into his eyes.

"Mr. Dawes, what is this strange, small room that has neither entrance nor exit?"

Jeptha could only answer with a stricken look.

"And I can see here that the earth has been recently turned," she went on. "And I do, likewise, surmise that something has been buried and that this slab of granite rock has been placed upon it." She glanced up at him with large, greenish-brown eyes. "What is it that lies buried here, Mr. Dawes?"

Jeptha stared down at the large square rock beneath her feet and thought of the thing that lay beneath it. He said, "May I first ask you my question, Miss MacDonald?"

She nodded.

Jeptha glanced up to where she stood silhouetted against the darkening sky and said, "Miss MacDonald, I have, I mean, I feel, I mean, I have feelings—"

"Yes, Mr. Dawes?" she said quietly.

"Ever since that first morning I saw you—in the doorway of Mr. Frost's house—I have felt...." He swallowed, his throat suddenly dry. "I-I love.... That is, I want you to be...my wife."

The tiny, Scotts-Irish maid in the severe black dress blushed for a moment and finally looked up. "Yes, Mr. Dawes, and I do think that I likewise have 'those feelings' for you as well." She paused and gazed into his eyes. "But...."

"But?" Jeptha's heart seemed to shrivel.

"But I can see in your face—in your eyes—that there is something there, some terrible secret. Some terrible burden you force yourself to bear." She drew a deep breath. "And unless I know what, I cannot know you. And I will, Mr. Dawes—Jeptha—know the heart of the man I marry."

Jeptha took two steps towards her. He reached out and touched a strand of her long dark hair that spilled from underneath her bonnet. He tried to speak, but nothing would come. He swallowed and finally stuttered, "Miss...Miss MacDonald."

"Fiona, Jeptha," she said softly and pulled him towards her.

He dropped to his knees in the sandy soil of the hilltop next to Skaket Creek. She put her hand on his cheek as he buried his face in the starched folds of her black dress and told her everything.

Well, almost everything.

* * * *

Skaket Creek
Skaket Harbor, Cape Cod
May 1ˢᵗ, 1858
6:42 p.m.

A blood red sun was dipping into the ocean by the time the surrey began the long journey down the rutted sand track back to town.

Red sun at night, sailor's delight, or so went the old saying.

And the seagull circling and gliding on the increasing wind off of the ocean probably would have thought: There goes one *delighted sailor* with his new bride-to-be.

That is, if the seagull could have thought, which, having a brain the size of a walnut, it of course couldn't.

Instead, it glided down to the partially timber-framed house and searched for any stray goodies that the two visitors might have left behind. It hunted and pecked its way up to the little open room at the top of the hill, cocked its head to one side so it could focus one black, beady eye on the gray stone slab.

The eye saw something. Was it food?

The bird hopped closer to investigate and...the stone moved.

Or maybe it didn't.

But the bird gave an angry, terrified squawk and flew off toward the gray-green waves breaking against the deserted shoreline.

The wind blew harder, and the drifting sand slowly started to cover the slab of granite—and whatever lay beneath it.

Nothing moved on the hilltop except the wind and the sand. The sand and the stone and—something else—were patient.

They were very good at waiting.

Chapter Nine

Skaket Creek Inn
Skaket Harbor, Cape Cod
August 17th, 1968
2:11 a.m.

Pounding on the door woke Bridget from her nightmare, which at first had seemed to blend in with the terrible dream she was having. In her dream, there was something at the door—something horrible. Evil. And it wanted to get in. It wanted to come into the room, to the bed where Bridget lay moaning and clutching her pillow in terror. In her dream, something—he...it—leered at her with an obscenely slobbering grin and a long, snake-like tongue that twisted and curled towards her body. The fingers on each hand had long filthy nails and they motioned to her. It wanted to draw her close. It wanted to reach out its claw-like hands and wrap them around her body and her slender white neck and....

"Bridget!"

She sat bolt upright in bed with a gasp.

"Bridget. Unlock the door. It's me, Mick."

She jumped up from the bed, fully awake now. "Mickey?" she called.

"Yes."

She almost unlocked the door and then remembered. "So where is yer bleached-blonde honey, then? Is she all done with ya and thrown you out?"

"Bridget," came the strangely hollow reply. "I'm tired. Let me in."

The banging on the door started up again.

"Stop it now!" Bridget hissed through the still-locked door. "You're poundin' fit to wake the dead!" She paused and listened as her words seemed to fall at her feet like dry, brown leaves.

The banging ceased, the last thump fading with a muted sound.

A chill slithered down Bridget's spine. She reached out, and her fingers touched the cold brass doorknob. "Mickey?" she whispered through the door. She felt strange, uneasy—frightened. "Mickey?" she whispered again.

Silence, and then a cold, rough voice on the other side of the door said, "Yes. Let. Me. In. Now!"

Bridget drew her breath in sharply. "Mick? Mickey? What...what is the matter with you? Why are you talking that way?"

"Open this door now, you bitch!"

Bridget backed away from the door. Angry, frightened tears burned

55

at the corners of her eyes. What was happening? This wasn't the boy she loved. She'd seen him drunk before but never like this. It wasn't... it couldn't be her Mick.

Frightened, confused, she said, "Who are you?"

Silence for a moment, and then the voice whispered seductively, "I'm what you need."

The voice seemed muffled through the thick door and empty sounding as though speaking to her from a deep well. One minute it sounded like Mick and the next—like another voice. A voice she'd heard but couldn't place...a voice just outside of her consciousness, teasing her, mocking her. She couldn't quite place it. Maybe she didn't *want* to place it.

"Bridget," the voice outside the door continued on in the seductive tone, "open the door. I want you. You want me."

"Mickey?" Dizzy, almost nauseous, she wanted so much for it to be Mick. Her sweet, loving Mick. Her hand hovered over the doorknob. She reached for the old-fashioned brass key in the lock.

Suddenly the door buckled and shook as an incredibly powerful— fist?—or something, smashed against it.

"I. Said. Now!"

Bridget jumped back, her heart pounding. "Stop it! Get away from here, whoever or whatever you are! Get away from me and go to the devil, or go to...Hell!"

A cold, sea-dank wind blew underneath the door, and then... silence.

She shivered as skeletal tendrils of chill crept up her legs. She shook her head and ran back to the old four-poster bed, pulled the covers over her head, and buried her face in the pillow.

* * * *

On the stairs leading to the second floor landing, Mick heard Bridget's muffled shout of "go to hell!" and the sound of another door opening. He cleared the railing just in time to see a door click shut at the far end of the hall. The end of the hall...someone had told him about a room at the end of the hall. Who was that? A girl, just before he'd passed out on the couch in the lobby, a whispered voice and long silky hair brushing over his face.

"Come to my room at the end of the hall...." A seductive voice—a blue-eyed voice. The voice had said that they could.... But he couldn't. All he wanted was bed, the sleep kind of bed, a bed with Bridget.

He walked unsteadily towards the door to their room and turned the knob. "Bridget?" he whispered.

He heard the sound of muffled sobs, and a choked voice said, "Go away, I told you! Go to Hell!"

Mick leaned his forehead against the door. All he wanted was a place to lie down, any place. Any bed, any room. He turned and took two steps towards the room at the end of the hall. No. No, that was the wrong place. And it seemed like Bridget's sobbing came from that room too. Sobbing and pleading, almost like someone in pain.

It was too much. It must be him. Everywhere he went he caused sobbing and probably pain. What was wrong with him? He was drunk but he also felt like lead encased his body and scorpions and snakes filled his clothes. He couldn't stand it.

Mick staggered back down the hallway and stumbled down the stairs into the dark lobby. He barely made it to the old horsehair-stuffed couch before his knees buckled. He sprawled face first onto the worn upholstery as a deep well of darkness filled with all of his nightmares rose up to meet him.

Chapter Ten

The Skaket Creek Inn
August 17th, 1968
8:16 a.m.

"Okay, kid, wake up!"

Something smacked against Mick's feet, and he sat up. Opened his eyes. Not a good idea. The room wobbled and spun, like the toy gyroscope he'd had as a kid—just before it ran out of centrifugal force and began to teeter on its axis. He shut his eyes again and opened them slowly. Where was he? He looked around, blinked and yawned. A big room with a long wooden counter, old-fashioned chairs and tables, and a stiff, ancient horsehair-stuffed couch that...that he'd apparently been sleeping on. And a big beefy guy stood in front of him. He owned a florid red face, a very unpleasant scowl, and held a long black nightstick. He wore a blue uniform and a badge that read: Town of Skaket Harbor – Police. And just now, he drew back what Mick knew as the son of a former Boston cop, was a billy-club, to give Mick another whack on his feet.

"I said up!" the man in blue barked.

Mick stood up. Quickly. A little too quickly.

"Okay, I'm up. I'm up, but I gotta warn you, if you keep me standing up, I'm liable to throw up."

The cop paused for a moment and grunted, "Okay, sit down."

Mick collapsed back onto the couch and put his head in his hands. "What the hell is going on?" he muttered.

"That's what you're gonna tell me, hot shot," the cop snapped back.

Mick tried to look up, but the action only made the room appear to spin faster. He swallowed hard and tried to think about something other than the eight—ten—mugs of last night's beer that seemed determined to rise up to meet the morning light.

"So where were you last night? Who were you with? What time did you leave the bar? Who did you leave with?"

The questions came rapid fire, like his old M16 on full automatic, spitting words like bullets from the angry face of the way-too-intense example of Skaket Harbor's *finest*.

"Aw, shit, man...I mean, I'm sorry, Officer—"

"Frost. Chief of Police, Arthur Frost."

Frost! The same name as that....

The big beefy cop raised an eyebrow at him.

"Ah, yeah, Officer—Chief—I mean, sir."

"Who were you with last night? Were you up on the second floor?"

"Yeah. Sure. I think I was. Shit, yeah...oops, 'scuse me. Yeah, I must have been. I was going to my room."

"Really? Then what were you doing sleeping here?"

"Here? I'm not sure. I...oh, crap! The fight...me and Bridge, we had this fight, and—"

"Bridge, who's that?"

"Bridget. Bridget Connolly. She's my girl. At least, she was. I mean, I hope she still is."

"Really.... Well, why don't we ask her? Miss...?" the chief called over to a slight figure sitting huddled on the stairs, her face almost hidden by a terry-cloth bathrobe several sizes too big for her, "will you please come over here?"

* * * *

Bridget Ann Connolly was *not* going to cry. She was the only daughter of an IRA major. And she was sister to five tough, hard-ass brothers who ate fat, bloated, self-important, puffed-up, petty little tyrants like the red-faced, small town constable standing in front of her, for breakfast. She got up, tied Mick's old bathrobe tighter around her waist, and almost marched up to the knot of people standing around the lobby couch.

"Well, Missy?" the chief asked. "Did *lover boy* over there spend last night with you or not?"

Bridget only hesitated a moment. She remembered Father McCauley and Sister Margaret drilling the fear of God and lying into her with stern admonition and a heavy ruler respectively. But even those lessons of her County Cork girlhood weren't enough to stop her from drawing herself up to her full five feet, one-and-three-quarter inches and answering defiantly, "Yes—yes, of course he did. He is my...my... we're in love."

A look of salacious contempt crossed the fat old chief's face.

The dirty minded old Proddy bastard!

And, before she could stop herself, she blurted out, "We're going to be married, you know!"

The chief raised his eyebrows and smirked in her direction. "Are you now, Miss...?"

"Connolly. Bridget Ann Connolly, you friggin' bastard!" Mick shouted, pushing off of the couch and covering the distance between himself and the chief in two staggering strides. And that was as far as he got. From out of nowhere, a nightstick smashed into his solar plexus, doubling him over in helpless agony.

Mickey! Bridget cried and started forward, but the chief held up his hand.

"Stay down, pal, if you don't want another one." An acne-scarred face snarled at Mick from where he lay gasping on the floor, trying to draw a breath.

"Thanks, Dougie." The hereditary chief of the Skaket Harbor Police Department smiled. "You can put your 'come-along' away; I think he's got the message."

Deputy Douglas Frost stepped around from behind the couch and looked at the chief. "I don't know, Uncle Art, this guy thinks he's some kind of a bad-ass. Are you sure?"

Chief Arthur Frost, son of First Selectman Samuel Frost, the Director of the Skaket Harbor Bank and Realty Trust (among other titles), glanced over at Bridget and nodded with complete confidence. "Yeah, Dougie, I'm sure."

"Now then, young lady," he said, turning back to Bridget. "I'm waiting for an answer."

She gave one last worried look at Mick before turning back to the chief. She nervously fussed with the too-big bathrobe that kept slipping off of her shoulders, revealing what she was using as a nightgown—Mick's old freshman lacrosse jersey, one of his few souvenirs from Harvard, before he was kicked out for fighting and packed himself and the giant chip on his shoulder off to Vietnam. The jersey was large, and Bridget's shoulders were small. So it had a tendency to slip off of one shoulder or the other and play peek-a-boo with her breasts. Bridget knew that was why Mick had given it to her in the first place. And she didn't mind at all—when they were alone. But right now she wished that she had been wearing an Old Mother Hubbard nightgown that stretched all the way down to her toes.

But the jersey was what she'd been wearing—all she'd been wearing—when twenty minutes ago, she was dragged almost gratefully from more horrible dreams by more insistent pounding on her door. In her half-awake and still terrified state, she hadn't been able to leave the dubious safety of the bed and cross the early morning, sunlight-speckled floor to open the door. So it was probably a good thing when the master key was inserted into the lock and the door pushed open by a triumphant and smug Helen Dawes.

"There she is, Chief!" The old harpy from the front desk had sneered and added maliciously, "And if you ask me, that young fellow she *claims* is her husband, hasn't been in this room tonight. But I'll wager a bushel of Wellfleet oysters that there's another room on this floor that he *has* been in!"

Bridget had jumped out of bed, desperate to throw off the remnants of her nightmare. "What do you mean?" she'd called in a panicked voice, pulling on Mick's old bathrobe and the faded, fuzzy pink slippers that she'd worn every night in her Radcliffe College dorm.

She grabbed the arm of the salt-and-pepper-haired cop and asked, "What's happened to Mick? Where is he?"

The man in blue had motioned her towards the stairs and said, "Downstairs, Miss. Let's go."

Now he turned towards her again and said, "Let's cut the BS, Miss. Loverboy here doesn't seem to be interested in cooperating, so why don't you tell us?"

The sound of Mick getting hit with the billy-club had been all too familiar. It was a sound from her youth. A sound common to the jail cells she'd waited outside as a girl in Ireland—waited to help her mother carry her father home from. It was the sound of a lead-weighted stick smacking into bare flesh.

She pushed past the chief and was on the floor cradling Mick's head in her arms as he lay there struggling to draw in a deep, ragged breath.

"You bleedin' bastards," she hissed. "You're just like the bloody Black and Tans at home!" She leaned over and brushed a sweaty lock of his hair out of his eyes. The terry-cloth robe fell open, dragging the lacrosse shirt off of her right shoulder.

Deputy Douglas Frost stepped around his uncle and grinned down at her. "Well, good morning, sunshine."

Bridget looked up. Her stomach lurched as she fully realized who it was.

The chief walked over and prodded Mick with the toe of his polished black shoe. "Get up."

"Leave him alone!" Bridget snapped, tears smarting in the corner of her eyes.

"Okay, girly, have it your way," the chief said. "Dougie, read him his rights."

The chief's nephew smiled a shark-tooth grin and slowly began to read from a small laminated card that he produced from his top pocket. "You have the right to remain silent. You have the right to—"

"What?" Bridget gasped, her face turning, she was sure, chalky white. "What in Heaven's name are you charging him with?"

The eyes of Helen Dawes watched the couple huddled on the floor in the middle of the old inn's lobby with obvious, smug satisfaction.

But the chief's eyes were impassive as he said, "Charging? He's being charged with the rape and murder of Karen Randolph."

Chapter Eleven

Skaket Harbor Police Department
August 17th, 1968
7:42 p.m.

"Hey, McCarthy."

For a long time, there was no sound. At last, Mick looked up through the bars of the Skaket Harbor Police's sole tiny jail cell and answered quietly, "Hey, babe."

The silence stretched on. Mick stared at the floor and finally said quietly, in a husky voice, "I didn't do it."

Bridget walked up to the cell. Mick's hands clenched around the bars. She put both of her hands around his. She didn't say anything as his eyes searched her face.

"Bridge...you don't believe that I could...?"

"No, Mickey. Of course I don't."

Mick drew in a ragged breath. "Listen, I know that I acted like a real jerk last night. I-I don't know what got into me...."

"About six beers too many." Bridget smiled wryly.

Mick startled her by grabbing her arm. "No!"

She stepped back a half step, but he still held on to her arm.

"I. Didn't. Do. It!" he said from between clenched teeth.

Bridget put her right hand over his where it held her arm. "I know, Mickey."

"Know what?" he answered bitterly. "That I didn't do it, or that I'm a big jerk?"

"Both, luv." She smiled.

He leaned his head against the cold iron bars and laughed sadly. "You got that right, babe."

Bridget reached out her other hand through the white, chipped, enamel-paint iron bars and ran her small fingers through his long, tangled hair.

"I...didn't...do...it," he whispered again.

"Hush, I know you didn't." She put her thumb and forefinger under his jaw and raised it up until his blue-gray eyes gazed down into hers.

"Mickey, don't you know how much I love you? You're the only boy I've ever let inside of me. Let into my thoughts, my dreams, my mind, my heart, my body, my soul, inside of...me."

Mick glimpsed her through stinging eyes. "Bridge, I swear to you, I don't know what the hell was happening last night. That...that wasn't me."

"She was beautiful, Mickey."

"Yes, she was." He nodded. "And if I wasn't just ape-shit crazy in love with the most beautiful friggin' girl in the world, I would've gone to bed with her in a heartbeat." He put his other hand through the bars and gripped hers. "But I am. So I didn't."

"I know that too, Mickey," Bridget said with a catch in her throat and lifted his scarred, jail-grimed hand to her lips and, one by one, kissed each of his fingertips.

They stood like that—hands through the cold iron bars—for a long time. Suddenly the cocoon of each other that they had wrapped themselves in was pierced by the sound of voices coming from the chief's office outside the cell room. Footsteps scuffled in the corridor. They stopped as voices rose just outside of the connecting steel door. Mick's hand tightened over hers.

"But I gotta tell you, Bridge, before anyone comes...I don't remember...anything after I left the bar with her!"

Bridget glanced up at him. "The drinkin', the flirting, I-I forgive you, Mick. I know it didn't mean anything to you." She added in a small voice when he didn't answer, "It didn't—did it?"

Mick stared at her with a desperate intensity. "The drinking? Yeah, I'll take the hit for that. Sure, that was me and a few dozen generations of McCarthy's sloshing down those brews. But the rest—the flirting; Karen; me sitting next to her with my tongue hanging out..? Yeah, I suppose that was me too, but it was...it was like I was under some kind of spell. Hell, my professor of Medieval History would've said that I was...bewitched."

Bridget drew in a sharp breath. "When I was a girl growing up in Ballykill, there was this old woman who lived in a thatched roof cottage down by the peat bog. One afternoon, after school when I was fourteen, we all went down to see her with sweets and pennies because we'd heard that she was well-versed in the 'old ways'. They said she could see the future, cast spells, and make potions to bring you wealth, fame, success and...love."

Despite all that had happened, Mick always had to smile when Bridget told him her stories of fairies and magic spells. He asked gently, "And did she?"

But Bridget wasn't smiling. She looked up at Mick with an intensity that wiped the grin off his face. "Yes, Mickey. She could and she did. Maureen Donahue wanted the O'Connor boy, so the old woman whispered in Maureen's ear and gave her something. And Maureen gave the old woman all her sweets money and her mother's old cameo brooch."

"And did the girl get her boy?" Mick asked, unsuccessfully trying to keep it light.

Bridget gazed past Mick—at her memory—and answered, "Yes, she

63

did, but not in the way she wanted. Not at all."

"What do you mean?" he asked, uneasy.

"Well she...."

Raised voices in the other room interrupted Bridget. The chief and his nephew. They must've been yelling, because the sound was audible even through the heavy steel-covered outer door.

"I don't want any more lip from you, Dougie. You get your ass in there and do just what the hell I told you! Besides, it's not gonna be what you'd call particularly tough duty. In fact, we both know that it's probably right up your alley, eh, Dougie?"

The sound of laughter filtered in from the corridor and a fumbling at the lock in the outer door.

Bridget glanced up at Mick. "Just answer me one thing, Mickey." She clutched both of his hands and stared at him through the bars with a lurking fear behind her green eyes. "Last night, did you come to my door? Do you remember?"

Mick answered uncertainly. "I think so."

"You said that you wanted...me. And you wanted to come in. And I was just about to turn the key and let you in and then...then I called your name, and at first you didn't answer, and then...finally you did. But the voice—it wasn't like your voice. It was harsh and rough and—cruel." She watched Mick, her face tight with fear. "That wasn't your voice. Tell me it wasn't, Mickey."

Mick closed his eyes and tried to think. Finally, he shook his head from side to side. "No, Bridget, it wasn't."

"Aw, well isn't this sweet."

They looked up, hands still locked together, and saw the sneering face of Skaket Harbor's Deputy, Douglas Frost.

"Well, Dougie," said a lower voice from behind him, "don't be too critical. Maybe if you could find yourself a girl as pretty as that one, you wouldn't have to spend every Saturday night beating your meat alone with a stack of girlie magazines."

"Uncle Art!" Douglas Frost whirled around to the man behind him.

Chief of police Arthur Frost hooked his thumbs into his wide black service belt and walked into the cell room. He swaggered up to Bridget and said, "You recall what I said when you asked me if you could come back here and see your boyfriend?" He put two chubby fingers under her chin and pushed it up towards him. "I said there would be a price, and that price is called cooperation, remember?" he said softly.

"Get yer hands offa me!" she hissed.

Mick's knuckles whitened on the cell bars.

"Quite the little spitfire." He chuckled. "Dougie, don't you wish you had one like this?"

"Yeah, Uncle Art, as a matter of fact, I do. I most certainly do." Dougie Frost wiped his mouth with the back of his hand.

Never taking his gleaming, piggy little eyes off of Bridget, Chief Arthur Frost said, "Well then, Dougie, why don't you take our Little Miss Spitfire here into the storeroom and see if you can't get her to... cooperate. And maybe that might work faster if you and her could become...better acquainted."

Douglas Frost needed no further urging. He took two steps forward and grabbed Bridget around the shoulders. He sneered at Mick. "See, I told you we'd be seeing each other again." His arm tightened on Bridget's shoulders. "C'mon now, little chick." He licked his lips. "Why don't you and me go have our own little love-in, and you can show me some of the things you do at those hippie parties, huh?"

Mick's right hand flashed through the bars and snagged the sleeve of Dougie's blue uniform. He pulled it from Bridget's shoulder with the sound of tearing cloth as the sleeve of Dougie's uniform peeled away in Mick's grip.

"Get your fucking hands off her, you bastard!"

There was a sickening sound of a hard object striking flesh, and Mick's arm went numb.

"The next time you put that arm outside these bars, McCarthy, I'm going to break it."

Mick's arm hurt like hell, but he wouldn't give the bloated bastard holding the billy-club the satisfaction. He just glared at Dougie and repeated through pain-gritted teeth, "Get your goddamn hands off of...."

Chief Frost gave his nephew a nod, and the hand on Bridget's shoulder fell to her breast—and squeezed. Bridget twisted quick as a cobra and raked her fingernails down the left side of Dougie's face.

"Ow, you bitch!" he screamed.

Chief Frost moved surprisingly fast for a fat man. With one swift movement he grabbed both of Bridget's wrists, and there was sudden click. Bridget whirled around to strike out but found that both of her wrists were immobile. She had been handcuffed.

Frost smiled slowly and maliciously. "Okay, Dougie, think you can handle her now?"

"Yeah, Uncle Art, I sure as hell do," he said, rubbing the long scratches on his cheek and mimicking his uncle's sadistic, leering grin.

Mick shook the bars in impotent fury. "When I get out of here, you bastards are dead!"

"Ah, but you're not getting out of here, Sonny-Jim. Unless...."

"Unless what?"

"Unless you sign a confession that you met Karen Randolph last night in the Scrimshaw Pub. You put the moves on her. She flirted, but you wanted more. You wanted to get into her pants."

"Liar!" Bridget spat. She struggled with her handcuffs as Dougie fondled her breast and pulled her closer.

The chief just laughed and sneered at Mick. "And when she wouldn't go along with it, you got pissed and in a drunken rage, raped and strangled her in her own bed."

"Fuck you, you twisted sack of shit!" Mick snarled.

"Okay, smart ass." Chief Frost shrugged. "Have it your way. Dougie, why don't you take Miss Connolly back to the *interrogation room* and see if you can't convince her to be more...cooperative."

Mick swore and pounded on the bars with his good hand.

The chief laughed, and Dougie tugged the struggling Bridget through the outer door.

"And Dougie?" the chief called after him, "Make sure you do a thorough job of convincing the young lady. So take your time."

"All right, you son of a bitch!" Mick screamed. "Bring me your goddamn confession. I'll sign it. I'll sign whatever the hell you want. Just get his fucking hands off of her!"

"I will, sonny." The chief chuckled. "And you're right, you will sign. But first we got to let Dougie have a little fun, don't we?"

Mick screamed like a wounded animal.

Chief Frost gave a deep rolling laugh that jiggled the small folds of fat underneath his chin. "Yeah Dougie," he called through the open door, enjoying Mick's torment, "Take your time."

There was a smack, then a gurgle and retching sounds from the other room.

"Dougie! You idiot! Take it easy. Have fun, but don't leave any marks that'll show! Damn boy," he muttered, "got no more sense than a clam."

More sounds of distress floated in from the outer office.

"Hey, I said take it easy, you idiot," he called again, glancing at Mick. "Damn—he's got to leave some for the rest of us." He smiled maliciously. "Who knows, maybe I'll even carve myself off a piece of that little cutie, before we call it a night."

He leered at Mick, who clutched the bars with hate-filled eyes. No answer came from the other room.

"Dougie?" Frost shook his head and started moving towards the door muttering, "Goddamn kid can't get anything right. The hell with him, he's just lost his chance. I'll take care of the little bitch myself."

As the fat façade that passed for law and order in the clan-dominated seaside town reached the doorway, a huge scarred fist came out of nowhere and buried itself in the middle of his jelly-roll gut.

The chief's breath left him with a sudden whoosh, and he raised his head just in time to see a size eleven black, thick-soled shoe rise up and smash into his testicles like a place kicker kicking a field goal. His scream was almost too high to hear.

A pair of wide shoulders, supporting a broken-nosed face, filled the doorway.

"Hi, Mickey."

"Pop?"

Chapter Twelve

Jeptha Dawes reached up to lift his brand new bride down from their brand new surrey in preparation for carrying her across the threshold of their brand new house. Just as he was about to clasp his hands around her tiny waist, he hesitated. A silvery sheen reflected from his palms in the late afternoon sunlight glinting off the ocean.

I'm just like a schoolboy! he thought with dismay as he looked at his damp, sweat-covered hands. And it wasn't the heat of the beautiful blue-sky June day. He was nervous. In all honesty, he was terrified. He'd fought cannibals and braved typhoons, but in truth, he'd never had a woman.

Those nights in the stews and port taverns of Shanghai and Siam, the other men of the crew had gone upstairs with the brothel whores, but Jeptha had just smiled shyly, shaking his head while the women sat on his knee and whispered in their silky sing-song voices, "Nice sailor-man. You come with me—I love you long time."

He'd always said no. Some had cursed him in strange languages and some had looked at him with sad, hurt eyes. And some of those—the sad, hurt ones—he'd even given coins to. But he'd always said no.

And now? His new bride of three hours stood on the step of the surrey, waiting for her new husband to sweep her up and carry her over the threshold, and his hard, calloused hands dripped with nervous sweat. Would he stain and ruin the beautiful white Irish lace wedding dress that the Frost's had given her as a wedding present? An incredibly generous gift, but it certainly hadn't started out that way.

Six weeks ago, Fiona and Jeptha had asked to see Mr. Isaiah Frost the first night they declared themselves to each other. His reaction had been anything but generous.

Fiona had told him of their intent to marry and that she'd be leaving his service. He had cursed her and called her an ungrateful Hibernian.

Jeptha told him in cold but measured tones that, rich though he was, he'd better mind his tongue. Isaiah Frost looked ready to explode and barked at Fiona to collect her belongings at once and leave his house. She ran in tears up to the tiny room under the third floor eaves and returned carrying a faded carpetbag with everything she owned. Or so they'd thought at the time.

She took a room at the same boarding house in town where Jeptha was staying while he built his—their—house, and they never thought of—or cared to see—Mr. Isaiah Frost again.

Thus their surprise was total when three weeks later he rode up to the boarding house in his fine carriage, contrite smile on his face, and his arms overflowing with expensive gifts.

Jeptha watched through the boarding house window as all four members of the Frost family descended from the carriage and walked up the crushed shell pathway leading to the house.

He called Fiona from her chair in the parlor, where she sat embroidering her one plain shawl with bright flowers so as to have at least one festive thing to wear on her wedding day.

She joined Jeptha at the open window and looked on with astonishment as Isaiah Frost mounted the wooden steps to the porch, followed by his bovine wife, Millicent, his equally porcine son, Edward, and his sullen, sloe-eyed daughter, Chastity, who, if the town rumors were correct, practiced anything but.

They all lined up behind Isaiah Frost like a gaggle of plump geese while he raised the boarding house door knocker and let it fall back on its striker plate.

Mrs. Bascom, the widow who owned the house, came in from the kitchen muttering until she opened the door. She gave an awkward curtsy and said, "Oh my. Mr. Frost. Oh, well, good day, sir. I wasn't expecting.... Well, do come in. What do you...I mean, to what do I owe the pleasure?"

Still smiling his unaccustomed, contrite smile, he said, "Ah, dear Mrs. Bascom. Thank you, thank you. Actually, we're here to see a former employee of mine—ours. Or I should say friend—or rather more, like one of the family."

He beamed and used the phrase again as if testing it. "Yes." He chuckled. "That's it exactly: one of the family. We've come to see our own dear Fiona, to wish her well in her upcoming marriage."

He stepped inside and walked to the open parlor doors where a stunned Fiona and a puzzled Jeptha watched in disbelief as all four Frosts trooped in, their arms bulging with elegantly wrapped gifts.

"And to show just how fond of our little Fiona we all are and to make amends for my own rather hasty words," he shook his head with a contrite and, Jeptha felt, contrived smile, "we've brought a few small gifts to help brighten up the wedding day." He motioned his portly son forward, and Edward Frost awkwardly handed Fiona a large beribboned box.

She opened it and gave a gasp of astonishment. A beautiful white Irish lace wedding dress lay inside, hand embroidered with hundreds of cream-colored seed pearls.

"Yes!" Isaiah Frost chuckled again with what Jeptha thought looked far too much like a calculating gleam behind the benign smile. "Just like one of our family."

* * * *

Skaket Creek
June 14th, 1858
6:38 p.m.

"Is there something wrong? Mr. Dawes…Jeptha…Husband?"

Jeptha looked up in confusion at his hours-old bride and shook his head, partly to answer no and partly to try to clear it of the cobwebs of remembering. Finally he forced a smile onto his face and shook his head again. "No, Miss MacDonald…Fiona…I mean, Mrs. Dawes. No, there is nothing wrong, nothing at all."

He surreptitiously wiped his damp palms on the trousers of his new five-dollar suit and fastened both of his hands around the tiny waist of his new wife. He lifted her off of the single step of the shiny new surrey and carefully hooked his left arm behind her back while his right arm straightened to support her legs and a half-dozen yards of white Irish lace that made up the long train of her wedding dress.

"Is everything all right, Husband?" Fiona asked, an uncertain frown on her young face.

"Yes, of course," Jeptha answered with his best attempt at a reassuring smile.

But it wasn't. Something still nagged at him around the dusty, uneasy corners of his mind. He tried not to think of it and instead to focus on the lovely young woman in white that he carried up the newly laid, red brick walkway to the threshold of the raw, un-weathered shingle house. But it didn't work. The thoughts came despite his best efforts and perched like tiny black vultures in the dark closets of his inner most secrets.

He mounted the wide wooden porch steps, and as his newly purchased, shiny black boots touched the freshly cut oak threshold, the conversation that he'd had just twenty-four hours ago with his then bride-to-be came back to him.

They had driven out to the barely completed house on Skaket Creek to distribute some new furniture and the pitifully few personal possessions that each of them owned. They'd been unpacking a crate of books that Jeptha had purchased through a factor/lawyer in Boston, and Fiona placed them one by one on the freshly milled walnut shelves of the house's library. As the majority of the books had been shipped direct from the printer, Fiona dutifully cut the pages before placing each one carefully on the library shelves.

Suddenly she stopped and frowned. Concerned at her expression, Jeptha had asked, "What is it, Miss MacDonald? Is there something wrong with those books?"

She shook her head. "No, Mr. Dawes. It's just that.... It's just that these books reminded me...of another book."

"What other book, Miss MacDonald?"

She frowned for a moment longer and shook her head again. "Not a book exactly. A journal; my diary."

"You kept a diary, a logbook, as it were?" Jeptha's thoughts flashed back to that last terrible night on board the *Elizabeth James*.

"Yes, Mr. Dawes—Jeptha." Fiona continued, "Nothing so grand as a captain's log book, or even an explorer's journal. Just the random thoughts and tedious daily happenings of a lonely girl in service in a strange country far from family and friends."

"And what secret talks and momentous happenings did you confide to your diary, Miss MacDonald—I mean, Fiona?" Jeptha smiled gently.

"Things of no great import." She smiled back. "Except for...."

"Except for what, Miss Mac—Fiona?"

She looked down at him from the stool she stood on while placing the books on the tall library shelves and answered, "Except for the joy I felt the evening that you asked me to become your wife."

Jeptha kept smiling as she continued.

"I had confided to my diary, the very tender feelings that I had for you and how I would do everything in my power to make you a good and proper and loving wife."

"I know you will, Fiona," Jeptha whispered.

"And yet," she went on, almost as if she hadn't heard him, "and yet, I did confess to my diary that there was a small dark part of your soul that you kept walled off from me. A secret kept locked behind a door or buried...."

She didn't seem to notice that Jeptha had most certainly turned pale.

"And I said to my diary that I had to somehow find the key to open that dark, walled part in your soul. And I speculated as to how I knew that it had much to do with what is buried beneath the gray granite slab in that tiny room that now lies forever hidden beneath the foundations of this house."

Jeptha grasped both of her hands with an unconscious force that made her wince. "Miss...Fiona. I must ask you—command you—no, beg you—to never mention that room and that which lies buried under the gray stone slab *ever again*."

Despite the pressure of his hard, calloused hands, she remained silent for a moment before answering. "Of course I won't. I swore to you that night you confided in me that I'd never tell a living soul. And I haven't—at least not any *living* soul."

"Meaning?" Jeptha asked with a frown.

"Meaning," Fiona answered, not meeting his eyes, "not a *living* soul, only...only the pages of my diary."

"You wrote it down?" Horrified, Jeptha gasped.

"No, no!" Fiona shook her head. "Only hints, musings to myself. References to the secret room and something buried."

"But you didn't say what, did you?"

"No. I swear it, my love," Fiona said, visibly steeling herself against the unrealized but increasing pressure of his hands on her own.

Slowly he began to breathe easier, and his grip relaxed. "Then all is well." He drew in a deep breath.

She didn't answer for a moment. Finally, she shook her head. "I-I am afraid not, Mr. Dawes. That night we told Mr. Frost that I was leaving his service and he shouted at me to pack my belongings and leave his house on the instant? I'm afraid that in my distress and haste to vacate the garret room on the third floor I forgot something."

Nausea had pervaded Jeptha's throat. He didn't need to ask what she had forgotten but now he knew what had prompted the armloads of gifts and beautiful white wedding dress on that day three weeks ago.

Now, he looked again at his young bride in his arms and tried to drive the memory of her confession of the missing diary from his mind.

He crossed the threshold and set her down in the spacious front hallway.

"Welcome to your new home, Mrs. Dawes."

He did his best to smile, and Fiona did too. But she knew him too well by now and could almost certainly tell what he was thinking—and remembering.

They walked deeper into the house and clasped hands to try to dispel each other's fears. But they both knew as the early evening shadows closed in around them that the consequences of the missing diary and the mysterious hints it contained were just beginning.

Chapter Thirteen

"You're dead meat, McCarthy!"

The threat might have sounded more ominous, Mick mused, if the fat, red-faced chief of the Skaket Harbor Police Department hadn't been simultaneously rubbing his stomach and his testicles while he delivered it.

Mick's father, "Big Mike's" only response to the threat, was an amused smile.

When it appeared that his words didn't seem to be registering, the chief reluctantly stopped massaging his aching private parts and glared up at Big Mike.

"And I'm gonna start by making a call to the chief of the Boston Police Department and telling him to pull your PI license."

Big Mike looked at the phone. "Would you like me to dial it for you? That way you could use both hands to go back to doing what you seem to like best." Big Mike's grin got even wider. "And after getting a good look at you and your nephew, I can understand that's probably the most useful thing that the two of you could do with either hand."

Chief Frost grabbed the phone out of its cradle and dialed a string of numbers.

Big Mike leaned against wall and watched with the same amused smile.

After a few seconds, Frost said, in his most official tone, "This is the chief of Skaket Harbor Police, Arthur Frost. Put me through to...," he looked down at the sheet of names of Massachusetts's cities and towns, listing the ranking officers of every precinct in the Commonwealth, "Captain Dennis Gilmore." He held the receiver to his ear and glared at Mike as he waited.

After a few minutes he said, "Gilmore? Is this Captain Dennis Gilmore? Yes, this is Chief Frost down on the Cape. I believe you were the issuing officer who approved a PI license for a Michael McCarthy operating out of a Cambridge, Massachusetts location? Yes? Well, I'd like to the start the paperwork rolling to pull that license, and while you're at it, I suggest you pull his license to carry as well.

"Why? Why? 'Cause I've got him and his son in my office and under arrest for assault and battery on a police officer; in fact, two police officers. And resisting arrest! And.... What? Yes he is. As a matter fact, he's standing right in front of me. Why! Okay, okay. All right, here."

Arthur Frost warily handed the phone to Big Mike.

Big Mike took the phone and spoke casually into the receiver. "Hey, Denny, how's it hanging? Yeah. Yeah...that's right, I sure as hell did! Yeah, and just in time too as it turns out.... The charge? Oh yeah, I'd *love* to talk about the charge. But first, d'you wanna do me a favor, Denny? Will you give a quick call over to Judge Parker and tell him that I need a bench warrant—for two people. Yeah, I got their names. Arthur Frost and Douglas Frost, both of Skaket Harbor. The charge? Yeah, very serious—attempted rape. And if my son's darlin' girlfriend hadn't called me this morning after these two fine examples of law and order arrested him...," Mike looked at Bridget, and she nodded solemnly, "I'm pretty damn sure that by now the charge would be attempted rape and *murder*."

All of the color drained from the face of Skaket Harbor's Chief of Police.

"You wouldn't dare," he whispered.

"Watch me," Big Mike said coldly.

"Wait!"

Big Mike paused, still holding the receiver.

"Wait...let me have the phone."

Big Mike looked at him for a moment and then spoke into the phone. "I think he wants to speak to you again."

Chief Frost held out a hand for the phone, but Big Mike turned away and answered into the receiver, "Yeah? Well, okay, Denny, if you think so. Yeah, I guess I could live with that. Okay, yup. Here he is." Mike let the phone fall into Frost's outstretched hand so that he fumbled for and almost dropped it.

He glared up at Mike again and barked, "Chief Frost here! Yes, well no, no! Of course not! What you think I am! What? No, that's ridiculous! I don't care how long you've known him, I demand.... Errr—no, sorry, I mean...of course, *request*. A professional courtesy between department heads. How many? Well, there's me and Dougie and...well, yes, he is my nephew, but that doesn't mean.... He didn't! And no, I didn't! Of course not. Well, no, I certainly don't want that. No, no, you're right, a misunderstanding. Okay, and yes—yes I do. I withdraw the charges."

He looked at Big Mike again and then over to where Mick stood in the corner of the room, both of his arms wrapped protectively around Bridget.

"But," Frost said, staring maliciously at Mike, "I still need to hold the son. What? Why, on suspicion of murder! Yes! Yes! And, and the girl too as a material witness. Oh, but you're wrong, I can and...."

Mick heard the sound of a voice rising on the other end of the line. Tiny beads of sweat rose on the chief's slowly reddening forehead.

"No! Well, I mean, of course I don't. No...I mean yes...yes, yes. Well certainly. That makes more sense. Okay, yes, yes. All right."

Frost, his face a tight mask, held out the phone to Big Mike. "Here," was all he said.

Big Mike took the phone. "Yeah, Denny?" He listened for a second or two and finally grunted, "Okay, and Denny? Thanks."

He handed the receiver back to Frost and proffered his hand. "Give me the keys to the cuffs."

Frost's face grew redder, but he snarled, "Here!"

Big Mike went over to Mick and Bridget and unlocked the single handcuff that still dangled from each of their wrists.

Mick rubbed his left wrist and took two quick strides over to where Dougie Frost still retched into the wastebasket between his knees. "Get up, you piece of shit!" he hissed.

Dougie rubbed his stomach where Big Mike had hit him when he'd burst in and found him pawing Bridget. He looked at Mick, moaned again, and threw up into the wastebasket—again.

Mick reached for Dougie, but Big Mike's hand on his wrist stopped him.

Big Mike slowly shook his head. "Uh-huh, Mickey, I promised Denny."

"Well I didn't frigging promise him anything, Dad!" Mick snarled, reaching for Dougie again. "I'm gonna make that little prick pay for what he tried to do to Bridget!"

Big Mike didn't let go. He shook his head again. "But not now, Mick, not just yet."

Mick breathed out heavily as his fists clenched and unclenched. He nodded. "Okay, Pop. Okay. Not just yet."

Deputy Douglas Frost looked up at him between retches, the expression on his face showing that he was just beginning to realize that there might be worse things than throwing up into a wastebasket.

Much worse.

* * * *

As the door of the cinder block building that did double duty as town offices and police department of Skaket Harbor swung closed, the three people walking up the cement steps heard the angry voice of Chief Arthur Frost call after them. "Remember, McCarthy! One week—seven days. And then your kid's ass is mine!"

Mick stood on the top step of the basement entrance to the small mean rooms of the Skaket Harbor Police Department and drew a deep, cleansing breath of the fog-laden, salt air. Bridget rubbed her wrists where the handcuffs had been closed around them less than an hour before. She didn't realize that Mick watched her as she unconsciously smoothed the generous curve of her small, firm breasts where they molded to her sweater. Seemingly without thinking, she wiped her hands on her skirt as if to wipe off the touch of where Dougie Frost had pawed her in the holding cells.

Mick's hands clenched once more, and he turned back towards the Skaket Police Department door, but Big Mike clamped a hand on his shoulder and shook his head.

"I told you, Mickey, not now, not yet."

"Okay, Pop, then when?"

"Soon, I promise you."

"Uh-huh, that's not good enough. Do you know what he—they... those bastards—tried to do to her?"

"Yeah, I do, Mickey."

"And you can just stand there and tell me not here, not now?"

"I gave my word."

"To who? What did you promise? What's the deal, Pop? I'm not a friggin' kid anymore. And I'm not just your son—I'm also your partner. And I've got a hunch that Frost's parting remark about 'One week' concerns me—big time."

Big Mike looked straight up into the sky, until the fog-wet clouds parted for a moment and he got a glimpse of the moon. "Yeah, Mick, it does."

"Okay, Pop," Mick said softly. "So what's the deal? What are we in for?"

Big Mike kept on looking up at the sky. The night wind blew in clouds again, and the moon disappeared.

"Denny—Captain Gilmore—bought us a week. No more. Most of what I told Frost was BS. But as a gutless piece of crap, in a long line of gutless pieces of crap, he didn't have enough balls to challenge it."

Mick laughed. "That's because you flattened what little balls he had, Pop."

Big Mike smiled. "Didn't take much to do that."

Mick got serious again. "So you promised your old station B buddy that in one week we would what?"

Big Mike took his eyes off of the now invisible moon and put both of his large, rough hands on his son's shoulders. "I told him that within one week—seven days from today—we'd have the killer of the Randolph girl, not just identified, but bagged, tagged, and delivered."

"And if we don't?"

Big Mike McCarthy gazed at his son for a minute and said in a voice too low for Bridget to hear, "Then you turn yourself in to Frost. No fuss, no hassle, and stand trial for the murder of Karen Randolph."

Mickey glanced up to where the moon poked out from behind a cloud, illuminating the three of them standing there, and wondered if it would be shining on this same spot seven days from now. He shook his head. "One week."

Chapter Fourteen

"Mickey?"

A breath exhaled, as soft as the passing of the cloud over the moon that shone through the big bay window of the second-floor room overlooking Cape Cod Bay.

Mick slowly twisted his head up to the right until Bridget's pale white face became visible in the flickering moonlight. Was it pale from the moonlight, pale from exhaustion, or pale from fear?

The moon gave no answers. It just shone over the equally impassive, uncaring sea as two friends, lovers, and sometimes mysterious strangers, tried to put the fractured pieces of their lives back together again.

Bridget came around the old wingback chair where Mick sat staring out the bay window at the ocean and knelt down on the floor next to him.

She tucked her legs up underneath her and leaned her cheek against the worn denim of his jeans.

"Mickey?" she said again.

"What, babe?" Mick still stared out at the ocean.

"Tell me again. What did your Da promise his mate back in Boston, then?"

"You mean Capt. Gilmore, Denny?"

"Yes."

"He gave him his word that we'll find the real killer of Karen Randolph and present the Barnstable County D.A. with irrefutable evidence of his guilt, before midnight on the 23rd of August. One week from today."

"And if we don't—if we can't find the killer?"

"Then at 12:01 a.m. on August 24th, Pop hands me over to the 'tender mercies' of Chief Arthur Frost and his inbred, idiot nephew."

Mick looked down at Bridget. She wrapped both of her arms around his legs, her cheek still pressed tightly against the blue jean fabric covering his right leg. She remained silent, but he just barely made out the small, sharp movements of her shoulder blades. The cloth pressed into his leg next to her left cheek felt damp. She was crying.

"Bridge...? Baby? Don't. Please don't. I'll figure out something. We'll...we'll figure out something. It'll be okay. I promise."

She didn't look up. She kept her head down, stared at the floor, and said softly, "If they take you, Mickey, I don't know what I'll do. I've seen what prison can do to a man. When I was just a girl, back home in Ireland, I saw men that I'd known all of my life. Good men. I saw them after they came out. I saw what they'd become and what happened to their families. To the ones that loved them. And the ones that they had loved...." She gazed up at him, her face streaked with liquid silver tears that glistened on her pale skin in the cold metallic moonlight.

"If that happened to you, I wouldn't want to live anymore, Mickey. I'd-I'd...." She angrily rubbed her left hand across her wet eyes and stared at Mick with a fierce determination that he'd come to know only too well. "I'd take the .38 that your Da gave you. The very one that rests in the bike's saddle bags right now. I'd take it and kill both of those evil spalpeens."

And Mick knew that she would.

"And then—and then I'd turn the gun on mys—"

"No!"

"It would be a bloody blessin'!"

"No!" He grabbed her by the shoulders. "Stop it! Don't ever let me hear that from you again. You're strong, goddamn it! You're fighter, a survivor! No matter what happens you've got to promise me that you'll stay free and strong for both of us." His fingers dug into her shoulders, and he held her at arm's length. His gray-blue eyes bored into hers. "You hear me, Bridget? I mean it, damn it! I mean it!"

Suddenly he realized he was hurting her. But she didn't acknowledge the pain. She never even winced. She just shook her head and said quietly, "I *was* strong—I was a survivor. Back when I had all of those cold stonewalls that I had brought from Ireland wrapped around my heart. Back before I cared. Back before I met you." She shook her head once more. "Caring and loving can be a terrible curse darlin'. But I can't change it now. And I don't want to."

Two tiny drops traced paths from the corners of each of her wide-open green eyes and over the twin arches of her high Celtic cheekbones. He looked down at his hands where they gripped her as though he'd forgotten they belonged to him. His knuckles, white above his fingers, dug into her flesh. He pulled his hands away as though they'd been on a hot stove.

"Oh, my god. Bridge. I'm sorry. Did I hurt you, babe? I didn't mean to. It's just that I love you so frigging much, and to hear you talking crazy like that.... And this whole stupid fucking day with those two bastards putting their fucking hands all over you, and me being locked up in a goddamn cell where I couldn't do anything about it. And...and... son of a bitch!"

Mick jumped up and in blind frustrated rage rammed his right fist into the old wooden wardrobe next to the chair. The dry wood splintered, and his right arm went straight through the closed front cabinet door and into the wooden back panel. It was so old and brittle, and Mick was so angry and frustrated, that it felt like little more than paper to him. That is until he withdrew his arm and saw the blood dripping from his knuckles. He stared down stupidly at his bleeding right hand as if he couldn't understand what had happened and where all the dripping red liquid came from. He turned back to Bridget. "I-I...."

"Hush." She took his hand and kissed each bloody knuckle. Then she drew him close to her and laid her wet cheek on his.

His cheek was wet, too, he realized. She tugged him towards the old four-poster bed. "Make love to me," she whispered.

Mick looked at her breasts—they pressed against his chest—and couldn't burn away the image of the last hand that had touched them. His jaw tightened.

"No, Mickey," Bridget whispered. "That pathetic, dirty little boy didn't touch me. He never could. Only you can, darlin', only you."

She pulled her sweater over her head, unsnapped her bra, and let it fall to the floor. "Only for you, darlin', only for you." She took his bloody hand and put it deliberately on her breast.

"Bridge...." He breathed heavily. "My hand...the blood...."

"Yes!" she said fiercely, taking his hand and rubbing the bloody knuckles over her white breasts. "Your blood on my body, like the old ways, the ways of the Druids and Celtic priestesses. The blood of my man, it makes me his—his alone!"

She held out her arms, drew him down onto the bed and rolled on top of him, then slowly lifted his T-shirt over his head and unbuttoned the top button of his Levis.

He reached up and ran his hands over her beautiful white skin. The bright red blood on her moon-pale breasts mingled with his sweat as they rocked together, and she said over and over again, like an ancient Celtic chant, "Only you...only you...only you."

* * * *

Mick opened one eye and glanced at the gray light stealing through the window.

The moon had grown tired of watching the lovers and decided to pack it in for the night. But apparently the sun's celestial alarm clock hadn't gone off, or he was sleeping in this morning, because the water stretching out from the bay was still a cold, gray-lead hue.

Mick turned and opened the other still sleepy eye to find another pair staring into his own. Bridget watched him, her head propped up on the pillow next to his, her tiny fingers laced underneath her delicate chin.

"What're you doing?" Mick mumbled sleepily.

"Watching you."

"I can see that. Why?"

She looked at him with large, serious eyes. "To make sure the fairies don't steal ya and leave a changeling in your place."

Mick rolled on to his elbow and said, "You don't really believe that," and added with just a tiny tinge of unease, "do you?"

The serious look remained for a few heartbeats before her eyes crinkled and the corners of her mouth turned up. "No." She smiled. "But I used to."

"Yeah, well I used to believe in Santa Claus and the Easter Bunny, and a fat lot of good that did me."

"Oh, come here, you old grouch." She giggled, pulling him on top of her.

"I swear, babe," he grinned, "by the time the sun finally comes up, there won't even be enough left of me to cast a shadow."

She giggled again and brought his hand, still sticky with dried blood, towards her lips. Suddenly, she hesitated and then frowned at his hand.

Mick looked at her expression and then at his hand.

"Yeah, sorry, babe, I forgot about that. Hang on a second, let me run some cold water over it." He got up from the bed, moved over to the small sink washstand in the corner of the room, and turned on the tap. He let the water run for a moment before pushing his scarred knuckles towards the flow.

"Wait!" Bridget called.

"Huh?"

She jumped up from the bed and grabbed his right hand.

"Wait," she said again. "Come over here." She dragged him into the pale of the predawn light streaming through the big bay window. Gently, she turned his hand over and held the side of it up to the window. "There," she said.

Mick looked. Something stuck to the side of his hand—something yellowish and stiff that had almost been glued by the blood and ran all the way along the edge of his little finger.

"What the hell...?"

"Shush.... Wait, don't move." She ran over to her suitcase, knelt down, and came back with a small nail file. "Sit." She pushed Mick downed onto the big wingback chair. "Now hold still." Gently, she inserted the nail file under the stiff, brittle film on his right hand and lifted it away from the skin.

Finally, she said, "There," and held it up to the increasing dawn light. It was a thin strip of paper, or cardboard, or parchment. And through the stain of dried blood Mick saw...writing.

"Where the hell did that come from?" Mick said.

They both stared at the splintered door of the wardrobe closet.

Bridget jumped up and tugged the battered door open. A few more slivers of wood fell out, but no paper. She wrenched the other door open and peered at the back where the force of Mick's rage had carried his fist through the door and cracked open the back of the old armoire. She peered in and worked two thin fingers into the six-inch crack in the back panel. She strained to push her fingers in further, and then a tiny rustling sound, the sound of something old and thin and brittle, kissed the air. She eased it through the crack and brought the object out into the growing pink dawn light. She placed it on the bed, and they looked at it. It was a packet of wrinkled brown-yellow papers, curling at the edges and tied with a faded red ribbon held in place by the shattered remains of sealing wax.

Bridget carefully lifted the ribbon away from the packet and scraped off the remaining pieces of sealing wax that Mick's fist had shattered. She opened the first page and smoothed it out on the bed.

Dawn's light broke through the big bay window as they began to read.

Chapter Fifteen

I must set down these lines on random bits of paper as I have given my solemn word to my own dear husband that I would never again keep a diary. And yet, I am so often alone, living this far from town, and Mr. Dawes—I now chide myself and must remember that as his wife, I may call him by his Christian name, Jeptha. But he—Jeptha— being gone so often, I do confess to a certain loneliness. And thus the need to confide in something, be it only a few sheets of common paper.

* * * *

Skaket Creek
September 22ⁿᵈ, 1858
5:14 p.m.

Fiona sat on her "special" driftwood log and stared out at the ocean.

This was one of her favorite times of the day to watch the sea as it swept in and out of the tidal creek. She especially enjoyed watching the never-ending changes in sea and marsh from the enormous old weathered driftwood log that some violent storm had pushed well beyond the high tide mark, long forgotten years ago.

It must have been a mighty tree, Fiona had often thought, perhaps even one of the primeval giants that had awed the Pilgrims when they first set eyes upon Cape Cod Bay and the rocky shores of the Plymouth colony. Some ancient pioneer had hacked part of the huge tree away before giving up a job that had apparently proven to be beyond his strength or tools—or both.

However, probably unknown to that long ago woodsman, he had weakened the giant old tree just enough so that the next big storm had snapped the trunk off at the base and torn the stump out by its roots. Who knew how long it had drifted until it had been washed up here by some storm and left to bleach in the sun and salt wind. Over the years or centuries, not only the bark and broken branches had been scoured clean, but the constant action of the wind and sand had left the surface as smooth as silk. And in a strange trick of nature, the broken stump had been deposited on the beach fully upright.

Perhaps it was her imagination or the fanciful Celtic tales of her childhood working overtime, but to her eyes, the smooth, salt-white old stump looked just like a fairy throne. There was the seat, hacked out by the long ago ax. And the back, formed by a four foot, gracefully tapering piece of wood where the trunk had splintered off from the stump. Finally, the old roots themselves, as they radiated away from the stump and poked out of the sand like skeletal claws, gave the whole scene an eerie, other-worldly effect.

Fiona liked to sit in the natural throne formed by the weathered stump and imagine that she was an ancient Celtic queen who ruled a mythical land of sea sprites and Silkies. And during the many long weeks that Jeptha left her alone while he pursued his mysterious business in Boston, she would sit on her smooth, white throne on the beach in front of their house at sunset and watch for the packet boat that might be bringing him back to her.

Most nights she didn't see it, of course. There was fog or rain or haze. And most of the few times she did, it was empty. But one or two times during the past three months, when the weather was clear and the light just right, she had seen it. And on those nights, she was a happy young queen in her royal seaside court.

On those joyous nights, she rushed up the winding pathway through the dunes to make ready "the ocean hall" to receive her consort, like Venus welcoming Neptune home.

She smiled sadly to herself. Marriage and a home of her own had seemingly turned her back into a girl, complete with silly notions and romantic fantasies. And although the nights when Jeptha was home were truly magical, during the long days when he was gone, her loneliness seemed sometimes unbearable.

She scrubbed and cleaned the wood-shingled house from attic to porch until it sparkled in the late September sun. But when all of her chores were done in the house and all in it was perfect, she was still lonely.

That's why, she thought guiltily, *I broke my solemn promise to my husband, to keep no more diaries.* And Fiona MacDonald—now proudly Dawes—had been raised that each promise given was indeed a solemn vow.

The breach bothered her terribly. And so she tried to rationalize it in her own mind. It wasn't a diary. It was just...musing. The silly, lonely musings of a silly, lonely young wife.

But still, in the warm September dusk, she hoped and dreamed that soon her husband would be home, and maybe, just maybe, there was a way to keep him home with her. At least those were her hopes and dreams when she looked up from the sand and seagrass at her feet and saw...a speck appear on the horizon, was it? No, just more of her wishful thinking, wanting it to be so, and so seeing what she wanted to see.

"Stop it, girl!" she scolded herself. "Look with your eyes as well as your heart. And see the truth as God meant you to see it." She strained her eyes. Yes, for certain, it was the evening packet boat!

Her heart beat faster, and she unconsciously held her breath as she focused her gaze on the stern of the boat. And, yes, her luck still held. A small dot on the stern of the boat, in the spot that Jeptha always occupied when the Boston Packet began its southeast turn into Cape Cod Bay. Now, there was only one thing more till she could be certain that it was her own dear man coming home to her. Fiona raised her right hand to shade her eyes from the sun's slanting rays reflecting off the still surface of the bay. Her eyes watered from the glare—or maybe it was tears of need and longing. She didn't care.

"Oh, please," she whispered. "Dear Lord, I know you've little time for silly, lonely girls, but if you could just spare the tiniest moment and in your great compassion...please let it be him." She bowed her head, shut her eyes, and opened them once more. As the boat drew closer, the small dot on the stern of the packet elongated to something that vaguely resembled a human form. And then...it moved. Just the tiniest flicker of a straight line reaching up formed the faraway silhouette swinging back and forth like an upside-down pendulum.

She gave a shriek of joy. It *was* Jeptha! That was his signal to her when he was returning on the packet. He would stand on the stern and wave his tall beaver hat above his head. He was coming home!

She jumped up from her make-believe throne and ran up the path to the house. Not only did she want to have the dinner hot on the table for her returning Neptune, but she also needed to put something away. A packet of paper filled with her lonely thoughts and dreams and sometimes puzzled and fearful thoughts about her husband and his secrets. Thoughts that she shared with no one but herself and those stiff sheets of inexpensive writing paper that lay on the small writing table in the front sitting room upstairs.

She rushed into the room where the setting evening sun washed the walls with pink and began gathering up the pages strewn about the table.

She looked out the big bay window to the sand-rutted road that Jeptha would soon be riding down and firmly tied the bundle of papers with one of her hair ribbons.

She walked over to the cherry wood wardrobe in which she'd stored all of her old coats and servant's uniforms from her former life and slid them behind a loose board in the back of the wardrobe. She smiled as she paused to put away what she had come to think of as her "loneliness companion".

I have no need of you now. She smiled. *My husband is coming home.*

* * * *

Skaket Creek
Early Evening
September 22nd, 1858

Before replacing these papers back in their hiding place, I must add a hasty postscript. While watching out the front window of this room, I've seen my own dear husband pull the surrey up to the front porch. He looks so handsome and yet so melancholy all at the same time. I will do my best to cheer him when I greet him in a moment, so I must put away these papers and go to him now.

But wait—there is one thing more. As he steps down from the surrey, I see that he carries a large black leather satchel, rather like a doctor's bag. It is filled with small parcels wrapped in plain brown paper.

I wonder...what can they be?

* * * *

The Skaket Inn
August 18th, 1968
6:47 a.m.

Bridget carefully placed the yellow, brittle piece of paper on top of a half dozen others she'd read aloud and looked at Mick.

He shook his head, whistled softly through his teeth, and glanced over at the splintered wardrobe in the corner. "So that's why she hid those papers in the back of that thing. She was afraid that hubby was gonna come home and find her making like 'Brenda Starr, girl reporter' and throw a hissy fit."

Bridget sighed and shook her head too. "I love you, Michael darlin', but you do have a talent for boiling the romantic right down to the trivial."

"Oh yeah?" Mick grinned. "Come here, my little Irish lass, and I'll show you just how romantic I can be!"

Ric Wasley

"Romantic doesn't always have to mean tickling the back of my neck with your tongue, you know."

Mick stopped doing what she had so accurately described and concentrated on looking thoughtful. Then he said in his best phony Harvard accent, "You know, my dear Miss Connolly, I do believe you're right. I have been paying far too much attention to the back of your neck lately. And yes, I do agree that it is high time I started giving equal attention to some even more delectable portions of your anatomy." He pulled her backwards until her shoulders rested on his left arm lying on the bed sheets, while his right hand reached around and slowly undid the buttons of her nightgown one by one.

"Ah-ha, just as I thought." He smiled as the loosened nightgown fell away to reveal her creamy white breasts. "These poor, neglected little beauties are just crying out for some of Dr. McCarthy's famous TLC."

"McCarthy—Mickey. Stop it. The sun's almost up, and we need to get on with things."

"My sentiments exactly, Miss Connolly." Mick grinned and went back to covering the upper half of her body with wet and increasingly intimate kisses.

Bridget sighed and said, "If you keep that up, McCarthy, in another five minutes I'm gonna forget all about these papers and...."

Mick winked at her and whispered, "I'll see if I can make it happen in two."

The last of Bridget's resistance evaporated, and she put both of her arms around Mick. "Time's up," she whispered back.

A knock sounded at the door.

They froze.

A voice on the other side of the door called out softly, "Bridget? Mick? Are you up? It's Kathy."

Mick held one finger to Bridget's lips, but she shook her head and answered with a sigh, "Yes, Kathy. We're...up."

"I'm...I'm sorry to bug you so early, but can you meet me downstairs in ten minutes? I've got something to tell you. It's really important."

Bridget looked over at a very unhappy Mick and responded with a wry smile that appeared to hide a disappointment as great as his. "All right, Kathy, we'll be there."

* * * *

Skaket Creek Inn
August 18th, 1968
7:36 a.m.

87

When Mick and Bridget got down to the lobby, they found a red and puffy-eyed Kathy Dawes standing in front of the entrance to the dining room waiting for them. She looked like she'd been crying.

Aunt Helen stood in her usual spot behind the registration desk, where she could observe all comings and goings with her perpetual frown of disapproval.

She greeted Mick and Bridget with a *cheery,* "Harrumph, are you still here? I thought that Chief Frost was going to lock you up and throw away the key." She gave a contemptuous shake of her head and muttered, "Fat pea-brain never could do anything right. So now I'm supposed put up with a murderer and his bimbo in my inn? Ha! I don't think so. I want the two of you packed and out of here before ten a.m. Do I make myself clear?"

Bridget's face turned a bright crimson with equal amounts of embarrassment and anger. Mick felt none of her embarrassment— only the anger. And he opened his mouth to tell the old biddy just what she could do with her insults and orders, but Kathy spoke up from the doorway. "The thing you're forgetting, Aunt Helen, is you don't own this place. It belongs to my mother—and me."

"Well! I'm going upstairs to talk to her right now," she snapped at Kathy. "And when I get through telling her about these two, she'll send them packing so fast it'll make your—"

Kathy took three quick strides to the front desk, leaned against the counter, and hissed into her aunt's stunned face, "If you upset her with any of your spite and malice, I will see that it comes back to you threefold." She glared at her aunt and whispered, "And you know that I can do it too!"

The old woman backed away from the counter, a look of fear replacing that of smug contempt. She dropped her gaze and muttered in a voice now oozing with wounded self-pity, "Harrumph, *I* might as well pack my bags and go for all the appreciation I get around here."

Kathy looked at her aunt with a level expression and responded softly, "You're always free to leave, Aunt." She turned back to Mick and Bridget and, grasping one of each of their hands, pulled them through the dining room towards the pub beyond. "C'mon, guys, I think we need a little privacy." She stopped, turned, and looked at Mick for a moment before speaking. "I know all about what happened last night. And if it's any comfort," she gazed into Mick's eyes, "I believe that you're innocent."

Mick swallowed hard. "Thanks, Kathy. We really appreciate having at least one person around here that doesn't think I'm some psycho killer. Right, Bridge?"

She nodded. "Yes, thank you, Kathy. It feels good to have someone on our side."

"Yeah." Mick smiled. "Welcome to the Mick Isn't an Ax Murderer club. It's got a pretty small membership, but we're wide open to new recruits."

Kathy mustered a tiny smile.

"In fact," he continued, "I'm thinking of opening another ancillary branch that'll be called something like: The Frosts Are a Bunch of Perverted Creeps." His smile faded, and he set his mouth in a hard, thin line. "And I've appointed myself president of this particular club and I plan on taking care of some unfinished business, with those two right at the top of the agenda."

Kathy tried desperately to smile herself, but it looked like she had just about reached the limit of her stiff-upper-lip façade. She nodded, and two small teardrops traced a path down her cheek, which now appeared pale under her salt-air tan.

She stayed quiet for a moment and then said, "You may not be as alone as you think, Mick." She looked over his shoulder, back towards the inn's lobby. "You're not the only ones who have had trouble with the Frosts."

"What do you mean, Kathy?" Bridget asked softly.

Kathy shivered, as though a cold draft had suddenly brushed her. Her eyes turned grim. "They've plagued our family for more that one hundred years. They've even...." She shook her head and seemed to change her mind about whatever it was she had been going to tell them. She took a deep breath. "But the bottom line is that Karen Randolph was my friend. And now she's dead. Yes, I know that she could be kind of ditzy and was a terrible flirt, but she was also my friend." She stared at Mick and Bridget and added in a voice made all that more surprising by its harshness, "And I'm going to make sure that the evil bastard who murdered her pays for it!"

Bridget, still holding almost protectively onto Mick's arm, took a step backwards. "But...but you do believe what you just told us, right? That Mickey didn't do it?"

Kathy nodded solemnly. "Yes, I know he didn't do it."

"How?" Mick asked. "I mean, I'm really glad you feel that way, but how can you be so sure? And whatever it is, can we bottle it and sprinkle a little on the Frosts and maybe a judge and jury or two?"

"Yes, Kathy," Bridget said. "We're very grateful for your support, but if you don't mind my asking, why are you so certain?"

With the same solemn look, accompanied by the tiniest bit of a twinkle in her eye, Kathy answered, "My mother told me."

Puzzled, Mick asked, "Your mother? But she's never even seen us!"

She pulled them by the hands again.

"C'mon. I've got something to tell—and to show you. And maybe even something that can help."

Chapter Sixteen

Jeptha looked up from the half empty bowl of oyster stew that he had been ravenously devouring and said, "Fiona, you're not eating. Why?"

Fiona leaned forward across the plain plank table they sat either side of and wiped a drop of oyster broth from the edge of her husband's silky black mustache. "I am more content to watch you eat, my love."

"Then have a slice of this fine Stilton cheese that I brought from Boston," he said while spooning up another mouthful of Fiona's delicious, rich stew. "It's imported from England, you know. From Yorkshire, or so I was told."

"Yes, I remember," Fiona said. "When I was a girl in Belfast, we would have it every Christmas. A treat, as it were. Though if truth be told, I never fancied it much as a girl. I only longed for it when I went into service and had to fetch and carry throughout the long meals that the family had—seven or eight courses—and my supper could not be tasted until their dinner finished and all was cleared away."

She stared off into space. "It was then, by the time I was serving the ladies their sweet and the men and their brandy and port and cheese, that I would be so hungry that the ripe smell of the Stilton as I cut each slice affected me so much that my mouth watered."

The lines around her mouth hardened. "Once, I was so hungry that I cut and ate a slice on the way back to the kitchen. The pantry maid saw me and told the cook." She looked down at the rich, ripe cheese with its dappled veins of blue and said bitterly, "They stopped two pennies of my wages for that slice, and the cook fed my dinner to the dog that night. Since then, I've never been able to abide the sight of Stilton cheese."

Jeptha stopped eating and put down his spoon. He came around the table and wrapped his arms around her. "I am sorry, Fiona. I have known of a rough life of often deprivation and danger. But you, my love, have known a hard life. And yet, throughout all, you have maintained a good and loving heart."

Fiona leaned her head on his chest and said quietly, "I am glad to have you home, Husband. Very glad."

They stayed like that for a long time, until the wicks burned low in the whale oil lamps on the plain kitchen table.

Finally, Fiona said, "Come, let's go into the parlor."

"Yes." Jeptha smiled. "I have some small gifts for you. Things from

Boston that I thought might please you."

They walked into the large front parlor, and Jeptha pulled brightly wrapped packages from his black leather bag. He placed them one by one on the lace-covered tabletop in front of Fiona.

She unwrapped the first one, a beautiful tortoiseshell brush and comb set, chased with finely worked silver and engraved with the initials F. McD. D.

"Jeptha," she gasped and shook her head, "it's beautiful."

"Not half so beautiful as you, wife." He smiled and rummaged through the black bag again. As he did, he pulled out several oddly shaped packages and placed them to one side of the table.

Fiona stared. They were the parcels she had seen from the second floor window.

"Ah," he said, smiling, "here's another." He placed a small box with red velvet ribbon in front of her.

Fiona looked from the bright box and then to the half dozen objects wrapped in plain brown paper and tied with coarse twine that rested ominously on the other side of the table.

"Jeptha," she said softly, "what is in those packages?"

* * * *

The Skaket Creek Inn
August 18th, 1968
7:52 a.m.

Bridget picked up the oddly shaped pieces one by one and turned them over in her hands. She held one up to the filtered morning light streaming in through the small semicircular window set high up in the basement wall. She shook her head and blew a stray wisp of jet-black hair from her eyes. Finally she turned back to Kathy Dawes standing in the doorway, leaning against the heavy oak door. An old fashioned brass key dangling from a faded, red velvet ribbon hung from her right hand.

"All right." Bridget sighed. "I give up. What are they?"

Before Kathy could answer, Mick asked quietly, "Do you remember what you asked me the first time we walked into the pub upstairs?"

Bridget glanced up at the heavy beams overhead that supported the pub's wooden floor. Yes, she remembered, the night before last. Had it really been so short a time? Time enough for their lives to be horribly changed. She gave a tiny, involuntary shudder and said, "Yes, I think so."

She frowned and tried to recall the exact words. "We'd just come in,

91

and I was looking over at the bar, and there was a sign above it and... yes—the sign. I asked you what that word meant. Scrimshaw."

Mick nodded and pointed his right index finger to the yellowed, cream-colored object in Bridget's left hand. "There's your answer, babe," he said softly.

She stared at the object for a moment and then stepped back from one of a dozen heavy dark walnut cabinets that completely lined the cellar. She swept her gaze around the octagon-shaped room again. Cabinet after cabinet, and each one filled with dozens and dozens of the fantastically carved yellow, brown, and dusky-white ivory objects—a room directly under the bar, a locked room with but one small window. A room dedicated to and filled with hundreds of objects that gave the name to the pub above. Scrimshaw.

Bridget held the curved tooth of a long-dead sperm whale up to the dappled light let in by the basement room's single window and studied the thin black lines and the odd patterns that had been etched into the old ivory. She turned it over in her hands until she finally saw one recognizable shape in the intricate and vaguely disturbing patterns. A three-mast ship under full sail. It appeared to be running from a pursuing storm or a giant wave or a....

The room began to spin, and the yellowed piece of ivory fell from her fingers. She reached out to grab hold of the walnut display cabinet in front of her, but the shelf somehow jumped forward into her hand. She stumbled back, but the shelf seemed attached to her hand like some sort of ectoplasm taffy and kept moving towards her. She screamed, pushed desperately at the shelf, but the more frantic her movements became, the faster the scrimshaws slid towards her, tumbling down the shelf and striking her shoulders and chest. She felt a sharp pain and looked down in horror. One small, pointed scrimshaw had lodged in the center of her chest, sticking through the fabric of her sweater. She tried to brush it off but the more she pulled at it, the deeper it worked itself into her flesh, like a fishhook. Its point squirmed into her skin.

"No, no! Get it off of me. Mickey, help me, please!"

She took a frantic step backwards, but instead of finding solid pine planking beneath her feet, she stepped and stumbled over dozens of irregular objects that littered the floor—scrimshaws. Her ankle turned, and she began falling backward. She grabbed the central brace of the cabinet for support, steadied for an instant, and heard a creaking sound. She looked up. The entire massive six-foot high cabinet started to fall...right on top of her. She gasped as in the same heartbeat she knew that with no solid footing and off balance as she was, there was nothing she could do to prevent the entire thing from crashing down and squashing her like a bug. Her throat paralyzed, she couldn't even scream.

There was a tremendous thud as she slipped to her knees, eyes screwed shut, and one arm thrown over her head in an instinctive if futile gesture to protect herself.

But nothing happened.

She opened her eyes. The cabinet hadn't fallen. And she realized that Mick stood next to her, his legs braced in a classic football lineman's stance, left shoulder wedged against the X formed by the two main crosspieces of the antique cabinet. He leaned in with his shoulder, breathed heavily through his nose, steadied his feet, and pushed. Slowly, the cabinet moved upright and finally settled back into the worn grooves in the old pine flooring where it had rested for over a century.

Mick let out his breath with a whoosh and slid down beside her.

"You, okay?"

She nodded.

"You know, Coach Mazzichano would be proud of me. He always told me that all those blocking drills we did in JV football would come in handy." He rubbed his shoulder and winced.

"Are you okay, Mickey?"

"Sure, nothing that a little Ben Gay and TLC won't cure. What the hell happened anyway?"

"I-I don't know. One minute I was examining one of the scrimshaws, and the next...."

"Oops, hang on, babe. Let me get that off of you."

Bridget looked to where his hand was moving and screamed. The small scrimshaw...it was still embedded in her sweater. It was still working its way into her skin and it would keep gouging and squirming all the way through to her heart.

"Ahhh!" She shivered in revulsion and snatched at the object but suddenly realized it wasn't embedded in her sweater at all. The thing had just caught on a tiny thread. She flicked it with her finger, and it dropped to the floor and lay there harmlessly with the dozens of other scrimshaws.

She stared dumbly at it. Just a bunch of old whales' teeth—just like Mick said. She had been hysterical over nothing. A bad case of the vapors, as her grandmother would have put it. She felt embarrassed, foolish.

Kathy, who'd come running just a few steps behind Mick, knelt down beside her.

"Kathy, I-I'm really sorry about all of this. I don't know what got into me. I thought...I mean, it seemed like...I really don't know...I must be coming down with something."

"Bridget, please. Don't apologize; it's okay, really. I'm just glad that you're okay."

"Well, I feel like a proper idiot and that's fer sure."

"No, don't say that. It's not your fault."

"Well, you're a good egg for saying that, luv, and I appreciate it." Bridget started to get up. "And if you'll show me where they all go, I'll help you tidy up." She reached out for the nearest scrimshaw.

"No!"

Bridget snatched her hand back and stared at Kathy.

"No," Kathy said a little softer. "Leave them where they are." She got up, looked around the room, and moved to the door. "Leave them and come upstairs with me."

Mick and Bridget gawped at one another and slowly got up. Mick started to speak, but Bridget shook her head and motioned him towards where Kathy stood in the doorway. As they filed up the stairs, Kathy slammed the heavy door behind them all and locked it.

* * * *

Skaket Creek Inn
August 18th, 1968
8:36 a.m.

Bridget sat down in the old green rocking chair that was flanked by a dozen others layered with the same peeling and chipped, weathered green paint. They lined the front porch of the Skaket Creek Inn like battle weary soldiers of a hundred summers spent rocking aimlessly back and forth in a losing battle with the sun and salt and a thousand well-fed and amply rounded bottoms that had left the woven cane seats split and sagging. Bridget's slight form perched so lightly on the tired old rocker next to the big front parlor picture window, that had the old chair been possessed with the power of speech, it would have murmured a grateful thank you.

Bridget closed her eyes and snuggled deeper into the welcoming old chair as the rising sun washed over the long front porch of the Skaket Creek Inn. Despite the sun's increasing warmth, she hugged her arms for a moment and shivered.

Mick watched her out of the corner of his eye but didn't say anything. He knew what was wrong. Hell, she could've been killed down there. He hadn't seen the whole thing. Just the huge cabinet as it started to fall. But something had sure spooked Bridget. And if he was going to be honest, it had affected him too. That room in the cellar below the pub, with cabinet after cabinet, shelf after shelf, all lined with hundreds or thousands of sometimes intricate and sometimes disturbingly carved scrimshaws, gave him the creeps.

Kathy Dawes sat on the white porch railing opposite them and saw the look that passed between them.

"I know what you're feeling," she said, her tone soft, "a vague uneasiness, a prickling of ominous premonition between the shoulder blades. And maybe a bad case of the 'creeps'." She glanced down at the floor. "Yeah, I know the feeling. I've been feeling it all of my life."

No one spoke for a long time. They just gazed at the beach stretching away from the seagrass-covered dunes just beyond the porch. Finally Kathy said, "So I guess I don't need to ask you how you liked Great, Great Granddad's...collection?"

"Well," Mick began, "it was kind of...."

"I didn't," Bridget said flatly, interrupting Mick's half-formed attempt at a polite response.

"Well at least that's honest." Kathy gave a wry smile. "And I can't say as how I blame you."

"There's something...something that's not right down there," Bridget continued, frowning. "Something old and ancient and...evil."

"C'mon, babe," Mick said quietly and leaned forward in his chair. "It's just a bunch of dusty old whale bones."

Bridget shook her head. "No, Mickey, I tried to make myself believe that, but it isn't. There's something else there—something waiting, watching, lurking in the dark corners. I-I can feel it. Something's happened. It's awakened. Someone or something has awakened it." She stared at Mick with eyes haunted by a thousand years of Irish myths. "I think...I think maybe that someone is...us."

Mick forced a laugh. "Okay, my superstitious little pixie, what comes next? Darby O'Gill and the Little People?" His laughter fell as flat as the still blue waters that covered the tidal flats of Cape Cod Bay. Mick tried again. "C'mon, Bridge, you don't really believe that a—"

"No, Mick," Kathy interrupted, "she's right." She pulled up both of her feet and stretched them out on the flat, white porch railing and leaned back against one of the wide, white-painted posts. She studied her tanned toes through the leather lacings of her handmade Province Town sandals and finally said, "I took you down there for a reason. It has to do with me and the inn and whatever is buried underneath it." She paused, looked at them, then stared back down and continued in a low voice, "And it has to do with a family legend and a curse and maybe...you."

Chapter Seventeen

Skaket Creek Beach
August 18th, 1968
11:42 a.m.

Mick had been watching the same seagull circling in the cobalt blue sky for the past ten minutes while Bridget had been looking at an eight-year-old boy chasing his sister around the beach with a handful of wet seaweed. Finally, Bridget raised her cheek from where it'd been resting on his chest and sighed. "Okay, McCarthy, tell me that I'm wrong. Tell me that it's just a product of my over-active Hibernian imagination. Tell me I'm not some superstitious, little bog-trotting Irish wench from the back end of nowhere, but an intelligent, highly educated young woman from one of the best institutions of higher education on the whole bleedin' North American continent! Tell me...."

"Yes!"

"Yes what?" She smiled. "Yes, I'm a highly educated young woman, or yes I'm a superstitious, bog-trottin' little Irish wench?"

Mick started to open his mouth but closed it with a smile. "Oh, no, my little angel from Erin, you don't get me that easily."

"Oh, so then you don't think I'm highly educated and highly intelligent, eh?"

Mick grinned. "Highly educated, highly esteemed...," he put his arm around her shoulders and pulled her head back down to his chest, "and highly desired...by me."

She sighed and nuzzled closer until her soft black hair brushed his cheek. She stretched sinuously in the hot August sunlight as Mick slid his other arm around her shoulders.

"What d'ya say we go back up in the dunes and find a nice, cozy, quiet little spot and—"

"No," she murmured.

"Why not?" Mick said with the uncomfortable beginnings of frustration.

Bridget picked her head up and looked out at him with eyes that had now grown serious. "Because you said to me not three hours ago that we had to be on the road and headed for Boston by noon at the latest."

Mick's desire floated away like the retreating seagull on the midday breeze. She was right. Damn! He gave one last half-hearted try. "Are you sure, babe? Maybe a little nookie up behind the dunes and then a quick swim, and then we can—"

"Mickey, we've only six days left."

As the 650 BSA roared over the Sagamore Bridge, around the rotary, and headed up Route 3 towards Boston, Mick thought back to the bizarre story that Kathy Dawes had related to them that morning.

"It all started with my great, great grandfather, Jeptha Dawes," Kathy had said. "The family history has it that he came from a small farm somewhere near Hancock New Hampshire and for some reason decided that he didn't want to be a farmer. So he signed on board a coastal schooner out of Portsmouth and eventually wound up in Nantucket where he shipped on board a clipper. I think the name of the ship was the *Lady Elizabeth* or something like that. Well, anyway, he eventually became second mate, and everything seemed to be fine until the spring of 1858. No one really knows what happened that April night in Nantucket harbor, but for some reason my great, great grandfather left the ship with a small fortune in gold coins and a heavily padlocked sea chest. Strangely enough, when he landed here in Skaket Creek the next morning, local legend has it that he buried the sea chest but not the gold coins."

"Where did he bury the sea chest?" Mick had asked.

"Supposedly in a tiny sealed room," Kathy drew out the word, "right under this house."

Kathy had talked for almost an hour. Telling them about how her ancestor had met and married a young parlor maid in the employ of one of the then—and still today—most powerful families on the Cape: the Frosts.

Mick gripped the rubber pads of the bike's handlebars tighter as he grimly catalogued the score he still had to settle with the Frosts of today. Kathy had also commented on the strange relationship their family had had with the Frosts over the intervening generations. Sometimes an uneasy truce, but more often foes. Sometimes gifts and bribes, but more often threats.

Mick shook his head as the wind whipped his long brown hair around. Yeah, he could understand the foe part.

And behind it all, Kathy explained, was the Frosts' unwavering obsession to regain Skaket Creek and whatever lay underneath the house.

"So why hasn't your family just dug up the chest and whatever else may be hidden in that sealed room?"

"Because of old Jeptha's will," Kathy said. "It states that if that room is ever disturbed, the family lawyers have the power of attorney to seize the house, have it torn down to the floorboards, and cover it over with slabs of New Hampshire granite."

Mick whistled. "Damn, he was really serious about no one messing around with that chest!"

And then Kathy had told them about the scrimshaws. The hundreds and hundreds of scrimshaws locked up in the strange, dank room underneath the pub. The room with the floor laid with double thick pine planks and fastened with four inch iron spikes that, as legend alluded, covered and sealed forever a tiny room with a mysterious chest double-bound with iron chain.

The legend and family history also said, Kathy told them, that shortly after Jeptha married the young parlor maid from Belfast, he began taking long trips to Boston, where he met with a lawyer. And, upon his return, he always had a black leather satchel filled with scrimshaws. Week after week, and month after month, he added more and more carved scrimshaws of every size, hue, and pattern to the ever-growing collection in the basement room underneath the pub. All purchased with his seemingly inexhaustible supply of gold coins.

"No one ever knew why he collected them," Kathy said, "as they never seemed to give him any pleasure. The room was always locked, and no one but himself was ever permitted to enter. After he died, his wife, Fiona, took possession of the room and its contents—and the key. And the room housing the collection remained locked until, on her deathbed, she gave her oldest son the key and told him to pass it down to the eldest of each generation of Dawes."

Kathy had paused there and twirled the big brass key around her finger. "So I guess that's me." She'd smiled sadly. "Not only am I the eldest of my generation, I'm the *only* one of my generation. And, just like old Chingachgook in *Last of the Mohicans*, I'm the last of the Dawes."

"So why did you show it to us?" Mick asked.

"Two reasons. First of all," Kathy said, "my mom isn't well. It's not just physically, but it's spiritually too. It's like something is draining the life force from her body." She paused and looked up at them. "I think it's caused by what I just showed you in that room down there." She added grimly, "I've got to get her away from that room—and the contents of that room away from her. As a matter of fact, I showed the collection to a couple of curators from the Peabody Museum about a month ago, and they said those scrimshaws are worth a small fortune."

She drew her knees up to her chin, leaned back against the square cut porch post, and continued, "They conservatively estimated the value at over three-quarters of a million dollars."

Mick whistled softly. "That's a helluva lot of bread for friggin' whale teeth. Well then, why don't you and your mom cash in those whale molars and split for the French Riviera or something?"

"Because of the punch line of the family tale." She smiled sadly. "It seems that after Great, Great Grandma Fiona died, the lawyer read the family her and Jeptha's final will. They'd added another clause just before Jeptha died. In addition to the destruction of the house if the sealed room was breached, the will also stipulated that none—not even one—of the scrimshaws could ever be sold or could ever even be taken from the cellar room!"

Mick and Bridget stayed silent for a moment and watched Kathy stretch her tanned legs below her cut-off Levis along the wide porch railing.

Finally, Bridget asked, "You said there were two reasons you showed those things to us. What was the second?"

"Because I think that you found something in Fiona's old sitting room—the room that you're staying in."

Mick and Bridget exchanged a quick glance.

"You found an old journal—a diary of Fiona's, didn't you," Kathy said, not as a question but a statement of fact.

Bridget nodded slowly. "Not so much a diary or journal, just some old papers."

Kathy swung her legs off of the porch railing and sat down cross-legged in front of Mick and Bridget. "Did the journal—the papers—did they mention anything about a lawyer? A lawyer in Boston?"

Bridget looked at Mick, and he nodded.

"Then that's where you need to start," Kathy said.

"Start what?" Mick asked. "In case you forgot, I've got less that one week to prove I didn't commit a murder that the Frosts have already got me railroaded for."

Kathy nodded. "That's why my mother told me to tell you that you've got to track down the final scrimshaw that Jeptha was seeking all those years ago. The last one, the one that really mattered. The real object of all of his searching and gold spent buying up one after the other in hopes he could finally get the one he'd been told to get."

"Told to get? By whom?"

Kathy shook her head. "Mom said it wasn't time for me, or you, to know that yet. But she said that just like she knows you're not guilty. She also says that if you can find that last scrimshaw, it will point you directly at Karen's murderer."

"I'm not crazy about riddles, Karen, especially ones that play with my life and maybe even Bridget's, as the punch line."

"I'm sorry, Mick. I know it sounds whacked-out, but you've gotta trust me, or rather, my mom. I swear to you, she really does know things like this and she does believe in you and wants to help."

Mick glanced at Bridget.

She nodded solemnly. "I believe her, Mickey."

Mick shrugged and said, "Well, I guess a crazy lead is better than none at all. Okay, so where do we start?"

"Where Fiona's old journal mentions," Kathy said, "at a law office in Boston."

Bridget reached down into her macramé shoulder bag and pulled out the packet of papers.

"Hang on a sec, Bridge." Mick took a quick look over her shoulder and moved her hand holding the papers up until it was level with his eyes. A smile spread across his lips.

"What?"

"Our odds of getting into that law office just got a whole lot better."

"Why?"

"Because I just figured out what the name of that old law firm is today, and it just so happens that I know a real big shot who works there."

"Okay, McCarthy, I'm all done playing Twenty Questions, so give."

"Just one more, babe."

Bridget sighed. "All right, Mickey.... Who?"

Mick's smile turned into a grin. He winked and said, "My brother."

Bridget raised an eyebrow. "You do have a talent for having family members in all the right places, McCarthy." She shifted the papers in her lap. "All right then, let's see what the journal has to say about this lawyer in Boston." She glanced up once at Mick, then at Kathy. She picked up the journal and began to read.

Bridget lowered her voice so that the narration wouldn't be heard by any of the octogenarian guests dozing or rocking in the morning sun.

* * * *

And none of them did hear.

But someone else did.

Someone who'd been standing quietly and listening at the parlor window for quite some time.

Mrs. Helen Dawes.

* * * *

Kathy Dawes continued to stare down Skaket Beach Road long after the big metallic blue motorcycle had roared off towards the Mid-Cape Highway and Boston some ninety miles to the north.

The sandy dust had floated away on the August breeze before she finally said, without turning around, "How long were you listening at the window, Aunt?"

There was no answer except for the faint tinkling of the wind chime at the other end of the long porch.

Kathy didn't move from her perch on the porch railing—she just kept staring down Skaket Beach Road. The screen door creaked open, and she heard footsteps behind her. She still didn't turn around.

At last, the clipped voice of her aunt answered, "Long enough." After a moment she added, "And they don't stand a chance of finding what they're looking for!"

Silent for a moment, Kathy finally said in a low, cold voice, "Then for your sake, you'd better hope that they don't."

Chapter Eighteen

Quincy Elliot paused for a moment at the sound of footsteps in the hallway and the polished brass doorknob turning.

Quincy, described by his 'lady friends' as handsome and his rivals as arrogant, sat up straighter behind his small oak desk and raised his head expectantly.

The newly hired clerk of the law office of Messrs. Cabot & Saltonstall smiled as Jeptha walked towards him. But the smile gradually twisted into a sneer of contempt. Quincy had quickly learned to rate the importance of a client by the condition of his shoes. A shiny, clean pair of boots meant that a valet, or personal servant saw to it every night, that the mud and manure of the sometimes cobbled—and sometimes not, but always dirty—Boston streets, had been removed. A gentleman never left his house in the morning with yesterday's soil on his boots.

Therefore, when young Quincy saw the filthy, scuffed boots and rough, hard-knuckled hands of the young man standing in front of his desk, he wrinkled his nose and asked, "Yes...sir. May I be of service?"

"I believe Mr. Cabot is expecting me," Jeptha said quietly.

"Is he now?" Quincy Elliott drawled, his Harvard College accent dripping with barely masked contempt. "And who may I tell Mr. Cabot is inquiring?"

"The name is Dawes. Jeptha Dawes."

Quincy looked down his long aquiline nose at the stolid figure standing in front of him, whose one red, rough hand folded over the other. Then he looked around the cold, bleak outer office where he was forced to spend ten hours each day clerking for the venerable firm's two senior partners. And Quincy was quite obviously not pleased about his new situation—not at all. He had no sooner returned from a golden summer spent touring the capitals of Europe, than his stern Presbyterian father had secured him a position in the firm that handled all of the Elliott maritime company's legal affairs. And the arrogant clerk made it all too obvious to Jeptha that he thought it most unfair that he, Quincy Elliott, with the ink barely dry on his diploma from Harvard, should be thrust out into the grubby world of commerce.

Thus, here sat Quincy on a bright, warm October morning, staring across his cluttered clerk's desk, as he twisted his mouth into a sneer of his disdain for some nondescript nobody named Jeptha Dawes. The clerk gazed at the yellow-gold October sunlight pouring through the office's dusty windowpanes and grumbled peevishly, "I should be out promenading on the Boston Commons right now, with a lovely young lady on my arm. Not stuck here dealing with some uncouth and unlettered yokel who probably wants to file suit for a lost pig or prize heifer that strayed into his neighbor's corn crib."

"It's nine a.m."

"What? I beg your pardon?" Quincy glanced up at the quiet young man who had so rudely interrupted his daydream.

"I said, it's nine a.m. I have an appointment with Mr. Charles Cabot at nine a.m.," Jeptha said quietly.

Quite put out, Quincy said, "Well, I'm afraid you must have gotten it wrong. Mr. Cabot is in a meeting right now and cannot be disturbed. Why don't you come back this afternoon. Or perhaps tomorrow, or—"

"Mr. Elliott!"

Quincy jumped.

"What, may I ask, are you doing keeping Mr. Dawes waiting out here when we have a nine o'clock meeting?"

Quincy Elliott stood up so quickly that he banged his left knee on the edge of the small desk. He limped painfully around the front of the desk until he stood facing the fuming senior partner of the firm.

"I-I...well, I was just telling Mr., ah, Dawes, that I thought you were, ah, I mean, I thought that perhaps you were...."

The white-haired member of one of Boston's most influential and powerful families stared at the stammering clerk and growled, "Elliott, if it wasn't for your father, I'd.... Oh, never mind. Just show Mr. Dawes into my office and then finish up the details for the Hawthorne brief."

"Yes, sir, of course, sir. Ah, right this way, Mr. Dawes—sir. Yes, so sorry to have kept you waiting. Just have a seat in Mr. Cabot's office and—"

"Mr. Elliott!"

"Yes, sir?" the young law clerk answered, all thoughts of Europe and young ladies driven harshly from his head.

"I expect that Hawthorne brief on my desk by noon sharp!"

Charles Cabot ushered Jeptha into his office and firmly closed the door.

* * * *

Boston
High Street and Tremont
August 18ᵗʰ, 1968
1:36 p.m.

"Watch it, kid!" a taxi driver called, flipping Mick the bird as he swerved his cab around the BSA.

Mick didn't even bother answering back. He just stared up at the tall buildings on the edge of Boston's financial district. He turned back to Bridget and said, "I think that's it—that big, gray building with the spire on top. And you see where the wall juts out and there's a big picture window facing Boston Harbor?"

Bridget stood up on the back footrests and shook her head. "No, luv, I don't. Where?"

Mick turned until her cheek touched his. He pointed and said, "There on the very top floor."

Bridget sighted along the length of his arm and nodded. "Yes, yes. Now I do."

Mick put the bike into gear and slowly edged back into the traffic.

"Mickey?" Bridget yelled, straining to be heard over the city sounds of honking horns and roaring engines. "I know that Kathy said that we had to look for old records about Jeptha Dawes and the search he hired the law firm to do for one particular scrimshaw. So that's what this trip is all about, right?"

"Yeah," Mick yelled. He revved the bike and pulled in on the clutch handle. "And about Jeptha Dawes's last mysterious trip to Boston when he received a telegram asking him to come as quickly as possible to the offices of a Boston law firm—the great, great grand-daddy of the same law firm that you see in front of us."

"And these lawyers of today are going to help us, right?"

"That's the plan."

"Because your brother works there?"

"He's a real important guy, Bridge."

"Well, that's sweet, Mickey. I think you should always be able to turn to family in time of need."

Mick twisted around and smiled. "My sentiments exactly, Bridge."

He turned back and gripped the bike's throttle, feathering it slightly so Bridget didn't hear him mutter as he let out the clutch, "I just hope to hell that Frankie feels that way about it."

* * * *

Boston
111 High Street

Tweeeet!

A loud, high-pitched steel whistle cut through the din of the downtown Boston traffic. Mick froze halfway between sliding the 650

104

BSA down on to its kickstand and then let inertia take over as the bike's front tire slid back down onto the warm asphalt.

The cop who'd been directing traffic on the corner stamped over to where Mick still held the motorcycle's handlebars.

He did not look happy. "What the hell do you think you're doing?"

Mick thought of a dozen really cool retorts, but his long-time experience with angry cops—starting with his father—counseled him to wiser action.

"Ahh, just parking my bike, Officer...," Mick squinted and read the nametag above the badge, "Kilgore."

The traffic cop pulled a crumpled handkerchief from his back pocket and mopped his perspiring, red face.

He was definitely not happy.

"Well, are you blind or just plain ignorant of the traffic laws of the Commonwealth of Massachusetts?"

Mick looked around and, uh-oh, saw the big red stripe running along the curb just as the overheated and pissed off cop pointed to it with his nightstick. Crap!

The cop now pointed to the white stenciled letters just above the curb.

"What does that say, kid?"

"Oh, yeah. Sorry, Officer," Mick said, trying for contrite.

"What was that? I didn't hear you." The cop cupped a large beefy hand behind his ear and said in a soft, menacing voice, "Come again?"

Mick cleared his throat and answered in a carefully modulated, neutral tone, "It says 'no parking'—sir."

"So then what are you doing trying to leave this Hells Angels piece of junk here?"

It was hot and humid, and the cop's bad mood was becoming worse.

As a matter of fact, Mick thought that perhaps the mood of the day might be catching because he sensed a cranky spell coming on himself. His fingers clenched.

A soft voice dripping with the lilt of County Cork spoke up from the sidewalk. "We're so sorry, Officer Kilgore." Bridget smiled her most winning smile. "We didn't mean to break any rules. And I'm afraid it's mostly my fault. You see, we've been ridin' so long, and I was so tired and...and...well, I told my boyfriend that I...." A schoolgirl blush infused Bridget's white cheeks. She leaned forward and whispered modestly, "I-I really have to use the little girl's room."

Oh brother! Mick wisely kept his mouth shut.

The cop rubbed his sweaty jaw for a few seconds while he gazed at the black-haired beauty looking up at him from beneath long dark eyelashes.

"Okay, one block up on the right, Kennedy Shoes. You go on in and tell Brian Kennedy that patrolman Kilgore says to let you use their... facilities."

"Yeah, that's great, Officer," Mick broke in, "but why can't we just leave the bike here for fifteen or twenty minutes while we run upstairs to see my brother, and my girlfriend can use the, ah, *facilities* up there while I—"

"You really are determined to piss me off, aren't you, kid!"

"Mickey...." Bridget shook her head and turned back to the traffic cop with her hundred watt smile. "I'm sorry, Officer. We'll move the bike right away, and thank you so much for your help."

The cop breathed heavily through his nose for a few moments. Eventually, he turned back towards Mick and growled, "You're damn lucky you got such a nice girlfriend, kid." He gave a curt wave of his nightstick and snapped, "Move it out!" and shuffled back over the hot street to his traffic beat.

Mick blew a sweat-damp strand of hair from his eyes. "I thought he was gonna write me up for sure. Nice act, Miss Manners. And by the way, do you really have to use the little girl's room?"

"As a matter of fact, the power of suggestion notwithstanding, now I do!"

"*Little girl's room!*" Mick shook his head and shrugged. "But I gotta admit it, kiddo, you've got the touch."

"Okay, so maybe I was laying it on a bit thick for the officer, but it certainly sounds better than your *high class* announcement after your third or fourth beer, that you've got to go 'take a leak' or 'tap a kidney'." She wrinkled her nose in disgust.

"Okay, okay." Mick laughed and held up both hands in mock surrender. "You win! It's off to find the 'little girl's room' and hope that there's no 'little boys' already using it."

Bridget stuck out her tongue at Mick and climbed on the back of the bike as he fired it up. The toe of his boot clicked the foot shift into first, and he gave one last look at his brother Frankie's office building. "Damn!" he muttered, "it'll be another half hour before we can find a parking place and get back here and...."

"Hey, man." A tall, skinny hippie with long, greasy blond hair ambled towards them. He'd been standing on the sidewalk in the shade of the tall building while Mick had been having his friendly little *chat* with the *nice policeman*. But now he walked towards Mick and Bridget, still clutching the grimy tambourine that he'd been jingling at passersby, mumbling his bored mantra of, "Spare change, man?"

He paused and leaned against the NO PARKING – TOW ZONE signpost that Mick had recently tried so hard—and so unsuccessfully—to ignore.

"You looking for a place to park your bike, dude?"

Mick looked back warily. "Maybe."

The skinny guy leaned closer. The humid August day hadn't done much for his appearance—or his smell. Mick leaned back.

"I know a place right around back of the building, man." The hippie smiled.

Mick observed that street life also hadn't done much for his dental health either.

"And for just two bucks, I'll watch it and make sure that nothing happens to it."

Oh, fantastic. If you can't get Brinks Security, just call in the hippie patrol.

Still, they were running against the clock. "Okay." Mick sighed. "Lead the way. What's your name?"

"I'm like the Moon Dog Man. It's Moon Dog, 'cause when the sun goes down, like, I really howl. Can you dig it?"

Crap! Moon Dog! Mick rolled his eyes, clicked the bike into first gear, and slowly followed the shambling hippie down the shadow-strewn alleyway.

As they turned the alley corner, the hippie rattled his tambourine and thumped twice with the palm of his hand. He grinned back at Mick and Bridget. Or least that's what they thought.

Mick turned. Three guys in black T-shirts and construction boots lounging against a hot dog stand on the other side of the street nodded and began walking towards the alley.

Chapter Nineteen

The coach lurched as the four-foot, iron-rimmed wheel dropped into a large pot hole in the road and bounced out. A cloud of dust swirled through the coach, and the fat man seated beside Jeptha coughed and spat nosily into his handkerchief. The prim woman in the severe black dress seated opposite Jeptha, looked down her long nose with disgust and turned away.

The fat man coughed again, and his enormous Beaver top hat swayed dangerously on his head.

Jeptha edged another inch away and sighed. He should have taken the train. But by the time he'd emerged from lawyer Cabot's office, he'd already missed the 11:10, and the next train to Framingham wouldn't be until 4:21 p.m. And then he'd still have to hire a buggy and drive the seven miles north to the town of Sudbury. But the Boston Post stage was leaving at noon and went straight down the Old Post Road, right past his destination. The Wayside Inn.

Jeptha unfolded, for the tenth time, the letter that lawyer Cabot had given him, and read the crude and painfully formed block letters making up the barely intelligible words:

> dear Mr. Kabut
> my shipmate Benj. Quinn said as how you had a man what pays big monie for scrimshaws. U tell him I be staying at wayside inn in Sudbury town Til 19 October. I got a Injun half breed With me. He just come back after two years Whalen in the South sees. He says he got speshul Scrimshaw. Real speshul. U tell yer man to bring his monie. Lots of it. We will wait til 19th. No longer.
> Signed
> zeke Tanner

Jeptha folded the grimy piece of cheap writing paper and put it back into his pocket. He looked out the coach window at the red-and-gold-colored leaves that swirled around the dust raised by the speeding coach. The signboard nailed onto one of the enormous old elm trees that lined the Boston Post Road read: ENTERING EAST SUDBURY.

Jeptha turned to the portly man beside him. "Are we near the Wayside Inn?"

"No, no," the heavyset man said, his jowls wobbling as he shook his head back and forth. "No, we've still got a good six miles to go. They ought to change that sign. After all, the real name of the town is Wayland now. No, settle back, still a ways to go before we reach the inn."

Jeptha bit his thumbnail and stared unseeing at the beautiful New England fall scenery unfolding outside the coach window.

"Settle down, young fellow." The fat man laughed. "The old inn will still be there when we pull in."

Yes it will. But will a man named Zeke and a half-breed Indian harpooner still be there? And, more importantly, after so long, will they have what I've been seeking? What I have to find.

* * * *

Boston
Behind 111 High Street
August 18ᵗʰ, 1968
2:01 p.m.

Mick knew they'd been set up before they reached the end of the alley. He'd walked into enough jungle ambushes to sense one even before the first AK-47 slugs started to fly. It was just too damn bad that the old jungle instincts left over from 'Nam hadn't kicked in a little bit earlier, he thought, as he heard the footsteps behind him.

Their new *pal*, good old Moon Doggie, started to sweat, and the tambourine made little jiggling motions in his hand that obviously had nothing to do with any preparation to shake the stupid thing in front of some tourist's face while he asked them for spare change. No, Mick was pretty damn sure that he knew just where Moon Doggie's next donation of spare change was coming from. It was coming from the three sets of heavy footsteps that closed the distance between him and Bridget in the hot, damp alleyway.

Mick locked eyes with Moon Dog. "Peace and love, eh, man?" Mick said bitterly.

Moon Dog shrugged his skinny shoulders. "Sorry, dude. We all, like, need bread, you know."

Mick grabbed the greasy tie-dyed T-shit and cocked his right first. "And silly me, I thought it was just anyone over thirty that we weren't supposed to trust," he said as Moon Dog tried to wiggle away from him.

"Don't do it, man—please!"

"Mickey—no!" Bridget said from behind him.

Mick shook his head in disgust and pushed the skinny hippie away.

Moon Dog leaned against the alley wall and began muttering, "Bad vibes. Bad, bad-ass freakin' vibes all over the place. Time for ol' Moon Doggie to make like a banana and split."

"Let's see you try that move with me, hot shot," a heavily muscled guy about twenty-five years old in a black bodybuilder's T-shirt sneered as Mick turned towards him.

Yup, there were three of them. And they all looked tough and they all looked mean. And they also all looked like they were playing for keeps.

The guy in the black T-shirt stood about five feet away from Mick and flexed his muscles for effect.

"Very impressive," Mick said. "You guys making a commercial for Jack LaLane?"

"Smart ass," the guy in front of Mick snorted contemptuously.

Nope, Mick thought, as the guy on Muscle Man's right pulled a three-foot length of steel chain from the back pocket of his dungarees. The taller guy to the left pulled a twelve-inch pipe wrench from his tool belt and hefted it in his right hand. They sure as hell weren't making any commercial unless the rules of advertising had changed and the sponsors had decided to beat the customer into submission with blunt objects rather than boring them to death with words.

"Bridge," Mick whispered out of the corner of his mouth, "there's a steel door about ten feet to the left and behind us. Do you see it? At the top of those three cement steps. It must be the back entrance to my brother's office building. And hopefully it's unlocked."

The three guys took another step towards Mick, and he backed up a step.

"When you see me move, you run like hell up those three steps and through that door. And then you start screaming like bloody murder. 'Cause that's probably what it will be," Mick muttered under his breath and whispered to Bridget again, "Okay?"

"I'm not leaving you here, Mickey," she hissed.

"Bridge." Mick shook his head. "There's nothing you can do. Believe me, they'll get to me quicker if they get their hands on you. You've gotta get inside that door and scream—loud. And run and get help and get it back out here as quick as you damn friggin' can."

She didn't say anything for a moment, but he heard her breathing behind him.

"Okay...okay?"

Finally, a sigh and a strained single word, "Okay."

Mick backed up another step and, with his hand behind his back, motioned Bridget to start moving backwards towards the door.

"Mickey, I love you," she whispered, her voice breaking.

"I love you too, babe," Mick replied harshly, trying to keep his voice from doing the same thing as hers. "And Bridge.... Please—run. And don't look back."

And then they were on him.

Mick managed to dodge the length of chain as it came in over his head, but the pipe wrench from the guy on his left caught him in the side, just below the third rib, and knocked the breath out of him. The only thing that saved Mick from getting his brains beat out in the first ten seconds of the fight was a mistake Muscle Man made in coming up and grabbing Mick by the front of his frayed, drab, olive T-shirt. It allowed Mick's jungle training to break through the fog of pain, and he put both hands on the straps of Muscle Man's T-shirt. Thrusting his cowboy boot into the bodybuilder's hard belly, he rolled backwards, with the forward momentum of his adversary's charge, in a full somersault and wound up sitting on the overconfident guy's chest.

The guy had just enough time to say "What the f...?" before Mick wrapped his left hand around his right fist and jabbed the side of his elbow down into the guy's windpipe. Mick had been told by his judo instructor in 'Nam that it was a blow designed to kill in close combat. But the last second he pulled the force of the blow. He didn't want to kill anybody—at least, not yet. He left Muscle Man gasping for breath on the alley pavement and turned to the other two.

Oh shit!

Either the door had been locked, or Bridget hadn't made it that far, because the guy with the pipe wrench stood on the cement steps, his heavily muscled forearm around her slender white neck.

Mick picked up the heavy length of chain and started towards them.

"Drop it or she gets cut." Wrench Guy's left arm clamped around her throat as his right hand came up holding a black-handled switchblade. He pushed the silver button on the side, and the blade sprang open with a frightening *snick*. He moved the blade slowly towards her face.

Mick stopped—frozen.

Bridget looked at Mick, and he knew they were both dead unless....

She bit down on Wrench Guy's left arm. Hard.

As he screamed and whipped the arm away, she twisted and stamped the sharp little heel of her black boot into his ankle—also hard.

"Run!" Mick screamed.

She bolted up the last step towards the rusted steel door. She had almost made it when the third guy swung himself up by the iron railing and grabbed her around the waist. She struggled and tried to get a grip on the old iron door handle, but he slowly pulled her backwards.

And then, just as the handle slipped out of her grasp, the door moved. Just an inch. She strained towards it again, and the man holding her around the waist backhanded her. She fell back against the hard steel door, and...it swung open.

A tall man in a tan summer suit stood in the doorway. He held a small caliber handgun. He pointed the cocked gun at the man holding the knife behind Bridget. In a calm, cool voice he said, "I think that will be quite enough."

Chapter Twenty

Franklin (aka Francis/Frankie) Prescott (aka McCarthy) put on his best solicitous, lawyerly smile as he held out a Waterford cut-crystal glass half filled with amber liquid. "Here, Bridget," he said to the still visibly shaken girl, "try a sip of this."

The petite black-haired girl seemed even smaller and more vulnerable curled up in the large red leather client chair that faced Franklin Prescott's massive, solid mahogany desk.

"No thanks," she said. Her smile appeared forced. "I'll be all right in a minute or two."

"Certainly." Franklin smiled back. "Well, I'll just put it down here in case you change your mind." He set the glass down carefully on a Harvard alumni coaster on the side of his immaculate desk and turned towards Mick. "Michael, how about you. Would you like one?"

Mick hooked one leg over the padded red leather arm of Franklin's other client chair, flopped down into the seat, and gestured towards the matching antique brass and mahogany, small but tasteful, liquor cabinet. "What are you serving, Frankie? Got some of Pop's old Bushmills Irish whiskey in there?"

Franklin Prescott winced at the unwanted use of his childhood moniker, Frankie, as Mick knew he would, and slowly shook his head. "No, Michael, it's a very fine old single malt Scotch."

"Naw, in that case I'll pass. Unless you got a cold can of Papst's Blue Ribbon or maybe a Schlitz?" Mick added hopefully.

Mick's older brother shook his head again. "Sorry."

Yeah, I'll bet, Mick thought, but kept his mouth shut. He needed Frankie's help, now more than ever.

Franklin Prescott walked over to his floor-to-ceiling plate-glass window and looked out over Boston Harbor.

Although Franklin and Mick shared the same set of parents, they shared very few other similarities. Mick, for better or worse—and a lot too often, for worse—was almost a carbon copy of their South Boston, Irish, whiskey-drinking, ex-cop-turned-detective father.

Frankie—Franklin—on the other hand, was a self consciously molded product of the fondest hopes and aspirations of Miss Felicity Parker Prescott, who, for a few tempestuous years, had also worn the McCarthy name, tacked like a nonchalant afterthought, onto the rest of her more impressive heritage. Franklin had done everything that Miss Felicity had dreamed of for both of her boys. He had gone to Andover then on to Harvard and finally into the family connected law firm of Elliott and Delbert.

Mick had reluctantly gone to Andover also and had even more reluctantly been pushed into Harvard. But like a bad paint job on a dented, street hot-rod, it hadn't taken. Whether trying to impress his tough guy dad or trying to prove something to himself, Mick had gotten kicked out of Harvard for fighting at the end of his freshman year. Knowing that the loss of his 2-S student deferment would mark him as 1-A, prime meat for the draft, Mick had figured "What the hell!" and joined up. His eighteen months in the Vietnam jungle had almost resulted in his death at the hands of a Black Ops rogue CIA agent and had left him with some memories that he still woke up from in a cold sweat. But it had also toughened him and made him grow up—sort of. Still, on the rare occasions when the two brothers got together, the oil and water somehow seemed to mix—sort of.

Franklin turned away from the window and glanced back at his younger brother. "So tell me again, exactly why were those guys in the alley after you?"

"Damned if I know." Mick shrugged.

Somewhere just short of exasperation, Franklin turned to Bridget. "Bridget, do you have any idea what they wanted?"

She shook her head. "It all seemed to happen so fast. One minute we were following this strange Pied Piper flower child down the alley, and the next, poor Mickey was fighting for his life. And then one of them grabbed me and pulled a knife and...and he...."

Bridget's hands started to shake again, and she gripped the chair arms to steady them.

"But why would they...?" Franklin started again.

"Frankie!" Mick stood up. "That's enough; cool it!"

Franklin drew in a deep breath and gazed at the ceiling.

"Let's just put it this way," Mick continued, "it's a damned good thing that your buddy here," he nodded to the man in the tan suit across the room, "opened that alley door when he did, or we would have been...."

Oops! Mick watched Bridget's pale face as she tried to still her shaking hands. He walked over to her and put his hand on her shoulder. "Hey, babe, I was just about to dazzle them with some fancy footwork and Bruce Lee karate moves."

Bridget smiled back weakly, and Mick tried to return what he hoped was a confident, no-sweat wink.

"But all that aside, I guess we owe you a big fat thanks." Mick nodded to the tall figure in the tan summer suit leaning nonchalantly against the walnut paneled wall. The tall man smiled, straightened up, and walked over to them. "No thanks necessary. All in a day's work. Besides," he smiled, "I consider it good, on-the-job training for my new assignment."

"Which is?" Mick asked.

"Oh, sorry, my fault." Mick's brother gestured toward the man in the tan suit. "Bridget, Michael, allow me to introduce one of my oldest and closest friends—and the new assistant district attorney for Barnstable County, Mr. E.F. Westlake."

E.F. Westlake walked over to Mick and shook his hand with a firm, dry handshake. Not a bone-crusher, but not fish-limp either. Just right. He smiled at Mick. The smile was just right too. Not too phony and not too flashy. Just right.

"Great smile," Mick said. "Nice teeth."

"My orthodontist thanks you." Westlake flashed the easy smile again. Then he turned the same charming smile on Bridget, curled up in Franklin's big leather client chair. "I hope you're feeling better now, Miss...?"

"Connolly." But Bridget's normally lilting alto came out in an uncharacteristic squeak. She blushed and cleared her throat with a lady-like cough. "Excuse me. I mean, Connolly. It's Bridget Connolly from Ballykill, Ireland. And...and," she stammered and caught herself. She drew in breath and smiled almost shyly. "And thank you for saving our lives, Mr. Westlake."

Westlake held her sea-green eyes with his deep blue ones. "It's E.F., Miss Connolly from Ballykill, Ireland, and thank *you*."

Chapter Twenty-One

Harvard Square
Cambridge, MA
August 18ᵗʰ, 1968
4:04 p.m.

Mick eased off the throttle grip of the BSA.

"Mickey," Bridget shouted so that she could be heard over the roar of the twin tailpipes.

"What, babe?" Mick called back without turning his head.

"Why are we turning off here?"

Mick clicked the foot shift down into second gear and leaned the bike left onto Palmer Street just off of the square. He quickly snapped the gearshift lever down again into first and put both legs out for balance. The bike slowed to a fast walking speed. He concentrated for a moment on keeping the bike's front wheel steady while the shocks struggled to absorb the worst of the jouncing from the uneven cobblestone street. Finally Mick slowed to a stop, turned his head back to Bridget, and said, "Because we gotta make a quick stop."

"What for?"

"Part business, part family duty, and part...promise."

"At the risk of sounding like a freshman in journalism class," Bridget said, leaning forward, "who, what, and where?"

"My sister, for a book she has, and I think, right about...there!"

Mick pointed to a third story window about half way down the block, edged with bright purple curtains. He put the bike back into gear and slowly coasted up to the rough granite curbstone underneath the window.

As they got off the bike and Mick pushed the kickstand down, Bridget looked up at the window and murmured dryly, "I think I forgot the most important question."

"What's that, teacher?" Mick smiled, raised his finger, and pressed one of the apartment building's intercom buzzers.

Bridget joined him in the building's tiny front hallway and said, "Why?"

"Like I said, for a book she has."

"So then my question still stands. Why?"

"That old letter and the copy we made of the stuff we found in the old store room in Frankie's office building? The stuff we read about the place old Jeptha Dawes went to—The Wayside Inn?"

"Yes but—"

"Yeah...*glixmiczzle zzmxple*...there?" crackled from the dented speaker grill set just underneath the building's mailboxes.

"What?" Mick and Bridget shouted in unison back to the squawking and hissing coming from the intercom speaker.

"I said," *Bzzz-pop-crackle.* "There?"

"Mickey, I think they're saying: Who's there."

Mick yelled back into the speaker grille as loud as he could, "It's Bronwyn's brother, Mick, and Bridget!"

"Okay, well, she's...." *Crackle-crackle-hiss-pop.* "But come on up."

The lock buzzer rattled loudly in the old door lock. Mick pushed the rickety glass-and-wood hallway door inward, and they started up the stairs to the third floor.

The building smelled of old paint, long ago cooked cabbage, and more recent curry. Plus, the faint but unmistakable smell of Mexican pot that conflicting scents of sandalwood and strawberry incense couldn't quite mask.

They got to the third floor landing, and Mick banged on the door.

"C'mon in, it's open."

A girl with long, straight, reddish-blonde hair stood in the middle of the room in front of a small easel and held a paintbrush. She waved the paintbrush in their direction and said, "Hi, guys, I'm Laney Hewitt. I just moved in with Brom." She made several more dabs of the paintbrush on her canvas and then looked over at them.

"So you're Brom's brother Mick?"

Mick pretended to pat himself down as if looking for identification and finally turned to Bridget and asked in a stage whisper, "Whaddaya think, babe, am I him?"

"Oh yeah, luv." Bridget nodded with a sarcastic half smile. "You're him, sure enough." She held out one small, delicate hand to the strawberry blonde and with the other, gestured towards Mick. "Meet Mr. Michael Prescott McCarthy, the 'wit' of Harvard Square."

Mick bowed, his long hair falling forward over his eyes.

"Or as some others might say who've sampled his rather sophomoric brand of humor, the—"

"Ah-ah-ah!" Mick broke in, wagging his forefinger in her direction, "don't say it!"

But she did anyway, finishing with an elaborate curtsy in his direction, "The half-wit of Harvard Square!"

"I told you not to say it." Mick sighed.

Bridget stuck her tongue out at him.

Laney Hewitt laughed and clapped her hands as if at a play. "Bravo, bravo! Better than *Midsummer Night's Dream.*"

"I hope so," Mick muttered, "I never could understand what the hell old Will was talking about."

"So anyway," Laney said, flopping down in an old, faded print, overstuffed chair, "like I said, Brom isn't here, but you're welcome

117

to—"

"She isn't here?" Mick and Bridget said almost in unison.

"Ahh...no. Remember when you buzzed, and I said...."

"Snap–crackle–hiss," Bridget said.

"Glixlezizzle zzmxple," Mick replied with a slight smile.

Laney giggled. "Yeah, that intercom is pretty useless, isn't it?"

Mick sighed again and asked, "Any idea where she is?"

"Not really, but I think she said she was going somewhere with your mom."

"Mom?" Mick raised his eyebrows. That could mean anything from a shopping spree to a debutante ball, the former of which his sister seemed to care little about, and the latter she hated like poison. He thought for a moment and turned back to Laney. "Do you know where she keeps her books?"

"Sure," Laney said. She got up and pointed proudly to a small alcove off of the apartment's main room. "We made a shelf for all of our books right there. Pretty cool, huh?"

Mick looked down and, yup, there it was, the mandatory pine board supported by two milk cartons—the obligatory "college apartment bookshelf".

"Nice," he deadpanned. "Hey, babe, why didn't we think of that?"

"Mickey!" Bridget hissed under her breath.

"Great." Mick squatted down and ran his fingers over the titles on the books. "Well, anyway, if you don't mind, I'm gonna take a peek to see if she's got this book that I seem to recall—"

"What was the title?"

"Umm, I don't remember, but it was all about old country inns."

Laney paused for a moment and smiled. "Oh yeah, I know the one, it's right...here!" She bent down and lifted a large thick book with faded black binding and handed it to Mick.

"This is it?" Mick looked at the title on the spine: Famous Country Inns of New England. "Yeah." He smiled and straightened up. "That's it. I remember when she got it. She was in the sixth grade and was doing a report on old inns and their history. So Pop went out and bought her this book. It probably cost him half a week's pay on a cop's salary." He thumbed through the pages and then stopped. Yeah, there it was. The inn he remembered seeing in Bronwyn's book. The very same inn mentioned in the letter they'd found in the old files of Frankie's law firm.

Mick pulled a crumpled dollar bill out of his jeans pockets and put it between the pages as a bookmark and turned back to Laney. "When Brom comes back, wouldja tell her that I needed to borrow this for a while?"

"Sure, no problem."

"Thanks." Mick tucked the book under his arm and motioned Bridget towards the door.

"Should I tell Brom that you'll stop by again?"

"Yeah," Mick said as they started down the stairs, "on our way back."

"From where?" Laney called down to their echoing footsteps.

Mick opened the front hall door and yelled back, "Sudbury."

* * * *

Laney went back inside and picked up her paintbrush. She dabbed at the green oil paint on her palette and then mixed it with a little yellow to make a soft, early-spring sort of green. She began painting tiny green leaves on the tree in her picture.

"I hope I don't forget to tell Brom that her brother was here," she murmured. "Maybe I should write it down. Or leave her a note in case I'm out when she comes back from...."

She ran over to the open window, palette and brush still in hands, and stuck her head out. Mick and Bridget sat on the metallic blue BSA, and Mick had his foot poised over the kickstart lever.

"Wait!" Laney yelled just as Mick's foot came down. "I just remembered where she was going!"

But the 650 cc engine roared to life.

She put down the brush and palette and ran down the stairs in time to see the BSA turn right at the end of Palmer Street and join the flow of traffic heading west out of Cambridge.

Chapter Twenty-Two

Sudbury, MA
The Red Horse Tavern
October 10th, 1858
6:22 p.m.

"I got a nice room upstairs on the east side, overlooks the garden, and it gits the mornin' sun—nice and cheery." The old man looked at Jeptha with a calculating air.

Jeptha, a solidly built man in his early twenties, wore a dark brown suit, plainly cut but of good quality.

"I can let you have it for dollar a day, and it's worth every penny too."

Jeptha shook his head. "No, I-I...."

The old man's smile faded. He leaned forward over the heavy scarred-and-stained oak counter that doubled as a bar top as well as a registration desk for the tavern's half dozen rooms and peered myopically into Jeptha's pale blue eyes. The cold, rocky fields of northern New England and even colder gray waters of the Atlantic Ocean stared back at him. The old man seemed to realize that this was no young dandy from Boston. No rich man's son making his way leisurely down the Old Post Road to New York City. He shook his head as he seemed to realize that dollars would not fall easily from those blunt, strong fingers.

The old man leaned his elbows on the ale-wet oak counter and said in an almost conspiratorial tone, "You can bunk upstairs in the Drover's Room for four bits—two if'n you want to share the big bed. Them two farm boys what were sharing it with that sailor man left this morning to go to help with the hayin' up in Acton town, so you'd have it nearly all to yerself." He looked at Jeptha and nodded, almost as if encouraging him to do likewise.

But the Jeptha didn't nod his head. Instead, he showed his first animation at something that the old man had said.

"You said a sailor? What is his name?"

"How's about you answer my question first. You want the room?"

Jeptha thought for a moment and then asked, "Is there another coach bound for Boston that stops here tonight?"

The old man pulled his elbows off of the counter and shook his head. "You got the damnedest way of never answerin' a question, young feller."

Jeptha kept looking at him.

Finally, the old man sighed and nodded. "Yep, there's one that comes through here around eight-thirty. It carries mostly mail for the small towns along the route and a few of the more old-fashioned folks who don't like all the noise and smoke of the train."

Two hours. That should be enough time. Provided that the sailor is....

"This sailor, is traveling with an Indian—a half-breed, perhaps?"

"Still asking questions, and you still ain't answered one of mine. You want the room or don'tcha?"

Jeptha shook his head.

The old man drew in an exasperated breath. "Well, you gotta eat, don'tcha? I got shepherd's pie and some new, spiced autumn ale." The old man folded his arms across his scrawny chest and waited for the answer to what had now become his final ultimatum to his diminishing hopes of realizing even the tiniest bit of profit from this infuriating stranger.

Jeptha was silent for a few seconds and a small smile turned up the corners of his lips. "Yes, that sounds fine."

The old man beamed at this small triumph. He came around the other side of the counter and wiped his hands on his greasy apron. "You come on over here, Mr...?"

"Dawes, Jeptha Dawes from Skaket Harbor on Cape Cod."

The landlord pointed to a small dark pine table next to the window of the taproom. He pulled out one of the two Hitchcock chairs on either side of the table and motioned for Jeptha to sit. "Cape Cod, eh? You're a long way from home. What brings you out this way?"

Jeptha put his hat on the opposite chair and sat down. "Business, Mr...?"

"Hows. It's Hows, Mr. Dawes. And my family has run this here tavern and hostelry since seventeen-hundred-and-sixteen. As a matter of fact," the old man pointed to the massive brick fireplace across the room, "this was where my great grandma Hepzibah did all the cooking and caring for seven children when the original two-room house was built by my great granddad, David, way back in seventeen-oh-seven."

Jeptha let his eyes sweep around the room; small and paneled in a dark wood aged with the patina of a century and half of wood smoke and the guttering flames of a thousand tallow candles. Jeptha imagined how cozy this room would be when the chill autumn air began to settle outside and the fire snapped and roared up the old chimney.

This would be a fine place to pause. Spend the evening drinking ale, listening to stories from men with pipes in their hands and tales to tell. Then go upstairs and fall into a soft bed and sleep a dreamless sleep—a dreamless sleep, untroubled by dark promises and even darker consequences. Bed....

He shook his head. *No, not with vows still unfulfilled.*

The old man—Hows—had gone into the small kitchen while Jeptha had been daydreaming and now returned with his ale and food. He placed a large bowl of steaming shepherd's pie and a cold pewter mug of autumn ale in front of Jeptha and turned back towards the bar.

"Mr. Hows—a moment, if you please." The old man turned back towards him. "The name of the man upstairs...the sailor?"

A harsh voice growled from the doorway, "It's Tanner—Zeke Tanner. And who the devil wants to know?"

* * * *

Sudbury, Massachusetts
Wayside Inn
August 18ᵗʰ, 1968
5:47 p.m.

The BSA made a low rumbling sound as it coasted slowly up to the old, rambling, red-painted clapboard inn. Mick looked at the hand-painted signboard and leaned back to Bridget. "This is it, Bridge."

Bridget slid off the back of the motorcycle and stretched her hands over her head. "It's pretty, luv, but I'm stiff and sore and I think I've had just about enough of motorcycle riding for one day." She unbuttoned her fringed suede jacket and ran her fingers through her short hair. "And," she continued, "my rump feels like it's been bounced black and blue, so—"

"And such a lovely little rump it is too." Mick grinned. "Would you like to have kindly old Doc McCarthy check it out?"

"So-o-o-o, as I was saying...." Bridget fixed Mick with a stare somewhere between exasperation and amusement. "I'm just gonna settle back under that lovely old elm tree and rest for a bit, if you don't mind."

"Not at all, babe." Mick smiled and started to let the BSA down on to its kickstand. Suddenly he stopped, aware of a half a dozen pairs of eyes on him from a group of blue-rinse-haired old ladies who stared at the big blue motorcycle with disapproval. They had paused in the middle of the brick walkway leading up to the inn's front door and now whispered to one another with little outraged clucking noises.

Bridget inched towards Mick and murmured in a low voice, "I don't think you're supposed to be parking large blue motorcycles at the front door, darlin'.""

"Hummm," Mick said, smiling and giving a little *too-da-loo* type wave with his finger tips to the ladies at the front door. "What tipped you off?"

"All right, Mr. Smart-ass, just don't come crying to me when those grannies start whacking you over the head with their canes."

"I don't know about canes, kiddo. They all look pretty spry me. They're probably gonna come over here and kick my ass with those *sensible* little shoes."

Bridget sighed. "Just move the bike, luv." She looked around. "There," she pointed, "across the street. You can park it next to that old barn."

Mick touched the tips of his fingers to his forehead. "Your wish, as always, milady, is my command."

Mick started the bike, put it in gear, and slowly rolled over to the faded red barn on the other side of the street. He parked the bike next to the barn and draped his denim jacket over the handlebars, then walked back across the quiet street and lay down in the cool soft grass under the tree right next to Bridget.

"Mmm-m-m this is lovely, isn't it, darlin'?"

But Mick didn't answer. He was sound asleep.

In Mick's dream, he and Bridget had fallen asleep beneath some American version of a haunted Irish Myth tree, transported in time back to 1776—to the time of the Revolutionary War!

As Mick tried to struggle up from the deep well of sleep, he saw and heard colonial minutemen and their ladies as they passed by the tree. The men wore knee britches and tri-corn hats and most of them carried five-foot long flintlock muskets. Their women, dressed in long striped or calico dresses, most with aprons, wore straw bonnets or white caps. And, from somewhere he heard—yes, it was—the sounds of a military fife and drum corps rattling out an ancient marching tune.

Oh, man. It's finally happened, Mick. The jungle—'Nam—too many tokes off too many joints. You've checked out of reality for good, dude! Maybe I'm in some psycho ward somewhere. Maybe I'm....

"Mick! Mickey! Wake up!"

Bridget shook him, and he struggled up from his half awake state and fully opened his eyes. And then he clapped them shut again—tightly.

Bridget was there. And so was he. And so was the inn and the tree, and he was awake, except...except he must truly be tripping out in some psych ward somewhere, because all of the colonial characters from 1776 were right there too.

Chapter Twenty-Three

Sudbury, MA
The Red Horse Tavern
October 10ᵗʰ, 1858
7:14 p.m.

Jeptha stared at the angry, disheveled little gnome of a man standing in the doorway to the taproom, belligerently clenching and unclenching his fists.

"I'm gonna ask you just one more time, Mr.—whoever the devil you are. What d'you want with Zeke Tanner?"

Jeptha fingered the smudged, crudely written letter in his pocket as he opened his mouth to speak. But the fifth generation of Hows tavern keepers, came around from the backside of the bar/counter and pointed a bony finger at the figure in the doorway. "Tanner, you mind your tongue, you hear me? This feller's come all the way down from Boston. No, even further, Cape Cod, just to find someone—and I reckon as how that someone is you."

"Shut your mouth, old man, if you don't want me to shut it for you. Or if you wanna keep flappin' them gums then maybe you can tell me just who is this here Boston man who wants to...." He stopped, and a feral calculating look replaced the angry, antagonistic expression. "Boston, you say?"

Jeptha finally spoke. "I haven't said anything—yet—Mr. Tanner."

Zeke Tanner continued to stare at Jeptha as he rasped, "Git out," to the old man in the stained apron.

"I'll be damned if I will!" the old man muttered.

"I said git!" Tanner hissed from between clenched teeth.

The old man looked at Tanner with an expression that wavered between contempt and speculation. "So this is the Boston man that you've been waiting on for the past two weeks."

"I told you to get! It's none of your damn business, you old—"

"Oh, but it, is Mr. Tanner. If this here is your Boston man what you been telling me is gonna pay the bill for you and that damn lazy half breed you got sleeping in my barn, then it's my business as much as yours. Maybe a whole lot more!"

The belligerence ran out of Zeke Tanner like a breeze floating through a torn sail. "Mr. Hows," he said in a raspy, whiskey-ruined voice, "give me leave to talk with this here Boston gentleman and you'll git...you'll git everything you got coming to you."

"That suit you, Mr. Dawes?" The old man looked over at Jeptha, and he nodded silently.

Without waiting to be asked, Zeke Tanner pulled out the chair opposite Jeptha and sat down at the table.

The old man took off his apron and started to leave to the pantry in back of the bar.

"Wait," Tanner called. "Bring me whiskey. No, no, rum. Yeah, that's it, hot buttered rum." He rubbed his scrawny hands together and cracked the knuckles. "Seems like every time I feel the frost comin' on this time of year, the only thing that can drive it out of my bones is hot buttered rum." He rubbed his hands together again and muttered, "I ain't gonna spend another winter in this cold, damp New England, or hauling ice-stiff lines on some dirty fishing boat. No, it's gonna be Barbados and rum and black-haired senoritas with dark eyes and soft hands."

The slam of the thick stone jug of rum on the table made the little man jump.

"Here!" The old man grinned with a glint of satisfaction. "I got no hot irons in the fire just now, so you'll have to make do with hot water and...," he let a small crock of butter clatter onto the table beside the rum and another jug of steaming water, "you can butter your own damn rum yer own self."

Zeke Tanner nodded once and said, "Now git."

Hows shook his head. "Not till I get paid; your bill's overdue enough as it is. Who's paying?" He sneered. "You?"

"No. Me," Jeptha said quietly from the other side of the table.

Both men watched in astonishment as Jeptha pulled his worn, lambskin wallet from his inside coat pocket and dropped a handful of $20 gold eagles on to the center of the table.

* * * *

Sudbury MA
The Wayside Inn
August 18th, 1968
6:29 p.m.

Bridget knelt behind Mick and rested her chin on his shoulder as she continued to curiously examine the scene unfolding in front of them.

Mick just stared. He sat cross-legged in the mid-summer grass underneath the enormous old elm tree and shook his head.

Yeah, he'd figured out that they hadn't fallen down Alice's magic mushroom rabbit hole or stepped into some kind of a time warp. And best of all, he wasn't tripping out or flashing back, but on the other hand, plain old reality was just about as weird! Apparently, all of these overgrown adult-type boys and girls had decided to play dress up for the day. Or maybe they were practicing for Halloween two months early. Or....

"Maybe they're shooting a movie, luv."

"Maybe. C'mon, let's go find out." Mick stood up and gave Bridget's hand a slight tug, but she was already on her feet in one graceful motion. She followed Mick as he sidled up to a large man in a brown waistcoat with pewter buttons.

"Ahh, excuse me, ah, Colonel?"

The man turned and gave Mick a pleasant smile. "Hi."

"Hi," Mick smiled back. "So what gives? Are you guys making a movie or something?"

"No, no, were just practicing drilling for the battle next week."

"Battle?"

"Yeah, we're going up to Fort No. 5, up in New Hampshire, for a battle reenactment."

"Battle reenactment? So you guys put on shows and stuff? Like mock battles?"

"Reenactments."

"Oh, yeah, right. Reenactments. How come?"

"We like to keep history alive," the colonel said as the command, "prime and load!" came from the captain of the troop. "We're all a bunch of local guys from Sudbury, Framingham, and Wayland, and we do this 'cause we like history and it's a lot of fun."

"Fun?"

"Yeah. Watch."

"Make ready!"

The line of men standing in front of the inn came to attention; there was a clicking sound as the hammers were drawn back on a dozen muskets.

"Take aim."

The muskets' muzzles came up.

"Fire!"

An ear-shattering crash and a simultaneous belch of flame followed by clouds of sulfurous gray smoke shattered the quite afternoon.

The small crowd that had gathered on the lawn to watch the demonstrations screamed and jumped back. A few small children started to cry, while the older ones clapped, and in the distance a dog started a frantic barking.

The colonel turned back to Mick with a big grin on his face. "See what I mean."

Mick smiled. "Yeah, so what d'you guys call yourselves?"

"We're the Sudbury Companies of Militia and Minute," he said proudly.

"Then you must know quite a lot about the inn and all," Bridget said.

"A fair amount," the colonel replied. "But if you want to know about the furniture and clothing and stuff like that, my wife probably knows a whole lot more. Hey, Annie!" he called.

An attractive, middle-aged woman with wisps of curly brown hair straying out from her white cap walked over.

"This is my wife, Annie—terrific at sewing, made my whole outfit—knows lots about the inn too."

"You want to know about the inn?" she asked pleasantly.

"Yeah, we do." Mick nodded. "Especially any bedrooms where people might have stayed, say, a hundred years ago. Maybe rooms like this." Mick opened the big book that he'd borrowed from Bronwyn's apartment and pointed to several black-and-white photographs of colonial bedrooms with massive four-poster beds.

"I think I can help...c'mon." She pushed open a black-painted heavy front door with a big brass doorknocker, and they stepped into the cool dark shadows of the inn's long front hallway. The woman pointed to a small, pub-type room on their right. "That's the old bar room where you could of gotten a meal or a mug of ale a hundred years ago."

"What about the bedrooms?" Mick asked.

"Well, there are some very elegant bedrooms at the end of the hall on the second floor. That's where the ladies and gentleman would of stayed if they were taking the coach to New York."

"Where would the common folk have stayed?" Bridget broke in.

"Yeah." Mick nodded. "Say, like a sailor and an Indian half-breed."

"Half-breed? Sailor? My, you do have interesting questions. Writing a book?"

"No, we just—"

"Annie!" said the colonel. He stuck his head in the door and yelled, "Captain Taylor was showin' 'em how to thrust with a bayonet and split a big rip right down the backside of his breeches! You got your sewing kit with you?"

She smiled and shook her head. "Yeah, it's in the car. I'll go get it."

She turned back to Mick and Bridget and said, "Gotta go. Costume emergency, but I see someone who can show you the room that I think you want. Ahh...umm, Miss?" she called out. "Oh, and I'm so sorry, I forgot your name, but I've got some people over here and was wondering if you could help them."

She turned back to Mick and Bridget and pointed to a graceful feminine shape in a long, blue, striped silk gown standing at the end of the hallway, partially obscured by the shadows. She started walking towards them.

"I met her briefly this morning. She's with the D.A.R., you know, the Daughters of the American Revolution. They're having their meeting and colonial crafts exhibition at the inn today."

The trim figure approached. Her face was still in the shadows, but Mick saw that she was in her late teens and very attractive too. He shot a quick, guilty glance at Bridget, but her eyes were fixed on the approaching girl.

"I'm sorry I forgot your name, dear. But would you mind showing these people the old Drover's Room. I think that's probably the room they're looking for."

Bridget looked intently at the girl.

Uh-oh. Did she catch me staring at this cute looking chick, 'cause I really just.... Oh my god!

The girl stepped into the light and looked back at them with an expression as surprised as theirs.

Bronwyn!

"Sis! What the hell you doing here?"

"I could ask you the same thing, Mick!"

"And what's with the get-up, kiddo?" Mick started to laugh. "Why on earth would you drag yourself all the way out to Sudbury just to dress up in colonial duds?"

"For the stupid D.A.R.," she sighed.

"But why?" Mick asked again. "You don't even belong to the D.A.R. Hell, the only one I know who'd get involved with something like that is—"

"Yeah, you got it." Bronwyn nodded glumly.

Just then, a slightly taller and even more elegantly gowned figure glided out of the shadows.

"Michael! What a pleasant surprise."

"Ah.... Hi Mom."

Chapter Twenty-Four

Sudbury Mass.
The Red Horse Tavern
October 10ᵗʰ, 1858
7:15p.m.

It was hard to tell whose eyes had grown wider or shone with more naked avarice, those of Zeke Tanner or the stunned innkeeper who stood behind him.

Jeptha let the handful of carelessly spilled gold eagles lie in the center of the table where they had fallen. Neither man opposite him made any move to pick them up—or to even touch them.

Jeptha silently berated himself. This wasn't the way to negotiate for what he wanted. He knew that he should have held the gold hidden in his pocket until he had found out if and what the sailor actually had, and then how much he wanted for it. But having been raised in a home where hard money was as scarce as good crops from the thin rocky soil of their New Hampshire farm, he'd never grown familiar with the shrewd ways of using wealth. And the stacks of $20 gold eagles that rested in the strongbox beneath the floorboards of the room back on Skaket Creek which housed the rapidly growing collection of scrimshaws, also seemed unreal to him. He had but one purpose and one purpose only. The pursuit of scrimshaws and the fulfillment of the promise he'd made to his dying captain when he'd lowered both the strong box and the chained and padlocked sea chest down to Jeptha six months ago outside Nantucket harbor.

As Jeptha had untied the longboat's bowline on that moonless night, he'd taken one last look at his captain's face in the flickering light of the ship's stern lantern. He hadn't been able to see his eyes anymore. They'd sunk back into the captain's sockets so far that his entire face had taken on a skull-like appearance.

"Mr. Dawes," the captain had croaked.

"Yes, sir?"

"Remember your promise, your solemn vow. You must have that iron-bound chest underground before daybreak."

"Yes, sir. I know."

"And then," the captain continued, "you are to use the contents of the strong box—the bulk of my fortune—in pursuit of the scrimshaw which I have described to you. It is the only means of defense from the contents of that chest." The captain gripped the railing and stared down at Jeptha with his sunken, burning eyes.

Jeptha looked back, suddenly filled with doubt. "But Captain James, sir. You yourself have said that you have never seen this scrimshaw and have but heard of it from one of the men who were with Foster on the island. And that man himself had likewise never seen it, but had only heard it described by the tribe's dying shaman who Foster had tortured to learn of its whereabouts."

The captain breathed heavily and nodded. "Aye, Mr. Dawes, you have the right of it, I'll not deny."

"Then," Jeptha said, close to despair, "how will I tell the one that was described from all others? There must be hundreds of scrimshaws scattered in taverns and sailors' boarding houses throughout the New England states. And many must have strange carvings of whales and the lines of etching you described to me. How shall I know that I have the right one?"

Captain Palmer James of the ship *Elizabeth James* stared over Jeptha's head towards the bright lights of Nantucket Town. Finally, he answered, "All I can tell you, Mr. Dawes, is that once in your possession, the object will reveal itself to you."

Jeptha stood in the gently rocking longboat and shook his head. "How, sir? I still don't understand; how will it be revealed and when?"

"I cannot answer those questions for you, Mr. Dawes." He shifted his gaze from the town to the young second mate in the longboat. "It is said by the natives of those islands that a man who is dying is sometimes given to know things that he cannot explain, nor would have the opportunity to within the time he has left."

The captain's breathing grew labored. He struggled to continue. "And though I fear I am now that man, yet there is one thing more that I must tell you...." A racking spasm of coughing shook the captain. He held his blood-spotted handkerchief to his mouth, but it no longer staunched the great gobs of blood and fluid steadily filling his lungs. He looked around for a moment, as if confused. "I-I must tell you.... But it has slipped away, as am I," he said softly, staring at the dripping handkerchief in his hand. "No matter." He shook his head. "You must do as I have said."

"Sir?"

Captain Palmer James straightened up and sucked in one great ragged breath. He gripped the rail tighter as a glowing red spot infused his chalk-white face on each cheek. "Yes, Mr. Dawes, Jeptha, you must seek out and obtain every scrimshaw that fits the description given. And do not cease until you are certain—dead certain—that you have the right one, the final scrimshaw, and have it locked and barred below ground as a sentinel against the evil that lurks within this chest." The captain's voice lashed out. "Swear it! Upon your honor, swear this final vow to your captain who now places all trust in you. Swear!"

"Yes, sir, I swear."

Jeptha had remembered his vow and had let nothing deter him from its fulfillment. Not even his marriage to the young, former parlor maid from Belfast whom he adored.

Now perhaps, just perhaps, he was closing in on the end of his search. If this man, Zeke Tanner, and his yet unnamed Indian friend, had what Jeptha prayed they had.... But he feared now that he'd overplayed his hand with the pile of gold coins. Then again.... He watched the scrawny sailor sitting opposite him. Both hands gripped the table, and both eyes focused hypnotically on the small pile of gold glinting in the candlelight.

No, maybe he hadn't. Because Zeke Tanner, it was apparent, would do anything to get his hands on those coins.

Anything.

* * * *

The Wayside Inn
August 18th, 1968
6:34 p.m.

"Well, Michael, as delightful as it is to see you and your little friend, Bethany...."

"It's Bridget, Mom, Bridget."

It didn't register—or at least it didn't seem to. It never did.

Felicity Parker Prescott—the McCarthy filed away in the musty attic of sentimental but useless things—continued, "I do have to confess to being a trifle curious as to just what brings you out to the Wayside Inn. Have you developed a sudden interest in history, or are they holding one of those 'hootenanny' things that you sing at, out in the barn?"

"No, Mom." Mick gritted his teeth. "We have to find a—"

"It's for history project, for me, Mrs. McCarthy."

"It's Prescott now, Bethany."

"And it's still Bridget, Mom!"

Despite the fact that the "queen" of the Prescott clan had met Bridget several times, she always seemed to develop a bad case of amnesia whenever Bridget was around. And Mick knew all too well that even though Bridget was attending Radcliffe, the same college as his sister and the Alma Mater of Miss Felicity herself, she could never forget or accept that her youngest son was dating as she termed it, "a little Irish waitress". Only four months ago, Mick had gotten into a verbal bout—well, he had shouted, and she merely ignored—with his mother over just that subject.

"Mom, she's not a waitress!" Mick had yelled. "She works part-time for a catering service and is going to you and your daughter's school, on full academic scholarship!"

Now, as then, Miss Felicity continued to ignore.

"Hmmm? What's that, dear? Oh, yes, Bridget, of course. Now I remember. Do forgive me, dear Betha...I mean, Bridget." Miss Felicity flashed her million-dollar smile, which, considering what the Prescotts of Beacon Hill had laid out for those thirty-two, beautiful white-capped teeth, probably wasn't far from the mark.

Mick bit down on his tongue—hard—and said, "Yeah, that's why we're here with this book that we borrowed from Bronwyn."

Mick's sister gave him a sidelong glance.

"So we've got to go hunt up one of these old rooms for...ah, for Bridget's...paper."

"Well, you and Beth—Bridget—run along and have fun. I have to get back to the D.A.R. ladies. Come along, Bronwyn."

"Ah, actually, Mom, Mick and Bridget asked me to show them around the bedrooms upstairs."

Now it was Mick and Bridget's turn to exchange glances.

"Oh, oh, all right, then. Well, enjoy yourself. But don't forget, dear, were having dinner in the main dining room with the D.A.R. at 7:30 p.m. sharp, so do try not to be late. Well, toodles!" A three fingered wave, a flash of the perfect smile, and Miss Felicity glided away in yards and yards of flowing silk and lace.

Bronwyn let out a pent-up sigh and, tugging at the too-tight bodice of her 18th century gown, turned to her brother and his girlfriend and said, "Okay, guys, what's up? What are you really looking for?" She looked at both of their faces and nodded slowly. "It's just like the last two times, right? Something weird, dangerous...." She smiled mischievously. "And exciting!"

Chapter Twenty-Five

Sudbury Mass
The Red Horse Tavern
October 10ᵗʰ, 1858
7:31 p.m.

Zeke Tanner hadn't added the butter to his rum, after all. In fact, the small crock still sat in the center of the stained dark pine table, in the same spot where the fifth generation of Hows tavern keepers had dropped it.

For that matter, the skinny sailor hadn't bothered with the hot water either. Once Jeptha had spilled the gold eagles onto the table, it seemed that Zeke Tanner had lost interest in everything except that gleaming golden horde and his mug of rum. He took a long pull from the pewter mug and wiped his lips with the back of his hand.

He glanced back at Jeptha as if trying to discern what was going on behind the slate-gray eyes. But mostly Zeke Tanner stared at the twenty-dollar gold eagles with calculating lust.

Zeke's watery blue eyes caressed each shiny gold coin while he laboriously tallied them up. Fourteen, fifteen, sixteen, seventeen… *seventeen*! The sailor slowly smiled as he realized $20 gold eagles equaled a fortune!

"Enough for passage to Barbados with a few left over to keep me in whores and rum for another year or two," he muttered.

"So the sight of my gold pleases you, does it, Mr. Tanner?"

Zeke squirmed in his chair. He looked up at the thoughtful man watching him and dropped his gaze back to the table and the pile of gold coins.

"Well, Mr. Tanner," the quiet voice of Jeptha asked, "You have something to show me? Something that perhaps you'd like to trade for these gold coins?"

"How many of them?" Zeke asked.

Even though the tavern's taproom was empty, the quiet voice dropped even lower. "If you have what I am seeking and what you've hinted that you have, all of them."

Zeke's gnarled fingers moved toward the coins, but a strong hand with sandpaper-rough fingers like iron bands closed over his own.

Jeptha, the quiet man in the brown suit, shook his head. "Show me, Mr. Tanner. Show it to me."

Zeke swallowed hard and nodded. "The Injun's got it."

"What Injun?"

"The one what was harpooner on the whalin' ship with me. The

133

Perseus."

"And how did he come by this...object?"

Jeptha stared across the table at the sailor.

"There was this village."

"Where?"

Zeke shrugged. "Somewhere in the Fijis."

"Go on."

"We put in for water and fresh fruit to fight off the scurvy. But when we got to the village, we found as how there'd been a Dutch East Indiaman put in there six weeks before us. They'd been carrying the small pox, and now that whole village was down with it. They was all dying when we got there." Zeke's fingers traced small meaningless patterns in the thin film of rum left by the bottom of his mug. "Or for the most part, dead."

Jeptha didn't speak.

"The chief of the village, a big, fat old bird, was still half alive, but his woman and his oldest brats, a boy and a girl—twins of about twelve or thirteen—were in a real bad way. 'Bout nine tenths gone. Well, this old heathen, he commences to blubbering something fierce and he tells us if'n we can give his two youngins something to cure or at least ease their suffering, we could take our pick of anything he owned."

Zeke's eyes unfocused with remembering. He shook his head. "We didn't have nothin', of course, nothing that would cure the pox anyhow. But we all made noises like we did so as we could help ourselves to whatever he had. One of the boys give the old chief a Bible and told him to start prayin'. Another give him a plug of strong tobacco and told him to chaw on it and then spit it out into some lime juice an' drink it—which actually ain't a half bad cure for scurvy."

"What did you give him?" Jeptha asked.

Zeke Tanner shrugged again. "Half a bottle of rum and a couple tots of laudanum that I'd wagered and won from a drunk old ship's doc in Singapore."

Jeptha stayed silent.

"What!" Zeke muttered, slamming the pewter mug down on the table. "All right, it wouldn't cure any of them, but it would sure as Hades ease their passin'."

He went on. "The old chief didn't say nothin'—sorta' like you," he grumbled. "But we figured as how we'd made a fair trade and started to help ourselves to his goods." Zeke's eyes glazed with avarice and lust as he remembered. "He had gold and trade silver and silk and teak from China...and no end of carved and woven goods. But the best, the very best of all, was them pearls. My god, Mr. Dawes, he had pearls as big as robin's eggs. Pearls as big is yer fist!"

Zeke's breath came in ragged gasps. "And then...and then there was this one pearl, different from all the rest. It were black, as black as the Ace of Spades. And it had carvin', some kind of funny writing all over it. It was...beautiful."

He paused and swallowed. "It seems that we all must have reached for it at once. But just then, them two—the twins—they give a terrible shriek, and their eyes rolled back in their heads, and it's plain as the nose on your face that they were dyin'."

"So, your 'cures' couldn't save them, eh, Mr. Tanner?"

"How could they?" Zeke snorted. "They weren't nothin'." He shrugged. "And this old boy, well, he's still got two big warriors who're alive and kickin' and he yells at them to c'mon over and shove their spears through our guts. And for a minute there, I gotta tell you, Mr. Dawes, I thought as how our game was up. But just then, the strangest damn thing happened." He looked up at Jeptha. "That there Injun half-breed drunk that I got sleeping over in the barn, steps up and says to the chief, 'I kin ease your youngin's pain and make sure their spirits go and join your ancestors in the great ocean of life.' And then he puts one hand on each of their foreheads and starts in singin' some damn heathen Injun chant, and these two youngins who've been burning up with the pox and pain, get these big peaceful-like smiles, and just like that, they close their eyes and they's gone."

Zeke shook his head. "Well, I thought as how we were done for, for sure then. But the chief, he's smiles all over and gets these big tears running down his old tattooed face. And he turns to John Twin-Hawks—that's my Injun friend—and says to him, 'You done helped my youngins. I don't give two hoots for the rest of these scum with you,' (that's us) 'but you, you can take anything you want.'"

Zeke clutched the edge of the table. "We all know'd what he should take, an' we kept whispering to him, 'John, ya silly red heathen, take the pearl, the big black pearl!'" The tips of Zeke's fingers whitened now. "But he didn't! He just shakes his head and points to this strange hunk of whale tooth that the old chief had around his neck. 'That,' says John Twin-Hawks, 'I'll take that.'"

"Well, for a minute I didn't think that the old boy was gonna part with it. But finally he nods his head, pulls up the cord hanging round his neck, and hands that old whale tooth to John. 'Go,' is all he says."

"And what about the rest of the...'treasure'?" Jeptha asked.

"We had to leave it!" Zeke spat. "All of it. All of it and...and that black pearl!"

He stared down at the table and muttered to himself, "That was something that shouldn't have been...couldn't be left there. Left to molder in some heathen native hut! No, it had such...such...beauty. It—"

"So the whale tooth that your Indian friend took in payment, where is it now?"

Zeke looked up, perhaps surprised at the ragged emotion on the young man's here-to-fore tightly controlled face.

"It's...it's in the barn, across the road, around the neck of the Injun, John Twin-Hawks."

"Show me!" Jeptha rasped.

* * * *

At first Jeptha thought that the Indian was sleeping, but as they drew closer to where he sat cross-legged in the straw in the barn loft, eyes focused on nothing, Jeptha realized that he was in some sort of a trance.

"John!" the scrawny sailor barked. "John Twin-Hawks! Wake up, ya damn drunken savage. I got a man here from Boston what wants to see that heathen thing you got hangin' round yer neck."

Slow and calm, the Indian opened his eyes and regarded the two men.

"You be good now and show it to this feller, you hear me?" Zeke's voice had degenerated into a whining wheedling.

The Indian watched with impassively calm eyes and finally stood up. He took two steps towards Jeptha and put both his hands on his shoulders. He stared intently into Jeptha's gray eyes as a few seconds or a hundred years went by.

Finally, and still without speaking, he nodded and slipped the intricate, carved scrimshaw from around his neck and placed it around Jeptha's. He nodded once more and sat back down in the straw and waited.

He didn't have long to wait.

"I'll take my payment now, Mr. Dawes," Zeke Tanner said.

"You've already got it," Jeptha said without turning around. "I gave it to you. There in the tavern, seventeen $20 gold eagles—three hundred and forty dollars."

"That was just the down payment, Mr. Dawes, now I want the balance."

"And what do you reckon that is, Mr. Tanner?" Jeptha said, turning around.

Zeke Tanner, his lips drawn back in an evil grin, pointed a six-barreled pepperbox pocket pistol at Jeptha.

"I reckon, Mr. Dawes, that it will be the entire contents of that sheepskin wallet that you carry. Everything."

"So this was the plan all along?" Jeptha shook his head in disgust. "You and your Indian friend are just common thieves bent upon robbery?"

"Oh, no, Mr. Dawes." Zeke kept smiling. "Old John Twin-Hawks there is the genuine article, and he done give you what you came fer. Not that it'll do you much good," he muttered.

"Now get over there and stand beside him!" Zeke snarled.

Jeptha didn't move. Instead, he said, "So you mean to cheat him too then? Your partner!"

"No partner of mine!" Zeke snapped. "Now move, I said!"

Jeptha still didn't move. But someone else did. John Twin-Hawks got up from the straw and for the first time spoke. "Zeke Tanner," he rumbled, his voice a low growl. "For a long time now I have known you have a bad heart, an evil heart. But I don't care because you buy me rum. I still don't care, but let this man go. He has what he came for. What I have to give him, and what he has to have. It is important to many people that he has this. Let him go and keep all the gold for yourself. I don't want it."

"Okay, John, okay. You was always fair minded even for an Injun. That okay with you, Mr. Dawes? You keep the tooth. I get the gold." His eyes grew hard. "All of it!"

Jeptha took the worn leather wallet from his inside coat pocket and threw it down in front of Zeke. "You're still a thief, Mr. Tanner."

"No I'm not, Mr. Dawes. Ya know why?" Zeke grinned.

Jeptha was silent.

"Because you're gonna write me out a bill of sale." He pulled out a crinkled piece of cheap paper from his pocket along with the stub of a pencil. He tossed them to Jeptha. "Now pick 'em up an' write: 'I hereby do pay to Mr. Zeke Tanner the sum of....'" Zeke shook the rest of the gold coins from the wallet and counted. "Six hundred and...forty dollars in gold, for one real special scrimshaw." He sneered at Jeptha as he pocketed the gold.

"You know, Mr. Tanner, even if the law or I don't find you, I don't think I would sleep easily knowing that I cheated a man like John Twin-Hawks."

"Yeah? But that's where you're wrong, Mr. Dawes. Cuz I plan on sleepin' real easy, fer a long time. And so will you, John. Sorry."

The pepperbox pistol barked out twice, and two red splotches appeared in the center of the Indian's chest. He looked down at them and then took three deliberate steps across the barn hayloft towards Zeke. The gun banged out a third time, and the Indian crumpled to the floor. Jeptha knelt down and placed his ear on the Indian's chest.

He was dead.

"You treacherous bastard!" Jeptha spat.

Zeke looked at Jeptha, and the mocking grin had disappeared from his face. "And I ain't gonna spend the rest of my life lookin' over my shoulder fer you either, Mr. Dawes."

One more shot rang out in the barn. And then there was silence.

Chapter Twenty-Six

The Wayside Inn
August 18ᵗʰ, 1968
6:46 p.m.

"This is it?" Skeptical, Mick turned towards his sister.

Bronwyn nodded, and Mick turned back and looked into the primitive colonial room. It wasn't that it was necessarily so small, although the massive two-foot wide beams that ran the length of the ceiling did give it a rather ominous ambiance. No, Mick decided. It was the three beds and assorted rickety chairs and tables crammed into the second floor space that made the room seem claustrophobic and crappy.

"Huh?" his sister said.

"It looks...crappy. Are you sure this is the one?"

"Sure I'm sure; at least that's what the brochure says." Bronwyn waved the accordion-folded pamphlet that read: *Longfellow's Wayside Inn – a Self-guided Walking Tour* in front of Mick's face. "If you don't believe me, take a look in here."

He did. Yeah, there it was, Room number 3 in the brochure, the Driver's and Drover's Chamber. It was notated as the "sleeping quarters for the drivers, drovers, peddlers, and merchants who traveled the Boston Post Road". Mick read it to himself and then read it again, aloud, to the two girls standing next to him in the cramped viewing space just off the second floor landing. "They left out one category," he announced after the second reading.

"What's that, luv?" Bridget asked, peering into the dark-shadowed room.

"They left out sailors—sailors with very bad handwriting." Mick held a Xerox copy of an old envelope up to the light. "And even worse spelling."

Bronwyn pulled Mick's hand around so she could see what he was holding. It was a photocopy of an old envelope. It read: To Mr. Kabut of Kabut lawers of Bostin Citti.

"What's this?" she asked, wrinkling her nose.

"It's what we came to find, Sis."

"But it's just an envelope?"

"I know." Mick nodded. "It was all we could find in Frankie's old files. And we were damn lucky to find this."

"Huh?" his sister said again.

Mick sighed and gave her the condensed version.

He told her about the Skaket Creek Inn and the murder, but by the time he got to his own tipsy infatuation with the sultry charms of the late Karen Randolph, Bridget's sea-green eyes had become tiny little emerald daggers, so he left out any further descriptions of the girl with the platinum-blonde hair and the enormous.... Yeah, he skipped right over that part. But he told about the arrest and those two inbred cops and his temporary reprieve. He ended up with a quick gloss over the fight in the alley and when he got to the meeting in big brother Frankie's office, he stopped.

His sister shook her head and smiled a slight smile as she recognized that this was indeed promising to be another wild escapade of her older but reckless brother. "Oh, wow, Mick. When you step into it, you do it with both feet, don't you?"

Mick shrugged. They'd been down this road before.

"So what did big brother Frankie have to say?"

"The usual. You know, when am I gonna grow up and crap like that. But then, just as me and Bridge were gonna pack it in as a lost cause, this friend of Frankie's—the new Barnstable County Assistant D.A.," Mick glanced at Bridget, but she didn't look up, "pipes up from the corner, that he may have an idea."

"What?"

"You tell it." Mick nodded at Bridget.

Bridget nodded back slowly. "Well, I was still in the process of collectin' meself after that...that bleedin' close shave in the alley." She drew in a deep breath. "And all I really wanted was to get back out into the fresh air and away from the city and office buildings and alleys. So Mickey nods to me and says 'let's go.' But just as we reached the door, this dapper lookin', rather handsome young lad...." Bridget must have seen a dark cloud pass over Mick's face; she quickly dropped her gaze back to the floor before continuing, "Ah...his name was Mr. Assistant District Attorney, E.F. Westlake." She glanced up at Mick. "I do have that right then, don't I, Mickey?"

Mick didn't answer for a moment. He studied tiny twin spots of red blush on her cheeks and thought about the way the "handsome young lad" had looked at Bridget and started to wonder about the *look* she had given back to him. Then he stared at her long black eyelashes and emerald green eyes and thought about a fool who had jeopardized the love and passion that lay behind those eyes by chasing after platinum-blonde hair and enormous.... And decided not to think any more about what he might have been thinking. So he nodded and said, "Yup, that's right, babe."

Bridget let her breath out and smiled. "So this fella says, 'Wait, I think I may know something that can help you or at least point you in the right direction.'" She turned to Bronwyn. "You see, we'd told them— him and Frankie—everything. Well, almost everything, about the inn and the legends and Kathy's great, great grandfather and Jeptha and his mysterious trips to Boston in search of scrimshaws."

Bridget began pacing up and down in the narrow hallway and, as she spoke, her words flowed in a rapid staccato and her tone became more intense. "So he takes us down to this big dark old musty room all filled up to the ceiling with all of these dusty old wooden file cabinets and he says, 'I think you should have a look at these, they might give you a clue as to what old Jeptha Dawes was looking for when he came to Boston a century ago.'

"And I says, 'Well certainly!' but all the time I'm lookin' around at the dark and the shadows of that musty old place and I can't stop thinkin' about the story Kathy told us and the poundin' on the door of my room two nights ago and the evil thugs in the alley and...."

Mick reached out and stopped Bridget's nervous pacing with a hand on her shoulder. Her County Cork brogue had deepened with every word. She was still spooked by what had happened. And what *was* happening. So was he.

He pulled her in until her cheek was level with his shoulder. He felt her relax a little. "May I?" He smiled.

She nodded.

"Well, amazingly enough, what Westlake knew that not even Frankie did, was that Elliott and Delbert was actually a fifth generation offshoot of the old Cabot and Saltonstall law firm. And, as such, had all of the old records going all the way back to the 1840s."

Bronwyn shook her head and sighed. "Is this going somewhere, Mick?"

"Yeah, right here." He held up a photocopy and pointed to the old envelope reproduced on the sheet of white paper. "Westlake found this envelope in one of the old files. The letter was gone, but we also found an entry in the law diary of Mr. Edmund Cabot, the firm's senior partner. It was dated October 10th, 1858. Here, I made a copy of that too." He pulled another piece of Xerox paper out of his back pocket and showed it to his sister as he read:

"October 10th, year of our Lord, Eighteen Hundred and Fifty-Eight. Met this a.m. with one Jeptha Dawes of Skaket Creek on Cape Cod. Mr. Dawes has proved himself to be a good and God-fearing Christian and a man who pays promptly and in gold during the six months that he has been a client of this firm. This day, I assisted him once again in his seemingly fruitless and never-ending quest for strangely carved bits of marine ivory. But I must confess that I have never seen him so agitated over a possible addition to his collection. I did give him a crude letter that I had received by personal messenger—a sullen, half-breed Indian—that directed him to go to a rustic inn out in the town of Sudbury in West Middlesex County. There, the letter alleged in its barely legible prose, he would find 'very special Scrimshaw.'

"Mr. Dawes became very excited and betook himself straight away to the Boston Post Road coach with barely a farewell to me. Only the hasty, parting words that he would have, if God pleased, perhaps have the end to his long and dire quest.

"The entry ends there," Mick said, folding the photocopy and putting it back in the pocket of his jeans.

"And so that's why you and Bridget are out here," Bronwyn said. "But why this room?"

"Because," Bridget said softly, "this looks to me the sort of a place that a poor sailor would stay while awaiting his benefactor-to-be."

Bronwyn shrugged. "I suppose. But what do you expect to find here?"

"Nothing," Bridget answered. She stared at the far wall of the bedroom. "Unless...." With one quick, graceful movement, she slipped under the hand-woven rope strung across the door to the bedroom.

"Ah...I think that rope means, like, keep out, you know?"

"Absolutely right, Sis." Mick smiled, unclipped one end of the rope, and handed it to Bronwyn. "So you stand right there and keep everyone else out until we find...well, whatever it is we're looking for."

Bronwyn rolled her eyes and blew out an exasperated but resigned breath as Mick joined Bridget at the far corner of the room.

"What are you looking for, babe?" he asked, coming up behind her.

"I'm...I'm not sure. I thought I saw something sparkle over in this corner, just as the setting sun passed through the windowpane a minute ago." She stood on tiptoes and stared at the massive two-foot oak beam over the ancient pine plank bed. "Look, Mickey, the beam. It's all charred. There's been a fire in here."

"Brom," Mick called to his sister at the doorway, "That book of yours. Does it say anything about a fire?"

Bronwyn opened the thick black book.

"Yes," she called back, "about fifteen years ago. Most of this old place burned down, and they rebuilt it to keep it open as a historical landmark." She closed the book with a snap and looked over at her brother. "So whatever it is that you're looking for, and whatever the heck that is," she muttered almost under her breath, "it would have been...."

Bridget's shoulders slumped. "Then any clue we might have hopes of finding would have been burned up in the fire."

"Maybe, maybe not. Come here. You see this beam? It's charred on this end but it's still sound and two feet thick and—"

"And over in that corner by the big bed." Bridget pointed with growing excitement at the four-foot-wide double trundle bed. "The beam and the wall are completely untouched! And that's where I saw the sparkle." She ran over to the dark cobwebbed corner above the bed and climbed quickly up onto the thick pine headboard.

"Ahh, Bridget," Bronwyn called nervously from the doorway. "I got a hunch that's probably a big no-no too."

Bridget ignored her and strained up on her tiptoes while she tried to fit her tiny fingers into the space between the beam and the wall.

"Mickey," she said, "do you have that Swiss Army knife thing with you?"

"Sure, kid." He grinned. "Complete with handy bottle opener."

"Give it here." She opened the smallest blade on the knife and slipped it in between the beam and the wall. She worked the blade back and forth.

"What? What do you see?"

"Shush! I'm trying to listen."

Mick heard the faint crinkle of paper. Then a soft clank as the blade struck something metal. Bridget slowly pulled the blade out and... *clunk*. Something struck the floor and started to roll. It rolled through the puddles of late afternoon sunlight and flashed a reflected, bright yellow. Mick started after it, but Bronwyn reached down and scooped it up. She gasped.

"Mickey," she breathed opening her hand. "It's...gold!"

* * * *

The three of them sat outside under the big elm tree and watched the sun begin to dip behind the hills.

"Like, wow!" Bronwyn said, staring at the two yellow coins and shaking her head. "There's only two of them, but I'll bet they're still worth a fortune."

"Could be, Sis, but that piece of paper that Bridge found could be worth a whole lot more—at least to me."

"How so?"

"Well, if it helps us to prove who I think is really behind all this mess, then it could keep my sorry butt out of jail."

"Jail? You didn't mention that part. Oh, Mick, now what've you gone and gotten yourself into?"

"It's a long story, Brom. Maybe we'll come by your place tomorrow, and I'll explain the whole stupid thing."

"But that piece of paper." Bronwyn looked at the crumpled yellowed document spread out on the ground. "I don't get it. It says 'Bill of Sale' and it's dated 1858. So how can that help you?"

Mick picked up the paper again. "It's a bill of sale saying that Jeptha Dawes bought a 'special scrimshaw' from one Zeke Tanner for $640 in gold—a small fortune in those days. And yet this Zeke Tanner left the bill of sale and two of the coins hidden in his room. Why?"

Bronwyn shrugged.

Bridget stared at the document and the two gold eagles. Finally she said, "Because he hid them for safekeeping. But for some reason, he never came back for them. He took the bulk of the gold and he ran."

"But why. And where?"

Bridget shook her head. "I don't know, Mickey."

"I'm totally confused," Bronwyn said. "How will finding out where this Zeke Tanner ran off to keep you out of jail?"

Mick stretched and leaned back against the tree. "Well for starters, it will—"

"Bronwyn! You-hoo, dear!" Miss Felicity stood at the doorway of the inn. "It's time for dinner, dear. Come along. We don't want to keep the D.A.R. waiting, you know."

"Mommm!" Bronwyn drew the word out from between gritted teeth. "Mick?" She looked at her brother plaintively.

"Sorry, kiddo. I can field strip an M-16 in the dark, but I can't do anything when Miss Felicity has her mind made up."

Bronwyn stood up slowly with a long-suffering sigh. "Come over tomorrow and tell me the whole story, okay, guys?"

"Sure, Sis. And give those old D.A.R. ladies a big wet kiss for me."

She stuck her tongue out at him and gloomily let Miss Felicity lead her back into the inn's dining room, now filled with blue-rinsed hair and many, many yards of ancient silk, ribbons, and lace.

Mick and Bridget smiled at one another, and Mick said, "C'mon, babe. We better get a move on if we wanna get back to Cambridge and pick up a couple of Vitto's great meatball subs before he closes."

They walked across the street to where the BSA rested against the barn. Mick pulled the ignition key out of the watch pocket of his jeans, but it slipped through his fingers and landed in the soft dirt. Without thinking, Bridget bent down to pick it up, and as she did something struck the side of the barn, exactly where her head had been a second before.

She'd started to straighten up with a puzzled look on her face. Mick jumped off the bike and threw himself on top of her just as a second thud threw a small shower of splinters out from the side of the old barn.

"Mickey, what...?"

"Sniper!" Mick hissed, swiveling his head back and forth. "He's using a silencer and probably got a scope too."

A third shot kicked up dirt just inches from the toe of Mick's right boot.

He wasn't waiting for more. He got up in a crouch, grabbed Bridget, and they ran towards the half open barn door. "Quick! Inside!"

He looked around. Whoever had the sniper's rifle was a pro. And he wouldn't just give up and go away. He'd be coming for them.

Mick took Bridget's hand, and they moved to the back of the barn. A solid wall. They were trapped. No way out, and the .38 Police Special that Pop had given him still rested out of reach in the bike's saddlebags—a definite bullet through the brain if he made a try for that. Shit!

He looked around again. "C'mon, Bridge," he whispered, "the loft."

He pushed her ahead of him up the rickety ladder and into the far corner where several old hay bales were stacked amid disarranged piles of rusty farm tools and rotting leather harnesses. They burrowed under a pile of old burlap sacks behind the hay bales. They waited, but not for long.

Mick gripped Bridget's hand, and she held her breath. The barn door slowly rolled open and then closed all the way. The dim sliver of fading sunlight disappeared.

In the semidarkness, they heard footsteps approaching and the unmistakable sound of the heavy bolt being drawn back on a sniper rifle.

The footsteps reached the foot of the ladder to the loft and stopped.

Silence for a moment, then the sound of heavy breathing and the faint tap of shoes on wooden rungs as someone began to climb.

Chapter Twenty-Seven

The Red Horse Tavern
The Drover's Room
October 10th, 1858
8:03 p.m.

Zeke Tanner stuffed the last of his few shabby possessions into his stained old sea bag and pulled on his coat. He took the contents of the lambskin wallet and the bill of sale and thrust them into his inside pocket.

He started to leave. He paused. Suppose someone found Dawes and the Indian? Was this piece of paper proof that he'd been with them tonight? Slowly, he realized that while it could save him, it might also hang him. He couldn't get caught with the paper on him, but he didn't want to destroy it. Just in case.

He'd hide it, somewhere in his room, where he could come back for it. He took the paper out of his pocket along with two pieces of gold, again, just in case. His eyes swept the room then roamed over to the bed and the dark corner.

There.

* * * *

The Wayside Inn barn
August 18th, 1968
7:32 p.m.

Bridget's right hand cramped from clenching the single strand of coarse twine that Mick had handed her before silently moving off into the shadows on the other side of the barn loft. As soon as she'd heard the footsteps approaching the loft ladder, Mick grabbed a small bail of twine from the old junk pile next to them. He'd quickly tied one end around the rotting harness hanging on the rusty nails behind them and put the other in Bridget's palm. She repeated his whispered instructions in her mind.

"Wait for my signal. When he starts to move into the loft and has his back turned towards me, I'm going to step out of the shadows and do this." Mick had pumped his right fist up and down twice. "That's your signal. And what are you gonna do?"

"Pull," Bridget whispered to herself again. "Hard!"

A creaking noise and then a heavy thump erupted as a booted foot stepped onto the loft floor.

Bridget held her breath and repeated silently to herself, "Pull, pull, pull. Come on, Mick, where's your signal?" She strained her eyes to pierce the shadows on the far side of the loft. Mick should have stepped into view by now. He should be signaling.

"*As soon as his back is turned towards me....*" She slowly raised her head until her eyes drew level with the top of the hay bales that hid her. The gunman stood in front of the ladder, but his back wasn't facing Mick—it faced her.

She watched with horror as he raised the rifle stock to his cheek and pointed the muzzle at something in the corner of the loft. Something—someone—trying not to move. Or even breathe. Someone praying as hard as her, that the rifle's telescopic scope wouldn't pick up the faint glimmer of slivers of fading daylight reflected off of a belt buckle or a pair gray-blue eyes frozen in the shadows.

The sound of chromed steel on steel broke her silent prayers. The metallic sound of a rifle bolt sliding forward as it chambered a half-ounce of steel-jacketed death.

* * * *

The Red Horse Tavern Barn
October 10th, 1858
8:20 p.m.

"Where the hell is he?" Zeke Tanner muttered and searched the barn for the third time. Finding only the dead body of John Twin-Hawks where it lay in a cold puddle of congealing blood, he savagely kicked the corpse in frustration.

The mounting panic in his chest reflected all too clearly the only possible answer. "Ya jest wounded him, ya damn fool!" he hissed into the darkness. "But then again, maybe he's crawled off some place to die," Zeke mumbled back to himself.

"Or maybe I just grazed him, and he's all hale and hearty and hiding in a dark corner." Zeke franticly swiveled his head from side to side looking for a crouching figure just waiting for him to lower the pistol or turn his back or....

Zeke ran to the barn door and rushed out into the cold night air. He looked at the lights of the tavern shining across the road. Of course!

"That's it! That damn Dawes come to and he done go'd across the road to that damned old man. He's probably waiting fer me right now. And he's got some big ol' blunderbuss filled up with lead shot. Yeah, gittin' all primed and loaded to blow ol' Zeke to kingdom come the moment he steps through the tavern's front door. They's probably...."

147

Zeke stuffed the pistol into his belt and ran around the side of the lamp-lit tavern. Quietly, he lifted the latch to the rear door and let himself in. He carefully tiptoed through along hallway and into the kitchen. He stopped next to the cook stove and checked the six barrels of the pepperbox pistol. Four of the barrels were empty. Four shots fired. That left only two. He cursed himself for not reloading.

"But then again," he murmured, "Two shots? Yeah, that'll be enough."

* * * *

The Wayside Inn Barn
August 18th, 1968
7:35 p.m.

Bridget was never sure if she consciously pulled on that sweaty piece of twine, or if it was just the reaction of nerves wound too tight for too long. But one way or another, when she saw the finger tighten on the rifle's trigger, she pulled. Hard. There was a soft plop as the ancient rotted harness ripped from the wall and dropped to the barn floor with a loud clatter. The barrel of the rifle swiveled a hundred and eighty degrees until the crosshairs of the scope centered directly on Bridget's forehead peeking over the top of the hay bales.

She froze like a quail in a hunter's sights.

The rifle fired. And at the same instant, a rusty pitchfork jabbed out of the shadows and ripped through the arm of the gunman's black leather jacket. The steel-jacketed slug passed so close to Bridget's face that she felt its heat.

But the gunman wasn't paying any attention to Bridget. He quickly chambered another round and brought the rifle barrel up level with Mick's stomach. Except...except the damn kid with the gray-blue eyes in the sweat stained T-shirt wouldn't let go of the damn pitchfork!

The gunman strained to bring up the rifle barrel, but every time he did, Mick pushed the leather-jacketed arm stuck to the pitchfork back down again. They continued this deadly tug-of-war like a demented barn dance. Waltzing in a silence punctuated only by a few desperate grunts and the scraping sounds of boots on the loft floor. And it seemed as though the dance would go on forever. The gunman straining to raise the rifle and Mick forcing it back down.

* * * *

Suddenly the man took a quick step backwards, and Mick, unprepared, stumbled forward. That was all the gunman needed. His eyes glittered through the slits of the ski mask in brutal victory. And Mick knew that if the hitman couldn't get off a killing shot, he'd settle for a wound—then the kill.

The black-clad figure's finger tightened on the trigger, and as Mick desperately tried to regain his footing, the black-gloved finger squeezed.

The muzzle flash illuminated Mick's face as the bullet struck.

Mick tried to twist out of the way as a burning pain flashed from his hip down to the heel of his boot. His right leg buckled. If the gunman's face hadn't been hidden by a black ski mask, Mick was sure he'd have seen a triumphant grin spread across it. Instead, all he heard was a whispered, "Goodnight, McCarthy," and the sound of the bolt drawing back to chamber the final round.

The gunman screamed. Mick looked up. A small, lithe figure had suddenly attached itself to the gunman's back. Bridget!

"You bitch!" The gunman howled. "You bit me!"

She had. And she did it again. Right on the back of his neck, like some pixie vampire.

He screamed again and with one savage move reached over his shoulder and pulled her off. As she struggled to regain her footing, he backhanded her, and she rolled to the edge of the loft floor, stunned.

Mick yelled, "Bridge!" and made a desperate lunge with the pitchfork just as the gunman leveled his rifle at Mick's stomach and rammed the bolt home.

* * * *

The Red Horse Tavern Taproom
October 10th, 1858
8:21 p.m.

"Where is he, you old bastard? Talk or I'll splatter yer guts all over this bar room!"

"Where is who, ya miserable Devil's spawn! I know'd you was a wrongun the moment you set foot in here. Shoulda throwed you out two weeks ago. My own damn fault for being too greedy fer lodgin' money," the old man muttered.

Zeke looked around the empty room. "I can search this whole place if I have to, old man."

"Go ahead, and bad luck to ya! Say, what've you done?" The old tavern keeper's eyes grew wide. "By God. You've done gone and murdered him, ain't you?"

"You got a real big mouth, old man." Zeke drew the pepperbox from his belt. "And I don't want them noisy gums of yours flappin' when I'm gone."

The old man took a step backwards as he realized Zeke's intentions.

Zeke thumbed the hammer back on the pepperbox.

He paused. A noise came from the road outside. Faint at first, then louder. The sound of horse's hooves and coach wheels.

The 8:30 Post Road Stage! He made a sudden decision, prompted by the weight of gold eagles in his coat pocket. It was time to git!

He lowered the pistol's hammer back slowly to half-cock. Not the time for a pistol shot. But he didn't want this nosy old coot raising a ruckus either. So.... The heavy barrel of the pistol lashed out, and the old man collapsed with a moan.

Zeke pushed the pistol back into his belt and stepped out to the waiting coach. "Say there, driver, does this here coach stop at any train stations on the way to Boston?"

"Well...." The grizzled coachman fingered his jaw and looked down at his scruffy potential passenger. "Fer ten dollars I kin make a detour of a few miles to Saxonville station."

Zeke handed him a gold coin. "Here's twenty dollars. We're leaving now."

Chapter Twenty-Eight

Skaket Creek
October 13th, 1858
11:14 a.m.

Fiona's hands had been trembling ever since the clerk at the general store had handed her the stained, smudged envelope. He'd finished filling her order and was just opening up the account book for her to sign for the $2.37 that she'd spent on this week's groceries, when he'd said, "Oh, I almost forgot. You got a letter that come for you, just yesterday." He held up the letter and read the return address. "From Framingham town; that's somewhere west of Boston."

Fiona stared at the letter.

"Got two cents postage due on it."

"Just add it to our account, please, Mr. Baker."

"Think maybe it's from that wandering husband of yours, Mrs. Dawes?"

"Thank you, Mr. Baker." Fiona had stuffed the letter into her bag and stumbled red-faced from the store.

All the way home down the dusty sand track back to Skaket Creek, she thought about the letter. It wasn't from Jeptha. Even though she'd only seen him sign his name a few times, she'd know his handwriting anywhere. No, this wasn't his. And it didn't look like the perfect copperplate script that she'd observed on the letters that came to him from those lawyers in Boston. This envelope had been addressed by someone who didn't write very often, or very well.

Now she was down in her special place on the wide sand-dune beach, seated on her fairy throne. Time to open the letter, which somehow she knew that although it wasn't from her husband, it was about him.

She squeezed both of her hands together until the trembling stopped.

"Buck up, girl!" she scolded herself. "You crossed a wide ocean and have worked for demanding masters. Whatever it is, you can deal with it!" She pulled open the flaps of the envelope and began to read:

> *dear Mrs. Dawes*
> *I take pencil in hand to tell you I got News of your husbind.*
> *He come up to our door two nights ago more dead than alive.*
> *Me and my wife, Martha, we nursed him for two days and with the Lord's help his life wuz sparred.*
> *he is gettin better now but is fretting something*

awful Cuz he says he cannot pay uS for saving him as he wuz shot and robbed.

I tole him we don't want no money Cuz we are good Christian folk and believe the Lord rewards a kine deed. But even though he is still weak as a newborn kittin, he says he got to be after this man wat robbed him of something real important. So he give me this note to send to you by the Boston Post coach and he is now gone. Here is his note.

very Truly youres
Mr. Thomas Jensen
Jensen farm
Framingham town

Another piece of paper fluttered down from the envelope. Fiona grabbed for it and missed. A sudden gust of wind blew the paper out of her hand towards the white foam surf. Fiona shrieked and stumbled forward after it. She ran like a madwoman as the teasing breeze blew the precious paper closer to the water's edge. As it reached the foam she made a desperate lunge and fell to her knees as a wave curled up and soaked her dress. But she held the paper up in her right hand, damp but safe. Tears ran down her cheeks as she broke the seal.

My Dearest Fiona,
I do hope that kind Providence continues to smile upon you, my darling girl, and has kept you safe and well during my absence. Once again I must beg your pardon and indulgence for being so often away from you. Believe me, my love, when I tell you that each day away from you tears at my heart worse than the cruelest barb that a Nantucket harpooner could ever thrust.

I must implore you to trust me just a little while longer. I am so close to the end of my quest—my burden and obligation. I am so close! It shames me to admit that I had the object of my search in my possession. In my hand! And I allowed it to be taken from me.

I curse my clumsiness and gullible nature. But I did not think that the wretch who calls himself Zeke Tanner would shoot. But he did. He shot and killed a blameless Indian by the name of John Twin-Hawks.

He likewise shot me and left me for dead.

Please, my dear, I know that I should not be telling you this, for I do not wish to cause you worry or distress. But I only tell you to demonstrate that the good Lord is sparing me to fulfill my vow. And because, as I have continued to do every hour since I first met you, I need you now, my darling wife.

The thief and scoundrel, Tanner, has fled. But I know where he has gone. After the kind farmer Jensen and his wife nursed me back to health, he drove me back to the tavern to collect my things. There I found that Tanner had clubbed the old innkeeper and had made his escape on the Boston Post stage. But innkeeper Hows had searched his room and found a newspaper under his pillow. It was the Shipping News, and among the columns of the names of ships departing from New England ports, he found one had been circled. It was The Perseus, sailing in five days' time from Nantucket town. Bound for Valparaiso with a stop for rum in the port of Barbados. The very place that Tanner had let slip that he fancied. Mr. Hows also told me he discovered the Boston Post Road coachman had been paid $20 in gold—my gold—to take Tanner to the train station at Saxonville.

Further, I learned that trains leaving from that station do not run east to Boston. No, they run south, to the Port of New Bedford. That is where he will take the packet boat to Nantucket Island and the Perseus. And that is where I will find him and reclaim what he has killed and stolen for!

Fiona put her hand over her heart. It was beating so fast, she was afraid that it was going to break free from her chest. She drew a deep, shuddering breath. Calm, be calm, girl. He is alive and well—or least on the mend—but alive. Alive! And she needed to be strong—for him, for them. She drew in another deep breath and willed herself to be steady. "That's it, girl," she told herself. "You're not a highborn lady given to fainting vapors. Now read on and see what your husband will need of you." It came in the very next sentence.

This brings me to what I must ask of you, my loyal wife. Were there some other way, but there is not. I am now bereft of all of my funds as the thief

The Scrimshaw

Tanner left me not a single coin. I have been forced to borrow the price of a train ticket to New Bedford from innkeeper Hows. I swore to him that I would repay him, but he would have none of it. He said to just bring the thieving black dog back to Sudbury to stand trial for the murder of John Twin-Hawks. I promised to do all in my power to bring him to justice. And that is where I need your help, my dear one. You must go into the room in the cellar where I keep the scrimshaws, which I know you despise, as please believe me, so do I! There, go to the northwest corner of the room and pull up the third floorboard from the right-hand wall. You will find a strong box containing a portion of the gold eagles. You must bring them to me in New Bedford so that I may continue my pursuit of Tanner.

Once you reach New Bedford, take a goodly room at the Bristol Hotel down by the harbor. It is there I will come to you.

One final instruction—nay, a plea—from one who loves you more than his own life. Leave today, my love. Do not linger another hour in the house on Skaket Creek.

Upon finishing the reading of this letter, go straight to the house. Pack your valise. Then while the sun still shines through the cellar window upon the scrimshaws, go to that room and retrieve the gold. But I implore you. Do not tarry! You must be out of that house and away before sunset. I fear that in his selfish and cruel greed, Tanner has set something in motion that only the hand of God, with my poor help, can set right.

Come to me with all speed, my own dear wife.

Your devoted and loving husband,
Jeptha

Fiona's hands trembled again. But this time she was afraid that no amount of willpower could stop them.

The pages fluttered from her fingers into the sand. She reached down absently and gathered them up. Then, stuffing them into the damp pocket of her still wet dress, she started up the path to the house.

She looked up at her home, but for the first time with fear. A dark cloud passed over the sun, plunging the house into wavering shadows. It looked somehow sinister. As though there was a dark and brooding presence waiting there. Something evil, waiting. Waiting for her.

She thought about the noises she'd been hearing at night recently. A shuffling and a creaking sound. And now they no longer seemed like the normal, friendly sounds of a new house settling on its foundation. They seemed dark and...evil.

Calling on the last remains of her Scotts-Irish courage, she walked hurriedly into the house. She threw clothes into her old carpetbag and rushed down the stairs without even bothering to change her sea-stained dress.

The worst part was entering the cellar room.

Clutching her tiny gold crucifix in one hand and reciting the Lord's Prayer in a continuing litany, she quickly located and pulled up the floorboard. She grabbed the strongbox, tore it open, up-ended its contents of gold coins into her carpetbag, and walked to the door. She had just reached the threshold when a wind from nowhere blew it shut—right in her face. She stretched out her hand, slippery with the sweat of cold fear, and turned the handle. It wouldn't budge.

No. Oh no!

Once again, a spiteful cloud passed over the sun, and the room was thrown into shadows. The creaking noise began.

"Oh, sweet merciful Mary, mother of God," she prayed. "Please help me. Don't let me die here in this awful place, I pray you. My husband needs me. I must go to him. He needs me. And you know, sweet Mary, that I-I am, and will, be needed by.... Oh, please, help me!"

The tears poured down her face as the sounds of creaking timbers and rising wind became louder. "No! Please!" She gave one last desperate tug on the door handle. And it turned.

Still blinded by tears and goaded by terror, she fled blindly up the stairs, out the back door of the house, and into the carriage shed. She threw the carpetbag into the surrey, dragged their old mare into the harness traces, and frantically urged the poor old horse into a trot.

"Come on, old Bess, please, girl. Run, yes run! That's a good old girl," she sobbed gratefully as the horse picked up speed.

She didn't look back as the ocean wind blew the sandy dust away from the surrey's tracks. But all the way down the dirt road, she felt the stare of something evil watching her leave.

And waiting.

Chapter Twenty-Nine

Cambridge MA
Inmann Square
August 18th 1968
9:42 p.m.

"Ow-w-w! Dammit, Bridge, that hurts!"

"Oh, sush up, you big baby." Bridget turned to their downstairs neighbor, a medical student from India, and sighed. "Here, Gupta, I think maybe you better finish the bandaging."

Gupta looked down to where the green-eyed girl knelt in front of her boyfriend with a long strip of white gauze in one hand and a bottle of iodine in the other. He shook his head. "No, Bridget. If Mick insists on not going to the hospital, then you are going to have to change the bandages every day for the next week. However, in my professional opinion...."

Bridget tried not to smile as Gupta practiced his bedside manner.

"I still think that Mick should go to the hospital."

"Hey, man." Mick grinned through gritted teeth. "I think you did a great job. So what the hell do I need with some nosy hospital?"

Gupta swelled with pride but then looked troubled. "That's a gunshot wound, isn't it, Mick?"

Mick shrugged. "Nah, I was just playing a little softball with some buddies and slid into home plate."

"Softball? A gouge from your hip all the way down to your foot?"

Mick shrugged again. "We play rough."

Gupta shook his head. "That's okay. I don't think I want to know." He sighed and walked over to the door. "Well, just remember, I'm right down stairs if you need anything."

"Thank you, Gutpa," Bridget said.

"Yeah, like, thanks, man. I owe you one."

The Indian student nodded and closed the door behind him.

Bridget bit her lower lip and went back to her bandaging. She continued winding the gauze around Mick's leg until she came to the spot where the crease that the gunman's bullet had left in Mick's leg was still oozing.

"Take a deep breath, luv, this may hurt." She dabbed some iodine on the spot and then wound the gauze over it as gently as she could.

Mick's breath hissed from between his teeth.

"I'm sorry, luv," she whispered.

Mick let the rest of his pent-up breath out and unclenched his hands. Bridget finished the bandaging, climbed up on to the old green sofa next to Mick, and put her head on his shoulder. She sighed. "As me old

Da used to say, it's been one bloody bollocks of a day, hasn't it?"

"That just about sums it up, babe."

Mick slumped back into the broken springs of the couch and put his arm around Bridget. He still couldn't believe that they'd managed to get out of that barn alive. When the gunman had pushed the barrel of the rifle into Mick's stomach and then thrown the bolt home, he'd thought he was a dead man.

As he stumbled back, he saw that the gunman had a clean shot. The barrel swung around until the muzzle pointed directly at his stomach, and the gunman levered a round into the chamber. As the bolt slid home, Mick made a last desperate lunge with the old pitchfork. The bolt stopped and jarred. The gunman cursed and slapped his palm down on the bolt lever, and the rusty old tip of the pitchfork's tine snapped off, jamming the breech block.

Suddenly the gunman found himself with a useless rifle and a wounded but very mad gray-eyed kid pushing a pitchfork towards his guts. He dropped down the loft ladder and was out the barn door before Mick realized what had happened.

Bridget had helped him down the ladder and then started to run to the inn for help, but Mick had stopped her. "Uh-uh, Bridge. Go get Bronwyn. Just tell her that I need her, but don't tell her why."

Bridget had yelled at him and called him an idiot—and a few other things. But in the end, she'd grudgingly done what he'd asked.

When she returned with Bronwyn, Mick's sister had added her own choice assessment of her brother's judgment before finally asking what he needed.

"Two things," Mick said. "First, how attached are you to that dress?"

Bronwyn laughed.

"Great, then rip me off about four feet from your hem."

She looked puzzled.

"Bandages," he said.

Then he told her what he wanted her to find out from the inn's old historical files.

* * * *

New Bedford, MA
Central Train Station
October 15th, 1858
6:14 p.m.

Fiona jumped and dropped the heavy carpetbag that she'd been clutching tightly in both hands ever since leaving the small railroad siding that the locals sometimes jokingly referred to as 'Skaket Harbor Station'. In truth, it was just a crude wooden platform where the trains from Boston and Fall River unloaded milk and mail and picked up oysters and salt cod twice a week. But Fiona had been lucky enough to catch the local milk train after a wait of only two hours. And for that entire time she'd sat trembling on the hard wooden bench that some village carpenter had been kind enough to erect for the handful of passengers who caught the occasional train each week. Only when she had changed trains in Hyannis for New Bedford had she been able to calm the shaking that had racked her like a palsy victim ever since her blind flight from the house on Skaket Creek.

But obviously those sharp little talons of terrified panic still lurked just beneath her self-imposed demons of forced courage. Because all it took was the sibilant, sinister hiss of steam escaping from the boilers of the enormous black-and-red trimmed locomotive engine beside her to make her shriek and drop the precious satchel.

"I beg your pardon, Miss, have you dropped your valise?"

Fiona whirled around. A tall, distinguished looking man stood in front of her. His elegant brown beaver hat tipped politely as he held out Fiona's old, travel-stained carpetbag.

"Oh! Oh yes! Aye, it tis." Fiona snatched the bag from his outstretched hands, her Belfast accent thicker in her distress.

The tall man kept his hat tilted towards her and spoke softly. "Glad I could be of assistance, Miss."

All at once, Fiona felt embarrassed. How common she was behaving, like a factory girl snatching at her lunch pail. Her poor parents would be turning in their graves. Poor they'd been, but she'd been raised better than that. She took a deep, calming breath, forced a smile to her lips, and inclined her head in the best curtsy her mother had taught her. "Forgive my bad manners, sir. I was raised better. I have had a very...trying day. I do thank you for your kindness."

"My pleasure, Miss...?"

"It's Dawes. Mrs. Fiona Dawes."

"Mrs. Dawes. It is I now who must crave your pardon. But I hope you will not think me too bold to observe that you almost seem too young and too lovely to be a married woman."

While a highborn lady might have blushed and simpered at such a compliment, Fiona had been thrust into the world at too young an age to have taken much stock in pretty but meaningless words. She stiffened.

"Well, once again, I thank you, sir. And now, if you would be so kind as to point me towards the direction of the harbor, I will bid you a good day."

"I am devastated—Mrs. Dawes, was it? My poor attempt at courtly phrases has offended you."

Fiona shook her head distractedly as she clutched the carpetbag's handle once more and began to move towards the station's stairs.

"It's nothing, I assure you." She began to descend. "Thank you again—and again, good day, sir."

"No, no, Mrs. Dawes," he said, hurrying after her. "Please allow me to make amends."

"There is nothing to make amends for—really." Fiona glanced nervously at the long cobblestoned street. Which way was the harbor and the hotel?

"Then please, I insist, allow me to see you safely to your destination."

Fiona finally looked up at him uncertainly. He was tall, with angular handsome features, skin of an almost olive shade, silky black hair, and fastidiously groomed muttonchop whiskers. And when he smiled, what surely was a charming smile, there was something in his eyes that made her....

"Mrs. Dawes?"

Fiona gave a small start and pulled her eyes away.

The smile widened just a fraction.

"Here's Robert with the carriage."

The driver climbed down from the high coachman's seat and opened the gilt edged door for her.

"Please," he whispered softly. "Where are you staying in New Bedford?"

Fiona heard her own voice reply as though it was something separate from her, with the will of its own. "Staying? I am meeting my husband at the Bristol Hotel near the harbor."

She allowed herself to be helped into the carriage. The dark interior smelled of leather, cloth, a man's sharp pomade, and something else.

He slid in next to her. Not so close that she felt his form next to her, but she sensed his presence without even looking at him.

"Robert, the Bristol Hotel."

The carriage began to move.

Suddenly, Fiona turned and stared at him. His slight smile seemed to radiate in the carriage's dark interior.

"Your name, sir!" Fiona blurted out in an almost panicked voice. She took another deep breath and asked again in a voice that she willed to calmness, "I beg your pardon, sir, but I don't believe you've given me your Christian name."

The small smile turned up slightly at one corner of his mouth. "My name? Ah. Yes. Forgive me, Mrs. Dawes. My *Christian* name is Simon—Mr. Simon F. Westlake."

The Scrimshaw

* * * *

Cambridge, MA
Inman Square
August 18th, 1968
10:17 p.m.

"No shit!" Mick whistled when Bronwyn had finished relating what she'd learned from the current innkeeper and amateur historian of the Wayside Inn.

"Mickey—language, luv."

Mick raised his eyebrows. "What? You gonna wash my mouth out with soap, Mommy?"

Bridget brushed her hair back from her forehead and said, "Don't make me come over there, lad, or I might have to spend the rest of the night bandagin' yer other leg."

"Whew!" Mick held up his hands in mock surrender. "I'll be good. Cross my little black heart."

Bridget ignored him and turned back to Mick's sister. "So you even got him to make copies of all these old newspaper clippings?"

Bronwyn smiled and tossed down the Mexican, hand-woven bag she was carrying. The blue-striped silk dress she'd been wearing at the inn spilled out. "Men are all the same, whether they're sixteen or sixty. And it doesn't matter if it's bellbottoms or an 18th century ball gown, as long as it's tight, it gets their attention." She winked. "And their cooperation."

"Sis!" Mick exploded.

"Mick!" she shot back, mocking his suddenly serious expression. "I mean, like, I'm not a kid anymore."

"Yeah? Well you're still my baby sister."

Bronwyn just rolled her eyes and turned back to Bridget. "What do you think? Is this the stuff you're looking for?"

Bridget slowly nodded and handed the photocopies of the old newspaper clippings to Mick.

Mick read through the copies quickly and then piled the rest in his lap as he started his summing up process out loud to the two girls.

"So.... According to the Framingham Weekly News dated October 15th, 1858, the sheriff of Middlesex County was called to the Red Horse Tavern on—"

"Red Horse Tavern?" Bronwyn broke in.

"Yeah, that was the original name of the Wayside Inn before Longfellow made it famous and gave it that nickname by publishing his 'Tales of...' in the 1860s." Mick continued. "So according to this, the

160

innkeeper of the place, a fifth generation of the original Hows family, told the sheriff that the night before, murder had been committed in his barn."

"Does it say who did it?" Bronwyn asked.

"Yeah, one Zeke Tanner, an itinerant sailor."

"And who did he kill?"

"An Indian."

"Indian? You mean like the Lone Ranger and Tonto type of Indian?"

"No, actually it says one of the last of the Nipmucks living around Nobscot Mountain. What they used to call a half-breed. A man by the name of John Twin-Hawks."

"How did he die?"

"Shot. Three times at close range."

Mick glanced up at Bridget and said softly, "Right across the road from the inn. In the barn."

There was a crash as an unexpected flash of lightning lit up the sky to the west over Somerville.

The two girls jumped, and Mick grabbed the arm of the old green couch.

All three stared at one another while the thunderstorm, which had been brooding all day long, finally broke. The wind blew rain through the faded white curtains.

"Take it easy, guys. Just a little rain."

Bridget looked at him with an expression that said, "BS" but she let it go—for the moment.

But Bronwyn didn't.

"Like, wow! The same place that you and Bridget almost got...."

"Anyway...!" Mick gave his sister the same *shut up* look that he'd used when they were kids.

"Oops."

"Anyway again," Mick tried to redirect the conversation. "But here's the part we need. It also says that the old tavern keeper told the sheriff that he'd suspected that Zeke Tanner had robbed and murdered a young man from Cape Cod. One Jeptha Dawes!"

"Kathy's great, great grandfather!" Bridget breathed.

"Yeah, and collector of strange scrimshaws."

Bridget jumped up. "But we know that Jeptha Dawes wasn't murdered. He must have returned to Skaket Creek, and because he fathered children—Kathy's ancestors, right, Mickey?"

Mick nodded slowly.

"So then where did Jeptha go from the inn?"

Mick thought for a moment and finally answered, "He would have gone after the man who had shot and robbed him. The man who had the object of his strange quest—the scrimshaw."

"But where, Mick, where did Jeptha go?"

"You mean where did Zeke Tanner run to?"

"Yes, where?"

"Sorry, babe. Right now that's the big fat missing piece of the puzzle."

"Maybe not," Bronwyn said, reaching into her bag and pulling out another photocopy.

"What's this?" Mick asked as she handed it to him.

"The current innkeeper said that after the fire in 1956, they had to throw out all the old bedding and when they moved the mattress on the big trundle bed in the Drover's Room, this fell out."

Mick looked at the photocopy of smudged faint newsprint. It was dated October 2, 1858, and the heading at the top of the page read: Shipping News for New England Port Cities.

There were dozens of entries in tiny six-point type, detailing the arrivals and departures of all sorts of ships from all over New England. But Mick's eye was immediately drawn to one notice. A wide pencil held in a shaking hand had circled it crudely. It read: Notice, the clipper ship Perseus bound for Valparaiso, by way of Barbados, on a three year voyage for whale and trade, seeks able-bodied seaman and mates. Sailing from Nantucket harbor on 19th of October 1858.

"That's it, Mick. Nantucket! That's where he went."

"Okay. But how did he get there? There were no trains, and he didn't swim."

Bronwyn made a motion with her hand. "The other side, Mick. I think it got stuck to the copy when he ran the original through the machine. And," she smiled guiltily, "I guess I sort of 'forgot' to give it back."

"You are my sister." Mick grinned.

He grew serious again as he peeled off the ancient yellowed pamphlet from the backside of the photocopy. It was an old railroad timetable. The same blunt pencil had circled the times for the trains running from Saxonville to New Bedford. And right next to their arrival times of the trains in New Bedford was printed a list of the packet boats that sailed from the harbor to Nantucket and Martha's Vineyard. The pencil line ran from the New Bedford station of arrivals and ended in a circle around the listings that read: Packet Boat Schedule for Nantucket Island.

"Bingo," Mick said.

Chapter Thirty

New Bedford Massachusetts
The Bristol Hotel
October 13ᵗʰ, 1858
8:42 p.m.

Fiona paced back and forth across the hotel room's plush Turkey carpet. She had tried to sit in front of the large bay window and wait for her husband's promised arrival. But every time she heard footsteps in the hallway, she jumped out of the chair and ran to the door listening, hoping. But her hopes were always dashed as the footsteps passed by and faded down the hall. She stopped pacing and felt a sharp pain in her stomach. She had to sit down. She pulled the chair closer to the window and sat—and waited.

Her mind kept drifting back to the disturbing image of the handsome stranger. Mr. Simon Westlake. Fiona gave a little shiver. She didn't know why. Was he threatening? No, how could he be? He'd only given her a ride to her hotel. They'd barely spoken in the carriage. And yet her thoughts kept returning to him, almost against her will. There was something. He had been so polite, an obvious gentleman. But there had been something in his sardonic stare, the way that he looked at her. An amused smile and a look that had made her feel...naked.

She blushed furiously. Shame on you! Shame, girl, for such wicked, sinful thoughts. You are a married woman and....

There was a knock at the door. Fiona jumped up, nudging over the small tea table next to the chair. Her head spun. She felt nauseous. "Who...?"

"Fiona," a low baritone voice echoed from the hallway, a voice that meant love, strength, and her own personal salvation.

"Jeptha!" she cried, tears starting at the corner of her eyes. She ran to the door and pulled it open. Her husband stood at the threshold with his shy, quiet smile.

She looked at his pale face for a moment and the pent-up dam of emotion, fear, and uncertainty burst, and she threw her arms around him, sobbing.

"When I got your letter, I prayed that you were not badly hurt. And then your warning to flee. And the darkness and the shadows of the house, they seemed to pursue me. The entire journey here, I feared I would be too late or you could not come. Or that your wounds were worse, or you were...." She clasped her hands over her mouth.

"Hush, my love, I am well, and you're safe here with me, and nothing can harm you."

She thought about the house and the noises and the shadows. And, quite unbidden, the image of the smiling, saturnine face from the carriage played across her mind. She shook her head fiercely. No!

She reached up on her toes and took her husband's solid face in both of her hands. "Jeptha, you must promise me that you will never leave me again. Never!"

He pulled back with stricken look. "I-I-I cannot, love."

"Why? Why?" Fiona slipped to the floor and knelt in front of him. "Why?" She kept shaking her head.

* * * *

Jeptha wanted to put his arms around her. Comfort her. Promise her that which she pleaded for and that which he wanted to give her more than anything in the world. But he couldn't.

"Because, my wife," he said in a low voice, "there is a man, an evil man, who has stolen something from me that I must recover at all costs. I know where he has fled. Two nights ago, he took the packet boat from this harbor for Nantucket town. There he means to take ship to Barbados or some island port where I shall lose him forever."

"Let him go then!" Fiona sobbed.

"I cannot."

Suddenly she was on her feet, the tears drying as her eyes became fierce.

"You cannot! You cannot? Does your gold mean more to you than your wife?"

"Fiona, my heart, no, no. It is not the gold. I care nothing for that. It is only a tool to secure what I must."

"What then?"

"The scrimshaw. This final but most important scrimshaw."

Her face crumpled with bewilderment and hurt. Suddenly, she drew herself up to her full five feet and stared at him through angry, wet eyes. "Then I curse that scrimshaw. As I curse every one of those evil things which blight our home. And if you insist upon leaving me again to do this, then I-I will curse you too!"

Jeptha felt the color drain from his face.

"Fiona, you don't know what you're saying."

"Yes I do!" she said fiercely and put her hands on her hips. "You cannot go. You must not go! Swear to me."

Jeptha shook his head. "I cannot, Fiona. You remember, I made a vow, my word of honor to my captain."

Her eyes never wavered. "You made a vow to me also, Husband, also a sacred vow—before God—when we married."

"Please, Fiona! Do not ask this. Do not ask me to break my word!"

164

Fiona stood very still. At last, she nodded. "Very well, I will not ask you to do this."

Jeptha breathed a sigh of relief and started towards her.

She held up a hand.

"At least not for me. Instead, I ask in the name of another. That which I have carried here to you in hopes of escaping the evil that now stalks Skaket Creek. Our unborn child."

* * * *

Cambridge, Mass
Inman Square
August 19ᵗʰ, 1968
12:10 a.m.

Mick's exhausted sleep was deep but not dreamless and most certainly not comforting. It was tormented by demons and indefinable, nameless things that hovered just outside of his dream perception. They flitted in and out of the haunted panorama in his mind, where the jungles of Company C's Vietnam—the place Mick had commanded as Sergeant—twisted and intermingled with a jungle clearing of some South Sea island.

He didn't know how he knew that it was a South Sea island, but he did. A big-bellied, native chieftain spoke to Mick and the men that stood behind him. Mick glanced around, and for some dream-logic reason, he wasn't surprised to see his old squad: Anderson, Begley, Walzac, Smitty, and all the rest shuffling up behind him, M-16s at the ready.

The old chief babbled something in a language that Mick couldn't understand, and PFC Begley kept murmuring to him, "C'mon, Sarge, give the order, man. Let's waste 'em."

Mick shook his head. "Cool it, Begley. And shut the fuck up. He's trying to tell me something."

The drums started up again. Softly at first and then louder and louder. In an instant, Mick's corporal from Kentucky and best friend, Smitty, stood at his side.

"Hey, Mick," he drawled in his East Kentucky accent, "I think we better get the hell out of Dodge. Them things is comin' for us."

"Things? What things, Smitty?" Mick swiveled his neck from side to side. VC—a jungle ambush?

"There." Smitty pointed to the ocean gleaming through the palms at the edge of the clearing. Mick's gaze followed Smitty's finger, which seemed to be growing more skeletal by the moment, but yes, there, in

165

the water.... Something. No, not something, some *things*—two very big somethings. Enormous, they threw up gigantic waves as they plowed through the surf towards the island. Mick couldn't quite make out what they were, but they were huge. Two colossal plumes of water shot from the massive objects into the sky. Whales—two gigantic whales! One was white. White as snow. And the other was black. Jet black, black as the Ace of Spades, black as the pits of Hell. Hell, where all company sergeants who'd pulled too many triggers on too many M-16s in too many *suspected* VC villages were bound for.

"Bridget!" Mick tried to call out of the jungle dream, "Get me out of here. Help me, please!"

The village drums got louder and louder, and the two shapes in the ocean rushed closer and closer to shore. Suddenly, the drums stopped.

"Bring them to me!" the old chief called.

Strong hands fastened around Mick's arms and dragged him to the center of the village's beaten earth square. He looked frantically behind him. His company was gone. He was alone. Well, almost.

There was another man there. A man of about his own age but dressed in an old fashioned brown suit. He had a full set of dark whiskers and a sorrowful expression.

"Do you have what he must have?" the old chief asked solemnly.

The young man nodded. He opened his collarless shirt and displayed a long, curved ivory tooth hanging from a golden chain around his neck.

The old chief eyed the young man and continued, "And do you give this thing freely? To this other one whose responsibility it will now become?"

The dark-haired, dark-eyed young man appeared even sadder and said quietly, "I do."

The old chief nodded once more and took the tooth from around the young man's neck. He reached out, and with the sharp point of the tooth, slowly cut a large round circle into the upper chest of the sad looking young man. Then he placed the blood-dripping tooth around Mick's neck and turned back to the other young man. "And do you also give this part of you freely?" he asked.

"Yes I do. I must." He gazed at Mick with a look of deepest pity and said, "I'm sorry. Good luck, and may God guide and bless you."

The chief thrust his hand into the bloody round circle that he had made with the tooth in the young man's chest and ripped out his still-beating heart.

Mick screamed, again and again. And as he opened his mouth for another scream, the chief pushed the bloody, beating heart into his mouth.

Mick struggled with the hands that held him, trying to scream and spit the horrible thing out at the same time.

"No!" the chief said. "You must consume it. It is now your burden. It is your responsibility."

"He's right, Mick." The young man with the bloody chest smiled as if a great burden had been lifted from his shoulders.

"No! No!" Mick tried to scream, but his mouth was full of blood.

"Look!" the chief said, pointing to the water. "They come!"

The two whales, one white, one black, filled Mick's field of vision. They were enormous and they were coming for him.

Mick tried to turn away, but the chief and the bloody young man put their hands on his shoulders and turned him to face the two shapes that loomed ever larger. They held his shoulders and pushed him forward.

"It all now depends on you," they said in unison.

"No! No! Let me go. I don't want this!" He pushed their hands away and struck out. And he connected. The hands loosened, and their grips fell away.

He sat up quickly, ready to deliver another blow. A killing stroke, he thought savagely. Crush their frigging windpipes! He jumped up out of bed and.... Bed?

He blinked, and reality came into focus. One foot was tangled in his bed sheets. Sweat drenched his shaking body. It was his bedroom, his bed. The jungle, his old company, the chief and the young man, their hands on his shoulders, the bloody heart...a dream. Only a dream!

But he was sure he'd pushed them off. It had felt so real, it felt like....

"If you wanted to sleep an extra hour, luv, next time just say so."

Bridget?

She got up from the floor, rubbing her backside where she'd landed when Mick had violently pushed her off as she'd tried to wake him.

"Bridge?" he croaked, "I-I'm sorry. I thought you were.... You see, there was this jungle and my old company from 'Nam and this native chief and...and...."

Bridget's sardonic look faded. "Is it the old dream again, Mickey?" she said softly.

"No...I...well yeah, I guess, or a part of it anyway. But there was something new. There was this island and these two huge things and the tooth they gave me and the...." He shuddered.

Bridget put her arms around him. "C'mon, luv, go throw some water on your face. Your Da has been calling all morning. He's over at your sister's apartment and he wants to see us right away."

She guided Mick into the small bathroom and turned on the sink tap. She wet a bright yellow washcloth and held it out to him. "Here," she said, "you must have bit your tongue or something while you were thrashing about in the bed."

Mick looked in the mirror. Streaks of thick red blood coated his lips and chin. But not like he'd bitten his tongue. More like he'd been chewing on a....

Mick pushed Bridget aside and stumbled to the toilet.

And violently threw up a bloody, red froth.

Chapter Thirty-One

Cambridge, MA.
The Oxford Alehouse
August 19th, 1968
1:12 p.m.

"Do you see him, Mickey?" Bridget asked.

"I'm not even sure just who the hell I'm supposed to be looking for," Mick answered, shaking his head.

"Your Da said that the guy'd be wearing, and I quote, 'A puke yellow T-shirt covered with big purple blotches that looks like some damn purple jackass crapped on it and died.'"

Mick smiled. "Pop always did have a way with words."

"Ummm, must be where you get your 'quaint expressions' from, eh, luv?"

"No comment." Mick shrugged and looked around the half-filled bar. What or who was he supposed to be looking for? Someone in yellow and purple? What the hell would that be, a...?

"A tie-dyed T-shirt."

"Huh?"

"A T-shirt Mickey. A yellow and purple tie-dyed T-shirt."

"And just what makes you so sure, my fortune telling gypsy queen?"

"Because, to paraphrase Goldilocks, there he is."

Mick swiveled his gaze to the far corner of the smoky bar. Yeah, must be. How many other puke yellow and purple, donkey-crap T-shirts were there in the room?

Bridget took Mick's hand and gently led him through the maze of tables and beer drinking customers, waiting for the next band to come on stage. For once Mick was happy to let her lead. He still felt pretty shaky from that damned dream. Christ! Dream? Nah, try two double scoops of pure nightmare. That frigging tooth and the bloody heart and....

"Hold up a sec, Bridge." Mick pulled a crumpled $5 bill out of his jeans and, as a passing waitress slid by, he reached out and grabbed a shot glass of amber liquid off the tray and swallowed it in one gulp. Better. Yeah, just a little bit better. "Here," he tossed the $5 bill onto the tray. "Buy whoever's Scotch I just drank another on me."

The waitress turned around and looked at him. "You got it, man. And I'll be right back for you."

Right back for me? They hadn't even sat down yet.

Still holding his hand, Bridget stopped and looked at him. "Are you sure you're okay, luv?"

"No, but at this point I don't see as how it'll make any difference either way. C'mon, let's go find out why Pop was so hot for us to talk to this guy."

Bridget bit the inside of her lip. With a worried frown, she nodded and started moving towards the corner again. As Mick trailed after her, he wondered if he should've told Pop or Bronwyn about the dream. Tell Big Mike McCarthy that his youngest son was getting spooked by dreams? Ha, as Bridget would say, "Not bloody likely!" But then again he had a strong hunch that Pop had known that something was up. When they'd gotten up to Bronwyn's apartment, Pop hadn't wasted much time in getting to the point. And his news was almost enough to drive all thoughts of the dream from his head. Almost.

"Those two inbred goat fucking.... Ooops, sorry, Bridget. Sorry, Bonnie." The two girls just smiled. "I mean that those weasels, *Chief Frost*," Big Mike snorted contemptuously, "and his idiot nephew, are trying to make an end run around Captain Denny. They've got some local state senator to put pressure on the commissioner and, well, anyway, you know how shit, I mean, ah, crap flows downhill. So Denny called me last night to give me a heads up." Mike looked at his youngest son. "Bottom line, Mick, is that Denny doesn't think he can keep the Frosts' paws off of you for any longer than three more days."

Three days? Crap!

But Mick had just shaken his head and said, "Well then, I guess that me and Bridge had better get our butts in gear and down to New Bedford."

"New Bedford? Explain?"

So Mick had. Frankie's office, the old envelope and clues, the Wayside Inn, and the bill of sale. When he'd got to the part about the barn, his father's eyes had grown cold. He'd asked a lot of questions about the gunman and the rifle he'd used. When Mick had gotten through, Big Mike nodded with that same cold expression and said, "I've got a few phone calls that I need to make, so you two get along down to New Bedford, but before you go there's someone I'm going to have you talk to. I busted him last year down on Tremont Street for dealing. I could have thrown his sorry butt in jail but cut him a break because, well, let's just say he owes me one. He might give you an interesting perspective on some of the characters in this little drama that we've gotten ourselves involved in."

Big Mike had made a phone call and grunted a few words into the receiver, followed by: "Don't give me any crap, you useless piece of.... Just get your scrawny ass over the Harvard Square and meet Mick in the.... Mickey, what's a close but public place around here?"

Mick only thought for a moment. He winked at Bridget and said, "The Oxford Alehouse." She smiled, too, at the good memories.

170

"Okay, did you hear that? The Oxford Alehouse, one half hour. And kid? Don't be late, or I may have to come looking for you. And I might not be in a good mood." Big Mike had hung up the phone and said, "Be careful."

Now Bridget pulled him around the last few tables and towards the dark corner to meet Pop's mystery man.

And what, if anything, is this scruffy looking hippie burnout going to be able to tell us about....

Mick bumped into Bridget. She had frozen four feet from the table.

"Hey, babe, what's the problem?" He looked over her shoulder.

The hippie—in the yellow and purple tie-dyed T-shirt—their own little personal Pied Piper of the alley.

Good old Moon Doggie himself.

* * * *

New Bedford Harbor
The packet boat
October 14th, 1858
9:06 a.m.

Jeptha stared at the slate gray water of the autumn New England ocean and tried to catch a glimpse of the Bristol Hotel through the morning fog.

Still nothing. Just a shifting gray mass of dirty-wool-colored sky and sea that blended together until it was impossible to say where one left off and the other began. He leaned his elbows heavily upon the wet wooden railing of the New Bedford to Nantucket packet boat and willed his eyes to somehow pierce through the gray gloom and.... There, yes, there it was!

A strong and fresh wind from the ocean blew the fog tendrils away for a moment, and he saw the dark stone of the Bristol Hotel outlined against the rooftops of New Bedford. His eyes quickly counted the floors of the hotel and stopped at five, focusing on the corner window. Was it his wishful imagination, or did a tiny form stand at the window, peering out to sea, watching the packet boat steam out of the harbor towards Nantucket Sound? He couldn't be sure, but he would choose to believe it. So he waved and whispered, "Goodbye, my love. I pray that God will keep you and our precious child in your womb safe and well until I return with my vow fulfilled and our future secure."

And then...well, he would also choose to believe that he saw the tiny figure in the window raise an answering hand, before the ocean wind abruptly died and the fog closed back in around him.

The Scrimshaw

* * * *

Fiona watched until the fog completely obscured the packet boat. Long after she knew that the boat would have cleared the headland at the harbor's mouth and entered the choppy waters of the sound, she stood at the fifth floor window and stared out to sea. She stared at the fog and thought about the previous evening. The look of wonder and love on his face when she told him that she was carrying his child. He had fallen to his knees in front of her and pressed his face into the soft folds of her dress, telling her that this was the most wonderful news he had ever received and that he would do all in his power to prove a worthy father to their child.

Fiona sighed and turned away from the window. She crossed to the other side of the sitting room and added a small scoop of coal to the fire in the blue painted cast-iron stove. Then she turned back to the window and drew the large padded rocking chair up to it. She sat down and stared out into the fog again.

She had been so happy when Jeptha had fallen to his knees in front of her. She was so touched and filled with love by his heartfelt joy that she was sure that now he would abandon the mad quest of the final scrimshaw. She had knelt down beside him and taken his weather-roughened face in both of her hands and said, "Then all is well, Husband. Mr. Dawes, we need never go back to that house on Skaket Creek again. We've plenty of money in the carpetbag that I brought you. A small fortune, you said so yourself. Let's use it to buy a home or perhaps a farm, far from the sea and scrimshaws and evil, hidden things. We'll go far away, far from Skaket Creek. Some place where whatever evil lurks within the walls of that house cannot find us."

She'd held him tightly, and he was silent for a long time. And then she thought she heard him whisper, "I fear there is no such place." It was so faint that she had to ask him again, but he only smiled his sad smile. He'd picked her up and carried her to the big four-poster bed and hugged her close until the gray, foggy morning light had broken through the bay window. He had known she was awake, but they both pretended otherwise as he packed a small leather valise and transferred two sacks of gold coins from her carpetbag into the satchel.

It was only when he stood over her to kiss her goodbye that she couldn't stand it any longer and jumped out of bed. She wanted to plead but she knew it would do no good.

"You know I have to do this."

She couldn't speak. All she could do was nod.

"Wait for me here and keep you and our child safe and well. I will return for you in three days' time...."

He seemed about to say something else but stopped. But he really didn't have to say it. Fiona knew what it was and completed the sentence in her mind. "Or I won't ever be returning."

And so she had kissed him and let him go. She had spent the rest of the morning staring out the sitting room window at the blank gray wall of fog.

It was not until the Seth Thomas clock on the cherry wood table struck noon, that she realized she hadn't eaten anything in almost twenty-four hours.

She had no appetite, but, remembering her condition, patted her still flat stomach and said, "Forgive your silly mam, little tyke, for moping about all morning and making you go hungry. Come, we'll go down to the dining room and have some lunch."

She put her hand on the doorknob, but suddenly turned and focused on her carpetbag at the foot of the bed. She'd better not leave it. She opened the bag and quickly transferred the remainder of the coins to her large handbag. It was heavy, but then again she smiled wryly to herself, she'd spent the better part of the past two years lugging trays up and down three flights of stairs every day that weighed almost as much as she did.

She slowly made her way down the gas lit stairs that led to the hotel dining room. But when she got to the second-floor landing, she noticed that the gaslight had gone out. She didn't want to risk a fall so she carefully edged her way along the wall holding on to the stair railing. She just made out a dim light shining up the stairwell from the dining room beyond. As she started down the last flight of stairs, her right arm brushed the large potted fern on the stairwell landing and it reached out and grabbed her.

Or something did.

Fiona jumped as a hand reached through the stalks of the potted ferns and pulled her towards it. She struggled, but the fleshy hand would not let go. She drew in a breath to scream, and the other hand clapped over her mouth.

"Where is it?" a voice hissed in her ear. One hand remained over her mouth, pressing her against the wall, while the other fumbled for the pocketbook she gripped tightly in her left hand.

"We will have this!" the voice panted, while the hand continued to tug at the bag.

Fiona felt the handle rip as the bag slipped from her wrist. She clutched at it, but the portly man—for that was what he looked like in the darkness—pushed her away.

She saw that he had a scarf wound around his face and a broad cap pulled down almost over his eyes.

Fiona stumbled from the push but recovered quickly and yelled,

"Stop! Thief!"

He did stop.

Not because Fiona had yelled, but because a silver-tipped walking stick slashed out of the dark stairway behind her and cracked down on his wrist.

The would-be-thief howled and dropped the bag. A tall figure moved swiftly from behind Fiona and lunged for the thief's scarf that was wound around his coat collar. But the man twisted away and half-ran, half-tripped, down the last flight of stairs. She heard the side door on the first floor slam, and suddenly her knees felt weak.

She put her hand out to steady herself, and it was taken by another hand with long slender fingers encased in kidskin gloves. She looked up.

"Mrs. Dawes? Are you quite all right?"

Fiona stared. Mr. Westlake? Yes that was it, the man from the station.

Mr. Simon Westlake.

* * * *

"Are you feeling better now, Mrs. Dawes? Are you sure you won't have a brandy? It will help settle your nerves."

"No, thank you very much, Mr. Westlake, the tea will do just fine."

Westlake turned to the waiter hovering at the curtain in front of the private dining booth. "Then that will be all." He nodded, dropping a silver dollar into the waiter's hand. "And close the curtain," he added.

The waiter began to slide the two halves of the curtain along their brass rings when Fiona yelled in a panicked voice, "Wait!" and in a calmer tone said, "Leave them open, if you please."

She thought she saw an amused smile working around the corner of Simon Westlake's lips. But he nodded and said, "Of course, Mrs. Dawes, how thoughtless of me. You're still feeling nervous from that footpad's assault."

"Footpad? I don't know, Mr. Westlake. I've not had much experience with cities and footpads, but he seemed to be awfully well dressed for a common thief."

Westlake's amused smile returned. "Perhaps, Mrs. Dawes, he is a very good thief."

"Perhaps, Mr. Westlake, and yet...." She picked up the dark blue silk scarf that lay on the booth table between them and fingered the material. "And yet it seems as though I've seen a scarf like this before."

"Have you now, Mrs. Dawes. Where?"

Simon Westlake let his fingers run along the length of the scarf that he had ripped from the thief's face just before he'd made his escape. The fingers continued sliding up the silk until they touched Fiona's. She felt a tingle pass through her hand and continue all through her body. She pulled her hand away as if it had been burned and stifled a gasp. Her heart raced, but the man sitting across from her didn't seem to notice—or pretended not to. The room spun. She picked up the teacup with trembling fingers and took a deep swallow.

Westlake looked at her with concern, but was there something else lurking behind his dark eyes?

"Are you quite certain that you are all right, Mrs. Dawes?"

Fiona nodded slowly. "Yes, thank you, Mr. Westlake."

But she wasn't. The tips of her fingers still tingled from where he had touched them.

"It's too bad you didn't get a look at the rascal's face when I pulled the scarf off.... You didn't, did you, Mrs. Dawes?"

Fiona shook her head. "No." But in that same instant, she realized that she had. And that was why the blue silk scarf lying on the table between them looked so familiar. She'd washed and ironed it often enough in her former life. It was one of her many duties as maid in the household of Isaiah Frost. And the last time she had seen the fleshy hands of the scarf's owner, they had been filled with wedding gifts—for her!

The scarf belonged to young Mr. Edward Frost, the only son of her former master.

Chapter Thirty-Two

Cambridge, MA
The Oxford Alehouse
August 19th, 1968
1:43 p.m.

Mick was starting to get *that look* each time he stared across the table at Moon Dog. It was the look that Bridget knew all too well. It usually preceded someone being hit—hard. So, being a realist as well as having developed a finely honed instinct for potential trouble—especially violent trouble—she had the foresight to sit between Mick and the skinny, pathetic, and rather nervous-looking hippie who called himself Moon Dog. *He really is what my mother would have called "a sad case".* His purple and yellow T-shirt was stained and frayed around the collar, and his sallow, pale face had the waxen pallor of someone who been laid out in the undertaker's parlor for two days running.

Yes, agreeing with Mother's probable judgment, most definitely a sad case.

Unfortunately, her lover sitting next to her appeared to be having no such compassionate thoughts. As a matter of fact, Bridget speculated, if looks could kill, poor old Moon Dog would be deader than last Friday's flounder.

Moon Dog seemed to sense it too and started to babble in a low, meandering monotone, "Ah, like, hey guys. Like, far out seeing you again after...I mean, what a friggin' coincidence that you guys know... errr, like, are you related to that cop dude?"

"He's my father."

Moon Dog swallowed and bobbed his head nervously up and down like a spastic marionette. "Oh, yeah. Ah sure, man, I mean, I can dig it. Yeah, you and The Big Guy. I mean, really, like he's actually not such a bad dude, for like, a cop, I mean. Uh, like, no offense."

Mick didn't say anything. He just stared.

A waitress came by wearing bellbottom jeans so frayed and tight they were almost transparent. She gave the center of the table a half-hearted wipe with her dingy gray cloth and dropped a large plastic bowl of stale popcorn onto the table. Moon Dog shoved his hand into the bowl before it had even stopped quivering. He pulled out a large handful of popcorn and crammed it into his mouth, chewing desperately like he hadn't eaten in days—which was probably true.

The waitress hooked the ragged cloth down over her wide, handmade leather belt and asked in a bored voice, "So you guys want anything?"

"A Coke," Bridget said.

"Make that two." Mick nodded, never taking his eyes off of Moon

Dog, and then added, "And a shot of Bushmills."

"Oh, Mickey," Bridget sighed and shook her head.

"And you?" The waitress pointed her chin at Moon Dog. He squirmed uncomfortably. What he probably wanted wasn't sold in bars—except maybe bars in Morocco. But he needed something. The shakes were starting. Real bad. He looked up at Mick with a pathetic, pleading look.

"Yeah, I'm buying," Mick said with disgust.

"Awesome, way cool, man. Okay, well then, something sweet—but strong—say like...Galliano. Yeah, that's it. Straight up, no ice." He smiled at Mick as the waitress shuffled off towards the bar's pickup station. "Hey, like thanks, man."

"Screw your thanks, Moon Dog!" Mick spat the words as if they left a bad taste on his tongue. "I expect something for my money—and for not pounding your frigging face into this tabletop. So start talking. Now!"

"Wow, easy, dude. Like, what you want me to say, man?" he whined and spread both of his grimy palms open on the table.

"Like who were those creeps you set us up for in the alley yesterday?"

Moon Dog reached for another handful of stale popcorn and started to raise it to his mouth.

Mick slammed his hand down on to the tabletop, and Moon Dog jumped. Popcorn spilled out into the small puddles of stale beer at the table's edge before continuing on to join the rest of the indefinable litter on the dirty bar-room floor. Mick held Moon Dog's now empty hand clamped to the tabletop.

"I said talk, not eat. Now!"

Bridget reached over and gently pulled the hard fingers of Mick's right hand away from the frightened hippie's wrist. "I think you better tell him what he wants to know," she said softly.

Moon Dog rubbed his wrist and looked at Mick. "Shit, man, take it easy. I mean, like, I'd never seen those dudes before in my life."

"Before what?"

"Before one of 'em came up to me while you were talking to that cop and gave me a twenty to tell you that I knew a place you could park down that alley."

Mick stared at him, and the nervous tick below Moon Dog's right eye started doing a little dance in time to the Ale House's newest band, who'd just opened up with a cover of the Buffalo Springfield's *Hung Upside Down*.

Mick stared at Moon Dog as though the song had given him some ideas as to Moon Dog's fate.

Moon Dog saw it too and squirmed uncomfortably. Finally, he

couldn't stand the silence anymore and asked, "Hey, man, like what?"

"Like bullshit!" Mick growled.

"Dude, I swear it's the truth!"

"You wouldn't know the goddamned truth if crawled out of the frigging popcorn bowl and bit you on the ass!"

Mick slowly pushed his chair back and stood up. "C'mon, Moon Doggie, you and me are gonna go outside and have a little *chat*."

"Mickey, no!"

Moon Dog stared at Bridget with a pleading expression and then back at Mick with despair. Bridget shook her head. No, she wasn't going to be able to stop him.

He sighed. "Okay. Okay, sit back down, man." Mick put one foot on the seat of his chair. "Talk."

"Yeah, I guess there is a little bit more to it than that."

"I'm listening."

"Well, believe it not, I got this cousin, who's like a real big shot in one of the construction unions. And he's kind of involved with a lot of those big scary dudes, ya know, like Mafia types. Anyway, he's always been good for a couple of bucks when I needed some burgers and... stuff."

"Yeah, like stuff you stuff up your nose," Mick said with disgust.

Moon Dog looked around nervously.

"No, my father isn't here, and I don't give a crap what you shoot or snort. Keep. Talking."

"Well, like I said, I can usually hit my cousin up for a five or ten, but this time he offers me twenty just for giving you guys some...ah... directions."

"Why?" Mick's eyes resembled gray granite tombstone chips.

Moon Dog took a deep breath, leaned forward, and lowered his voice. "Well, he said he got a call from some dude connected with the statehouse who wanted you pushed down that alley and, ah, kinda 'messed up'."

"You miserable little bastard!" Mick spat, reaching for the scrawny hippie.

Bridget's hand closed over his. "Mickey, please—for me."

Mick drew in a ragged breath through gritted teeth. "This guy connected with the statehouse. I want a name. Now!"

The scruffy pan-handler cast a pleading look at Bridget.

She shook her head. "You'd better give it to him."

He sighed and nodded. "Okay, man, he didn't tell me the dude's name but he did say that he worked for—"

"We didn't have any Galliano, so I brought you some Sambuca. Is that okay?" Against all expectations, the waitress had actually returned—and with their drinks!

"Here," she said, putting a large shot glass filled with thick, clear liquid in front of the skinny hippie. "Try it, you'll like it. It's sweet. Tastes like licorice."

Moon Dog sniffed the contents for a moment before taking the glass and swallowing it in a single shuddering gulp. A smile slowly spread across his face.

"Far out. Hey, Mick, can you spring for another, dude?"

"Keep talkin'." Mick gave a slight nod of his head to the waitress as she put the Cokes and Mick's Bushmills Irish whiskey down on the table.

"Ah, yeah. Sure. Okay, man. Well, there isn't a whole lot more except like I was saying. My cousin said that the dude who called him worked for the—"

"Oh sorry, I almost forgot." The waitress had just finished counting out Mick's change and was moving away from the table when she stopped abruptly and turned around. "Tim, the bartender, told me to tell you that you've got a phone call."

"Phone call? Who?"

"Beats me, man, but like, you're Mick, right?"

"Yeah," Mick answered warily.

Who knew they were here? Only Mick's father.

"And you're sure they didn't say who it is?" Bridget asked.

The waitress shrugged. "Sorry, the bartender just told me to tell you that the dude on the other end said it was real important."

"Better take it," Mick said. "Where's the phone?"

The waitress pointed. "Right over behind the bar."

Suddenly Bridget felt uneasy and she wasn't sure why.

"C'mon, Bridget, you come too," Mick said.

She nodded and got up.

Mick looked down at Moon Dog and leaned his face towards him. "Don't get any sudden urges to go outside and pick flowers in the Harvard Yard, 'cause I'm gonna be watching the door and I'd better find you here when I come back."

And Moon Dog was—unfortunately for him.

* * * *

Mick hurried back across the tiny, crowded dance floor, pulling Bridget along behind him.

Seeing Moon Dog slouched in his chair, staring out the window as they approached the table, he seemed to breathe a little easier. But by now Mick's suspicion was on full alert, and his eyes scanned the bar for their bell-bottomed waitress. Bridget looked too but she didn't see her.

179

And somehow she doubted that they ever would again.

When she and Mick had gotten to the bar and Mick asked for his phone call, the bartender had looked at him like he had two heads and one of them wasn't screwed on very tight. Mick had explained, yelling over the ever-increasing decibels of the band's rendition of *Wooden Ships*, and the bartender had just shaken his head.

"Sorry, man, we don't even have a phone behind the bar—just a pay phone on the wall."

"But your waitress—the one in the faded bellbottoms and bandana?—said—"

"Waitress? What waitress? It's only Kenny and me here until the six p.m. shift comes on."

Crap!

Now, as she and Mick finally reached the table, all he could say was, "Shit."

"Mickey? What?"

"Go over by the door and wait for me, Bridge."

"No, damn it, I won't. What's the matter with...."

She drew in her breath and put her hand over her mouth. Poor old Moon Doggie wouldn't be hitting anyone up for spare change anymore.

He was dead.

* * * *

Mick and Bridget only stopped long enough to run upstairs to Bronwyn's apartment. But Big Mike had already left. So Mick called him and told him the whole story as his sister's eyes grew wider, listening to Mick's terse explanation.

"So that's it, Pop," Mick finished. "The waitress was bogus, and when we got back to the table, we found that someone had stuck the needle into old Moon Dog's neck and pumped him full of—my guess would be pure heroin—'cause he hadn't even had time to fall over."

Big Mike was silent for a long time, but Bridget heard him breathing on the other end of the line as she pressed her cheek close to Mick's.

At last he said, "Get out, Mickey. Take Bridget and go. Now. Go to that place you told me about."

"You mean New—"

"Don't say anything more. Just go. And tell your sister to walk downstairs with you and then come over to my office. I'll meet her at the back entrance. Now move it. Understand?"

"Yeah, Pop we're outta here."

"And Mickey?"

"Yeah?"

"Be careful—real careful. And from now on, keep one eye looking over your shoulder."

Chapter Thirty-Three

New Bedford, MA
The Bristol Hotel
October 15th, 1858
1:14 p.m.

"Are you beginning to feel a little better now, Mrs. Dawes?"

Fiona looked up from the delicate tiny crystal glass that she'd been staring at. Her eyes searched the dark, handsome face watching her from the other side of the table. She studied the slight, white lines of amusement that always seemed to hover at the corners of his mouth. Still wary, she hadn't made up her mind what the almost imperceptible smile really indicated—sympathetic friendship, or contempt. She stared at her drink again.

He continued, "Yes, I do believe that I see the most welcome color of those crimson roses for which the country of your birth is so justly famous returning to your cheeks."

Fiona raised her eyes from the small glass of murky red liquid. "And how is it now that ya fancy yourself to know where I was born!" she angrily blurted. Then she smiled. "So I've still got the speech of County Mayo hanging on after three years in this country, do I then?"

Simon Westlake's amused smile broke into a full grin. "Only when your natural spirit breaks through and you momentarily forget that you are constantly reminding yourself to be a demure, proper married woman. Like now."

In spite of herself, Fiona smiled back. What was it about this man that seemed to make her forget herself? Like the drink in front of her. She had been strictly admonished by her mother to eschew strong drink and the company of those who indulged in it—especially male company. And yet, in the end, she'd been persuaded to accept a small glass of sherry, to calm "her nerves" as Mr. Westlake had put it.

"It is very nice to see you smile, Mrs. Dawes. And I hope that you will not think it too inappropriate to observe that you do it so charmingly, that you should favor the world with it more often."

Fiona smiled again and sighed. "And I hope that you don't think me too ungrateful to observe that honeyed words and flattering phrases are perhaps not the most appropriate fare to feed a young woman who is quite determined to be as you put it, 'a demure married woman'."

"Touche, Mrs. Dawes." Westlake inclined his head towards her.

"And just what is that supposed to mean, Mr. Westlake?" The County Mayo brogue came rushing back to her.

This time he laughed and held up his hands in mock surrender. "It is a fencing term. It means that your rapier wit, along with your flashing hazel eyes, have thrust me to the quick, Mrs. Dawes."

The set of Fiona's jaw relaxed a little, and she decided that while she still wasn't quite sure what he had said, it was probably well meant. Probably.

She started to get up from the table.

"Wait, Mrs. Dawes. Where are you going? Was I wrong in assuming that we were becoming fast friends?"

Fiona paused. "Friends, Mr. Westlake? Well, yes, I suppose that you could say so. I should be most ungrateful if I did not at least acknowledge that you have come to my aid twice in the past twenty-four hours."

Simon Westlake inclined his head towards her again. "I count it a distinct privilege, Mrs. Dawes."

"Well then, thank you again, and I really must be going...."

"May I deliver you to your destination then?"

This time Fiona smiled back wryly. "Not unless that fine carriage of yours comes equipped with a set of sails or steam-powered paddle wheels."

"I must confess that you leave me baffled, Mrs. Dawes. Are you a embarking upon a cruise?"

"Yes, you might say that, Mr. Westlake. I mean to take the packet boat and follow my husband to Nantucket Island."

All of a sudden he beamed. "But this is too perfect. It is meant to be! I, too, am bound for the harbor and the Nantucket packet boat this very afternoon. You see, I have a small summer estate on the island which needs my attention before winter sets in. Why, Mrs. Dawes, this is most benign fate at work."

Fiona's palms dampened. "That's...that is most kind of you, Mr. Westlake, but I really couldn't. I mean, I really shouldn't. I mean, I am a...."

"Yes, you are, Mrs. Dawes. A most charming and delightfully proper, married woman. Oh, how I envy your husband. He must be quite the man indeed to have captured the heart of one so steadfast."

Fiona's head spun. "I-I really must go—now, Mr. Westlake."

"Mrs. Dawes, may I presume upon our friendship by calling you Fiona?"

"I-I...."

He reached out a gloved hand and let it fall on her fingertips. That same electric spark ran through her body, only ten times stronger than before. It was all she could do not to sway where she stood in front of the table. The corners of his mouth turned up into a smile that was the picture of earnest sincerity.

Still smiling in a self-effacing way, he said softly, "Then would it be too much to ask, Mrs. Dawes—dear *friend* Fiona—if this humble acquaintance of yours could be permitted to share the same packet boat and ocean with you?"

Fiona felt foolish. She blushed and stammered, "Of course, Mr. Westlake."

"Simon, please."

"Yes. Simon. Yes, I mean, no. I mean, of course I didn't wish to imply that you couldn't share...I mean...after all, this is America and...no, I mean, I.... Oh, and then I'm not sure what I mean, Mr. West—I mean Simon." She felt the red flush of blood spreading from her cheeks down to her neck and beyond. *Stop it, girl. Stop this silly behavior right now!* she silently screamed in her mind. She drew herself up ramrod straight, took a deep breath, and answered, "Yes, Mr. Westlake. Simon. I would be very pleased to have your company on the journey over to Nantucket Island."

"You're most gracious, Mrs. Dawes—Fiona," he added, standing up and giving her an ingratiating half smile. "Wait right here. I'll have Robert bring the coach around." He flashed that charming smile once more then turned and walked towards the dining room entrance.

Fiona's gaze followed him as he stepped out onto the hotel's portico front porch and motioned to his waiting coachman.

Yes, she had to admit, *Mr. Westlake is certainly proving to be the most considerate of friends.*

* * * *

New Bedford, MA.
Nantucket Ferry Pier
August 19th, 1968
4:50 p.m.

Mick gunned the motorcycle's engine and eased the clutch out a fraction of an inch. The big bike rolled slowly forward between the two lines of overheated cars driven by drivers with equally overheated tempers.

Bridget glanced surreptitiously from side to side and then buried her face in the back of Mick's denim jacket, probably consumed by guilty embarrassment from all of the hostile looks they garnered.

Mick was entirely focused on the white painted ferryboat up ahead of the double line of slowly moving cars. It was almost filled, and his battered old Timex watch with the cracked crystal told him that the last ferry of the day to Nantucket would be leaving in less than fifteen minutes.

He revved the engine again and moved up another half dozen car lengths. If he could just make it up to the gate, they might have room for a motorcycle, even though Mick saw that they were starting to turn cars away.

He edged the bike past a dusty station wagon with all of the windows rolled down. Three kids screamed from the back seat, "Dad-deeee! Is the boat gonna go without us?"

Then another voice chimed in, "I'm hungry!"

And then another, "I've gotta go to the bathroom—real bad!"

A woman's exasperated voice said scathingly, "Oh, this is just great, Bob. We drive all the way down here, wait in this stupid line for two hours, only to miss the last ferry!"

The driver finally spoke, "Jan, there's nothing I can do about it. What do you suggest? Shall I pick the car up and carry it to the head of the line?"

"Well," the woman sniffed, pointing across his chest, "that young man there seems to have found a way to do it. Maybe the kids and I should have found some hippie biker to get us to Nantucket."

Mick tried not to be offended. He was certainly no hippie!

"You know, Jan," her husband said through gritted teeth, "maybe you should have. In fact, there's still time." He leaned out the window towards Mick.

"Hey, pal, you want four more passengers? Maybe you can tie them on the back of your motorcycle. As a matter of fact, I'll trade you. This bunch for the cute girl on the back of your bike."

"Oh, that's wonderful, Bob. Go ahead, make everything into a big joke just because you don't have the gumption to either do something to get us there, or at least stop him from cutting in line!"

"Shut up, Jan, just shut up," the sweating husband muttered.

"Mickey," Bridget whispered in his ear, "move away, can you?"

Mick nodded and started to coast up another car length.

The woman's voice drifted loudly out of the open car window. "Yes, a real man with some intestinal fortitude would at least do something!"

Fortunately, it seemed poor old Bob had been henpecked for too many years to do anything. Unfortunately, the guy in the battered dune buggy loaded down with fishing gear hadn't and did.

As Mick got opposite the driver's side door, the driver opened it. Mick squeezed the hand brake just as the bike's front tire kissed the open door of the dune buggy. A large man climbed out. He was very large and looked very, very unhappy. And right now, 99.9% of that unhappiness was focused directly on Mick.

"Where the hell do you think you're going, buddy?"

"Oh, brother," Mick muttered to Bridget.

"Mickey," she hissed back, "I think maybe we should just call it a day, darlin'—a very long and somewhat trying day. Let's see if we can't find

185

somewhere to stay tonight and give it another go in the morning."

"Bridge," Mick shook his head. "In case it slipped your mind, that big clock full of a world of hurt and crap, is hanging right over my head. And it's still ticking. And it's getting louder. I don't know what pathetic old Moon Dog was about to tell us when he got jabbed by a fatal dose of skag, but my hunch is that if it was coming out of state government it must have something to do with the Frosts. Or...."

"Or who, Mickey?"

"Aw, nothing, just my immature paranoia kicking in. Forget it. C'mon, let's see if I can get around this joker."

Mick pushed the bike back a few feet and tried to swing it around the open door, but the big guy took a step to the left and blocked that way too. Yeah, he was big, real big—and mean looking. He looked like he came from Quincy or Revere. Liked the surf casting on Nantucket, but probably wound up killing more cans of cold Bud than he did striped bass, and from what Mick could smell as the guy took a step towards him, he'd probably already started on the most important part of the trip: the cold Bud. He leaned his face toward Mick's and hooked both thumbs into his belt. A beer gut roughly the size of a pony keg hung over the belt and strained against the T-shirt that read: You don't like cops? Next time you're in trouble, call a hippie.

"Hey, you long-haired hippie faggot, who the hell do you think you are? You can just wait your goddamn turn like everyone else!"

He breathed heavily into Mick's face, and Mick started to get pissed. And Bridget seemed to know it too.

"Mickey...," she said in a low voice with more than just a hint of warning behind it.

So Mick took a deep breath and gave it one more try. "Look," he said in what he felt was the voice of pure reason, "we aren't gonna be taking up anyone's place in line." He gestured back to the long line of fuming drivers and their cars. "These are all cars, and in case you hadn't noticed, I'm driving a motorcycle."

"Mickey!" Bridget hissed again and punched him lightly in the back.

Mick ignored her and focused on the big guy whose face continued to get redder.

"Listen, kid, when I was in Korea, we killed little commie fags like you with nothing but a bayonet or sharp stick up your ass!"

Mick sighed and pushed the kickstand down with his left boot heel. He swung his right leg over the handlebars and leaned against the bike. He smiled at the red-faced beefy guy yelling at him and hoped his own eyes were ice cold.

"Really?" Mick's voice was dangerously soft. "I guess things have changed in the past ten years, 'cause when I was in 'Nam, all we killed were VC—that's if they didn't get us first."

Taken back for a moment, the big man sneered, "Yeah, and half your squad was probably made up of little hippie fags like you."

That was when Mick hit him.

Right in that enormous beer gut. Hard.

The big guy's knees buckled, and he leaned forward on the hot asphalt gasping for breath.

Mick climbed back on the motorcycle and turned to Bridget. "You know, Bridge, I think you're right. Let's go find a room and try this again tomorrow."

Bridget just shook her head and smiled wryly. "Glad to hear you're finally taking some good advice, lad."

"Always, babe." Mick grinned back.

He gunned the BSA's engine, let the clutch out, and roared back towards the old buildings of the harbor's waterfront.

Chapter Thirty-Four

Nantucket Town
Nantucket Island
October 15th, 1858
4:38 p.m.

"Please believe, Mrs. Dawes, that I do not wish to intrude, but are you truly certain that you know where you are going?"

Fiona stood on the long pier that jutted out into Nantucket harbor and looked uncertainly at the gray-shingled waterfront of the town. Simon Westlake stood patiently beside her, languidly holding his tall brown beaver hat as he waited for the stevedores from the packet company to finish unloading his many pieces of elegantly monogrammed luggage onto the dock. By now, they had started to make a small but impressive mound. The stevedores had almost finished unloading the final pieces and were beginning to shuffle up to the tall, imperious looking man who stood with sleek beaver hat in one hand and silver-headed walking stick in the other. They were obviously hoping that he would turn to them with a small gratuity, but Simon Westlake ignored them, all of his attention focused on the slight young woman beside him who kept peering at the darkening town at the end of the pier.

Fiona felt at once both hopeful and desperate. She hoped that a much loved and loving figure would somehow emerge from the gray buildings on the waterfront, run down the pier, and sweep her into his arms. But at the same time, despite her almost unbearable longing, she knew that this wasn't going to happen. Jeptha didn't know or even suspect that she was here. And worse still, she didn't know where he was.

Fool. Fool. Fool! she chastised herself. *What were you planning on doing, girl, trudge up and down the streets of town until you tripped over him?* She felt like crying. *What's happening to me? I was raised as no hothouse flower. I've always been able to take whatever life's trials required of me and overcome them with determination, hard work, and the grace of the Lord. But now, now I seem to be falling to pieces at every bump in the road.*

She bit her lower lip to stop its trembling. It must have to do with the changes taking place in her body. The life she was carrying—hers and Jeptha's.

She drew a deep breath and stood up straighter. *All right, girl, standing here sniffling won't help solve things. Soonest begun, soonest done.*

She picked up the carpetbag, took two steps toward the town, and stepped right in front of a huge dray wagon that seemed to materialize from behind a small mound of bales and casks. It bore down on her without a moment's warning. Fiona stood frozen as the huge carthorse reared in front of her, blotting out the thin red ball of fading sunlight.

She didn't even have time to scream before the horse and cart were on top of her, poised to trample her small frame and the tiny spark of life it harbored under a ton of horseflesh, wood, and iron.

As the iron-shod hooves descended, a small brown object, a beaver hat, flashed across the horse's eyes, and it shied, the twin forehoofs crashing onto the granite slabs of the pier, sending up a shower of sparks just a hand's breath from Fiona's still frozen figure.

"You damned ignorant dock trollop, what in blazes do you think you're doing, stepping in front of my horse like that! He could have broken a leg, tipped the cart over. And these here goods is worth whole lot more than some purblind, no account, dockside drudge!" The red-faced drayman stood up in the seat and raised his whip at Fiona. It descended towards her unprotected face.

A hand encased in expensive but functional kid-skinned gloves caught hold of the whip and pulled. The carter's eyes widened with astonishment and then dismay as the hand holding the other end of the whip reeled in sharply and yanked the considerable bulk of the beefy drayman over the edge of the wagon's footboard and onto the hard rock surface of the wharf.

The carter went down hard but was on his feet a moment later coiling the whip that the kidskin-gloved hand had contemptuously let slide to the pavement.

The cart man wiped some bits of blood and gravel from his face where he'd hit the granite paving stones.

"That will cost you, you perfumed popinjay. And if you and your trollop have caused any damage to the goods of the man who owns this load, half the town and the very dock were standing on, I'll.... As a matter of fact, I'm going to—"

The silver head of a walnut walking stick smashed into his mouth, abruptly cutting off the last sentence.

The big man screamed as Simon Westlake lashed his shoulders with the stick. He threw up his hands to try to forestall another blow, but the heavy silver head of the cane smashed through his outstretched hands, shattering his fingers. He screamed and moaned, trying to curl himself into a ball like an overgrown hedgehog, but the blows continued to rain down on his back.

"No! No! Please, Mister, fer pity's sake, no more. My hands! You done gone and broke all my fingers. In the name of mercy, sir, leave off. I didn't do nothing to you!" he wailed.

"Nothing?" Simon Westlake's face was a red mask of fury. "Nothing, you yammering cur? You almost ran down this lady and then used your foul tongue to berate her. Nothing? I should beat you to death like the rabid animal you are!"

"I-I'm sorry. Lady," he looked up at Fiona with pleading, broken eyes, "I-I didn't mean it. It was just that you stepped in front of the cart, and I had to.... Ah!"

The walking stick slashed down once more, and the man writhed in pain crying, "In the name of the Lord, Mister. I'm sorry...sorry. What can I do? Just tell me and I'll do it!"

Simon Westlake leaned his head down and stared at the prone figure and said very softly, "You will crawl on your miserable worm belly to that lady and you will kiss the toe of each boot. And if she sees fit to forgive you, then, and only then, will you have a chance of leaving this wharf without every bone in your revolting carcass broken."

The big drayman looked at the dark, bottomless eyes and painfully slithered to Fiona's feet where he slobbered his bloody lips onto first one boot and then the other. Fiona screamed with revulsion and backed away.

"You toad," Simon Westlake snarled. "You've drooled your swine blood onto her boots." He raised the cane again.

"No! No! Please, Simon, I am imploring you, no more. Let the poor man go. Please, I can't stand to see any man—"

"I would hardly dignify him with that appellation, Mrs. Dawes," Simon said, the flush beginning to fade from his cheeks.

"All the same, I cannot abide to see any living creature beaten."

Simon inclined his head toward Fiona and then turned back to the sniveling drayman. "Do you hear that, cur? The lady has just spared your worthless life. But listen well to me." He bent down to the prone cart man and said in a voice almost too low for Fiona to hear, "You may take this to your master as a warning. This lady is under my protection, and he would do well not to cross me or my interests again."

He straightened up and slowly let the tip of his right calfskin boot press down on the sobbing man's broken fingers. "Do you understand me?"

"Yes! Yes! Fer the love of God, yes!"

Simon Westlake looked down contemptuously and turned away from the bleeding body as if it no longer existed.

Fiona swayed on her feet. The brutal scene spun in front of her. She felt her knees buckling and her body falling forward. Strong hands caught her and swept her up as if she was a small child.

"You!" Simon called to one of the loitering stevedores. "Run to that carriage at the end of the dock and tell the driver to bring the coach here to me."

As the man ran down the dock to do Simon's bidding, Fiona could just barely make out the lettering on the drayman's cart as Simon

carried her past it.
ISAIAH FROST & SON.

* * * *

New Bedford
Harbor District
August 19th, 1968
8:31 p.m.

"Mickey, this is the fourth place we've tried in the past hour. Please, let's just get a room, any room!" She looked around the dim lobby of the seedy, run-down hotel and gave a little shudder. *Are bedbug bites worth a few hours of blessed sleep?*

Mick shrugged. "Hey, I was up for the Holiday Inn, but they were all filled up."

"Well, what was wrong with that big hotel back towards the center of town?"

"Oh, not one blessed thing, Miss Connolly, unless you think that they might have been a wee bit perturbed when they found out tomorrow that we couldn't pay the bill!"

Bridget tried to stifle a weary yawn and sighed. "So just how much do we have in our travel budget for the Grand Tour of Southeastern Massachusetts then, Mr. Rockefeller?"

Mick looked glum as he pulled out his wallet. He counted it out again, seemingly more for Bridget's benefit than to confirm the question that he already knew the answer to. "Eighty-seven dollars and...fifty-three cents."

"But Mickey, that's more than enough for a room—a nice room!" she finished almost indignantly.

With obvious patience, Mick turned around and gazed at her. She was tired. Crap, he looked it too. "Look, babe, that eighty-seven bucks has got to last us from here to Nantucket and back to...."

Didn't he want to say it because he knew what probably waited for them back there?

Bridget said the word they were both trying to put out of their minds, "Skaket Harbor."

* * * *

Normally Bridget was a sound sleeper. For many reasons she had to be. It wasn't just that she'd grown up in a small cottage in Cork, Ireland, separated by one flimsy wall from her five snoring brothers, she'd also shared a bed for the past year with a Vietnam vet who was plagued by occasional, but very violent nightmares. Those always woke her, and she would then do her best to bring Mick back from their depths, holding him until the shakes and night terrors gradually subsided. But the normal run-of-the-mill moans and groans, she'd learned to sleep through. Bridget, on the other hand, rarely if ever had nightmares. So Mick was slow to respond that night when she did.

By the time her mumbled cries of, "No, no, keep off of me. Keep away!" finally woke Mick, Bridget was in the full grip of a full blown nightmare.

Groggy, Mick sat up. "Bridge?" He shook her shoulders lightly, but she swatted his hand away.

"No! I told you no, sir. Do not touch me. Your familiarity is most improper. I am a married woman!"

Married woman? Now Mick was fully awake.

She moaned again. This time it sounded almost sensual.

Now her breath came in small shallow gasps. Her eyes were half open and glazed, her lips slightly parted. She looked like...?

Mick realized with shock that she looked like she did when they were making love! He was surprised, confused, and more than just a little turned on. Did girls really have those same kinds of dreams that had historically plagued the restless nights of boys' prep schools?

Bridget gave a low, sensual moan. Apparently so.

He put his hands on her shoulders once more. "Hey, babe, wake—"

"Please, sir. I am imploring you. You must not touch me."

Mick gently pulled her towards him and whispered, "It's okay. It's me, wake up, you're just having a dream."

Bridget's eyes flew open. "God forgive me. I can resist no longer." She rolled herself into his arms with an intensity that was almost frightening. She put both soft arms around his shoulders and dug her fingernails into his back. It would have hurt if his own rapidly rising desire hadn't been blocking out every sense except his need for her. Her moans increased as she covered his body with kisses and small, sensual bites. Time became blurred, and the whole while her body writhed next to his her eyes glazed with unfocused lust.

She kept gasping, "This is wrong...so wrong. But I cannot help it."

They rocked together one last shuddering time, and then Bridget rolled off of him, burying her face in the pillow, sobbing.

Mick, on the other hand, was very satisfied and pretty damn happy, but this sure as hell wasn't Bridget's usual reaction. He tried to turn her towards him.

"Bridge?"

"No!" she cried fiercely. "You must release me. Release me from

192

whatever it is that you have done to me! From whatever wicked spell you have woven to make me dishonor my vows!" She dropped her head back to the pillow and buried her face again. "My husband! My poor, loyal husband! How will I ever atone for this betrayal?" She looked up, her eyes wild and unfocused.

"Your pistol, sir, give me your pistol. If you will not release me, then allow me to end my shame." She let out a heart-rending wail. "But the child. The child I still carry, despite everything you say and have done.... I can't—I won't—put an end to an innocent life!"

Okay, this has gone far enough!

"Bridget!" Mick grabbed her shoulders with all his strength and shook. "Bridget! You are Bridget Ann Connolly. That's who you are. And I'm Mick, and you're going to wake up. Now!"

"No!" She shook her head and tried to twist away from him. "Take your hands off of me. Seducer! Liar!" She slapped him.

That did it. Freud or no Freud, this dream was coming to an end. Now!

Mick ducked his head under her flailing arms and picked her up. She struggled, but he held on and carried her into the small bathroom. He set her down on the cold porcelain surface of the claw-foot bathtub and before she could stand up, turned on the overhead shower full blast—on ice cold.

She gasped and stood up sputtering. "Bloody hell!" She looked around, confused for a moment, and then saw Mick. "Damn your eyes, McCarthy, what in bloody blue blazes do you think you're doing?"

Mick smiled. "Welcome back, babe."

* * * *

Two worn, cheap white hotel towels later, they were finally back in bed.

"Do you remember anything of that dream?" Even in the half dawn light that seeped through the dirty Venetian blinds, Mick could tell that she blushed.

Finally she said, "Mickey...did I.... I mean, did we...make love?"

Mick grinned from ear to ear and pulled her close.

"That's putting it mildly. Hey, if it was that bucket of steamers we had for dinner that was responsible for the dream, I'm gonna start ordering them by the bushel."

But she didn't laugh.

"Don't joke about it, Mickey. I...well, it wasn't me. I mean, it was my body, but I wasn't really me."

Mick stopped smiling. Yet he kind of knew it was something like that. "So who were you?"

She shook her head but didn't answer for a moment. "What...what did I say?"

Mick thought for a moment. "Strange stuff. Like you didn't want to do what you were doing but you couldn't help yourself. Kind of like someone that you really didn't like or trust was putting the moves on you and you knew he was a creep deep down, but like he had your head all messed up. You know, like some chicks who hop into bed with a guy who's bad news and then wind up feeling—"

"Used. Used and cheap and...," she gazed at him with still haunted eyes, "helpless to do anything about it."

"Whoa, hold up, babe. I mean, it was dynamite, smokin' hot lovin', but I think I'm starting to feel just a wee bit jealous. Just who the hell was this mystery dream date? Maybe I oughta hunt him up and give him a couple of good shots for messing around in my girlfriend's dreams."

"I don't know whether you're serious or joking."

Neither did Mick.

"But it wasn't anyone I know." She stopped and looked thoughtful. "And yet...."

"Who?"

She shook her head again. "No, no. I'm sure that I've never seen him before—at least not like that."

"Like what?" Mick's patience started to fray around the edges.

It seemed Bridget was trying to stare back into the dream. "He was dressed up like an old fashioned gent."

"A what?"

"You know, all of those old pictures of the gents in top hats and waistcoats."

"Yeah," Mick said slowly, "you mean like a Victorian?"

"Yes. And I was in this hotel. Right here in this very room. And then all at once I was someplace else, a vast, rambling mansion where I could hear the sound of the sea crashing beyond the windows. We...." She grabbed his hand and stared at him with a strange, spooky look. Mick almost pulled back. Bridget kept gripping his hand as the words flowed faster. "It was me, but not me. He was handsome—so suave, so cultured. But he frightened me. I felt that underneath all of the beautiful words and fine manners he was...evil."

Her grip tightened. Mick just listened.

"And yet...yet," Bridget seemed to choke on the words and tilted her head down in shame. "And yet I-I wanted him. I was helpless. I wanted him so." She gazed up at Mick with tear-speckled eyelashes. "Mickey, can you ever forgive me?"

194

Ric Wasley

"What's to forgive, babe?" Mick said, genuinely puzzled. "Hey, I was the lucky recipient of all of that, to quote the Rascals, *Good Lovin'*."

Bridget glanced at him for a moment as if she also knew that he was rationalizing. And that's what Mick wanted—at least that's what he was trying to convince himself he wanted. He was still uneasy deep down but trying to let it slide. Yeah, just let it slide. It was a dream, just a strange, disturbing dream.

Just a dream.

But when he stared into Bridget's eyes, he knew it wasn't.

She shook her head sadly. "No, Mickey, you deserve honesty, and I won't take the easy way out."

She watched him with a sad, solemn look and said softly, "It wasn't you that I was making love to. It was...him."

* * * *

Mick threw their packs on to the luggage bar of the bike and savagely kicked down on the recoil starter. He knew he was being childish, blaming Bridget for a dream she'd had, but he couldn't help it. He was pissed. He was jealous. Of a frigging phantom!

"Get on," he grunted back to Bridget without turning around.

"I'm sorry, Mickey," she whispered.

Grow up, Mick! he mentally shouted at himself. He was finally able to muster a half smile. "It's okay, babe."

But was it? One thing he did know, all he wanted to do was get away from this stupid, crappy, rundown old hotel on New Bedford's decaying waterfront.

He gave a last look at the faded, old red-brick forefront of the tired hotel as he put the bike in gear.

It would be a cold frigging day in Hell before they ever came back to the Bristol Hotel.

Chapter Thirty-Five

Nantucket Island
October 15th, 1858
7:42 p.m.

"Mrs. Dawes, please let me send Enoch in by himself to inquire at this establishment." Simon turned to her with a look that seemed to radiate nothing but deep concern.

Fiona just shook her head.

"Mrs. Dawes—Fiona. Again, I presume on the liberty you have granted me of calling one who I hope is becoming a dear friend, by her first name."

"Of course, Mr. Westlake. Simon," Fiona said hoarsely, her voice made thick with fatigue and confusion.

She stared down at the soft fur coach blanket with which Simon had covered her lower limbs. The onset of early fall darkness had dropped the temperatures of Nantucket's cobblestoned streets down to an uncomfortable damp chill.

After the terrifying incident with the cart and its brutal driver, Fiona had allowed herself to be carried to Simon Westlake's coach. He had gently placed her inside and covered her with the warm bearskin lap robe.

"Mrs. Dawes," he said, taking her hand and looking at her with utmost sympathy, "Please allow me once more to offer you the shelter and hospitality of my summer estate on the north side of the island. It is set upon a majestic high cliff that offers magnificent views, especially during the autumn gales, hence its rather dramatic name—Tempest."

His eyes became unfocused for a moment. He turned back to her and smiled. "May I not tempt you into becoming a most honored guest?"

Fiona was frightened at how much of her longed to say yes. She tried to focus on the gentle, solid face of her husband, but it kept blurring in her mind's eye and continued to metamorphose into the darkly handsome, concerned but sometimes just out of the periphery of her vision, mocking and amused profile of the man who occupied the opposite coach seat.

"Mrs. Dawes? Fiona?" He startled her out of her reverie.

"I-I'm sorry," she stammered. "I was wool gathering. I seem to be becoming more and more scatterbrained as my condit—" She stopped herself abruptly. She didn't know why, but she suddenly didn't want Simon Westlake to know that she was carrying Jeptha's child or anything about her *condition.*

He stared at her intently. Almost as if he knew. *He couldn't possibly.... Could he?*

He took her hand. She didn't pull away. She was so very, very tired and despondent.

Once again, he seemed to read her thoughts. "Do not berate yourself, my dear Mrs. Dawes...Friend Fiona. It is the lateness of the hour, your traumatic brush with that swine of a drayman." His fingers clenched for a moment and then just as quickly relaxed. "And general fatigue brought on by your delicate...."

Fiona's eyes widened. He knew?

Simon smiled indulgently and finished with, "nature. Yes, a most charming and delicate...nature."

Fiona felt as though she was falling into a deep pool with no bottom. Slowly sinking, no matter how hard she struggled.

"Enoch!" Simon rapped on the coach wall with his walking stick. "Go into this establishment and inquire after Mr. Dawes. Describe him and offer thirty silver dollars for confirmation of his lodgings or whereabouts."

"Yes, sir, Mr. Westlake," came the muffled reply from the driver's seat.

Fiona's head fell back on to the soft velvet cushions. It seemed so much easier to let someone else take charge. Make all of the decisions. She closed her eyes. Suddenly, the image of Jeptha's face leapt into sharp, clear focus. The cobwebs seemed to lift from her brain. "Wait!" she cried, pushing the coach door open. "I am coming too!"

* * * *

The shabby but clean parlor smelled of cabbage and codfish.

A hard looking woman of indeterminate age wiped her chapped hands on her coarse, stained apron and looked warily back at the three people who filled her small parlor. Fiona watched the woman sizing her up along with Simon and his cadaverous looking servant. The woman stared at them contemptuously. Especially at Simon and the tall, gangly man dressed in a plain but high quality frock coat who bobbed his head each time the elegantly dressed Mr. Westlake glanced his way.

"My name is Mrs. Amanda Coffin and I own this boarding house." She turned to Simon Westlake. "Who are you and what do want?"

Simon bowed curtly. "A moment of your time, madam."

The expression on the face of Mrs. Amanda Coffin made it plain that she didn't like him. But it was clear that Fiona, the tiny young girl-woman in the plain, dark gray dress, puzzled the owner of the boarding house.

Fiona stated that she had come inquiring after her husband, one

197

Jeptha Dawes.

But the look that the widowed proprietor of Mrs. Coffin's Bed & Board for Christian Ladies and Gentleman gave back to her said: Well then, what are you doing in the company of this arrogant looking dandy and his toady?

However, when asked a direct question, it was plain to Fiona that Amanda Coffin was not the type to lie. Thus, when Fiona took out a small oval daguerreotype of a serious young man with full dark whiskers and asked with a slight Gaelic accent if she'd seen her husband, Mrs. Coffin answered a terse but truthful, "Yes."

Fiona stepped forward eagerly, and the words tumbled out in a torrent. "When? W-where? Is he well? Is he safe? Is he here?"

Simon, his gaze appearing nonchalant, allowed his eyes to bore into Mrs. Coffin's for a split second. Amanda Coffin took a step backwards in surprise. Then the glare was gone, so quickly Fiona wasn't even sure if she'd seen it. But she knew that Mrs. Coffin had seen and that it frightened her. And the widow of a harpooner didn't look like she frightened easily. She turned back to Fiona, whose hands clenched together in hope.

"He was here until earlier this very night."

Fiona's hopeful smile crumbled. "He...he's gone?"

"Aye," she nodded. "And right sorry I was to lose him too. He was a good and proper Christian gentleman, was Mr. Dawes."

"Where...where is he? Did he say where he was going?" She looked at the floor and choked out the words. "Did he leave any word for me?"

"He did not," the grim landlady answered sharply and then added, "He only mentioned to me that he had a wife. And that she...," the thin, rawboned woman glanced scornfully at Fiona, "was waiting patiently and...," her lips pursed, and she looked directly into Fiona's eyes as she clipped out the word, "*loyally* in New Bedford."

Tears leaked from the corner of each of Fiona's eyes. She stared down at the floor and answered in a voice that was barely above a whisper, "Yes, that is what I promised him." She looked up with a flash of her old fire, jutted out her lower jaw, and put both hands on her hips. "And yet, though I break a promise and am honor bound to answer for it, I do know that he needs me. My husband needs me!" Her nostrils flared. "And so I will ask you one more time, Mrs. Coffin, did my husband say where he was bound?"

The harpooner's widow gave out with a snort, which was close to a laugh. "You've got sand girl, I'll give you that." She paused as if debating with herself.

Simon, possibly sensing an opening, nodded to his cadaverous looking servant. Enoch opened a heavy cloth purse and pulled out a handful of silver dollars. One by one he dropped them onto a plain pine side table with a solid clunk.

Widow Coffin looked at the silver pile contemptuously. "Get your tin trash off of my table."

Simon Westlake's mouth still smiled, but his eyes shone flat and lifeless in contrast to the shine of the silver coins. "I think, Mrs. Coffin, you will answer the question that Mrs. Dawes has put to you."

She gave him back stare for stare. Finally, she turned and, looking back at Fiona's expression, that Fiona was sure was in turn belligerent and pleading, answered, "I may at that. But," her left hand swept the pile of silver dollars off of the table, "not because of any bribes or threats from you."

Simon Westlake looked at her, his expression tightly controlled and unreadable. He didn't even glance at the silver dollars rolling and clanking across the worn wooden floor. Although Simon's stiff expression never wavered or changed, one glance at his servant sent the coachman scrambling around the floor on hands and knees to retrieve each coin.

With eyes still locked on Simon Westlake, the widow turned her body back towards Fiona. "I get two dollars a week for room and board. And sometimes, if I think it proper, I will share my observations with those of my borders that I like and respect."

Simon nodded, and his servant put two of the retrieved silver dollars into her hand. She turned her palm over and let them fall to the floor again.

"Those of my borders that I like and respect," she repeated.

Fiona fumbled in her purse and held out a $20 gold eagle. The widow took it, bit down once, and nodded. She then laboriously took coins from her apron pocket and counted out $18 in change into Fiona's small hand. "Your husband had come in looking for a place to stay while he awaited a former shipmate he was meeting. They'd decided to sign articles to serve aboard the ship Perseus bound for Valparaiso by way of Barbados, or so he said to me. He asked me if I had seen a man of slight build, ginger whiskers, and a twitching cast in one eye. Well, as I think you've seen by now, I am not a gossip and believe in keeping my own counsel." She glanced at Simon Westlake. "But your Mr. Dawes had an honest countenance." She shifted her gaze to Fiona, and her expression softened. "As do you. So I told him that I had just such a man who'd been boarding with me for the past three days."

"What...what was his name?" Fiona whispered.

"Your man asked me the exact same question. And this is the answer I gave him. Tanner. The man's name was Zeke Tanner."

Fiona swayed on her feet. She clutched the side of the table. "Then where did they—he—go?"

"Your husband sat in that rocker for upwards of three hours and waited. Just after the clock had sounded six bells, that Tanner fellow came slithering in—I never could abide the little weasel," she mumbled to herself. "As soon as your husband sees him, he jumps up and yells, 'Tanner, I will have that which you have stolen from me and justice for the murder of John Twin-Hawks.'

"Well, this Tanner, he bolts down the front walk like all the legions of Lucifer were after him, with your husband in hot pursuit, but by the time I got to the door, they had both disappeared into the fog."

"Then you don't know where he has gone?"

For the first time the widow's tone truly softened. "No, child, I'm sorry. I don't."

Fiona looked at the older woman. "Is there nothing more you can remember, any clue, no matter how small?"

"No. Wait. Yes, one thing. Does your husband own a pistol?"

Fiona shook her head. "No. He believes that a man should fight his battles with only the strength that God gave him."

"Oh, well then, never mind."

"What? What about the pistol?"

The older woman shook her head. "Sorry now to have mentioned it."

"Please, Mrs. Coffin, you must tell me all that you know. I-I beg you."

The widow started to turn away and then looked back at Fiona twisting her tiny fingers into knots. She sighed as if choosing the lesser of two evils.

"After they disappeared in the fog," she said slowly, "just as I was closing the front door, I thought I heard a...pistol shot."

Fiona's knees buckled, and she crumpled to the floor. Without a moment's hesitation, Simon swept her up into his arms and tersely barked to his servant to open the door.

"Not so fast, Mr.—whoever you are." Amanda Coffin moved to block the doorway. "This good lady has paid me $2 in advance for a room, and this is where a respectable, married Christian woman should be staying till her husband returns."

Simon Westlake never even paused. He brushed her arm aside and threw the rest of the silver dollars from the purse into the parlor and said, "That is for your room, your troubles, and your long nose, which you should learn to keep out of other people's business."

She ran to the open front door and called to the tall figure setting the semi-conscious young woman into the back of the carriage. "Where are you taking her?"

Her last few syllables were drowned out as the wheels of the coach began to turn and the whip-sharp voice of the man within the carriage called out to his driver a single word: "Tempest!"

Ric Wasley

* * * *

Nantucket Island
The Crown & Anchor Pub
August 20th, 1968
2:16 p.m.

"Two more, guys?" The perky, tanned waitress picked up the two empty bottles of Narragansett Ale and gave them her hundred-watt smile. Mick glanced up appreciatively—especially at the way she filled out her blue-and-gold lettered Crown & Anchor T-shirt—and nodded. "Sure."

Bridget noticed the tan, the sun-streaked blonde hair, and swelling T-shirt too—but not appreciatively. "No thanks, luv. We've got to be pushing on. Just the check, if you please."

The waitress cocked one cut-off, jean-clad hip and looked hopefully at Mick for an override. But Mick had made that mistake way too many times and still had the verbal scars to prove it. He knew when to order a strategic withdrawal while he still had his pride, ego, and both ears intact. So he wisely nodded. "Yeah, just the check."

Bridget hid a smile behind her hand at her small and perhaps even petty, but still satisfying victory. Mick knew it too and knew that she felt by his giving in, it showed he wasn't still pissed about her dream. And he wasn't, was he? He shouldn't be. After all, look at the dozen times each day she had to forgive him for watching a cute butt in a tight pair of jeans wiggle across the floor—like now.

The waitress disappeared through the kitchen door, and Mick sighed.

Why couldn't he let it slide that Bridget had an erotic dream about a mysterious stranger? Maybe he couldn't because it wasn't like her to act like this—not at all.

"So is that where you want start, then?"

Mick turned and looked at Bridget.

Yes, I was talking to you.

"Huh...what?"

"I said, McCarthy, is that where you want to start—in the town records and shipping news in the town hall?"

"Hmm? Yeah, right. That's where we'll start. C'mon."

Mick got up, threw some singles and change down on the table, and

201

headed for the door without looking back.

Bridget slowly got up and followed him, her tiny victory turning to ashes.

No. It still wasn't all right.

Chapter Thirty-Six

"Is this the one that you want, Miss?" The town clerk's expression said that he certainly hoped it was. At least fifty years of dust coated the old record books from one-hundred-and-ten years ago. And right now it appeared that he had to.... "Achoo!"

"Bless you," Bridget mumbled absently as she took the large, dusty book from his outstretched hands.

The clerk wiped his running nose on his sleeve and asked in a weary tone, "Do you need anything else or do you think that one will keep you busy for a while?"

Bridget opened the yellowed record book and sat down. Without looking up, she murmured, "Yes, for the time being. I'll sing out if I need more."

"Hummmph, well let's hope you don't," the clerk muttered and shuffled away to wash the offending dust off of his hands.

Bridget turned the musty, brittle pages and gave her own dainty little "choo" as the fine motes of dust and mold tickled her nostrils. She turned the pages to 1858 and carefully ran her index finger down each page until she came to the month of October. It recorded all of the births, marriages, and deaths on the entire island for the month of October. She looked under Deaths.

The chipped, bitten fingernail of her right hand traced the faded brown spidery writing, searching for a name. Finally, near the bottom of the page, she found it.

"Tanner, Ezekiel – Transient. Place of Birth – Unknown. Place of Death – Nantucket Township, Nantucket Island. Cause of death – Strangulation."

Strangulation? Bridget sat bolt upright. She had to tell Mick. She looked around the bowels of the old Town Hall and up to the thin metal catwalk that ran alongside one wall. She could just make out Mick's shoulder between the stacks of shipping records that went all the way back to the 17ᵗʰ century.

She opened her mouth to call him. No, wait. Better to gather some more information before she called him to make his way back down the rickety iron spiral staircase. She turned back to the book.

Proceedings of the Coroner's inquest held 16ᵗʰ

The Scrimshaw

October, 1858, at Town Constable's office:

One Ezekiel (Zeke) Tanner, was strangled to death by person or persons unknown. As closely as can be determined, the marks found upon the victim's throat did not indicate any rope tool or device had been used to affect the victim's death. The coroner speculates that the deep bruises could have been made by human fingers, although there is no other supporting evidence of this theory. A thorough examination of the victim's effects gave little additional information as to the deceased's place of origin. The deceased was found to be in possession of a large sum of money. Close to $600 in $20 gold eagles, thus giving rise to the theory that the deceased might have been engaged in some nefarious activity and could have possibly been murdered by his cohorts.

This theory, however, was immediately discarded as the gold was found upon his person thereby negating the motive of robbery. The gold was placed in trust with the constable until such time as any living relations of Mr. Tanner could be located. The other few effects found on his person were interred with him and they were: 1 pocket watch, a sailor's clasp knife, a brass whiskey flask, and a strangely carved scrimshaw.

A scrimshaw! For a moment, Bridget stopped breathing. Oh, good Lord! Now she had to call Mick. Wait.... First, where was Zeke Tanner buried? She turned the page.

It was missing.

* * * *

The Crown & Anchor Pub
August 20th, 1968
6:13 p.m.

"Come on, Bridge, try some. It's not bad. Here, toss some of these oyster crackers in it." Mick pushed the small cellophane packet of octagon shaped crackers across the table, but Bridget just kept staring at the two sheets of copy paper spread out on the table in front of her. She had put one on each side of her still un-tasted bowl of New England clam chowder.

"At least give it a taste, babe," Mick said and tilted his bowl to get the last spoonful. "This is actually the real stuff. You know, not that crap they make for the tourists, all crammed full of cream and flour that makes it about the consistency of wallpaper paste and almost as tasty." Mick snorted and pushed his empty bowl away. He waved at the passing waitress and held up one finger. She nodded and motioned at Bridget as she kept walking towards the kitchen door. "Bridge.... Babe? You want another beer?" The waitress paused for a moment and glanced back at Mick with a quizzical and impatient expression.

Mick looked at Bridget's almost full mug sitting next to her untouched bowl of chowder and shook his head. The waitress disappeared through the kitchen door.

Mick leaned across the table and gently lifted Bridget's chin with his thumb and forefinger. She gave him a distracted glance and then stared back down at the copies that they'd made of the one-hundred-and-ten-year-old town record book. Bridget kept reading the faded writing over and over as if she could somehow define a meaningful clue that wasn't there.

Mick knew what she was thinking and said what they both knew, "Bridge, give it a rest. Come on, kiddo, lighten up."

Bridget continued staring for a few more moments and pushed the stiff sheets of paper away, laced her tiny fingers underneath her chin, and sighed. "Oh, Mickey, I know it's there. I just know it."

"What's there, babe?"

"The bleedin' answer. I know it. I can feel it!"

"Where?"

Bridget sighed again and looked up at the ceiling. "The missing page—it's on that bleedin' missing bloody page."

"Which we don't have."

"Which we don't have," Bridget agreed glumly.

"Aw, chill out, babe, we'll figure it out. Eventually."

"Eventually? Mickey, we're running out of time."

Bridget bit the inside of her lip, and worry spread over her face. "We've only got two more days. Two more days to prove that you didn't do something that we can't prove. Two days to find something we're not sure even exists. Two days to connect an object we've never seen, to people who died a hundred years ago. Two days to prove that an object we've only heard about from a girl who's also never seen it, is somehow connected to an evil bunch of inbred spalpeens who have tried to rape me and frame you for murder. Oh, Mickey," she gazed up at him, eyes brimming with tears of worry and frustration, "what in the bleedin', bloody, damn hell are we gonna do?"

Mick tried to think of a happy, snappy comeback, but nothing came.

All he could do was spread his hands out on the table, look back at her, and try to grin with a confidence he didn't feel. "It'll be okay, babe."

"Mickey, if they take you. If...if they take you away from me I-I...."

"Hush." Mick put his forefinger to her lips. "They won't get me. We'll find this...this...whatever it is and...."

Bridget pulled his hand on to her tear-wet cheek and said fiercely, "If they take you, I swear by every saint's bones in County Cork that I'll—"

"I hope I'm not interrupting."

They both glanced up.

Mick's face surely showed puzzlement. Bridget's was stunned.

Then Mick started a cautious, slow smile as he recognized.... "Yeah, hey, ah, Westlake, right? Ah, what was it Frankie called you? BF? PF? Ah...?"

"It's E.F. E.F. Westlake."

"Right, and by the way, thanks again for saving our butts."

"My pleasure," the tall, nonchalantly good-looking man said, putting his hand on the back of an empty chair. His eyebrows rose quizzically. "May I?"

"Christ, where's my freakin' manners! Hell, yeah, sit man, sit."

"Thanks." He smiled. "Can I buy you a beer?"

"Jeez, dude," Mick shook his head, "we should be buying you one."

Westlake shrugged dismissively. "No, I invited myself over to your table. It's the least I can do. And I hope that you'll forgive me for butting in, but I never have been able to stand the sight of a woman close to tears. Especially when the woman is as lovely as...Bridget? It is Bridget, yes?"

Bridget, strangely out of breath, whispered back, "Yes."

He smiled and nodded, the tip of his finger brushing the back of her hand as he raised it to signal the waitress. Bridget jumped as if an electric shock had gone through her.

Westlake appeared to have caught the movement out of the corner of his eye and smiled an unreadable half smile. Bridget's face burned red, and she quickly dropped her gaze to the table.

"As I said," he continued while holding up three fingers to the waitress, "I was having a piece of that fresh bluefish that the local fishermen have been hauling out all day—it's quite good by the way...."

His eyes glanced towards Bridget again, but she didn't look up. "Anyway, I was at that small table over by the bar debating whether to have another piece, when I saw this beautiful young lady who seemed like she was about to burst into tears, and, well, as I said, I just can't stand to see a pretty lady sad."

Bridget's fingers twisted as the flush spread from her face, down her throat, and between the buttons of her blouse.

"And if I'm not being too nosey, Mick, you're kind of looking like you're getting ready for a funeral yourself."

Mick glanced at Bridget and then back at Westlake. He paused a moment before he answered in flat tone of voice, "Yeah, mine."

Westlake smiled again. "Well, if you don't mind a little well intentioned meddling, I think that I just may be able to help."

Chapter Thirty-Seven

Nantucket Island
October 16ᵗʰ, 1858

Fiona came awake slowly as if climbing out of a deep cold well. Her first sensation was the softness of something cool and smooth caressing her cheek. Without opening her eyes, she ran her fingertips down the surface of the fabric that her head rested on. Smooth. As smooth as....

She opened her eyes. Yes, it *was* silk. She raised her head from the silk pillow and then from the bed she lay on. She rested fully clothed on a burgundy-and-blue damask coverlet trimmed with gold silk.

She sat up in an enormous four-poster bed with heavy burgundy-and-blue curtains drawn back to take the full advantage of a warm fire of sea coal radiating from a marble-faced fireplace shot through with veins of soft pink and gold.

It was beautiful, but where was it, and how did she get here? The last thing she remembered was feeling dizzy and sick at the boardinghouse where they had ended their fruitless search for Jeptha. A vague, dreamlike memory of a carriage ride, followed by dreams of her own, some strange, others disturbing, floated through her mind. Dreams of being carried through long, dark corridors, and then sleep—a troubled, disquieting sleep, but for how long? She got up and went to the window. She drew the drapes aside, and sunlight struck her full in the face. Daytime, probably mid-morning judging by the position of the sun.

A knock rattled at the door. She crossed the room and opened it. "Mr. Westlake?"

"Good morning, Mrs. Dawes. I hope that I am not intruding. Did you sleep well? Please forgive me for placing you on the bed without benefit of proper nightclothes, but Mrs. Samuels, the housekeeper, was down with the ague when we arrived, and I didn't think it would be proper for the butler or the night porter to conduct so delicate a task."

"But please, Mr. Westlake, how did I come to be here, in this place?" She gestured to and then pointed at the window and the rolling waves that crashed against the rocks and pebble-strewn beach beneath it.

Simon Westlake smiled. "Welcome to Tempest, Mrs. Dawes."

* * * *

The Crown & Anchor Pub
Nantucket Town
August 20, 1968

When the three, dark golden beers arrived at their table, Mick reached for his wallet, but Westlake just smiled at the waitress and said, "Terry, be a doll and just put this on my tab, will you?"

"No sweat, Mr. W., you got it."

"Thanks, sweetheart," he said with a wink and slipped a five dollar bill into her hand.

"Thanks." Mick nodded at Westlake and took a cautious sip of the beer in the mug in front of him. He nodded again. "Not bad. German?"

Westlake continued to smile. "Dutch, actually." He glanced over at the waitress who was just walking back to the bar, scribbling something in her order pad. "Hey, Terry?" She snapped her head up. "Terry, another round, please. And this time just bring the bottles." She winked at him and disappeared behind the bar.

Mick felt a little annoyed that he and Bridge hadn't been asked if they'd like another. But on the other hand, he couldn't complain about the price—free. And as he took another sip, he realized that it was a damn good too. He smiled again at Westlake and said so.

"Glad you like it." Westlake inclined his head toward Bridget. She hadn't touched hers. His face crinkled with concern. "I'm sorry, Bridget. Or would you prefer Miss Connolly?"

Bridget glanced up under lowered eyelashes and whispered, "No, Bridget is fine."

"Then can I get you something else? Often people find the German and Dutch beers too heavy. Perhaps a nice light Pilsner, I know that they have both Papst and Carling Black Label on tap."

Bridget stared down at the mug in front of her and took a small sip. She snorted and looked back wryly at him. With a hint of her old sarcasm, she said, "You call this strong? My Da and brothers brush their teeth with brews stronger than this, and they tell me I was weaned on Guinness."

"Touché, Miss Connolly—Bridget. A worthy answer from a charming representative of the beauty for which your homeland is so justifiably famous."

Mick's interest now stood on tiptoe, waiting for Bridget to cut through this obvious bullshit with a tongue that could chop a phony line and its owner into verbal fish bait with a word or two.

But she didn't. For a moment it appeared that she was going to say something, but as she gazed across the table at the tall, hawk-faced man, the retort seemed to stick to her tongue. She mumbled something and then fastened her eyes back down at the tabletop and began to draw aimless doodles in the thin film of beer suds.

What the hell's going on? This isn't like Bridget at all. He could count on one hand the number of times he'd seen her flustered or at a loss for words.

He moved his head towards hers and started to say, "Bridge, are you okay?" but the question was clipped off by the waitress, Terry, clattering three large green bottles down on the table.

"Thanks, doll." Westlake winked and turned to Mick while pointing at the bottle. "This is it. What you liked. The Dutch beer I mentioned."

Mick picked up the bottle and analyzed the label. "Grolsch," he said, twisting the name around on his tongue. If he'd mispronounced it, Westlake was smart enough not to let on. Next, Mick examined the strange white stopper that was fastened to the bottle by a complicated looking wire device.

"What is this thing made of?" he asked, scraping his thumbnail across the white stopper.

"It's porcelain. Just like a teacup. Porcelain."

"Hmmm, cool." Mick put the bottle back down. "Thanks for the beers and the lesson in international brewing, but I seem to recall something about you being able to help."

Westlake's smile vanished, and he became serious again. "Yes I did, and sorry for rambling on for so long."

Mick didn't say anything. Westlake eyed him a moment more and then went on. "Well, as you may remember, when we were in your brother's office I believe he mentioned that I'm the new DA for Barnstable County."

Mick raised his eyebrows. "I guess I got it wrong. I thought Frankie said you were the assistant DA. Did I get my wires crossed, or was there a quick promotion?"

Westlake's expression turned bland. "I guess you could categorize it as a 'quick promotion'. The old DA had a sudden stroke. Very sad."

"Yeah, but not for you," Mick said under his breath.

"Excuse me?"

"Hmmm?"

"Sorry, I didn't catch what you said."

"Nothing. Just clearing my throat. Please, go on." Mick nodded, and Bridget continued with her distracted doodles.

Westlake composed his face back into the easy smile, leaned across the table, and lowered his voice. "Well, a friend of mine at the town clerk's office told me that you had been inquiring about a grave—one grave in particular."

"Go on," Mick said, keeping his tone non-committal.

"The grave you were asking about was that of a semi-literate seaman of dubious character by the name of Zeke Tanner." Westlake grinned. "How am I doing so far?"

Mick shrugged. "And so?"

"And so I think that I may be able to help you locate that grave."

"How?"

"Before I answer that, let me ask you a question."

Mick shrugged again and took another swallow of beer. "I guess that Dutch beer with porcelain stoppers at least entitles you to ask." He picked up his glass again.

"What do you know about the Frosts?"

Mick stopped with the glass halfway to his lips. Bridget paused in mid-doodle and glanced up.

Mick set the glass back down on the table and stared at Westlake before answering. "Look, some good beer and saving our butts does earn you the right to play Twenty Questions with us, but I'm only into fun and games up to a point, and I'd kinda like to know what this one is." His eyes narrowed. "And you already know about my beef with the Frosts and the cell they're warming up for me, from what we told you in my brother's office, so what's the game, man?"

Westlake shook his head. "No game, Mick. I didn't ask you what your problem was with the Frosts, although I may be able to help you with that too. I asked you what do you know about them?"

"If you'd have asked us a week ago our happy answer would have been abso-friggin'-lutely nothing!"

"And now?"

"And now I know that Frost is a synonym for scumbag and collective noun for inbred sons of bitches."

Westlake smiled and stuck out his hand. "Join the club, pardner."

Mick shook it warily. "You mean the club that thinks the Frosts are inbred sons of bitches?"

Westlake nodded.

"Must be a pretty big friggin' club," Mick muttered.

"You have no idea," Westlake said more to himself than to Mick.

"Okay, so now you know what I know about the Frosts. Now it's your turn. What do you know about them? And outside of maybe being a guy with a sensitive nose who doesn't like the stink that rubs off on everything they touch, why do you care?"

Westlake glanced around the room as if to make sure that no one was watching. He motioned Mick and Bridget to lean towards him. As Mick did, he also noticed that Bridget seemed to be trying to hold herself back. She either looked away or down at the table, but her eyes and face kept being drawn back to Westlake as if against her will, until her face, deathly white with one bright red spot on each cheek, appeared like a burning coal in the dimly lit bar.

Westlake studied them. The smile was gone, along with the easy good humor. In a flat voice that seemed to mask some underlying deeper emotion, he said, "The Frosts are dirty. Not just the chief and his idiot nephew, but the older brother, the selectman. The cousin, the building inspector who shakes down contractors. The aunt, the town clerk who charges illegal fees and forces people to have a license for everything but breathing. And the tax assessor, who can keep upping the valuation on your property until there's no way you can pay it. Then the town slaps a lien on the property and sells it at a forced auction, where the highest bidder—and often the only bidder—is the old man himself, Samuel Frost."

"Sounds like you've been doing your homework," Mick said quietly.

Westlake nodded and said, "And this is the part that I'm guessing at, but I think it's a damned good guess. Kathy Dawes told you the story of how the Frosts had been trying to get Skaket Creek back for the past one-hundred-and-ten years. And by running the taxes up on the inn, they're pretty close to succeeding. They want Skaket Creek for what they think Kathy's ancestors buried under the house all those years ago. And if they can't get it through taxes and intimidation, then they'll do it by hassling their friends and guests—like you, Mick—and intimidating everyone or driving them away until the inn is bankrupt. Or, if all else fails, by eliminating the last of the Dawes."

Bridget finally lifted her head and whispered, "Kathy."

Westlake nodded. "Yes."

* * * *

The Skaket Creek Inn
Skaket Creek
Cape Cod, Massachusetts
August 20th, 1968
8:25 p.m.

Kathy Dawes awoke with a start. She didn't know what had awakened her. She started to get up and then saw the familiar and pathetically shrunken form of her mother lying in her bed next to the worn settee that Kathy had fallen asleep on. She turned away from her mother who dozed fitfully, her matchstick-thin arms resting palms up on her slowly rising and falling chest, as though she was making one last futile stand towards holding off the evil that was, with increasing ferocity, consuming the house and the last of the Dawes matriarchs from the inside out.

Kathy knelt next to her mother's bed. "Mom? Can you hear me? Mom?"

No response.

"Mom, hear me. Please, you must. Let it go; it's killing you!"

No response.

"Pass it to me. Now. This very minute. You must. I can do it, Mom. I'm strong enough. Please, you must...let me!"

Her eyelids fluttered open. Her mother turned her thin, pinched face to her only child and with a tiny but loving smile shook her head. She began to speak, and Kathy leaned forward to hear her mother's soft but unmistakable words.

"No, Kathy. It's not time. Not yet."

* * * *

The Crown & Anchor pub
Nantucket Town
August 20th, 1968
8:37 p.m.

Mick still wasn't buying it—at least not the whole scene. But apparently Bridget was. She was sure hanging on to Westlake's every word. And Mick had to admit that what he was saying sure as hell should be sounding good to a couple who had just about run out of options.

"Look," Westlake said, spreading his hands palms up on the table. "You need help, right?"

Mick looked at Bridget. She solemnly nodded, so he gave a shrug but slowly inclined his head forward towards Westlake.

"Okay then, I'd like to provide that help."

"Why?"

"Let's just say I've got my reasons, Mick."

"Uh, ah, not good enough. We may need help, but were not desperate."

Well actually we are, but a little false bravado won't hurt right about now either.

It was Westlake's turn to shrug. "Fair enough. Could we just let it go, that it's part of something I'm working on, part of my job?"

"No."

Westlake turned to Bridget with a slight smile. "Is that your answer too? Couldn't you accept a little help from someone who'd like to be your friend?"

Mick stared hard. First at Westlake as he gently added, "If you'd let him."

And then back at Bridget who murmured without looking up, "I... it's up to Mick. Whatever he thinks is best."

Wh-a-a-a-at? Where was this coming from? This wasn't his

Bridget!

"Bridge? Hey, like, what gives? Where's that Connolly two cents worth of advice that usually adds up to ten or twenty bucks worth PDQ?"

She shrugged.

"Hey, babe, look at me."

Normally, a command like that would have earned Mick a sharp look and even sharper retort, but now? Now she didn't even want to look him in the eyes. He shifted his gaze to Westlake, who had molded his face into the image of a blond, Caucasian Buddha.

Mick blew out an exasperated sigh. "Bridge, I'm asking you. What do you think?" He wasn't sure why he was pushing this onto her, but he desperately needed to do something to snap her out of her strange behavior.

"Bridge...?" he said softly, tilting her face up with his forefinger.

"Yes," she said with an undertone of reluctance.

"Yes?"

"Yes we should...we've got to do as he says."

"Come again?" Mick's stare got harder.

"I-I mean, we should...we must. I have to.... No, no, I mean, we ought to take his very kind offer to...to.... Oh, bloody hell, McCarthy! I don't know what I mean! You've got me twisted all around every which way!" Her cheeks burning and voice cracking, she turned her head away from Mick and focused on the growing darkness beyond the window.

Mick shook his head. Something wasn't right. But then again, talk about being all out of options. He turned to Westlake and said, "Okay, Mr. DA, so we all agree that the Frosts are a pack of belly-crawling slimeballs. And you'd like to put 'em away, and I'd be even happier if you could arrange to do it before they throw my ass in jail. Which, according to trusty old Mr. Timex, is gonna be in about forty-eight hours from now."

Mick placed both of his hands flat on the tabletop and leaned forward.

"So what's your plan?"

Chapter Thirty-Eight

Nantucket Docks
October 16th, 1858
2:16 p.m.

Jeptha's muscles swelled and bunched as he strained against the knots holding the seawater-soaked ropes tightly around his wrists. It was no use. Men who'd spent a lifetime tying sheepshanks and bowlines in force five gales were not about to leave a knot loose.

Zeke Tanner had bested him again.

The scrawny, unkempt whaler's mate seemed to know what Jeptha was thinking, and he grinned and lifted the pewter mug of rum in his direction.

After all these days of shadowing him. He'd had him too. He'd tracked the vermin to his hole. He'd pursued Tanner from the boarding house to this dockside warehouse. But as he'd been following Tanner, it was now sadly evident that others had likewise been following him.

Tanner laughed and raised his mug in Jeptha's direction again. "Don't fash yerself so, Mr. Dawes, it will do you no good. Best be using what time ye've got left to makin' yer peace with yer god."

"He is your god too, Mr. Tanner," Jeptha said evenly. "And before long you shall stand before his throne and be forced to hear, catalogued, a litany of your black deeds of which I suspect this is just another. I will pray for your soul against that terrible day."

Zeke Tanner jumped up and ran over to him, hopping like an evil little gnome. "Pray? Pray for me, you mealy-mouthed son of a bitch? You better start prayin' fer yer own self!"

He stopped and waggled a dirty, broken-nailed finger under Jeptha's nose. He looked at him with the kind of smile that children get when pulling the wings off of flies. "In less than one hour's time these here two shipmates o' mine...." He pointed to the two expressionless seamen who sat playing dice on a scarred old table at the other end of the warehouse, and his grin got wider. "Well, when I gives 'em the signal, they're gonna dump you in the longboat waiting under this here pier and row you out beyond the jetty and cut ya up fer fish bait. So whadda think of that, Mr. Christian Prayin' Man! As soon as I snaps my fingers like this—"

"If there are any fingers to be snapped, Tanner, it is I who will be doing the snapping here."

Zeke Tanner looked up at the pudgy figure that had just entered the warehouse. He stared at the scowling, red-faced young man hurrying towards him and murmured, "You? Yer father more likely."

"What was that, Tanner?" A soft, fleshy hand grabbed Tanner's filthy wrist. Tanner shook it off and turned away angrily.

"Did you bring it, Tanner? Do you have it with you?"

Zeke Tanner didn't answer his question but asked instead, "Did you bring your end? My money? And it better be in gold too!"

The portly young man nodded and held out a heavy leather purse. Tanner reached for it, but the soft hand drew back like a white-fingered sea anemone.

"Let me see it first."

Tanner scowled and shrugged. "Aye, fair certain it's a valluble object, it is. And it be mighty pretty carved too." Tanner's features twitched as cunning caution warred with greed. "You're damned lucky that I'm such a soft touch and lettin' it go at a bargain price."

The fat young man yanked the collar of his greatcoat away from his face as he stared at the ivory-white object that dangled on a greasy black piece of rawhide from Tanner's outstretched hand. He bent forward to look at the intricate carvings etched into the five-inch tooth of a great sperm whale.

Tanner grinned and moved his hand back. He chuckled. "All the tales I heard o' this here gimcrack, seems they was like to be true after all. Most of 'em I thought was just drunk Injun talk, but if just half of 'em is true...." He smiled and closed his fist around the whale tooth. "Ya know, mebee I'm lettin' this go too quick. Why, young Mr. Dawes there was willin' to pay me three-hundred gold fer it." He sneered at Jeptha. "That was before I decided I'd rather have it all."

The heavy younger man's face reddened. "Do not think to cheat me because of my youth. You know my father and in whose warehouse you stand. My men," he nodded to the two seamen, "can filet two carcasses just as easily as one." He paused and slowly smiled. "In fact, yes, I think that perhaps that would please my father greatly—to bring him the scrimshaw and the purse."

He turned. "Caleb, Abner, bring them both to the boat."

"You lyin', cheatin' little pissant," Tanner snarled, pulling his sheath knife.

"Cut both of their throats," the young man said.

One sailor got up and strode over to Jeptha, pressing his clasp knife into his throat, while the other circled Zeke Tanner looking for an opening through Zeke's quick jabs with his sheath knife and the chance to bury the blade in the little man's stomach.

Suddenly, a clatter at the front of the warehouse and the sound of heavy doors being opened broke the tension.

The young man's face turned panicky, and he shouted, "That will be my father. He cannot abide unfinished business. Kill them both. Now!"

Ric Wasley

* * * *

Nantucket Island
Tempest
October 16th, 1858
5:21 p.m.

Simon Westlake entered the small informal parlor on the second floor where Fiona was reading and smiled at her. "Good afternoon, Mrs. Dawes. I hope you are finding Tempest comfortable, and please accept my deepest apologies for not being able to join you at luncheon today, but I had some rather urgent business to attend to in the town."

Fiona looked up from the very disturbing book that she was struggling to get through. She closed it with a secretly relieved snap and placed it on the small round pedestal table next to her chair.

Simon walked over and picked up the book. "So you've decided to brave Mrs. Shelley's frightening tale of a new Prometheus?"

Fiona shook her head. "I'm not sure which I find more unsettling, the monster, or that horrible Dr. Frankenstein who thinks to usurp the power of creation. The powers, Mr. Westlake, reserved for the Lord."

Simon's smile became a touch more sardonic. "Sometimes, Mrs. Dawes, the line between those powers becomes more blurred than we poor mortals care to admit."

Fiona's lips pressed together firmly. "Nothing is blurred, Mr. Westlake, if you put your faith in God."

Simon Westlake laughed and bowed. "I shall look forward to your continued instruction on this matter at dinner this evening."

"Dinner? Oh no, Mr. Westlake, I must be getting back to my search for my husband. And if you had but let me know of your intention to travel into town this afternoon, I would have happily accompanied you to resume my quest."

"But, Mrs. Dawes, dear friend Fiona, I—"

"Please do not misunderstand, Mr. Westlake. You have been the very soul of kindness and consideration, and I am most deeply grateful. But now I really must be on my way."

She started to get up from the chair, but Simon held up a hand and said, "Wait. I don't suppose that I could tempt you to stay for dinner if I told you that I was having a very special dinner treat brought all the way from Nantucket town, could I?"

"Oh, Mr. Westlake—Simon—I will never be able to repay you for all of your assistance and kindness, but I shall never forget them."

"And I hope that you may sometimes think upon me as a friend?"

"I-I, why yes, of course I will." *Why did I stumble so on that simple*

217

request?

"Then that is payment enough for me, dear Friend Fiona."

Fiona smiled and rose to her feet. "And could I impose upon your friendship one last time and beg a ride from your coach back to Nantucket town?"

Simon put his hand on the doorknob but paused. "And you're quite sure that I can't persuade you to stay for my surprise dinner treat?"

"No, no, I'm sorry. I cannot. I must resume my search."

She shifted her shoulders back so that she could slide through the parlor door without brushing against him.

He inclined his head towards her and stepped back, calling down the stairs after her, "Then if you won't stay for the dinner surprise, I will just have to bring the surprise to you."

As she drew parallel to the massive sliding oak doors that led to the formal dining room, Simon called, "Enoch!" to his manservant who pushed the heavy oak-and-brass studded panels back while making a forward gesture with his hand. A figure stepped through the gilt-framed archway and into the hall.

Fiona stared in disbelief and confusion until her mind finally realized what she was seeing.

"Jeptha!"

She threw herself into his arms.

Chapter Thirty-Nine

Nantucket Island
Cliff Line Road
August 20ᵗʰ, 1968
8:48 p.m.

"So, like, thanks again, man, for letting us crash at your place tonight." Mick felt he had to say it but he wasn't sure yet whether or not he meant it.

"Yes, ah...Mr. Westlake," Bridget stammered.

"It's E.F., ah, Miss Connolly."

Bridget giggled like a high-school girl while Mick did a slow burn in the back seat of Westlake's small but expensive BMW sports car.

When Westlake had made the offer to put them up, what could he do? They didn't even have enough money for the cheapest rooming house on the island. Then it started to rain, so naturally Westlake had said, "We'll take my BMW, and Mick, you can leave the bike parked here in the Crown & Anchor parking lot overnight. Don't worry; I'll fix it up with the owner."

Westlake had stepped inside and was back out less than two minutes later. By this time the rain had become steadier and heavier, so he had pulled the BMW up to the restaurant front entrance and then of course he had jumped out and opened the passenger door for Bridget, which left Mick sitting alone in the sports car's tiny back seat. And as if to pile on more insult to injury, every time that they hit a bump on the road that seemed like nothing *but* bumps to Mick watching from the back seat, Bridget practically slid right into Westlake's lap.

So Mick was getting pissed. Damn pissed, and getting more so by the minute. Worst of all, if he really wanted to be honest with himself—which he really didn't—he was also damn freaking jealous. And what happened next seemed as though it was custom made to drive the last spike into his rapidly deflating ego.

The BMW turned down a long, hedge-lined driveway, and Bridget gasped at the enormous structure that filled their entire field of vision: four stories of gray weathered clapboards, fronted by a white-pillared porch. And the whole mansion was topped off by a towering black iron weather vane spinning madly in the wind gusts that drove rain through the railings of a twenty-foot square widow's walk.

Bridget looked up through the rainswept windshield and sighed. "It's magnificent."

The youngest county DA in the Commonwealth of Massachusetts smiled at Bridget and said, "Welcome to Tempest."

The Scrimshaw

* * * *

Tempest
October 16th, 1858
5:33 p.m.

Fiona couldn't stop weeping. Jeptha held her and still she couldn't stop clutching onto the rough cloth of his coat like a drowning sailor to a spar. He was her spar she realized, the life buoy that she clung to, her own safe harbor. She hadn't realized until that moment that she had built an entire new life around this strong, quiet man. She had learned to stand on her own since childhood but now for the first time she felt there was someone who needed her and who she needed—so much. And she would never let him leave her again. Never!

She turned back to Simon. "How did you find him, and where?"

He smiled. "I find it prudent with my business interests to keep a number of locals on a small stipend in return for reporting to me any and all *interesting* activities that they see. And in this instance, this small pittance paid a handsome dividend. It allowed me to deliver, unscathed, the steadfast husband of a dear friend." He bowed slightly to Jeptha and Fiona.

"But how, Mr. Westlake, did you win through to aid my husband?"

"With the aid, Mrs. Dawes, of these." He drew two, heavy Navy Colt cap and ball, six-cylinder revolvers from under his coat. "The ruffians who sought to end your brave husband's life had knives, but a half-dozen rounds from these sent them packing. My only regret was that in my haste to assure myself that Mr. Dawes was unharmed, I missed the opportunity to capture, red-handed, the cowardly swine who had hired that scum. The Frosts."

Fiona gasped and turned to Jeptha. "Why, Husband, do they ply us with gifts one moment and then seek to do you murder the next?"

Jeptha started to speak but then shook his head and smiled. "Later, my heart, when we have dined and feel rested."

Simon turned towards Fiona and made another slight bow. "So that, my dear Mrs. Dawes, was the business in town that I spoke of that kept me from being a proper host at a luncheon this afternoon. However, I hope to make up for it with a fine dinner in which I likewise hope you will both join me?"

"We could do nothing less, sir," Jeptha said solemnly. "We are forever in your debt."

"Oh, yes, Mr. Westlake!" Fiona cried, whirling around. "May the Lord bless you, sir." She grabbed his hand in both of hers and said again, "Bless you, Mr. Westlake."

He smiled. "Simon."

She stood on tiptoes and kissed him on the cheek laughing, "Simon."

Just then, Mrs. Samuels came into the dining room and said, "Dinner, sir."

Fiona and Jeptha turned to follow the housekeeper, but as they passed through the wide double doors Fiona caught Simon's reflection in the gilt-edged mirror over the fireplace. Simon touched his cheek where she had kissed it.

Oh, how sweet! What a dear friend he has proven himself to be.

She moved towards the chair that her husband was pulling out from the table for her. And as she turned to sit down at the massive, polished mahogany table, she caught one brief glimpse of the small, strange smile that flitted around the corner of Simon's mouth.

* * * *

Tempest
August 20ᵗʰ, 1968
9:18 p.m.

"So what do you guys think of the old pile, the Westlake Island retreat for the past hundred-and-twenty years?"

"It's just beautiful," Bridget breathed. She swiveled her head trying to take everything in. "Isn't it beautiful, Mickey?" she said without turning to look at him.

"Yeah, bitchin'," Mick mumbled. But neither Bridget nor E.F. seemed to notice.

"It's lovely to see that you value old houses and keep them so perfect like this. Sometimes I think that everything in America was just finished yesterday."

Westlake laughed. "Well this one was actually built by my great, great grandfather, Simon Westlake. He made a fortune in the China and South Sea trade: tea, copra, silk, and jewels. And it's a family legend that he had a special fondness for exotic and unusual items. He had his ships bring him back trinkets and oddities from every port they touched."

He pointed to a mahogany door just off the main hallway. "Come in here for a minute. I think I've got something that's going to interest you."

"Like what?" Mick said glumly, "a nice big hole for me to hide in for the next fifty years?"

Westlake smiled and pulled the polished wooden doors open.

The Scrimshaw

"Hopefully something a whole lot better."

"Like what?"

"Like perhaps something that can help to prove your innocence."

Bridget stopped in the doorway. "Oh, Mr.—I mean, E.F., if you only could!"

"There's another thing," Mick growled, hating himself for sounding like some pouty, jealous high-school boy jerk. But that's about how he felt, so he snapped out, "What's with the E.F. scene? I mean, it sounds like you're playing some old tycoon on television. You know, the fat old dude chomping on a big black cigar. The guy who all of his uptight little yes men call J.P. or J.B. or...E.F."

"Mickey!"

Mick felt an unaccustomed flush spread across his cheeks as Bridget spun around, put her hands on her hips, and looked at him like he was something that had slithered into the room underneath the door.

"That is the rudest, nastiest, most ungrateful thing that I've ever heard you say. No, come to think of it, that's the rudest, most ungrateful thing that I've ever heard *anyone* say. Especially to a man who has not only saved our lives but is trying to help us now!" She shook her head and asked in bewilderment, "What is wrong with you?"

Mick couldn't meet her eyes. He knew what was wrong with him and he couldn't stand it. He was freaking, crybaby jealous.

He wanted to scream, "Yeah, I'm jealous! I'm jealous that Mr. E.F. Westlake here is tall, good looking, rich, successful, witty, charming, cool, brave, competent, smart and...jeez...have I left anything out? Oh yeah, and he's got you completely snowed!" But he didn't. His old man, Big Mike, had always told him, 'When you screw up and act like a jerk, kid, don't make it worse with excuses. Own up to it like a man.' So Mick took a deep breath, tried not to grit his teeth, and turned to Westlake. He held his hand out and said, "I wouldn't blame you if you told me to go screw myself, and it's probably just about what I deserve. But before you do, let me at least try to pry my big feet out of my mouth and say, hey, man, I'm sorry that I acted like a real jerk."

Westlake looked at him with amusement and said, "As a matter of fact, I'll second that—you did."

Mick's gut tightened, but he forced his expression to stay neutral and his hand to stay outstretched and steady. The seconds ticked by. Mick heard the echo of Big Mike again, 'Like a man, kid, like a man.' His hand stayed steady.

Westlake's amused smile broke into a grin. "Hey, Mick, don't sweat it. I've been there, done that myself." He shook Mick's hand with a firm, dry grip.

Mick swallowed hard and said, "Thanks...E.F."

Westlake laughed. "Yeah, I guess the whole initial thing can get a bit

222

much sometimes."

Mick let out his pent-up breath with a whoosh. "So if you don't mind my asking, is E.F. some sort of a nickname that you picked up at college or something?"

Westlake shook his head. "No, it's actually that I've got a couple of goofy family names that sound so clunky and old fashioned that I couldn't stand using them, so I just took the initials. But I understand that the initial thing can sound pretty pretentious, so a lot of my friends just call me Ed."

Mick smiled. "Yeah, Ed. Okay, I can dig that." He reached out and shook Westlake's hand again. "Nice to meet you, Ed. How's it going, man?"

"Just fine, Mick. Just fine."

Bridget beamed like a mother whose two squabbling children had just reconciled. "Well then, all's well. So, Ed, do you mind if I call you Edward? You do remind me of an Edward that I knew in Ireland. And he was quite a nice lad as I recall." She smiled again and leaned back, lightly resting her shoulders on the carved paneling of the hallway. "Well, be that as it may, I believe that you said you had something to show us?"

"Of course." He motioned them into a large study, crossed over to the huge walnut desk sitting in front of a floor-to-ceiling window, and pulled open the top right hand drawer. He took out a thick book bound with deep, blood-red burgundy Moroccan leather. It was fastened by a clasp with a brass lock. E.F. took a key out of the drawer and opened it.

"I found this last summer when I finally decided to clean out this old desk." He turned to them and held the book up. "It's the diary of my great, great grandfather, Simon Westlake." He handed the book to Bridget. She turned it over in her hands tentatively.

"Open it, Bridget, to the page marked with a black ribbon."

Bridget turned to the page. He leaned down and pointed halfway down the page. "Yes, right about...there. Okay, start reading."

Bridget blinked but began to read in a perfectly modulated, well-bred "Cliffy" prep school voice.

"*Tempest House. October 20th, 1858.*

"*I have, this day, performed a deed that should make the angels sing my praises. Or barring that, at least confound those more nefarious creatures that seem to beckon from below. I have saved the no doubt good-hearted and honest Christian who is the husband of one of the most attractive little stunners that I have run across in all of my jaded, if not unusual, life. What a woman like that could ever see in such a dull, plodding, milk-and-water fellow escapes me, but then again, most things connected with the middle class morals and respectability do.*

"Ah well, no matter. If by accomplishment of this deed I have won the admiration of the fair Fiona, then it is recompense enough. And, of course, there is that small service that they, especially she, can render me, which I am sure they will be fawningly glad to perform.

"Yes, the heroic rescue of Mr. Jeptha Dawes was not a solely altruistic act.

"Jeptha Dawes?" Bridget said, looking up from the page. "Why, that's the man who built the Skaket Creek Inn. The ancestor of—"

"Kathy Dawes," Mick said quietly.

Westlake nodded and said, "Keep reading."

Bridget did.

"Truth be told, the entire affair concluded well in all aspects for my interests.

"The dutiful Dawes is saved for the glittering little diamond peeking out from its rough setting, that is, Fiona. A dull, drab setting that only wants a good polishing to make the little jewel realize how enticing that setting could actually be.

"But more importantly at present, I have beaten and confounded the grasping, worm-like pestilence known as the Frosts."

Mick and Bridget looked at one another and said in unison, "Frosts!"

E.F. Westlake nodded. "That's what I was talking about. Keep going, Bridget."

"They thought, of course, in their own beef-wit arrogance, that they, by this one typically ham-fisted act, would be able to possess both Skaket Creek and the item which can call only be destined for me.

"But in this they were thwarted by myself, my man Enoch, and two of Mr. Colt's remarkable repeating revolvers. Though the Frosts, both father and son, in a typically cowardly fashion, sacrificed their hired cutthroats to save their own sorry skins, they left behind the odious Zeke Tanner and the object that he had stolen. The object of which the Frosts have only the barest inkling of its true value. The object that the stiffening corpse of Tanner still bears. But with the aid of the lovely Fiona, Tanner's corpse will only bear it until tomorrow."

Bridget put the book down. "The entry ends there."

E.F. nodded.

"What does it all mean?" Bridget asked. "The Frosts, the strange house on Skaket Creek, and Kathy Dawes? And what about the 'object' that your ancestor keeps referring to. Was it...?"

E.F. shrugged. "I don't know if it was *the* scrimshaw, but it sure as hell was *a* scrimshaw."

"Edward?" Bridget asked hesitantly, as if still shy about using his name.

E.F. smiled, put his hands in his pockets, and leaned back against the desk. He inclined his head towards Bridget. "You have the floor, Bridget."

She began to pace.

"If we assume that Zeke Tanner still had the scrimshaw when he was buried, then how did your great, great grandfather get his hands on it?"

"What makes you think he did?" Westlake asked quietly.

"Well, first of all, the diary. It talks about the object on Tanner's corpse."

"Yeah," Mick broke in. "Yeah, and just how did this Zeke Tanner guy all of a sudden graduate to corpse status?"

Bridget nodded. "And in the diary Simon makes mention that somehow he's going to get Fiona Dawes to help him. To do what? And why?"

She stopped pacing and looked at Westlake. "And for that matter, how was he able to get the town to allow him to dig up Zeke Tanner's grave? Wouldn't that be a tip-off to everyone that Tanner must have had something of great value?" She smiled wryly. "And if you don't mind me sayin' so, Mr. Wes—ah, Edward—yer ancestor does not strike me as a man who tolerated any prying into his personal business."

"You're right." He nodded. "And that's why he found it very convenient to be a very rich man in a very frugal island town. When he learned that Tanner had no next of kin, he made an offer to the town to bury him in the graveyard on the estate. And as that would save the town the cost of a coffin and a headboard, they agreed to his request and weren't too interested in asking what was behind his generous offer." He winked. "Especially when he suggested that the town keep the pouch of gold eagles for 'civic improvement'."

"In other words, he liked his privacy and was willing to pay for it," Bridget added.

"Right again," he said. "Simon Westlake was a man of many secrets, and you're right, he kept them close. Very, very close."

"Which means that unless you've got the freakin' little do-dad tucked away in that desk, we've got squat," Mick said glumly. He flopped onto a leather chair and draped one leg over the chair's armrest.

"And we're running out of time," Bridget whispered.

Westlake pushed himself off of the side of the desk and turned to her. "Maybe not," he said.

He moved to the far wall of the library and drew back a set of floor-to-ceiling drapes, revealing a pair of double French doors. Westlake made a beckoning motion to Mick and Bridget as he uncovered a long, antique, brass telescope mounted on a tripod of polished rosewood. He peered through the telescope and made a few minor adjustments before stepping back and motioning Bridget forward. He reached down and moved a two-foot step stool up to the telescope and said, "Come here, Bridget. Take a look."

She mounted the two steps and peeked through the eyepiece at the storm-wracked sea. "I can't see a bloody thing," she muttered. "It's black as the Hades pit itself out there."

"Just wait."

"Wait for what?"

"For the big flash of.... There!"

There was a tremendous crack followed by a roll of thunder, and the sky, sea, and the rain-swept lawn of Tempest illuminated as though under a strobe light at a rock concert.

"I still don't see any...." Bridget gasped. The light faded, and she looked up from the eyepiece. "What is it that thing out there? It was so strange it looked like a—"

"One more time," Westlake said, softly putting his hand on her shoulder until his cheek was next to her own.

The suave movement wasn't lost on Mick.

"Temper, boyo," he whispered to himself. "No sense in being a jerk twice in the same hour." But his right hand curled in an unconscious clinch. He watched helplessly as Bridget and Westlake stood cheek to cheek in front of the telescope's eyepiece.

"Okay, Bridget. I see a line of lightning flashes moving in from the west." Another jagged flash crashed closer, and Bridget gave an involuntary start.

Westlake squeezed her hand. "Okay, steady now. It's coming, just another moment or two." Unconsciously, she squeezed his hand back.

"Hold it...hold it, and.... Now!"

A deafening crash rattled the French doors, and the world turned into a black-and-white negative.

"There," E.F. shouted over the roar. "Do you see it?"

"Yes! Yes, I do. Clear as day. My God, it's the bones and the jawbone of some gigantic whale!"

* * * *

Tempest
August 20th, 1968
10:43 p.m.

They all sat in the cavernous living room. E.F. had made a fire in the enormous marble fireplace that looked like it could accommodate a Christmas yule log and a couple of roast pigs with room left over to toss in a few of the local peasants if they started to get as unruly as Mick felt.

Bridget sat curled up on a velvet settee that E.F. had gallantly pulled up to the fireplace to offer her maximum warmth. And then, to no doubt balance the small couch that conveniently only sat two—and obviously in case the couch with only Bridget on it suddenly decided to roll into the fireplace—he magnanimously sat down next to her. Quite close actually, Mick tried to observe impartially. Probably just being a good host, supplying some extra body warmth. Right.

The can of Narragansett Ale in Mick's hand gave off a crinkling sound as he spasmodically clenched his fingers, crushing the hapless can as if it were some scrawny tin neck—some scrawny, rich, charming, and handsome neck.

"Mick," E.F. called with easy good humor, as if he knew what ran through Mick's mind. "Hey, pull that chair up here by the fire."

"Nah, thanks anyway," Mick said, trying not to grit his teeth. "I think I'm probably just about as, ah, hot as I wanna get tonight."

"Edward?"

Westlake looked at Bridget.

"Miss Connolly?" He smiled.

Bridget put the book down. "The entry ends here."

E.F. nodded.

"But what does it all mean? I'm so confused. It seems so convoluted and obscure. Wheels within wheels as my freshman philosophy professor liked to say."

She let the book rest in her lap and said again as much to herself as to Westlake, "What does it mean? How do they all fit together? The Frosts, your great, great grandfather, Jeptha and Fiona Dawes, Kathy Dawes, the strange house on Skaket Creek, and the strangest thing of all, the scrimshaw?"

"I'll tell you how they all fit together," Mick snapped from his solitary chair. "They're all giving me a pain in the butt!" He motioned impatiently with his hand towards the wide staircase leading to the upper floors. "Come on, babe, let's hit the rack. I'm wiped out."

Bridget shook her head. "Not yet, Mickey. You go if you're done in, luv. I'd...I'd like to hear whatever Simon can tell us about the—"

"Who?" Mick broke in, sitting bolt upright.

227

"What? Oh...what did I say? Simon? Now why on earth did I say that name? I-I meant Edward, of course."

E.F. Westlake covered whatever expression he might have had by taking a long swallow of his coffee.

Mick concentrated on controlling his ragged, hyperventilating breathing by saying over and over to himself, "Cool it, cool it, cool it," like some sort of jealous lover's self-help mantra.

Finally E.F. put the coffee cup down and said, "Perhaps it's time to tell you about the legend of the scrimshaw."

* * * *

The Skaket Creek Inn
August 20ᵗʰ, 1968
10:47 p.m.

Helen Dawes paused with her hand on the doorknob and then turned it slowly. She winced and abruptly stopped when the loose screw holding the knob onto the shaft slipped a quarter turn and screeched against the spindle.

She shook her head at her over cautious timidity muttering, "Who's going to hear me anyway? My dear niece is wandering up and down the beach in a blue funk, and my saintly sister-in-law is probably past hearing anything."

With another snort, she wrenched the doorknob all the way to the right and pushed the door open. She stopped. Polly Dawes sat upright in her bed. Fully awake, fully conscious, and staring right at Helen.

"Come in, Helen."

Helen Dawes remained frozen to the spot.

"Please." She smiled, a faint ghost of her former smile. "Come in and close the door. I know you wouldn't want me to catch my death... of cold."

Helen Dawes advanced warily into the room.

"Sit," Polly said. "Have you come to comfort a sick relative?"

Helen tried to control the gleam in her eyes at the mention of the word sick.

"Or do you have some more...urgent business on your mind?"

"No...well, that is, I mean...yes. I did want to see how you were feeling." She tried unsuccessfully to sweeten her tone.

"Did you?" Polly answered with an amused smile.

Helen Dawes felt a flush burn her cheeks.

"Well then, Helen, thank you so much for your *thoughtful* visit, and now having had my spirits once again buoyed up with the loving best wishes of a devoted sister-in-law, I will, I believe, go back to sleep."

Helen Dawes rose but quickly sat back down. "No. I'm not leaving just yet. At least not until you tell me—"

"Tell you what, Helen?"

"Tell me what's to become of this inn and the property. And...and what's going to become of...me once you're gone!" She clenched her hands into fists.

"Heavens!" Polly said with an underlying hint of mockery. "Do I really look that bad? I guess Kathy is right. I should start wearing makeup again."

"You can smart mouth all you want, *Polly-Anna.*" Helen's voice dripped acid as she sneered out the derogatory nickname she'd devised years before to try to annoy her sweet-tempered sister-in-law. "But we both know what's coming and we both know it's coming sooner rather than later."

Polly Dawes looked at her with the same sad smile. "Ah, then I may assume that the *friendly* portion of the visit is over."

Helen Dawes looked at her contemptuously. "There was never much love lost between you and me so I guess there's no point in pretending anymore."

"No, Helen, there never really was."

"Stop! No more of your mealy-mouthed platitudes. I just want the straight answer to one question. What do I get?"

"I believe that you already know the answer to that question, don't you?"

"Yes! I've seen the will, and the answer is...nothing! I get nothing, you bitch!"

"Really? You've seen the will? How?"

"In the lawyer's office."

"You mean Chandler and Kramer?"

"Kramer's dead, and Chandler is nine-tenths senile. And if you paid attention to anything outside of your plants and *potions*, you'd know that last month your dear old demented family lawyer sold his business."

"Ah, and let me guess who bought it. Could it perhaps be the...?"

Helen Dawes, who had been born Helen Shirley Frost, gave a triumphant sneer and spat out, "Yes, my cousin Tommy, attorney Thomas P. Frost!"

"My, how industrious you've been, Helen. So then, if you've seen the will and have the answer to your question, what are you doing here?" She looked at her. "Were you thinking of perhaps of trying to speed up my departure from this world? No, that would make no sense. It wouldn't get you anything more than what you have right now—nothing."

"Yes," she hissed. "Nothing! Unless...."

Polly Dawes paled. "Unless...? No, not even you would be that awful!"

"Don't bet on that, Polly. Especially don't bet *her* life on it."

"You nasty, pathetic...."

"Enough! All you need to do is to decide how long do you want your daughter to survive your very imminent passing?"

"Spit your dried up, spiteful venom at me, Helen, but don't you ever, ever threaten my daughter!" The soft voice had become laced with steel, and the previously sad, gentle eyes hardened.

"Or what?"

"You know what I can do, Helen."

"Pah, your mind-game tricks and voodoo mumbo jumbo don't scare me."

"Well they should, Helen," Polly Dawes said softly. "And if you ever try to harm my child they will do more than scare."

Helen Dawes looked at her uncertainly for a moment and then snapped out, "Shut your mouth! I'm not listening to your nonsense anymore, do you hear me?" She lashed out, and her right hand connected with Polly's cheek. It left a red palm print on the death-white skin.

But Polly Dawes didn't make a sound or even touch her cheek. She locked her eyes with Helen's—and she didn't let go.

Helen turned away. That is, she tried to turn away. She gave the command to her feet to move, but they wouldn't obey. She tried to turn her head, but once again her muscles failed to respond.

"Stop it!" she screamed, but only in her mind. In the real world, no sound came out.

The walls started to waver and drip blood. The floorboards wiggled and squirmed. She looked down. Dark brown rats covered her shoes. "They aren't real," she kept muttering to herself. "They're only in my imagination!" And then the imaginary rats took small but very painful bites out of her flesh.

A scream convulsed through her throat and bounced off the blood-dripping walls.

"Please! Let. Me. Go!"

The terrifying eyes of the woman whom Helen would never again mock as Polly-Anna held her with eyes that seemed to pry open her skull and she said, "Remember, Helen, you will never threaten my child again."

Helen Dawes sobbed out a tortured, "Yes-s-s!"

Polly Dawes closed her eyes and lay back on the pillow as her sister-in-law stumbled sobbing, out through the bedroom door.

Tempest
August 20ᵗʰ, 1968
10:48 p.m.

E.F. Westlake threw a log on to the fire and sat back down on the settee next to Bridget.

Bridget took a sip of her cocoa and then curled her feet, cat-like, underneath her. "All right then, Edward you were gonna tell us about that scrimshaw legend."

"Yeah," Mick said, taking a long pull from his Narragansett Ale, "lay it on us."

"Well, here's what I've pieced together from family legend and old diaries.

"In April of 1858, one of the ships in which my great, great grandfather had a half interest, dropped anchor just outside of Nantucket harbor. Her name was the *Elizabeth James* and she had just returned from two years in the South Seas loaded down with tea, copra, spices, jewels, and the one thing that my great, great grandfather prized above all else—a unique curio."

"Curio?" Bridget wrinkled her nose.

E.F. nodded. "My ancestor was a passionate collector of all things to do with legend and the occult."

"Oh, brother!" Mick said. He rolled his eyes and helped himself to another ale.

"Hush up, Mickey," Bridget snapped. "I'm trying to pay attention. Sorry, Edward, do go on."

E.F. gave Mick a quizzical look but was met with only stony silence so he shrugged and continued, "It seems as though while stopped at some island in Micronesia, one of the crew's harpooners, a Nipmuck Indian by the name of John Twin-Hawks, did a great service for two dying children of the island's king. The king, as it was told, offered this harpooner his choice of anything on the island. And of everything he could have chosen, gold, jewels, all he took was a—"

"Scrimshaw," Mick broke in.

"Yes, so you know this?"

Mick shook his head. "Not enough. Keep going."

Westlake raised his eyebrows but nodded and continued.

"Well, according to the legend, the chief told John Twin-Hawks that the tooth came from a giant sperm whale. It seems that years before there had been terrible storms and the men couldn't fish so they were all starving. One day, after a particularly bad storm, they had come down to the beach and found an enormous white sperm whale washed up on the shore. The village shaman said that the whale had deliberately beached himself in the night so that his body would feed the village and save their lives. The whale only asked that they would remove a tooth from him and carve it with a series of images that he had given the shaman in a dream. So the people consumed the whale, and the shaman removed and carved the tooth in exactly the way the whale had told him in the dream, and from then on the village thrived and prospered. That is, right up until one month before the *Elizabeth James* had landed. The village had been visited by a Dutch East Indiaman, and two weeks after the ship sailed, the entire tribe was stricken with smallpox.

"John Twin-Hawks tried to give back the scrimshaw, but the old chief would have none of it. He said that John had brought peace for his children and thus had earned it. And before he died, or so went the forecastle rumors on the *Elizabeth James*, the chief told Twin-Hawks that there were other scrimshaws, but that he should avoid them at all costs, because just like all of life contains both good and evil, some were purely evil. And as the creator of all things always strove for balance, so were these two focal points always pushing against one another for dominance.

"His final warning was to never let go of the white scrimshaw until he felt his own death upon him. And then, and only then, he must give it to the one that he would know was prepared to receive it."

Westlake paused and looked at Bridget.

She stared at him with rapt attention. "Please, Edward, don't stop."

He smiled at her and glanced over at Mick who was trying to concentrate on the story while ignoring his girlfriend casting worshipful glances at Westlake. He nodded for him to go on.

"Well, two weeks later, the ship stopped at another island for supplies and water. The ship's log, which I also found in Simon Westlake's desk, says that the ship's first mate, one Ezra Foster, took a landing party ashore but somehow ran afoul of the natives who came howling out of the jungle for his blood. The captain said in his log that he believed that the first mate, Ezra Foster, stole something of great value from the island. He never identified the object but said it was pure evil and must not be allowed to leave the ship."

He touched the back of Bridget's hand with his forefinger. "Do you know what I think it was?" he asked.

"Yeah," Mick growled. "Another frigging scrimshaw."

Westlake nodded. "Yes, one of the others the chief had spoken of. Something evil."

"So what happened to them then?" Bridget whispered breathlessly.

232

Westlake shrugged. "One of the scrimshaws left with John Twin-Hawks when the ship docked in Nantucket the next day. The other? The one presumably stolen from its rightful owners by Ezra Foster? No one knows, because as far as anyone can determine, Ezra Foster never left the ship. The ship was thoroughly searched. The first mate's packed duffle bag was found but never any trace of him."

"He probably jumped overboard and swam for it before the ship docked," Mick said.

Westlake shook his head. "No, like so many other sailors of his time, he couldn't swim a single stroke."

"So then find out what happened to Foster, and we find out where the tooth is," Bridget said excitedly.

Westlake nodded. "And when we do, we'll have both of the scrimshaws from the legend, and they'll lead us directly to who or what killed Karen Randolph."

"Who," Mick mumbled, taking a long pull from his fourth Narragansett Ale. "Not what—*who,* damn it! This isn't some cheesy drive-in movie horror flick. It's who!"

Westlake, silent for a moment, looked first at Bridget then back at Mick and said softly, "Yes, you're probably right. And when we find the scrimshaws they will point the finger to whoever wanted to make it look like Mick murdered Karen Randolph."

Mick shrugged and said, "Let's hope to hell so." He stood up and stretched, swayed for a moment and yawned. "Come on, babe, let's hit the rack. I'm freakin' wasted."

"Ah, that's all right, darlin', you go ahead. I think I'll just enjoy the fire a bit more."

Mick drew in a deep breath, walked over to Bridget, and held out his hand. "Bridget, I'd really like you to come up with me." He looked at her and said in a clearly enunciated, level tone, "I'm serious." Then added softly, "Please."

Westlake also stood up. "Mick's right, Bridget. Get some sleep. Tomorrow's going to be a busy day."

"Busy?" Bridget wrinkled her brow. "I don't understand?"

"By this time tomorrow, we'll have half of the puzzle."

"How so?"

"Tomorrow we're going to dig up Zeke Tanner's grave."

Chapter Forty

A tree rattled its branches against a window, and Fiona awoke with a start—but she wasn't in her bed. She stood in a long, dark hallway lit by only one guttering whale oil sconce and the sporadic flashes of lightning from the fading storm. She looked down at her feet—bare. She caught a reflection of herself in the blackness of the windowpane as another lightning bolt flashed far out to sea. She saw a young woman, her white cheeks flushed. Her long dark hair unpinned and falling over her shoulders. And she stared in horror as she realized that the young woman standing in the hallway was clad in only her nightshift.

And then came the memory of the dreams. They started slowly at first, just confused images and vague, bewildering feelings. But as she backed away from the wavering reflection in the window, they began to coalesce and slither across her brain. She continued backing away, shaking her head as the images from the dream rushed over her and seared into her soul. She put both of her hands to her head as if she could squeeze them out, but they only became stronger. She had never had dream memories this powerful before. They seemed less like an insubstantial dream and more like...real memories.

But it was the substance of the dreams that had her shaking and pursued her down the hallway and into her dear, loving husband's bed. The vivid, soul-shattering, all too real memories of another man's hands on her breasts. His tongue all over her body. Her most intimate places...and hers on him.

Her face burned with shame as she murmured, "No," over and over. The most shameful memory of all was that of the face of the man who was touching and caressing her. The man who whispered things in her ear and to whom she wantonly and willingly responded. The man who smiled sardonically at her from the sinful shadows of her memory. The man she saw even now as she climbed into her bed and buried her burning face in the back of her husband's nightshirt.

Simon Westlake.

* * * *

When Jeptha and Fiona walked into the sun-dappled breakfast room, Simon was already seated at the table.

He quickly rose and called, "Mrs. Samuels. Our guests are down. Bring two more plates, if you please."

He pulled out an ornately carved chair with gilded pictures of seashells on the back and invited Fiona to sit.

As the plump, gray-haired housekeeper came in and placed a platter with eggs, scones, and a large rasher of bacon on the table, Simon said, "And so, my honored guests, I hope that Tempest has provided you with a comfortable night's rest?"

Jeptha picked up the silver coffeepot and said, "Yes, sir. Quite comfortable. Thank you for asking." He turned to his wife and asked, "Mrs. Dawes, will you have coffee or tea this morning?"

Fiona didn't look up. She gave a tiny shrug while staring down at her empty plate. "Either is fine."

Jeptha poured the steaming black liquid into her cup, added two lumps of sugar, and filled the rest of the cup with thick cream.

Simon pushed his plate back; the housekeeper removed it and left the breakfast room. "Well, I'm glad that you've found our rustic cottage comfortable and you are, of course, welcome to stay as long as you like. In fact, I have planned a scenic stroll around the estate to be followed by a late picnic lunch on one of Tempest's numerous promontories."

"Thank you, sir," Jeptha began, "but we are already too far in your debt, and I do wish that I had some way of repaying your kindness."

Simon leaned back in his chair and looked out through the French doors and onto the garden beyond. He appeared to be deep in thought. Suddenly, he smiled. "As a matter of fact, Mr. Dawes, I think that perhaps there may be one small but very important service that you and your charming wife may be able to assist me with."

* * * *

Tempest
August 21ˢᵗ, 1968
7:05 a.m.

The first rays of the morning sun slipped around the molding in the window frame and brushed the edge of Bridget's pale cheek. It traveled up the delicate high angle of her cheekbone and reached the still sleep-smudged corner of her right eye. She stirred restlessly.

Mick lifted his head off the pillow and watched her as she rolled away from the sun's alarm clock.

He smiled. Damn, she looked good. A little tired maybe, but damn good all the same. He turned over and put both hands behind his head and thought.

Would I be a completely horny, oversexed, typical male creep if I asked her to finish what I tried to start last night?

He bit the inside of his lip and thought for a moment, then mentally shrugged.

Worth a shot.

Bridget stirred restlessly again.

"Hey, rise and shine, sunshine," Mick whispered, kissing the tip of her ear.

She gave a small sound, like a whimper.

Well that wasn't a promising beginning.

He sighed and put on his best bedroom voice. "Hey, beautiful, think you might be up for something that's, ah, come *up* with me this morning?"

"Ummm...what's that, luv?" She yawned sleepily.

"You know, babe, last night I kinda wanted to get it on, but you said you were feeling kind of funny, strange, and just wanted to get some sleep. I started bitching about not wanting to start dating Mr. Hand again, like back in prep school. And you said, 'Tomorrow, luv!' just before you suddenly decided that you were gonna take a bath."

She gave a noncommittal shrug and yawned again.

Whoa, I'm really losing my touch.

Damn it. He really didn't want to plead, but it seemed like the farther away her interest drifted, the more he wanted her. And the harder it was not to get pissed all over again. He took a deep breath and tried to sound nonchalant. "Hey, don't blame me, babe. If I wasn't turned on waking up next to the sexiest, cutest little chick in the world, I'd have to be senile or dead or both." He lowered his eyelids and leaned over and stuck the tip of his tongue in her tiny pink ear.

She wiggled grumpily and said, "Mickey, don't. Stop it."

Now he was pissed.

"Jeeze, Bridge, what the hell's the matter? Do I need a shower or something?"

"No! Oh, I don't know...nothing is the matter, I-I just don't want to. I'm too tired."

"Yeah," Mick muttered bitterly. "That's just what you said last night."

He folded his arms across his chest and asked sarcastically, "Do you still feel *funny*?"

"Yes." She laid her head back down on the pillow and closed her eyes again.

Goddamn her. Mick fumed in silence. *She was in a pissy mood last night and then this morning and....*

And suddenly it broke through, and he almost laughed. *Oh yeah, it must be that time of the month. Okay, now everything makes sense.* Even though he'd seen Tampax wrappers in the bathroom wastebasket what seemed like only two weeks ago. Oh well, it was probably because he always wanted her so much it made any time it couldn't happen seem like an eternity.

Man, what a king-size, gold-plated jerk I am. Getting down on her just 'cause she's OTR.

He leaned down to her face on the pillow and said softly, "Hey, Bridge? Babe?"

She mumbled something.

"Ah, babe, I just wanted to say I'm, like, sorry. You know, for not getting it that you're on the r...I mean, having your period and all."

"What are you talking about?" she grumbled.

"What I just said, that you have your period. So like, that's why we can't, you know, get it on. Last night and like, now."

Bridget lifted up her head and turned over. She gazed at him with her still sleep-dark eyes. Eyes that appeared distant, like there was a blind drawn behind them.

"I don't have my period," she said flatly.

"Then why?" Mick asked, the hurt spilling out in his voice.

"Why, why? I don't know why. All I know is that I'm still bloody tired. I feel like I was up all night and the last thing I want to feel is some man's hands on my body and...." She yawned hugely and stretched her hands over her head. The covers fell away, and Mick stared resentfully at the taut little white body that he wouldn't be holding this morning. That face, that kissable neck, creamy shoulders, and firm white breasts. Just smooth white skin, interrupted only by the red-pink of her nipples and.... What?

Mick sat bolt upright and hissed, "Bridget, what the hell is that!"

"What is what?" She sat upright too.

Mick pointed to mottled gray marks ringing her breast. Bridget looked down, jumped out of bed, and ran to the large swinging dresser mirror set in a dark walnut frame. She tilted the mirror downward and stared deeply. Her already pale skin became chalk white. Ringed around her beautiful alabaster breast were five large bruise marks.

She turned around to Mick.

"Mickey...I-I don't know."

Mick was out of bed and standing in front of her now. He stood there for a moment, naked, bewildered. And then his expression began to change as the angry, red McCarthy rage started to throttle his calm.

"Well, *I* know what it is," he said from between clenched teeth. "It's fingerprints. The fingerprints of a man's hand."

237

Bridget took a step backwards.

"No! I mean...well, yes, it looks like.... I mean, it could be. It-it's yours. You must have...."

"It wasn't there when you got undressed last night. When you pushed me away and said you didn't want to and that you were going to take a long hot bath—alone. But you didn't, did you, Bridget?"

"Mickey, what are you saying?"

"I'm saying that I waited up for you until midnight when I finally fell asleep. But when I woke up and looked at the clock it was two a.m., and you still weren't back. I even went down the hall to the bathroom, but you weren't there." He took a deep, ragged breath. "And the tub was dry. No one had used it at all. I searched the house. I couldn't find you. But when I got back to our bedroom, there you were, laying in bed, your back towards the door. I tried to wake you, but you just pushed me away. So I kissed the back of your neck. It was damp, with sweat, just like it is after we've made love. But you didn't last night. Make love, did you?"

He stared at her for almost all full minute before adding in a flat, cold voice, barely above a whisper, "At least not with me."

Bridget kept shaking her head. "No, Mickey, no. I...it's...I was...."

"You were screwing that bastard Westlake!"

"No, Mickey! No, no, no! I couldn't. I wouldn't. I mean.... Oh, I don't know what I mean. I—"

"Yeah, it's all coming clearer now," Mick spat. "That bullshit story about your dreams and 'gents from the past'. They all had his face, didn't they? You've had the hots for him ever since he saved your pretty little ass in that Boston alley. And all those moans and groans in the night...you were dreaming of balling him the whole time you were doing it with me!"

She turned to him, tears streaming down her face. "No! Oh my god, how could you ever think that of me? Are you that petty and jealous? Just because an interesting, cultured man is gracious and friendly to me. Are...are you insane or just determined to live the rest of your life as a jealous, immature little...boy?"

With seemingly no conscious thought on his own part—almost as if his actions were not his own—Mick's hand moved in an upward arc, slapping the first three fingers of the back of his right hand against the side of her face.

The sound of the slap echoed in the high-ceilinged room. Then silence ruled as they stared at one another in stunned horror.

"Bridget, I'm sorry. I-I never meant to...to hurt you. I love you," he whispered.

"Bastard!" she hissed.

Suddenly the red rage roared back into him, stronger than ever. He stood before her, naked and shaking with anger. His hands clenched and unclenched into fists. "Yeah, that's right. I'm a bastard." The same mirror that reflected Bridget's horror and shock reflected his rage, torment, and pain. "And you're a fucking whore!"

"Get out," she said in a cold and lifeless voice.

He grabbed his T-shirt, jeans, and boots from the floor. Swinging the bedroom door open, he stared at Bridget as she stood naked and stunned, staring with obvious pain, guilt, disgust, and despair at five dark bruises around her small perfect breast.

He slammed the door behind him.

Chapter Forty-One

Tempest
October 17th, 1858
The Whale-bone Graveyard
Zeke Tanner's Gravesite
2:57 p.m.

The wind made an eerie, almost otherworldly wail as it passed through the bleached bones of what Simon had told them was the skeleton of a great sperm whale that had washed up on the beach below. Simon had said that his sea-captain father had ordered the bones carried up from the beach and arranged as a fence around the estate's small graveyard.

Fiona looked up as they entered the graveyard beneath a spectral arch formed by the upper and lower jawbones of the long-dead leviathan. A gray, brooding sky outlined each sharp, jagged tooth. The wind picked up and shuddered and swirled around the grisly archway. *It sounds like the wail of the banshees that my old gran used talk about.* Fiona shivered.

As if the wind's vengeful banshee spirit had heard the thought, a gust blew the corner of Fiona's dress onto one of the jawbone's splintered teeth where it caught and tugged at Fiona like a taloned claw. She gave a start and clutched at her throat.

Simon reached down and with an amused smile said, "Allow me, Mrs. Dawes." He removed the fabric of her dress from the piece of bone and bowed, holding out his right hand with a gesture towards a recently dug grave surrounded by piles of fresh earth.

"I am most embarrassed to have to ask you to assist me in so macabre a task, but there are no other members of the fair sex present upon the estate except for Mrs. Samuels. And she is a widow and hence, according to the culture where the object was formed, no longer considered to be married."

Fiona turned and looked back at him with a puzzled frown. "I am not sure that I understand you, Mr. Westlake."

Jeptha took her hand and nodded. "Yes, Westlake, what does my wife's marital status have to do with all of this?"

"Forgive me." He bowed again slightly. "There is, in the coffin below, an object which I have long sought. A scrimshaw."

"Then if I don't sound too plain in my speech, why do you not retrieve it yourself? Why do you need the assistance of my wife?"

Simon shook his head. "Would that I could, sir, but the history— or legend, if you will—that surrounds the object states that the thing may only be removed from a deceased owner by a woman who has

240

given herself in love to a man." He glanced at Fiona, and a dark smile flitted across his features. Just as quickly, it was gone, and he added, "And, of course, in our Christian culture that can only mean a married woman."

"Yes, of course," Fiona murmured.

She stared distractedly at the grave's open hole, looked down and saw the pinched, gray face of the corpse in the coffin. She swallowed back the bile gathering in her throat.

Jeptha saw her expression and said, "Perhaps, sir, I could go into the town and fetch back some woman, perhaps an undertaker's assistant, who I would gladly pay to do this service."

"There is not enough time." Simon shook his head again and glanced over his shoulder. "Already the sun begins its westerly course, and in an hour or two it will be dark. The particulars of the lore that I have gathered states quite clearly that the thing must be removed on the same day before the grave is closed. Before the sun sets." Simon studied their faces. "Please, Mrs. Dawes. This is very important to me."

Jeptha bit his fingernail, and Fiona realized his sense of honor and obligation battled with the protective feeling he had for her.

"Fiona, although I carry a personal debt of honor to Mr. Westlake, this must be your decision. If you feel that you cannot do this thing...."

Fiona glanced up and blew out the breath she had been holding. She squared her shoulders and said, "You are right, Husband. We do carry a debt of obligation to Mr. Westlake. And though this be not something that I'm looking forward to, I am no hothouse flower. And I've done many an unpleasant task before this day."

She took a pair of long white muslin gloves from her handbag and started pulling them on. She took a deep breath. "Well then, let's be about it. Soonest begun, soonest done."

"Wait!"

Her head snapped up in surprise.

"Wait," Simon called again, his tone silky. "Forgive me, Mrs. Dawes, but the legend likewise mandates that it must be your hand, your bare flesh, that removes the scrimshaw."

Fiona swallowed hard and her eyes sought Jeptha's.

He turned to Simon and whispered, "Mr. Westlake, is there nothing that I may do in her stead?"

Simon Westlake shook his head once more.

Fiona set her jaw in a determined line and climbed down the ladder into the grave until she stood next to the heavy brass and oak coffin. She looked up.

Simon breathed heavily. "Excellent, Fiona...Mrs. Dawes. Now simply reach down and lift the scrimshaw and its cord over his head."

Fiona's hand hovered hesitantly over the grimaced, gray-faced head,

241

revulsion burning her throat. She slowly moved her small white hand and grasped the greasy, black rawhide thong holding the scrimshaw. And pulled.

The lips of the corpse shrank back from its teeth, and a tortured moan hissed out breath like rotting carrion.

Fiona screamed and stumbled back against the side of the grave. "God have mercy!" she half sobbed and crossed herself.

"It's nothing!" Westlake snapped. "Trapped air in the lungs and nothing more."

"Westlake! She cannot do this! You must not force her to!"

Simon Westlake's face was cold as he glared at Jeptha with contempt. "Is that the scope of your gratitude, Mr. Dawes? The extent of your... honor?"

Jeptha hung his head, and his face burned while he helplessly watched his wife. She gazed up at him and tried to smile. "I-I can do this, my love. If-if I can just slip the cord over his head. If only...if only I did not have to touch him again."

Jeptha took out his pocketknife and dropped to the edge of the grave. "Fiona, cut it with this."

"No!" Simon roared. "The cord must not be cut or broken. The circle must remain inviolate!" He stared down at Fiona. "Mrs. Dawes," his voice lashed like a whip, "lift the cord over his head. Now!"

Fiona bent down again and put one hand on the greasy, stinking hair behind Tanner's head. She grasped the cord once more, and her hand brushed over the scrimshaw.

The sky appeared to whirl over her head. A roaring sounded in her ears. The sides of the grave closed in on her. She looked down at the face of the corpse and saw with horror that it stared at her with red flaming eyes. Laughing as the blood-filled eyes glowed—as if preparing to suck out her soul. The laughter filled her ears and rubbed her senses raw. Slowly, the black, swollen tongue began to inch out of the mouth, growing longer and longer. Reaching out for her. Moving towards her face, and all the while the deep, blood-red eyes burned and the lips drew back in a horrible grin. The snake-like tongue touched her hand.

Fiona screamed and threw herself back into the far corner of the grave. With tears of revulsion and terror streaming down her face, she vomited into the sandy soil.

Suddenly she felt herself being lifted from the grave by powerful, calloused hands. Then Jeptha's arms were around her, and she buried her face in his chest. Still holding her, he turned his head to Westlake and shouted, "Enough! Do you hear me? This is done!"

"Why? Because your woman got the vapors?" Westlake walked towards Fiona. "I thought you had spirit, madam."

Fiona looked up while wiping her mouth with her handkerchief.

"My God in Heaven. Did you not see his eyes? The horrid black tongue reaching out for me?"

"I saw nothing but a hysterical woman letting her imagination run away with her."

"If my wife says that she saw it, then it was so," Jeptha said, his voice low and dangerous.

Simon stepped back, his face red and teeth clenched. "So then this is how you repay me for your life? This is the debt of honor you owe me?"

Still holding Fiona, Jeptha said, "Ask anything of me. Be it not illegal or dishonorable, I will do it."

"Dishonorable? You forsworn cur. You have already forfeited your honor by allowing your wife to renege on the small task I set her."

Jeptha's mouth hardened. "Then so be it, Mr. Westlake. I would rather live my life as an honorless dog than to ever again see the expression of terror and loathing on my wife's face as she tried to fulfill your 'small task'."

Westlake's features contorted with rage, and he spat out, "Then there is one final service you may do me."

"And what is that?"

"Take yourself and your wife from my sight as quickly as possible."

"Gladly. If you will loan us your coach, we will leave this instant."

"The coach is not here. Enoch has taken it to the town for provisions. You may take my horse."

Jeptha looked at Fiona. She swayed on her feet.

"My wife cannot ride." Jeptha swallowed. "May...may she rest here while I ride to town to hire a sloop to sail us round Race Point and back to Skaket Creek? I will likewise hire a coach to take us to Nantucket town."

Simon thought for a moment and then nodded. He composed his features and spoke in a more normal voice. "Yes, of course, Mr. Dawes. Forgive my outburst of bad temper. This has been a trying afternoon for all of us."

He gestured towards the house. "Please, take Mrs. Dawes into the library. There is a comfortable divan there where she can rest until you return."

Jeptha gave Westlake a hard stare. Finally, he picked Fiona up in his arms and said as he walked towards the house, "I shall ride hard and return before the sun sets."

* * * *

The Scrimshaw

Tempest
August 21ˢᵗ, 1968
7:21 a.m.

Mick sat at the bottom of the wide formal stairway and pulled his T-shirt over his head. He picked up his boots from where he'd tossed them at the foot of the stairs and held them in his left hand.

He couldn't remember the last time he'd cried. Not when he'd gotten shot—twice—on that deadly jungle patrol. Not even in the bar fight in Saigon where he'd gotten his nose broken. God, how that had hurt, but this hurt worse.

"Yeah," he muttered, angrily yanking on his worn cowboy boots. "I'll take a broken nose or a 7.63 mm AK slug any day!"

His nose was running, and his eyes stung. He dragged a scarred, chapped knuckle over them and swallowed hard.

How could she do this to me? Was this payback for me playing footsie with Karen Randolph? Christ, what an incredible mess!

But, no, no, she doesn't do things like that. She isn't into playing games.

That only leaves one possibility, the worst one of all. The one that makes me feel like bawling like a frigging baby.

He held the thought and twisted it around and around like a knife in his heart but kept coming up with the same soul-searing answer.

She really was in love with the guy.

* * * *

Tempest
On the Shore
August 21ˢᵗ, 1968
11:49 a.m.

Mick wasn't sure how long he'd been walking, most of the morning judging from the sun's position in the bright August sky.

It was a beautiful day, but it was lost on him as he trudged up and down the rock-strewn beach, savagely hurling stones into the surf where each wave seemed to reflect E.F. Westlake's smiling, mocking face.

"Damn him! Damn him! And damn her too! I hope they go straight to Hell together. I hope they choke on each other. And I wish they...I wish she...." He stopped and let the stone fall from his fingers. "I wish she still loved me."

He looked up to the top of the cliff where that evil, unlucky pile of boards and bricks called Tempest loomed like a vulture.

A small bobbing speck with black hair moved down the path from the house. His heart jumped until he realized...she wasn't alone.

* * * *

Tempest
The Library
October 17ᵗʰ, 1858
4:56 p.m.

Fiona was jolted awake from the same terrible dream that had plagued her for the past week. The same dark saturnine features had leered down at her. The same seductive hypnotizing voice told her that she was his to do with as he pleased, all the while drawing her tighter into his embrace. The same horrid distressing dreams that now seemed to fill her mind every time she closed her eyes. But somehow, someway, she knew that this time, it wasn't a dream. This time it was real.

Fiona's eyes flew open. A face hovered just inches from her own. Simon Westlake's. The normally carefully controlled face was red and perspiring, and from the coal black eyes a naked lust burned with such force that Fiona instinctively pulled her own face away crying, "No, stop!" while pushing him away.

"You push me away? Me? The man upon whom you have so liberally showered your favors here-to-fore?"

"It's not true! I do not know how you have come to say these things, but I would never forsake my husband. I...I would never be unfaithful to him."

Fiona sat up from the couch where she'd been sleeping and pulled herself away from him. She stood up and quickly moved to the other side of the couch, putting it between her and the man who had awakened her with whispers of horrible foul things in her ear. His face flushed with anger, contempt, and something else—something that in her heart she knew was worse, far worse.

She tried to compose herself. "I know that we—I—have disappointed you. And I know that this has made you very angry. I am sorry that we cannot part as friends, but please do not make things worse by whispering horrid, shameful lies in my ear."

He smiled a smile that was more like a sneer. "Lies? Lies, my dear Fiona. What makes you say they are lies?"

"How could they be anything but? The things that you whispered to me. They...they are things that a woman would do only with her husband. And some of the other things that I thought I heard you whispering as I awoke I...I do not even know what they mean but they sounded.... Wicked."

"Oh yes, my little jewel, wicked they are, and wicked you were—with me."

"Stop saying these things!" Fiona banged her fist on the arm of the couch. "Even you, in your obvious desire to punish me for my weakness in not being able to carry out your task, could not think that I would ever be unfaithful to the man that I love more than the breath of life itself."

"But you have," he said softly. "Many, many times. With me."

She shook her head over and over.

"Come now, dear *friend Fiona*," he sneered mockingly. "Do not tell me that you don't remember?"

"I don't. You lie."

He arched his eyebrow. "How many mornings have you awakened with the perspiration of passion dried upon your brow?"

"Those...those were from dreams. Feverish fancies brought on by worry and my...my...." She clasped a hand in horror over her belly.

Simon whispered, "Your...condition?"

"Oh, dear Lord, yes! And what a foul creature you have proved to be to even think that I would do—"

"Ah, but we have, dear Fiona."

"No! No! They were dreams, I tell you. I cannot fathom the means by which you were able to peer into my helpless, wicked dreams, but they were only that. Dreams!"

"They were not dreams. And in your heart you know that they were not." He smiled at her knowingly. "But you are half right, Fiona. Although they were not dreams, they most certainly were...wicked."

"No," she cried but with less force than before. "I couldn't. I love my husband. I could never give myself to another."

"Never give yourself? Oh, but my dear, you did. Willingly, wantonly. Oh yes," he continued, the smile growing wider, "you have proven to be a most ardent little minx for such a modest package."

"No. I never...." Fiona backed away, her voice barely above a whisper.

Simon closed the distance in one stride and put his hands on her shoulders, the smile now gone.

"Yes, my passionate little hypocrite, you have come to me every night since we first met in New Bedford. And every night you have thrown yourself into my embrace with a lust that exceeded my own. And I have had you, little Fiona. In every way possible." The sneer deepened, and contempt dripped from every word. "Why, you have done things, my dear, that would make a Hottentot blush."

No words would come. She could only continue to shake her head over and over.

He reached down and grabbed both of her shoulders, lifting her until the tips of her shoes barely brushed the floor.

"And now, my wanton little harlot, my seed and my blood flows through your veins."

"What are you saying?" she whispered.

"Yes, it courses through every cell in your body. Through your heart, through your brain, through your belly, and into—"

"No-o-o!" She screamed, a low shuddering moan. "Oh, dear God, please no."

"Do not bother to call upon Him, Fiona. He has no more use for a faithless little slut like you. You have but one master now. Me. I own you and your whoring, lustful heart and soul."

He let her go and deliberately wiped his hands on the back of the couch as if ridding them of some contagion.

Fiona turned away. She couldn't bear looking at her own broken eyes reflected back from his gleaming ones. He stared at her with contempt as she slumped to the floor, sobbing.

"But most importantly, I am now a master of the child growing within your belly, nourished by your betrayal and my blood."

Fiona laid her cheek against the cold polished wood of the couch leg, stunned, shocked, crushed. Could she have a really done those horrible things? Was it true? Were they really more than dreams? She couldn't deny that the memories had felt so real. And the night she found herself wandering through the halls of Tempest clad in only her nightshift. Who had she been going to see...? Oh, dear God. If it was true, then she was surely damned, as Simon had said.

Her head fell forward on her chest as the tears dripped onto her modest gray dress. *Modest gray dress,* she thought almost hysterically, *how will I ever be able to wear anything modest again?*

As if Simon could read her thoughts, he reached out and pulled her up into his arms. "As you are now soiled beyond redemption, I will say goodbye in the way that you know best, while ensuring that more of my essence flows to the child who I now own."

At those words, a searing flash of her old spirit seemed to break through her despair. She screamed, "Go back to the hell that spawned you!" and lashed out with all of her strength. Strength won through a hard girlhood and years of service and work. The blow struck Simon on his right cheek, and he staggered back. His hand went to his face and came away dappled with blood drawn by Fiona's chipped fingernails.

He looked at her and whispered, "That was a foolish action, my little slut. But I will now ensure that you will never do another."

Chapter Forty-Two

Skaket Harbor Police Department
Municipal Town Building
Skaket Harbor Township
August 21ˢᵗ, 1968
12:07 p.m.

"What's today's date, Dougie?"

"Ah, it's the twenty-first, Uncle Art. Why?"

Chief Arthur Frost sat down gingerly on the hard, wooden office swivel chair. He gasped in pain as his plump thigh brushed against his still swollen testicles.

"Whassa matter, Uncle Art?" Dougie Frost asked with a smirk.

"The matter, you imbecile," his uncle snapped out from between pain-gritted teeth, "is that my goddamned balls are still swollen to the size of grapefruit. All thanks to you, you moron!" The shifted his weight. "I should have let that bastard McCarthy beat you to death in the booking room instead of taking one for you in the nuts."

Arthur Frost's mind had conveniently adjusted his memory until the chief had almost lost his "essentials" in a heroic attempt to rescue Dougie from Big Mike, instead of having had the very bad judgment of abusing the son and his girlfriend of a very bad man to cross.

"Jeeze, I'm real sorry, Uncle Art. Do you want I should get you another pillow?"

"No, Dougie," the chief shook his head with a martyred sigh, "just look on that wall calendar and tell me what today is."

Deputy Dougie Frost went over to the calendar hanging on the wall and looked at it.

After two or three minutes, his uncle prodded him with, "Today, Dougie!"

Douglas Frost sighed and tore his eyes away from Miss August, her very small bikini, and very large breasts. He picked up the grease pencil hanging by a string on the wall and crossed out August 20ᵗʰ.

"It's August 21ˢᵗ today, Uncle Art."

Skaket Chief of Police, Arthur Frost, gently massaged his aching private parts and smiled. "One more day, Dougie. Just one more day, and that son of a bitch's kid is mine!"

* * * *

Tempest – The Cliffside Graveyard
Zeke Tanner's Grave

Ric Wasley

August 21ˢᵗ, 1968
12:08 p.m.

Mick was panting when he reached the strange cyclopean gate made of twin-crossed whalebone jaws that led to the wind-swept graveyard. He focused on catching his breath after his headlong run up the cliff path from the beach far below and gave the strangeness of the whole scene a brief passing glance. But it was gone again a moment later as he desperately scanned the cliff top for Bridget.

There! Almost out of his line of sight, in a shallow depression and partially blocked by a section of rib-bone of what must have been an enormous sperm whale, he saw her jet black hair blowing in the wild, sea-borne wind.

God she was beautiful.

And she wasn't alone. *He* stood next to her, an open book in one hand and the other resting on her shoulder.

Mick pushed his long hair out of his eyes, impatiently rubbed the back of his hand over them, and walked towards the two people.

* * * *

Bridget gazed down into the open grave and stared at the gray lead coffin. The top half of the lid had been opened, revealing a shrunken shape partially covered by a rotting linen shroud.

She couldn't tell if she was more frightened or excited. Probably a little bit of both, she decided.

"I had Charlie Eldrich bring his backhoe this morning and open it up," E.F. said quietly. He glanced at Bridget again and asked, "Are you sure that you're okay with this, Bridget?"

She thought for a moment. Was she? But she nodded her head and smiled gamely. "Lead on, Macduff."

"I know how weird and creepy this must feel, digging up a grave, climbing down into it, and especially the part about—"

"The part about how only a woman who is married or has *known a man*," she blushed, "can remove the scrimshaw?" She gave a tiny shudder and asked, "And why didn't you tell us that part last night?"

Westlake looked sheepish. "I guess because I thought that you and Mick would think I was totally nuts and split."

Bridget wondered. Maybe that would have been better. If they'd left, *it* never would have happened and they wouldn't have had the fight, and he wouldn't have hit her, and she would still be in love with him.

Was she still? It was so hard to think with Edward Westlake standing there. Every time he gazed at her she felt her knees turn to jelly. And

249

that in itself was the strangest thing of all. No one, except for Mick, had ever produced a feeling like that. She had never been, like so many of the girls she grew up with, the kind of silly, flighty girl who developed a crush on every new boy they met. What was happening to her?

"And speaking of Mick," he said. "Where is he? I haven't seen him around this morning. Is everything still okay between you two?"

Her eyes burned. She didn't know whether to laugh or cry. She shook her head angrily. "No."

He put his arm around her. She let herself lean in until her cheek was next to his chest. He bent his head and murmured in her ear, "You are such a beautiful woman, Bridget. I can't stand to see you unhappy. Please, tell me, what can I do?"

"You can start by taking your fucking hands off her, you son of a bitch!"

They both turned around as Mick, with an expression of hatred and pain so intense that Bridget instinctively took a step back, advanced on Westlake.

"Mick, what's the matter, man? Take it easy."

"Shut your goddamned mouth, you sleazy bastard! All of this time, right in front of me, you've been putting the moves on my lady."

Bridget snapped, "I am not your 'lady' or chick or piece of property, McCarthy! I have my own mind and my own will and I will exercise them as I choose, not as you tell me. And if I want to be with Edward, then I bloody well will!"

Oh my God, I can't believe that I'm saying these words to the man that I've loved for the past two years. Why am I saying this? Why am I acting like this?

* * * *

Mick stopped and stared at the ground, his breathing ragged. He turned towards Bridget and back to Westlake. Something seemed to break inside of him. He shook his head and began to walk away.

Westlake glanced back over his shoulder and said to Bridget, "Thank you, Bridget, you made the right choice," and added in a voice just loud enough for Mick to hear, "I think that you'll be much happier with a man instead of a bad tempered little boy."

The words wrapped around Mick's gut like a whip. Without even thinking, he turned, took two steps forward, and slammed his fist into the side of Westlake's face. He staggered back a step, and Mick moved in, his left fist smashing into Westlake just below his rib cage.

Westlake swayed another step back, tucked his chin under his left shoulder, and jabbed straight out at Mick's jaw.

Mick took the punch and immediately shook it off. He didn't even feel it. He was past feeling anything except rage and the desire to beat that smug handsome face to a bloody pulp.

Westlake's longer reach connected with Mick's face again.

Mick's right eye was swelling shut. He put everything he had, all the frustration, all the rage, all the pain, into his right fist and swung it straight for Westlake's head.

Westlake ducked, stepped inside to the left, and Mick's driving fist brushed by Westlake's face and caught Bridget who stood right behind him, on the side of her shoulder.

Bridget gave surprised gasp, staggered back two more steps, and fell backwards into the open grave.

Mick heard a thump as her head struck the upraised coffin lid.

"Oh, Jesus," he whispered, letting his hands fall limply to his sides.

"What the hell have you done to her?" Westlake screamed, back handing Mick across the face.

Mick didn't move. Again, he didn't feel the blow. He just stood staring down into the open grave at Bridget's still form lying on top of the coffin.

"Oh, Jesus," he said again.

Suddenly, she stirred.

"Bridget!" ripped from Mick's throat. "Oh, my god, let her be okay, let her be okay," he kept repeating as he scrambled down into the grave. He landed on the bottom half of the coffin and pushed his feet along the lid until he reached Bridget. She was moving but seemed only semiconscious. Her eyes were unfocused, her complexion chalky white, and she kept muttering, "Where is it? I'm the one. I'm the only one...who can...."

"Hush, baby, don't try to talk. I'll get you out of here. I'm so sorry. I'm so frigging sorry, Bridge. Just be okay and you can do whatever you want to do, and I won't stop you." His voice cracked as he bent over her and the tears dripped onto her face. "I'll always love you, but I'll never try to hold you back from anything that makes you happy. Just please, please be okay."

He moved to pick her up, trying to be as careful as possible. She moaned, and he froze.

"No, no, I have to bring it. She...she needs it."

Her hand pushed aside the rotting fabric of the burial shroud until her fingers touched the thick black cord of the still white scrimshaw. As Mick lifted her up in his arms, her hand clenched around the tooth and pulled. The cord drew taut as Mick straightened up with Bridget in his arms. And with the snapping sound of a dry twig, the grinning, mummified skull snapped off of the pipe-stem neck, and both scrimshaw and cord came free as the head of Zeke Tanner's desiccated corpse rolled into the dirt of the grave.

Mick braced both feet and splayed them outwards, forcing his back into the side of the grave. He dug the toes of his boots into the sandy soil and, cradling Bridget in his arms, worked his way towards the top of the grave. He felt the back of his T-shirt rip away and the stones and pebbles grind into his bare skin. But he didn't stop.

At the top, Westlake leaned down and said, "Give her to me."

Mick didn't answer. He gave a final push with the toes of his boots and, still holding Bridget, rolled out of the grave. He got to his feet and, carrying Bridget, began to run.

Westlake called after him, "Mick, wait! I'll call for an ambulance."

He kept running.

He finally stopped when he got to the house. He looked at Westlake's BMW, and as Westlake caught up, Mick said, "Give me the keys."

Westlake shook his head. "Mick, I don't think you should move her. Please, let me call for an ambulance."

Mick shook *his* head. "Give me the keys," he repeated.

Westlake reached into his pocket and took out the keys. Suddenly he stopped. He gazed at Bridget's hand and whispered, "She got it. She got the scrimshaw." His closed his hand around the keys and withdrew. "A trade," he said, "my car for the scrimshaw. Her life for a bit of carved ivory."

Mick stared at him for a moment and then nodded. He gently unwrapped the cord of the scrimshaw from Bridget's fingers.

She moaned, "No, no, I have to...."

"It's gonna be okay, Bridge. You're gonna be all right. I'm gonna make sure that everything's all right."

Mick dropped the scrimshaw into Westlake's left hand and took the keys out of his right. "Choke on it, you bastard," he said and slid Bridget into the back seat of the car.

Westlake started to speak, but closed his mouth as Mick climbed into the front seat, started the engine, and drove off in a cloud of gravel and dust towards Nantucket town.

Mick glanced in his rear-view mirror.

E.F. Westlake, who had been known briefly as Edward by a fiery, black-haired girl with emerald green eyes, watched the car for a few moments. Emotions flitted across his face like a butterfly's wings: lust, longing, pain, anger, and regret. He lifted the scrimshaw and let the sun play over the strange carvings. His hand slowly closed around the object. He turned around and walked back towards the house.

Chapter Forty-Three

October 17th 1858
Tempest
6:03 p.m.

Jeptha Dawes was not by nature a violent man. In fact, by the tenets of his beliefs and upbringing (his mother had been a Quaker), he was a man of peace and of God.

But when he'd burst through the library door and found Fiona desperately trying to push Simon Westlake's leering face away from hers, something had snapped.

It was as though all thoughts of love and peace had retreated to a safe place, leaving only a cold hard command to "do what you must", and he did—with Old Testament vengeance.

Jeptha had heard the sounds of a scuffle coming from the small parlor where he had left Fiona sleeping. He'd walked up to the room and pulled on the heavy brass door handle. It was locked.

Suddenly, he heard the sound of breaking glass and Fiona's voice rising to a scream. "I said, get your foul hands off of me, you filthy... liar!"

Jeptha raised one heavy, hob-nailed boot and shattered both lock and door handle. The door flew inward, splintering against the wall.

He didn't think and he didn't stop to wonder about the strange scene in front of him. He didn't have to. All he had to see was that another man had his hands on his wife. He acted.

Two strides carried him across the room and put Simon Westlake's expensive, hand-tailored jacket under Jeptha's calloused hands. The same hands that were still able to raise a jib line in a gale caught Simon and sent him sprawling into the dying embers of the fireplace.

Simon got up, smacking out bits of smoldering cloth and blackening his soft, white hands. He glared at Jeptha, his breath coming in ragged gasps. "You dare to touch me? You fish-gut stinking, back country clod. I'll show you what I did to the last vermin who crossed me." His teeth pulled back in a sadistic leer. "In fact, I'll wager that your little slut probably enjoyed watching the hiding I gave that drayman. Didn't you, dear *Friend Fiona*?"

"You cruel, arrogant bastard," she whispered, shaking her head as in her anger her speech thickened back to her Belfast origins. "Cut from the same cloth as your great enemy, the Frosts. You're both grasping and greedy, crushin' all folks just tryin' ta live their life in a good and decent way. And you—you have to treat 'em like so much filth beneath your boots. Tryin' to grind 'em down to wallow in the same foul cesspool where you...you...."

Suddenly she screamed, letting out all of the anguish, guilt and fear that had dogged her for the past three days and rushed towards him. "You! You...!" She sobbed, flailing her arms as her small, clenched fists smacked against his singed coat.

"You common little bitch!" Simon grabbed the fireplace poker and raised it over his head, clenching his teeth as he put all of his force behind the blow.

Simon's forearm smacked into a steel-toothed bear trap. At least that's how it must have felt to him. He looked up from Fiona into the angry eyes of Jeptha Dawes, whose right hand squeezed the blood and strength out of Simon's right arm. The iron and brass poker clattered to the floor.

Simon Westlake had told them over dinner that he was not a weak man. He said he had never backed away from a confrontation and was supremely confident, as only arrogance and privilege could have made him. He had always proven to be more than a match for drunken bullies, street thugs, and unruly prostitutes.

But he has never come up against a man weaned on the backbreaking labor of wrestling crops from rocky New Hampshire soil. I suspect he has never tried to break the grip of hands that have held on to a frozen mainsheet for ten hours straight while battling around Cape Horn.

He couldn't. He twisted and turned, but the hand stayed clamped to his wrist—and continued to squeeze.

Simon's face turned red with effort, then white as the pain registered and the bones in his forearm began to crack. In one split second, his face reflected all of the beatings and pain that he himself had administered, and a scream broke from his lips. "Stop it! For the love of God! You're breaking my arm! Please!"

Jeptha glanced at Fiona.

She stepped back and glared down at Simon who had sunk to one knee, quivering. She drew a deep breath and nodded at Jeptha. "Come, Husband. Let's go home."

Jeptha's hand opened. He nodded back at her and took her arm as they walked to the door.

Fiona looked back, as did Jeptha. Simon Westlake scrabbled with his good left hand for something in his jacket pocket.

"Jeptha!" she cried.

Jeptha whirled around. Simon's left hand yanked one of his Colt revolvers from his coat pocket and thumbed back the hammer.

"I'll splatter your pig-farmer brains all over this room and then I'll take your whore of a wife and...."

Jeptha grabbed an object that hung on the wall next to the door, right under a portrait of a dour-faced man who had been Simon

Westlake's Whaler Captain father. A six-foot long harpoon. He aimed and threw it in one smooth motion, and the iron barb passed though Simon Westlake's wrist, pinning it to the cherry wood paneling next to the fireplace.

Simon screamed and hissed from between clenched teeth, "I'll. Kill. You. For. This. Both of you!"

Jeptha picked up the second of the pair of harpoons that had been crossed underneath the picture. He hefted it in his hand. "Know this, Mr. Westlake. My last voyage lasted near on three years. And while I was not a harpooner by trade, one of the old hands who'd served twenty years on board a New Bedford Whaler took to teaching me the mastery of this object to pass the time. I practiced almost every day for the best part of three years. I will hit what I aim at."

He turned to Fiona. "Mrs. Dawes, my sense of honor and to whom I should owe it has been set all adrift, but tis you who have been hurt. What would you have me do?"

Fiona stared at the white, perspiring face of Simon Westlake. "You know the only words I ever wish to hear from you, Simon Westlake."

His head flopped feebly like a speared fish on the end of a barb. But he raised it up and hissed out, "Never!"

Jeptha studied him and finally realized that Simon, driven by his own dark fantasies of power and domination, that crawled like spiders through his sick mind, would truly rather die than give Fiona peace and release by admitting he had lied. And he did lie! No matter what the scene he'd witnessed looked like upon entering this room, his heart told him Simon had lied. He was lying still!

She watched Simon's sneering, contorted face.

No, he would never admit it.

Jeptha narrowed his eyes on his target, but his hand was steady. He was right. He would not miss.

Did Fiona long to scream out the word "Yes!"? The word that would send the six feet of wood and iron into that sneering face and erase those hated features forever. And give him his final spiteful victory.

Fiona turned to Jeptha. "Come, Husband. The hour grows late, and we are done here—with everything. Let's go home."

Jeptha looked at his wife, the former little housemaid from Belfast. "You are a very great lady, my love."

He smiled for an instant and then turned back to Simon and, with a movement almost too fast to follow, sent the harpoon streaking across the room.

Simon screamed in terror.

The harpoon slammed into the cherry wood paneling and stuck there quivering between Simon's legs—less than half an inch from his crotch.

The Scrimshaw

The couple from Skaket Creek gazed at him for a moment. Then Edward's bladder let go, and a dark stain spread across the elegant, hand-tailored trousers.

Fiona and Jeptha turned away and walked out the door.

* * * *

The wheels of the coach and the swaying of the wooden frame on the iron-leaf springs should have been lulling Fiona to sleep. But she couldn't sleep or rest until her husband asked the question that she feared but expected would be at the forefront of his mind.

Finally, he did.

"What was he saying when I broke in?"

She drew in a breath, determined to answer as truthfully as her soul would allow. But in the moment before she opened her mouth, passion overcame reason and desperation, good resolve.

"Lies, Husband," she blurted out. "Foul, filthy lies, and deranged delusions! He said...he tried to...to make me believe that he, that I...."

Jeptha put his finger to her lips. "Hush, my heart. You have said it was all lies and the man's deluded ravings. And that is enough for me. We shall leave it there and will never again think upon that sad, evil man and his sad, evil lies."

Fiona threw her arms around him and kissed him fiercely. Tears stung the corner of each eye. And as the coach rumbled through the darkness, she held on to her husband and prayed. Prayed harder than she had ever prayed before—that it was as she had told her husband. That Simon Westlake lied.

Chapter Forty-Four

Nantucket Hospital
Admitting Desk
August 22nd, 1968
7:51 p.m.

"How is she?"

The nurse didn't answer. She glanced at Mick and continued walking down the hospital corridor.

"Nurse?" Mick called again, this time more insistent.

The nurse answered back over her shoulder, "The doctor will be out in a few minutes. Please have a seat in the waiting room."

Mick didn't want to sit. He didn't want to wait either. So he sure as hell wasn't going to have a seat in the waiting room. He gazed down the corridor at the double swinging doors that the nurse had just come through. He looked over at the reception desk. The receptionist glared over at him as if just daring him to try it. Crap! The hell with them. Let 'em call the cops or security guard or whoever they thought was going to try to stop him. He put his hand on the door. The old biddy at the reception desk must've had eyes in the back of her head, because she swiveled around and started to get up from her chair.

Just then, the outer door to the admitting room crashed open, and two frantic parents rushed in, half carrying and half propelling a screaming seven year old whose hand was wrapped in an ice-dripping wad of wet paper napkins.

The young boy yelled at the top of his lungs, an ear-splitting, continuous screech of, "Owwwww! Ow ! Ow-ey!"

The perspiring father ran up to the admitting desk, helplessly waving his hands. "Oh, my god, I don't know how it happened. One minute he was climbing into the back seat of the car, and the next he'd somehow closed the door on his hand. You...you don't think it could be broken, do you?"

The receptionist, who had obviously seen it all many, many times before snapped into the familiar routine. "I don't know, sir. The doctor will determine that." She pushed a clipboard with a long form attached to it across the counter. "Please fill this out and sign on the line with the X next to it."

"But...but you've got to get a doctor out here right now!" the mother wailed.

"As soon as we finish admitting him. Now, what is the child's name?"

"Brian," both parents answered in unison, and then the father stammered, lowering his voice, "D-do you...do you think he'll still be able to catch a baseball? You know, he just made shortstop on his Little League team."

"Billy!" the young, blonde-haired mother yelled accusingly, "Your son has slammed his hand in the car door and that's all you can think of?"

"Sorry, Sue," her husband mumbled, bending his head over the admitting form and trying to look busy. "Ah, where do I sign again?"

The receptionist stood up and leaned over the counter, pointing to a spot on the form.

Perfect. Mick quietly pushed open the swinging door and slipped through.

If he'd had more time to think about it, Mick would have realized that he stood out like a hippie at a bankers' convention. Half running, half walking from door to door dressed in his old jeans and ripped T-shirt, he peered into the tiny window to each room, muttering under his breath when Bridget wasn't there.

Think, Mick, think. Where would they take her? Would she be in some kind of operating room? Oh, Christ! Were they doing something to her? Were they doing some kind of horrible operation on her head? Was she...was she...?

He ran to the last room on the right and looked inside. Oh, dear god. There was an operating table with doctors and nurses clustered all around it.

The doctor yelled at one of the nurses, "Retractor, damn it. I said, retractor!" He held up a gloved hand for the tool, and as the gleaming surgical steel instrument was slapped into the palm, Mick saw that the hand was red with blood.

Feeling as though he'd been punched, he took a step backwards. He slumped down to the floor, pulled his knees up to his chin, and rested his sweaty forehead on his arms. He was still trying to keep the tears back. He didn't know why. *If she'd doesn't make it, then I'll....* What would he do? There would only be one thing. Pop's .38 in the BSA's saddlebags. He'd take care of Westlake and then himself. *No!* He shook his head. It wasn't Westlake who put her in that room. It was him.

Then Mick started to do something that he hadn't done since he was a very small boy, going to mass with Big Mike over on D Street back in Southie. He prayed.

"Excuse me?" Someone stood in front of him. "Ah, like, excuse me?"

Mick looked up and saw a teenage girl with long red hair in a ponytail and a red-and-white striped dress.

"Ah, like I don't think you're supposed to be here."

Mick didn't move.

"Please, like, I'll get in big trouble if they come out and see you, like, sitting here and all."

"I'm not leaving till I see if Bridge is going to be all right," Mick answered in a flat, tense voice.

"Who?"

"Bridge...Bridget Ann Connolly, my...my girl." The last word was whispered.

The red-haired candy striper looked at her clipboard and said, "But she's not in there. That's the operating room. But there is a Bridget Connolly right across the hall in number 204."

Mick jumped up, picked the astonished young candy striper up in his arms, and kissed her. "I love you, babe! You're an angel!"

He ran across the hallway and pushed open the door to 204. One bed was empty. Heart pounding, he pulled back the curtain separating the room's other bed. There was Bridget.

She lay there, her eyes closed, her soft black hair spread like raven's feathers on the pillow. The skin of her face and hands so pale that they showed white against the hospital sheets. He dropped to his knees, gently raised her hand to his lips, and covered it with kisses. He was crying now. He just kept saying over and over, "You're here, you're alive, and I'm not gonna let anything happen to you."

"Who are you, and what are you doing in here? This young woman is not supposed to have any visitors until we have fully diagnosed her condition. So I'm afraid that you're going to have to leave, sir."

Mick just shook his head and continued holding Bridget's hand as a blond-haired young doctor came into the room.

"Please don't make me call security."

"I'm not going anywhere until I know how she is," Mick answered without turning around.

The doctor came over and stood next to Mick. "What is your relation to this young woman?"

"I love her."

"Are you her husband? According to my information she is listed as 'Miss' Bridget Connolly."

Mick shook his head again. "I wish I was that lucky."

The young doctor paused for a moment, then held out his hand. Mick stood up and shook it.

"You know I can't let you stay here."

Mick turned towards Bridget then back to the doctor. "First you tell me what's wrong with her."

"All right, I'll make you a deal. You tell me just what happened, and I'll tell you what I know as of now."

Mick swallowed hard. "She...she hit her head. It-it was my fault."

The doctor stared at Mick. "She also has a bruise on her left arm.

259

Was that you too?"

Mick nodded. "For what it's worth, it was an accident. But it's still my fault."

The doctor looked into Mick's eyes, and his expression softened. "And it looks like you're beating yourself up pretty good for it, right?"

"With both fists, Doc." Mick managed a half smile then turned serious again. "Okay, Doc, your turn now. What's wrong with her?"

The doctor paused before speaking. "Concussion, that much we're sure of. But it seems more than a normal concussion, if there is such a thing."

Mick's heart sank. "What do you mean?"

"There is something else. We've given her intravenous and applied ice packs to reduce the swelling. The good news is that all of her body functions appear to be normal and all of her motor responses respond to the appropriate stimulus."

"And the bad news?" Mick asked softly.

The doctor leaned over and checked Bridget's pulse. "She seems to be in some sort of an almost catatonic trance."

"But you just said that she's responding to all of the normal stimulus?"

"Yes, her body is here, but her mind is...somewhere else."

"And...and the cure?" Mick held his breath, afraid of what the answer might be.

The doctor confirmed it when he turned back to Mick and answered softly, "At this point, we just don't know."

* * * *

Nantucket Hospital
August 22nd, 1968
5:41 a.m.

"Hey, kid. Hey you. Hey, wake up, kid."

Mick raised his head up off the back of the hard vinyl waiting room chair he'd fallen asleep in. He rubbed the back of his hand over his tired eyes and looked up at the big, beefy orderly who stood over him, poking him in the shoulder.

"Is your name McCarthy?"

Mick nodded groggily.

"Well, you got a phone call. You can take it on the white lobby phone." The orderly pointed to a phone hanging on the wall.

"Who...?" Mick started to ask, but the orderly was already walking away.

Mick stretched and walked over to the lobby phone and picked up the receiver. "Yeah?"

"Mickey?" came a soft voice over the phone line.

"Who's this?"

"Kathy. Kathy Dawes."

"Kathy? How...how did you know I was here?"

"I know everything, Mick. I know what happened at Tempest. I know what you did and I know how you feel. And you should stop. It's not your fault."

"But Kathy, I-I went nuts. And I was doing stuff and saying stuff and then I got all crazy and started going at it with Westlake and somehow, somehow I hit Bridge, and she fell and hit her head, and now the doctor says...."

"Mickey. I told you, I know all about it. There's more going on here... much, much more. You've got to forget about all of that and concentrate on just one thing."

"What?"

There was a pause on the other end of the line. Finally Kathy said, "You've got to get Bridget out of there and bring her to me right now."

"What? Why? The doctor said she's not supposed to be moved until they know what's wrong with her."

"I know what's wrong with her. And I also know that you've got to get her to me as soon as possible or—"

"Or what?"

"She'll die."

Chapter Forty-Five

Nantucket Ferry
6:36 a.m.

Mick watched as the ferryboat's mooring lines smacked into the water next to the dock and the boat began to pull away. He breathed a small sigh of relief. *Okay, first part done. We're on our way back to the Cape and Skaket Creek. But will I be able to get to the bike across the Cape to Skaket Harbor holding on to Bridget the whole way? Well, it's a case of having to.*

Getting Bridget out of the hospital had been tricky but not as hard as he'd thought it would be. He'd borrowed an orderly's uniform from the closet, put Bridget in a wheelchair, and wheeled her past the sleeping night orderly. Getting from the hospital to the boat had been the tricky part. Fortunately, at that time of the morning there were few people up to see Mick half walk, half carry Bridget back to the parking lot of the Crown & Anchor Pub where he retrieved the BSA. He'd dumped Westlake's car on a narrow side street a few blocks away, knowing that when they started looking for him and Bridget they'd be looking for them and that car. And when they found Bridget gone from the hospital they'd probably put out an APB for them. They might even send a black-and-white to check out the ferry when it docked. But they'd be looking for a red BMW, not a motorcycle. At least not yet, he hoped.

The real tough part was going to be when he had to put Bridget on the motorcycle. For that he'd have to use the same maneuver he'd used in getting Bridget and the bike on board the ferry. He'd taken a bungee cord, slipped one end around Bridget's left wrist, then pulled her other arm up tight around his waist and secured it with the other end of the bungee cord, putting on his jacket to cover the whole thing. Luckily, she seemed to have just enough motor skills to sit upright with her cheek pressed against his back. They'd made it through and onto the boat without a problem. So that's what he was going to have to do coming off the boat. He just prayed that if there were any cops they'd be too busy looking for a stolen BMW to pay a guy and his *sleepy* girlfriend much attention.

No matter. They'd make it. One way or another, he was gonna get Bridget to Kathy Dawes. Somehow, for some reason that he was still unsure of, he believed every word that Kathy had said. Bridget's life was depending on her.

* * * *

The Skaket Creek Inn
August 22nd, 1968
11:47 a.m.

"Mom! What are you doing up?" Kathy Dawes looked up at her mother gripping the hand railing of the second floor landing above the registration desk and shook her head. "Oh, Mom," she sighed, letting her pent up worry and concern spill into her voice. "You know that you're not supposed to be out of bed."

Polly Dawes smiled from the top of the stairs. "Well, I'd like to say that I feel fine, but I guess then you would probably want to know why, if I'm feeling so fine, I would really appreciate it if you could help me down these stairs, sweetheart."

Kathy Dawes moved quickly from behind the registration desk and up the stairs. She gently removed her mother's hands from the railing and put her right arm around her waist.

Her mother leaned her thin frame against her and gratefully sighed. "Yes, that's better."

"Mom," Kathy said, "please, let me help you back to bed."

Her mother smiled and shook her head. "No, I think that my bedtime is finally over. In fact, I think that the next time I lay down might be for a very, very long time."

"Mom! What are you saying? Don't talk like that. Come on, I'm taking you back to your room."

Suddenly the smile was gone, and Kathy felt her mother's surprisingly strong grip on her arm. "No, Kathy, I told you, the time for watching and waiting is over. They're coming—all of them. And we need to prepare, because we're going to need all of our strength."

Kathy paused, her eyes growing wider. "You said *we*?"

"Yes, Kathy." Her mother's mouth turned up slightly at the corner, but her eyes held something else. "Yes, it's time."

* * * *

Skaket Harbor
Cape Cod
No. 24 Frost Landing
11:59 a.m.

"That's it! I've had it!" Helen Shirley Frost Dawes snapped, slapping her palm down on the long polished dining room table where her father, Samuel Frost, sat eating his solitary lunch.

He looked at her from under his bushy white eyebrows for a moment before grunting and pointing to the antique Hitchcock chair opposite his.

"Sit."

She sat.

The old man took a large chunk of baked haddock off of the full platter of fish in front of him. He squeezed a half of a large lemon from the bowl next to him and doused the piece of white fish dangling from his fork.

"So what are you blathering about now, Helen?" He shoved the hunk of fish between his teeth and chewed.

Helen Dawes leaned forward and said, "I've just had it, I tell you! Had it up to here." She brought her hand up level with her chin. "I've had it with the whole lot of them. First it was the fourteen years I wasted married to that idiot, Dawes. And then living with that screwy goody-two-shoes Polly Dawes and her folk-singing hippie daughter! Well, it's enough to put anyone in the loony bin. And then...." Helen Dawes half rose from her chair. "Well, after what she did to me last night, I-I...."

"Have some fish."

"What?"

"I said, have some fish."

"I-I don't understand what you mean?"

"What I mean," Samuel Frost said, stuffing another chunk of baked haddock into his mouth, "is that you should sit your skinny rump back down in that chair and fill your mouth full of fish before you open it again and make a bigger ass of yourself that you already have."

Helen Shirley Frost Dawes slowly sat back down.

"But you don't understand, Poppa, she almost killed me last night," she whined.

Samuel Frost continued eating his fish.

"I-I think she's a witch!" Helen blurted out.

Samuel Frost stopped chewing. He put his fork down and looked at his daughter. "What did you say?"

"A witch. I think she's some of kind of a witch."

Samuel Frost said very quietly, "Do not ever say that word again and don't babble your vacuous blathering about things of which you know nothing. Powers which your shriveled little brain could never comprehend. Do you understand me?"

"Yes, Poppa, but...."

"No buts," he said and picked up his fork again. "Just do as you're told."

Helen Frost Dawes's face crumpled, and she wailed, "But...but Poppa, that's just what I have been doing for almost twenty years!"

Samuel Frost nodded. "And you're about to be well rewarded for it."

Helen sniffled and dabbed at her eyes with her handkerchief. "Well all I ever wanted, Poppa, was to make you happy and see that our family got what was rightfully ours."

"And we will, daughter, oh yes, we certainly will. Now stop your sniffling and have some fish."

* * * *

Nantucket Island
Tempest
August 22nd, 1968
12:06 p.m.

E.F. Westlake swiveled the library's big leather desk chair so that he faced the open window. He held the scrimshaw by the thick greasy black cord and let it spin in the sunlight. The longer he stared at it, the more the patterns etched into the tooth seemed to flow and slither across its surface. It even appeared to make a soft swishing sound as it turned around and around. In fact, there seemed to be other sounds in the room...other sounds blowing in on the sea air that flowed through the open window. Almost like a voice whispering to him. And the longer the scrimshaw spun, the faster the patterned carvings moved and the more distinctly the sea-wind voice whispered to him.

He glanced around the room. The voice was whispering his name. The name no one ever called him by.

He turned towards the fireplace. It seemed to be coming from there. From just above the fireplace where a portrait hung. A portrait of his great, great grandfather, Simon Westlake.

As he watched, the hard, cynical eyes appeared to stare out from the canvas, watching him. And now, as the painted eyes held his, the painted lips also seemed to move, and he heard a voice whisper, "Well done, my descendant and heir. You have accomplished everything perfectly. There is just one more part to be completed, and then everything—everything will be ours. Everything you've dreamed of. The power, the prestige. The Westlake family fortune, honor, and dominance—restored!"

E.F. Westlake had almost stopped breathing. The words inside his head echoed and hypnotized him.

"You can and will have everything you aspire to. You can be district attorney of the entire Commonwealth of Massachusetts, or governor or...president. You can have everything you lust for and desire!" The painted lips curled with a knowing leer. "Including the little black-haired beauty you seem so smitten with. She can be yours forever and hopelessly, helplessly in love with you and subject to your every whim."

E.F. Westlake finally drew in a ragged breath.

The voice continued. "There is just one last thing for you to complete, and then *we* will have.... Everything."

Westlake left the house and climbed into an old battered jeep next to the carriage house. And remembered the voice had said *we*.

* * * *

The Skaket Creek Inn
August 22nd, 1968
3:36 p.m.

Mick rolled the motorcycle up to the white, beach-plum-covered gate and turned off the ignition. He wiped the sweat and dust out of his eyes and gazed at the rambling two-story inn with its faded white paint and long, gray weathered porch. Had it really been just one week since he and Bridget pulled up in front of this same seaside inn? They had been laughing then. They'd been happy then. They had been...in love.

His eyes smarted. He shook his head. *No, damn it! I'm still in love. No matter what's happened or what will, I always will be.*

He eased the motorcycle onto its kickstand and gently helped Bridget off the back. He saw her deathly white face. She was so still, eyes unfocused and staring at something that only she could see. She seemed to barely be breathing. Mick pushed his long hair aside and pressed his ear to her chest. He heard a little sound like a small trapped bird trying to escape. Her heart faintly beating.

He picked her up in his arms, carried her up the front porch stairs of the Skaket Creek Inn, and kicked the door with his boot. It crashed open and banged against the wall.

A soft, amused voice from the dim interior said, "Welcome back, Mick."

* * * *

Skaket Harbor Police Department
Town Municipal Building
4:01 p.m.

"What time is it, Dougie?"

"It's four o'clock, Uncle Art."

"You got that court order ready to go?"

"Well, I called Uncle Matt this morning, and he said to meet him over at Grandpa's house at six. He said Uncle Tommy will be there and he has a foreclosure notice for the Skaket Creek Inn that he wants you to serve right along with the warrant for that bastard McCarthy kid's arrest."

Chief Arthur Frost grinned. "Perfect."

He got up from the metal desk swivel chair and walked over to the wall where his gun, handcuffs, and ammunition belt hung on a hook. "Come on, Dougie, let's mount up. It's show time."

* * * *

Skaket Creek Inn
4:09 p.m.

Kathy Dawes sat on the couch in the inn's front parlor with her arm around Bridget. Mick slumped in a faded upholstered chair trying his best not to fall asleep. Polly Dawes sat straight and upright, perched on the edge of a hard-backed wooden chair as she gently continued to coax the events of the past week from Mick.

"But how did you make it all the way from the ferry terminal in Hyannis to Skaket Creek?"

Mick shrugged. "Dumb luck? I don't know. Probably because we spent so much time pulled off the road and out of sight. I mean, poor Bridge; I had to keep pulling over so she could rest. And even with that, I don't know how she managed to stay upright on the bike all that time." He shook his head. "She is one amazing lady."

He stared at Polly Dawes and then across the room to Kathy. "Are you guys gonna be able to bring her out of this...this thing?"

Kathy glanced at her mother. Her mother nodded. "Yes, Mick. Yes, I think we can."

"Think? What is this 'think' crap? It's a question of gotta!"

Polly Dawes shook her head. "Mick, I know many of the things you've seen. The places you've been and what you've been through. So I think you know there is no such thing as certainty, or as you would say, 'gotta' in the real world. But as far as everything that Kathy and I can do, we will."

She pointed to a bookcase on the other side of the room next to the fireplace. "Mick, bring me the two books on the top shelf, the two old ones. The one bound in leather and the other that is tied with a red ribbon."

Mick retrieved the two books. He came over and put them in Polly

267

Dawes's hands. He pulled up another wooden chair and sat down next to her, and she opened the book tied with a faded red ribbon.

She motioned to her daughter who was still holding Bridget. "All right, Kathy, here are the things that we will need."

She bent her head back down and began to read.

Chapter Forty-Six

Skaket Harbor
Number 24 Frost Landing
6:56 p.m.

Samuel Frost eased his bulk down into his favorite leather wingback chair. He folded his hands over his paunch and said in a phlegmy but benign voice, "Well then, now that everyone is here, why don't you start us off, Tommy."

"Absolutely, Dad." Attorney Thomas P. Frost, the new owner of Chandler & Kramer, cleared his throat. "First of all, this has been a very productive week." He rubbed his hands together and smiled. "Yes, very productive." His smile was answered in varying degrees from the group gathered in the impressive Frost living room. He continued, "As I think you will all know by now, we have successfully completed the acquisition of the law firm that has been running interference for the Dawes for the past century."

There were a few nods, but no more smiles from around the room. But Attorney Thomas Frost smiled as he proudly announced, "However, I can assure everyone that there will be no further interference from now on. As a matter of fact," his smile widened, "under the firm's 'new management', all matters pertaining to the acquisition of the Dawes's property are going to run just as smooth as silk. Yes," he nodded at the assembled family members, "just as smooth as silk."

Samuel Frost beamed at his eldest son. "Excellent, Thomas. Excellent work indeed." He studied the faces of his family. Some were eager, some uncertain, and some frightened. "Ah, let me see. Who shall we hear from next?" His eyes lit on a small dumpy woman with mousey brown hair. He chose frightened. "Ah-ha, Gladys, the very one."

The dumpy woman who worked in the tiny Skaket Harbor Chamber of Commerce office tried to make herself fade into an amorphous brown lump, but her father's voice pierced through her reticence with a sharp, "Sit up straight, Gladys, open your mouth, and let's hear what you have to say."

"Yes...yes, Poppa. Well, what I was trying to do...."

Her father gave her a sharp look.

She sat up straighter. "I mean, what I did was to get the Skaket Creek Inn removed from all of the Cape Cod Chamber of Commerce listings. And with Helen's help," she looked over at her sister who nodded smugly, "we also got it taken off of the AAA Hotel listings as well."

Her father tossed her a rare scrap of compliment, "Well done, Gladys."

Her head bobbed up and down like an anxious marionette.

Samuel Frost hooked his thumbs into his belt loops and walked over to a tall, cadaverous looking man just slightly younger than himself. "Jonathan, is everything all set from your end?"

Samuel's younger brother, the Honorable Jonathan B. Frost, nodded slowly and said, "As long as Matthew has posted all those delinquent tax notices to the public record, this notice of foreclosure," he pulled a folded piece of paper out of his suit jacket pocket, "can be served at one minute past midnight."

Town Clerk and Assessor, Matthew Frost, popped out of his chair and nervously looked over at his father, the judge. "Ah, yes, sir. I got everything wrapped up this afternoon, Dad."

"Excellent team work, family." Samuel Frost beamed. "You see, it's like I always told you, when the family works together as a team, there is nothing that can stand in our way." He scrutinized the room and spotted his youngest son leaning against the fireplace mantel. "Well then, Arthur, I guess it all comes down to you. Are you ready to enforce the duly constituted laws and statutes of the Commonwealth of Massachusetts and the township of Skaket Harbor, bringing down the full weight of the law and order that we've so carefully crafted for the good citizens of Skaket Harbor?"

Chief of Police, Arthur Snow, chuckled. "You bet, Daddy. In fact, it'll be a damn pleasure. Right, Dougie?"

"You bet, Uncle Art! Especially with that little black-haired hippie bitch." Dougie unconsciously licked his lips.

Samuel beamed again. "Well done, my dears. I'm very proud of you all. It appears that everyone has completed his or her assigned tasks admirably, with perhaps one or two exceptions." He looked pointedly at his youngest son.

The Chief of the Skaket Harbor Police shifted his weight uncomfortably from one foot to the other.

"Perhaps, Arthur, you can explain to the family and especially your poor old doddering father, exactly why you took it upon yourself to have one of your miscreant acquaintances try to assassinate that attractive, albeit slightly scruffy, pair of young hippies?"

Samuel ensured his expression remained benign, but his eyes bored into his son's like a diamond-tipped drill. He smiled again. "But fortunately for us—and especially you, Arthur—you don't plan your murders any better than you do the affairs of the Skaket Harbor Police Department."

The back of Chief Arthur Frost's neck glowed a mottled red. After a pause, he finally looked up, took a deep breath, and said through gritted teeth, "You...you were the one that told me to call your old buddy, Bix Sullivan, in the Statehouse in Boston and arrange to get the pair of them 'mussed up' a little so's they'd back off looking for the gizmo you want."

"And what did I tell you to be careful of in relation to that...gizmo, as you so quaintly put it?"

Arthur shrugged. "Just to be careful that nothing could be traced back to us—and it can't!" he said defiantly.

Samuel snorted. "I also said to make sure that the girl, the one that Dougie seems so smitten with...," Dougie grinned, "was not to be harmed in any way."

"Well, she wasn't, Daddy."

Samuel sneered contemptuously. "Only because your five thumbed handling of the whole thing resulted in attracting the attention of the last man that we wanted to attract the attention of. At least at that time."

"Yeah, but what about you?" Didn't you tell me that *you* were going to have that drug-freak street bum—the only witness to the deal we made with those thugs that work for your pal's state-run construction company to mug those kids—taken care of? And a friend of mine on the Cambridge force told me that they found the freak in some bar in Harvard Sq. with a hot dose of pure skag sticking out of his neck."

"That's right, Arthur, and that's what you should be doing—observe and learn. And always, always keep it all in the family."

"What do you mean?" The chief's eyes narrowed.

"Do you remember your cousin Lois from Malden?"

The chief shrugged. "Vaguely."

"Well, you should. In fact, you should make it your business to maintain close contact with every member of the Frost clan. You can never tell when one of them might come in handy. Just like Lois."

He looked around, observing the equal amounts of puzzlement and interest on the faces that surrounded him.

"You see, by keeping in touch, I had also learned that poor young Lois had developed a nasty drug habit that required a minimum of $200 a day to support—which she did by prostitution and petty theft. Therefore, when I generously offered to keep her supplied with her favorite pharmaceuticals for the next six months in return for a small service...well, need I spell out the rest?" He chuckled jovially, but the doting smile switched off like a light when he turned back to his youngest son.

"But you, *you* Arthur, once you had succeeded in alerting young Westlake to our plans, your next brilliant move was...?"

The chief lowered his head again. "Well, I thought I'd make up for it by having a guy from the Winter Hill gang that I once helped out of federal beef, pop that motorcycle-riding son of a bitch for me. I mean *us*."

"And did you tell this hoodlum to be careful of the girl?"

"Yes!"

"Arthur, do remember what happened to you when you were a child and lied to me?"

In spite of himself, the Chief of the Skaket Harbor P.D. shivered.

Samuel's normally jovial voice dropped dangerously low. "Then I suggest you answer again and this time truthfully. Was it your explicit instructions or just dumb luck that kept the boy and his girlfriend from *both* getting their brains plastered all over that hayloft?"

Arthur Frost swallowed with difficulty and finally mumbled, "I guess just dumb fucking luck."

Samuel Frost's hand lashed out, and the crack snapped through the silence in the parlor as Arthur staggered backwards clutching his cheek.

Samuel took a step forward and hissed into his son's face, "Next time, Arthur, do what you're told, no more, no less. Do you understand me?"

Arthur Frost rubbed the bright red mark spreading over the left side of his face. The fingers on his right hand twitched over his holstered gun, but he swallowed hard again and said, "Yes, Daddy."

Samuel glared at him for another moment and then broke in to the huge avuncular smile that had become the personal façade that he hid behind.

"Excellent. Then it's all settled. It's taken years, my dear family, but tonight it will all pay off."

Samuel Frost stood up. "Now then, my happy little brood, let's all sit down to a nice supper, after which I believe I will take a bit of a nap, so as to be 'bright-eyed and bushy-tailed' when we leave here at eleven sharp for tonight's 'festivities' at the Skaket Creek Inn."

As the family filed into the dining room, Douglas Frost asked his grandfather, "Hey, what's for dinner, it smells good."

Samuel Frost laughed as he walked for his seat at the head of the table.

"Why fish, Dougie. Nice white, tender, helpless little fish."

* * * *

The Skaket Creek Inn
The Scrimshaw Room
7:49 p.m.

"All right, Mick," Polly Dawes said, "now you take Bridget's hand in your left hand and Kathy's hand in your right."

Mick held Bridget's cold, lifeless-feeling hand and grabbed Kathy's with his other so tightly that she gave a little wince. "Sorry," he mumbled.

Kathy gave him a slight smile and said, "Try not to worry, Mick. It's going to be all right."

She glanced over at her mother with a look that asked for confirmation, but her mother's expression was unreadable.

"Now listen to me very carefully, Mick. Now that we have joined hands you cannot let go until all parts of the ritual have been completed."

Mick looked at Polly Dawes sitting on the floor opposite him. "And just how will I know when that is?"

"Trust me, Mick, you'll know."

Mick bit the inside of his lip. He didn't like this. Not at all. It was a measure of the depth of his fear for Bridget that he had gone along with this at all. If he hadn't have been feeling guilty and desperate he would have walked out then and there, and had the two of them, mother and daughter, committed to a rubber room in some nut house.

But here he was, seated on the floor of the strange room beneath the house. The one that was filled with shelf after shelf, row after row of dusty, carved scrimshaws of all shapes and sizes.

The four of them sat cross-legged on the floor, each at one point of a compass that Polly Dawes had drawn on the wide pine planking with a piece of colored chalk. Mick sat at the point of the compass that was labeled with an N for north, with Polly at the west, Kathy at the east, and Bridget seated staring at nothing at the southern point of the compass.

Polly had a book open in front of her, the one that Mick had taken from the bookshelf upstairs and tied with a faded red ribbon.

"This is a book of South Sea Island lore, chants, prayers, and what some would call spells."

"Oh, Christ!" Mick blurted out.

Polly Dawes smiled wryly. "Yes, I rather suspected that would be your reaction. But whether you choose to believe it or not, there are things in this world, call them forces of nature, that can help or harm. The chants and incantations that have been gathered in this book help us to focus our positive energy on what some people would call white magic."

"That does it!" Mick said, starting to get up. "I'm outta here and I'm taking Bridge with me."

"No."

Mick froze. Bridget had spoken.

"Did...did you hear...?"

Polly and her daughter nodded.

"Yes, Mick, she spoke."

Still holding Bridget's hand, Mick eased back down.

Polly continued. "This book contains the accumulated wisdom, charms, and protection of the first Dawes woman to live in this house. She lived here before it became an inn almost seventy years ago. She moved into the house as a young bride just weeks after her new husband buried something underneath the house, built a room on top of it, double-timbered of solid oak. And then he sealed off the only entrance to the room so that no one could ever access the thing that he buried."

"I don't get it." Mick shook his head. "I mean, so what? What does that have to do with Bridge and whatever the hell has happened to her?"

Kathy Dawes spoke. "Mick, what is buried underneath this house and that thing that was in the grave on Nantucket are the cause of what's happened to Bridget."

Bewildered, Mick said, "I don't know what the hell you people are talking about. All I know is that you promised me that you could help Bridge." He gave Kathy a hard look. "And I don't take well to broken promises."

"And I don't take well to threats to my daughter—from anyone, Mick."

Mick matched Polly's hard stare for a moment and then let his breath out. "Okay, apologies. I'm just freakin' out over Bridge. And I gotta tell you, I'm just not into all this Twilight Zone stuff. I believe in what I can see and touch...and hold." He gave Bridget's hand a squeeze.

Polly Dawes smiled sadly at Mick. "Sometimes Kathy and I wish we didn't either." She drew in a deep breath and held up the faded diary. "But listen to what an eighteen-year-old former servant girl who was trying her best to be a good wife, mother, and a lady had to say one-hundred-and-ten years ago about her hopes, fears, and a legacy that has come down to us whether we want it or not. And I'm afraid, Mick, that you and Bridget have not only stumbled right into the middle of it, but quite unknowingly, may have unleashed a force that has been waiting for more than a century."

Chapter Forty-Seven

Number 24 Frost Landing
11 p.m.

Samuel Frost looked at his family gathered in the living room. They had all been waiting quietly and patiently, just like he had taught them, while he finished his after dinner nap. He got up slowly from the couch and stretched. "Dougie, hand me my jacket."

Douglas Frost ran to get the cream-colored suit jacket. "Here you go, Grandpa."

"Thank you, Dougie."

He looked around the room. "And so, my dear family, are we ready to go?"

Nods all around.

"Is everything in place? Are there any questions?"

Every member of the Frost family knew better than to have anything as dangerous as a question.

But Arthur Frost had an answer. "Daddy?"

Samuel Frost looked around, surprised. "Why, Arthur, do you have a question?"

"No, Daddy. But I've got some good news."

Samuel Frost raised his eyebrows. "By all means, do go on, Arthur."

"Well, Daddy, while you were having your nap, I did a little detective work."

"My, my." Samuel chuckled. "Just like a real policeman, eh, Arthur?"

Arthur Frost stiffened and forced himself to relax. *Someday, someday...and someday might be coming sooner rather than later.* He smiled. "Yeah, Daddy, just like a real cop."

He shoved the red raw feeling back down into his gut and continued.

"Anyway, I saw an APB out of Hyannis for a guy and girl on a motorcycle. So I started calling around and I just got a call back from Bill Mullins the park ranger who works over at Nickerson State Park. He says his wife—you know, she's the one who runs Bill and June's Gas and Grocery up on 6A—anyway, she says that a pair fitting those two's descriptions stopped for gas about three this afternoon. There's only one place they could be headed for."

Samuel Frost's eyes took on a predatory gleam. "Good news indeed, Arthur. So that means...."

"We've got them, Daddy, we've got them all!"

The Scrimshaw

* * * *

Skaket Creek Inn
The Scrimshaw Room
11:16 p.m.

Mick had felt his butt going to sleep more than ten minutes ago, and despite all of the strange South Sea Island or Tibetan or The Beatles frigging Indian guru chants that Kathy and her mother groaned out in a mind numbing monotone, it hadn't gotten any better.

He hadn't let go of Bridget's hand since Polly Dawes's admonition over a half hour ago. And though his rough, scarred palm was sweating more and more in the dank, humid room hidden deep beneath the Skaket Creek Inn, Bridget's hand still remained cool, dry, and lifeless in his.

Mick shifted restlessly. How damn long was this stupid game gonna go on? Were this mother/daughter tag team of A-1 wack-a-dos just gonna keep this bullshit up until his brain liquefied out of complete frigging boredom and ran out of his ears? Like the magic eight-ball in that stupid game said: Probability is high!

Damn, he knew there was lots of crap here that he didn't understand and he would do anything—anything—to bring Bridge back. But were these two just playing him for a desperate, gullible sucker? Wouldn't be the first time. No biggie, it had happened more times and more places than he cared to remember. So they could screw with his head all they wanted. Not a whole lot to mess up anyway. But when it came to Bridget...no way!

"Ohmmm...ohmmmm." The chanting had turned into a sound like a broken vacuum cleaner.

"Ohmmmm...."

Sweet suffering Jesus.

"Ohmmmm. Mick!" Kathy hissed. "Please, you need to chant too. And turn your palms upwards. And turn Bridget's up too."

Mick looked at Bridget beside him. At her pale waxy complexion, her shallow breathing, and thousand-mile stare. He started to turn her cold, fish-belly white, flaccid hands so that the lifeless-feeling palms faced upwards and....

"Fuck it! No more! Enough! This is bullshit. Kathy...you and your mother.... I'm sorry, I know you're just trying to help and I appreciate your good intentions, but Jesus. Bridge isn't getting any better—she's getting worse. And.... Well, you can screw me over, pull any kind of scam you want on me. Here!" Mick pulled the pockets of his dirty, torn jeans inside out, and the few lonely dollar bills fluttered to the floor.

276

"But you're not gonna mess with Bridge!"

He breathed out heavily through his nostrils. "So, well, thanks for the help you tried to give. But I'm taking Bridge to Cape Cod General." Mick shook his hand loose from Kathy's and in one fluid motion, pushed his legs, though numb from inactivity, into an extended upright position. And still holding on to Bridget's right hand, cradled her up into his arms.

"Mick! No! Don't! Don't break the circle!" Kathy Dawes grabbed for his right hand, but Mick pulled it away.

"Uh-uh, Kathy. Sorry, you're a nice chick and all, but I'm not buyin' it anymore—if I ever really did."

Holding Bridget's limp form, he started towards the stairs leading up to the first floor.

In a movement almost too fast for Mick's eyes to follow, he found Polly Dawes blocking the stairway.

"Mick, you can't. Please, for Bridget's sake—for your sake. For *our* sake, you must not...you *cannot* break the circle."

"Mrs. Dawes, Polly. With all due respect, ma'am, and gratitude for everything you've tried to do to help us, get the fuck out of my way or I'm gonna have to go straight through you."

"Mick...." Polly Dawes's breath now came in short, sharp gasps. "It's too late. If you leave here now, she...she'll...."

"She'll what, Mrs. Dawes?"

"She'll die, Mick."

Mick looked at her uncertainly for a moment and then shook his head.

"Like I said, ma'am, with all due respect, move out of the goddamn way or I'll move you in a way that you're not gonna like."

"I can't, Mick. Please...trust me. But if you can't...." He moved towards her. She stood up straight. Chin up, neck arched, as though offering herself for a sacrificial slaughter. "Then do what you feel you must."

Mick reached out. He hesitated. She was so frail. He didn't want to hurt her, but Bridget...nothing else mattered. "I'm sorry, Mrs. Dawes." He grabbed her shoulder in his right hand and pushed.

There was a horrible creaking sound as if ten thousand nails were being pulled from a thousand coffins. The floor of the room began to vibrate and then shake.

Polly Dawes looked back to her daughter. "It's happening, Kathy. Now they'll all be coming...all of them." She looked back at Mick. "The one-hundred-and-ten-year-old sleep is over. It's waking up."

* * * *

The Scrimshaw

Samuel Frost put his foot on the first step of the long weathered porch that ran the full length of the inn. "The next time," he said to himself more than to any member of his family, "that I set foot upon this porch, it will be mine."

He gazed down the long porch towards the waves breaking on the shore. His jaw set in a tight hard line. "In truth, this land has always been ours, since the first Frost set foot on the Cape over three hundred years ago. And it should have remained ours, if not for that jumped-up, sea-going farmer's son, Jeptha Dawes!" He gripped the porch railing and looked at his offspring shuffling nervously on the porch. "I know that you've all heard the legend that murder was done here one night a century ago." There were a few nods. "The story goes that late one night, old Jeptha Dawes shot and killed an intruder he discovered breaking into the locked room beneath this house." He stopped and looked again at the group. "But the rumors were wrong. At least part of them. The man found trying to gain access to what should have been our family's by birthright, was not killed—he was only wounded. But he lost the use of both of his legs and was forced to live the rest of his life as a cripple."

Samuel Frost stared at each one in turn before he finally said, "That man, my dear family, was your great, great Uncle Silas."

He walked up the front steps and into the front room. He glanced around as if taking a mental inventory. He nodded slowly and smiled. "Gladys," he said without turning around, "give me the book."

Gladys reached into her copious handbag and pulled out a tattered, cheaply bound, ancient diary. "Here, Poppa."

Samuel Frost took the book from her without looking back. "Arthur?" he said.

Arthur Frost opened the door behind the registration desk, and Samuel Frost led the way down into the dark heart of the house.

* * * *

The moment Mick had started to push Polly away from the stairs, his natural instincts had short-circuited his actions, and, still holding Bridget, he stepped forward to stop Polly's backward motion.

278

That was when Deputy Douglas Frost clipped the back of his head with his billy-club. Someone pulled Bridget roughly from his arms, and then a voice began speaking. The words seemed to echo through Mick's throbbing head and jumble themselves into the general confusion of his own a sense of unreality.

"Arthur, help Mrs. Dawes and her daughter up from the floor. It looks rather cold and uncomfortable down there. Besides, there is something that we will need to get. And it looks like they have been kind enough to draw some sort of a diagram exactly on the spot where you will need to rip up the boards and dig."

Polly Dawes stared back at him in horror.

"Oh, yes, Mrs. Dawes, I know all about the scrimshaw. Or should I say, scrimshaws?" He laughed. "Oh yes, it's all right here. Courtesy of your chamber-pot-scrubbing ancestor. The maid in my great grandfather's house, Mrs. Fiona McDonald Dawes."

Polly Dawes looked at the tattered book in Samuel Frost's hands. "You've got her...."

"Yes, her diary. The poor little thing was in such a rush to run off and get married that she quite forgot her most prized possession, tucked up under the eaves next to her bed. My great grandfather found it, and ever since then the family has decided that we changed our mind. We want Skaket Creek back."

He opened up the diary. "For a poorly educated little thing, she writes with a surprisingly fair hand. And more importantly, she seems to have been one of those romantic young 19th century girls who believed in confiding everything to their diary. Hmmmm, yes, makes for interesting reading, and more importantly, quite a lucid and compelling account of exactly what is buried underneath this house and why only my family will possess it."

Still holding the book, Samuel Frost crossed over to the center of the room. He peered down at the markings that Polly and her daughter had drawn.

"Fascinating. I assume that this is part of the ritual for summoning the power of the scrimshaws. But there is one thing that I do not understand. Perhaps you can enlighten me, Mrs. Dawes. How did you intend to use the powers of the scrimshaws when you possess only one of that very special pair that are reputed to bring an all-encompassing dominance when brought together?"

"What makes you think that I only have one of the scrimshaws?"

Samuel Frost clucked his tongue. "Now I believe that you are being disingenuous, Mrs. Dawes. We both know that you only have one of the scrimshaws."

"And how do we know that, Mr. Frost?"

"Because I know exactly where the other scrimshaw is, Mrs.

Dawes."

"As do I, Mr. Frost. It's on Nantucket Island, where it has been for one-hundred-and-ten years."

"Once again, your information is just slightly out of date, Mrs. Dawes. What's the matter, is your crystal ball a bit hazy tonight?"

Polly's hand went to her chest. "You...you have the other scrimshaw?"

Samuel Frost smiled again. "Well, not precisely. Not on my person, if that's what you mean."

A fraction of the tension went out of Polly's face. Samuel had been watching her carefully, and his smile grew more smug. "But let us say that I do know how I can put my hands on it in fairly short order."

"You're bluffing."

"Am I? Well then, perhaps you should call my bluff. Tell you what, you produce your scrimshaw, and I'll see if I can manage to scare up mine. Then we'll put them together and see what happens. Wouldn't you like that, Mrs. Dawes? Perhaps it could even help that vacant-eyed young lady over there." He pointed to Bridget.

"Mom! What *about* Bridget? Look at the time!" Kathy Dawes motioned to her watch. "It's almost midnight. We're running out of time!"

"Samuel, please, you've got to leave now. I know that our two families have not gotten along over the years but...."

"Ha! There's an understatement if I ever heard one, you treacherous witch!" Helen Frost Dawes spat.

"Quiet, Helen," Samuel said without turning around. "Go on, Polly."

"We...we have only a short time left to help Bridget."

Samuel Frost's eyes narrowed, and he took a step forward. "And if I let you do this, you will give me the scrimshaw?"

"I-I can't. The object is buried in a small sealed room under this one, and there is no way to get to it."

"Once again, you underestimate our resolve. That is why we brought crowbars and shovels, Mrs. Dawes."

Polly backed up until she stood directly in the center of the compass diagram that she had drawn. "I won't let you. Each generation of Dawes women has followed the instructions set down by Fiona more than a hundred years ago to keep the scrimshaws separated, isolated, and safe from anyone who would try to awaken their terrible power. People like *you*, Samuel Frost! Besides, there are still laws, and not even you would be so blatant as to force yourself and your greedy family into someone else's home and steal their property."

"Who said anything about stealing?" His hand went to his forehead in a mocking gesture of concern. "Oh dear, I must be getting forgetful in my old age. And once again, it seems that you have not kept yourself very well informed of events going on around you." He looked towards the stairwell. "Thomas, Arthur? Would you boys kindly hand your papers to Mrs. Dawes."

Thomas Frost stepped forward holding up two folded pieces of paper.

"This is a notice of foreclosure, and this one is a notice of eviction." He handed them to his brother, and Arthur Frost shoved both pieces of paper into Polly Dawes's hands.

"Mrs. Pauline Dawes, you have been duly served by an officer of the law of the township of Skaket Harbor. You have twenty-four hours to vacate the premises. You may take only your clothes and other small personal items that are not considered to be part of the property or contents of this house."

Samuel Frost looked at her. "Such a shame, dear lady. Perhaps you should have spent more time looking to the running of this business instead of puttering around with potions and spells. Quite sad really, the way you let a good business go to pot."

He stepped to one side and pointed towards the door. "Well, we don't want to keep you any longer. I suspect you'll have some packing to do."

"You can't get away with this, Frost. Even though you own most of the town and have stuffed your corrupt, contemptible family into every nook and cranny, this has got to be illegal. I'll get a court injunction and...."

Samuel put his hands behind his back and rocked back and forth on his heels for a moment. "Corrupt? Contemptible? Why, you do have a way with words, Polly, I will hand you that. But when you mentioned 'contemptible family', you obviously forgot the judicial branch." He laughed and waved towards the stairwell.

"Jonathan, Mrs. Dawes would like to know what the chances are of her getting a court injunction to stop us."

Judge Jonathan Frost folded his hands in front of him and shook his head. "I would say non-existent."

Polly Dawes bit the inside of her lip, obviously to hold back her tears.

Kathy walked up and put her arms around her mother. "It's okay, Mom. We'll think of something. But...Bridget. What about Bridget?"

Polly shook her head. "I'm sorry, Kathy, I don't think there's any way that we can help her now." She pulled gently on her daughter's hand. "C'mon, go help Mick up, and I'll guide Bridget up the stairs."

Samuel raised his hand. "Ah, but that's where your wrong, Mrs. Dawes. I never said that you couldn't help the girl. In fact, we intend to do everything possible to aid you."

"Why? What could possibly be in it for you?"

"Rather than asking questions, Mrs. Dawes, I suggest that you get busy doing whatever it is that you have to do to help that poor girl. You're running out of time."

Polly stood frozen for an instant, then whirled around and said, "Kathy, help Mick back to the compass circle and take Bridget's hand."

Kathy ran to Mick and brushed past Dougie Frost. He started to raise his nightstick, but his grandfather shook his head, and Dougie shoved the stick back into his belt.

Mick was still groggy, but Kathy got him seated upright and began chanting with her mother.

One minute passed, then two. Kathy glanced down at her watch. Mick peeked at his. Only seven minutes until midnight.

Suddenly, the lights began to flicker and then slowly dim. The room grew cold, the air damp and dank. The smell of the sea at low tide wafted in, and a low rushing noise like the pounding of surf on the distant shore.

Polly's breath again came in labored gasps. She stared at the center of the circle, and the lines on her neck stood out in stark relief as she seemed to strain every bit of concentration on the tiny point in the center of the compass circle.

Another noise cut through the sound of pounding waves. A long, drawn-out series of high-pitched squeals and clicks. The sound of a great sperm whale.

Then another sound, almost too faint to hear. A moan. A human moan.

Bridget.

* * * *

Her eyelids fluttered. Her breathing deepened, and finally she squeezed the hands on either side of her. "What...what is this place? What am I doing here?" She looked over at Kathy. "Kathy, what are you doing on Nantucket?" She turned her head the other way. "Mick! Mickey, what's happened?"

She saw his unfocused eyes and the huge red welt on the side of his head. "Mick?! Oh my God! What's happened to you?"

Without warning, her last clear memory came rushing back. The bedroom; the bruises; the horrible fight. The gravesite. Her angry words and the fight between Mick and Edward. And then something had happened. She had hit her head somehow, and there was the coffin, the horrid desiccated skull and...the scrimshaw.

282

All the memories tore at her all at once. She felt as if her head was going to explode. She dug both fists into her eyes. "Sweet Jesus, what is happening?"

"Bridget."

Bridget stared at the thin, pale woman across from her. "Who are you?"

"I'm Kathy's mother, and we have—"

"Fascinating, truly fascinating." Samuel Frost walked up to Bridget. "Welcome back, young lady. We are most happy to have you join our merry little band here tonight. I have a feeling that you are going to prove very useful." His small eyes gleamed, and he chuckled. "Yes, very useful indeed."

The smile dropped away from his face, and he called, "Arthur! Time?"

"Four minutes of twelve, Daddy."

"Dougie, Thomas, Arthur! Dig. Now!"

While Polly Dawes watched helplessly and Bridget shook her head in confusion, the three Frosts attacked the floorboards in the center of the room with crowbars and axes.

Samuel Frost watched them with obvious growing anticipation. He turned towards the small crowd behind him in the room. "Perhaps while they make their way to the prize underneath, you might be interested in another of bit of your family history."

He opened the diary again. "You see, your great, great grandmother had learned the true story of the scrimshaws from her husband, Second Mate Jeptha Dawes of the ship *Elizabeth James*. She set it all down in her diary exactly as her husband-to-be had told it to her. Now everyone around here has heard the old tales of Jeptha and the chest that he buried underneath this house, but few know what the chest really contained. In addition to the bulk of the gold that Capt. Palmer James had given to aid him in his search for the other scrimshaw, the chest below contains an object of dark, but great power.

"At first, I didn't believe it when I read this diary. But then one day I stumbled across an old ledger of my ancestor, Isaiah Frost. It was a copy of the manifest of the *Elizabeth James* in which he owned a half share. In the manifest, I found several letters written between him and one Ezra Foster, first mate on the *Elizabeth James*. It seems that this Ezra Foster had been working for my great grandfather as he suspected that Captain Palmer James was trying to cheat him. In the letter I found from Ezra Frost to my great grandfather, he stated that somewhere during the voyage on one or more of the South Sea islands upon which they landed, two objects that were purported to wield great power had come into his possession. He told my great grandfather of how he was using them to give him dominion over the captain of the

Elizabeth James and how he was making himself virtual master of the ship. Naturally, my great grandfather had an intense interest of examining these two objects and wrote back to the first mate to bring them to him the moment the ship docked in Nantucket. He promised him a thousand dollars in gold upon delivery of the items."

Samuel Frost studied the faces in the room. The room was silent except for the sound of ripping boards and the thunk of pickax against hard-packed sand and stone.

"Unfortunately, Ezra Foster never arrived with the objects. According to members of the crew whom he later questioned, no one saw Ezra Frost ever leave the Elizabeth James. But two of the crew swore that they had seen an Indian half-breed harpooner slip over the side. Captain Palmer James died that night the ship dropped anchor off Nantucket. My great grandfather also came to learn, too late, that the man to whom he had sold the ten acres surrounding Skaket Creek was the second mate who had taken the longboat and an iron-bound chest from the ship that night. Suspecting what the chest contained, my great grandfather tried to buy back Skaket Creek, but to no avail. And we have been trying to regain possession of our property for the past one-hundred-and-ten years."

Samuel Frost breathed heavily now.

The pickax struck iron.

Samuel Frost raised his hands and walked quickly over to the hole. "And now," he said slowly, "I believe we have."

Douglas Frost reached down into the hole and pulled up a heavy-looking mud-black chest about two feet square and wrapped in a rusted iron chain.

"Break it open, Dougie," the old man rasped.

Dougie raised the pick over his head and brought it down on the corroded old lock. A tremendous crack echoed as both lock and boards split open and the lid of the chest was knocked askew onto one hinge.

"Open it!"

Dougie strained. "It's...it's stuck, Grandpa."

"Arthur, get down there and help him."

The two men lifted the chest out of the hole and onto the floorboards.

They both pulled, and suddenly there was a creaking followed by a snapping sound. The lid fell back.

Samuel Frost scuttled forward. "It's true!" he breathed.

There, in the chest, resting on a mound of gold coins, was an almost perfectly preserved head, and around the severed neck was a scrimshaw on a thick black cord.

Everyone in the room stared, especially Bridget. Although this scrimshaw was similar to the one that she had seen in the grave

284

on Nantucket, there was one difference. One great and horrifying difference. This scrimshaw, with the strange carvings etched into it, was jet black.

"Ladies and gentleman, let me introduce you to, Ezra Foster, former first mate of the *Elizabeth James*."

He chuckled. "And it appears as though he told my great grandfather the truth. There were two scrimshaws, one black, one white. Each one powerful in its own right. But he swore, and this was confirmed once again in Fiona's diary, that if the two scrimshaws were brought together there was nothing—*nothing*—that the owner could not possess. Wealth, power, even...," he sighed the last words as though caressing a lover, "even youth and immortality."

"But you don't have the other scrimshaw, Samuel. Jeptha Dawes made sure that it stayed buried on Nantucket with the man who tried to steal it. And it rests there to this day where I pray it will stay until long after you have gone to your dubious reward," Polly said.

Samuel Frost shook his head and gave Polly a shark-like grin. "Once again, Polly, you're a day late and a dollar short with your comprehension of the situation. What makes you think, woman, that I would go to all this trouble were I not able to put my hands on the other scrimshaw?"

He turned around and called up the stairs, "Ezra, please come down and say hello to everyone."

Footsteps clattered on the stairs, and a tall, good-looking man entered the room.

"Friends, family, for those who may not have had the honor of meeting him, let me introduce you to our new District Attorney, Mr. E.F. Westlake. And for those who have met him and think they know him," his eyes leered at Bridget, "let me introduce him by his true name: Mr. Ezra Foster Westlake."

Chapter Forty-Eight

"You look confused, Miss Connolly." Samuel Frost laughed. "So you didn't know that Mr. E.F. Westlake here is actually descended from the illegitimate brother of Mr. Simon Westlake?" He shook his head. "As nasty a pair of double dealers and thieves as ever came down the pike. But they, and I, all had one thing in common. Simon, Ezra, even his reluctant young namesake here." Westlake looked at the floor. "We all wanted the power that the scrimshaws could give."

He looked at E.F. Westlake staring at Bridget and said, "Yes, I can see that my informants were correct, you are infatuated with this little thing, aren't you?" He turned back to Bridget with a sly smile. "And I do believe that our virtuous, young district attorney has been dabbling with the power of the white scrimshaw to turn your pretty little head, hasn't he?" He clicked his tongue. "Tish, tish, couldn't wait, could you? Didn't you know that when both scrimshaws came together, that which you could possess with its power would make this little Irish doxy look like last night's applesauce in comparison?"

He shook his head and sighed. "But that's just another reason why foolish young men shouldn't be allowed to possess things that they don't know how to use. Fortunately, for all of us, that won't be a problem."

He nodded to his two sons and grandson.

They walked over and grabbed Westlake by each arm. Arthur Frost whipped a pair of handcuffs from his belt and snapped them onto Westlake's wrists before he knew what was happening.

"What the hell is this, you double crossing—"

"Another young man who doesn't know enough about history. Even his own family's. Tisk, tisk, what is the younger generation coming to. You should have spent less time listening to the plea-bargaining caterwauling of long-haired hippies and more time learning the true relationship between your great, great grandfather and Isaiah Frost. But I'll sum it up for you in one sentence. They hated each other."

He turned away from the bewildered Westlake and walked over to where Bridget knelt, cradling Mick's head in her arms, whispering urgently to him as she tried to bring him back to consciousness.

"And now, young lady, you are going to have the opportunity to make yourself useful." He grasped her shoulder and pushed her over to the open chest. "My sources tell me that you've performed this task once before, so it shouldn't be too difficult." The old man squeezed Bridget's shoulder until she winced with pain. "Bring me the black scrimshaw."

Bridget, thought for a moment, terrified, jerked her shoulder out of

286

his grasp, reached up, and slapped Samuel Frost as hard as she could. "Take your bloody old hands off of me!"

Samuel Frost took a step backwards and rubbed his face. "I was afraid that might be your first reaction, so let me explain the consequences if you don't do what I say immediately. Arthur...?"

"Yes, Daddy."

"If this young lady has not done what I told her by the time I count to three, shoot her boyfriend and young Westlake."

"All right, ya bastard, I'll get the filthy thing, and may it bring ya nothin' but misery."

She walked over to the chest, knelt down, and gritted her teeth. She took one glimpse at the grinning, skull-like face that still had a few wisps of hair clinging to the partially mummified head. She shut her eyes tight, reached down, and lifted the scrimshaw and its cord off of the rotting stump of the neck. She pulled the slimy black cord and scrimshaw up away from the chest and then knelt and gagged as bile from her churning stomach filled her mouth.

"Quickly, Miss Connolly. We have only minutes left until midnight. Bring it here. Now!"

Bridget stumbled across the room and thrust the scrimshaw into the old man's shaking fingers. His hand closed around the object. He made a sharp, impatient motion to his son, Tommy, who ripped the white scrimshaw out of Westlake's numb fingers and placed it into his father's other hand. He held both objects up and hissed out an ecstatic, "Yes-s-s!"

"Now, let them go!"

"Go? Yes, of course, Miss Connolly. Which one?"

"What...what do you mean?"

"What do I mean? Oh dear, I don't think you were paying attention. I never said that I would let both of them go. I merely said that if you didn't get the scrimshaw I would kill them both. But I'm feeling very satisfied and consequently rather generous tonight, so I'll let you have one of them. They are both apparently madly in love with you, so you can't lose either way. So choose, Miss Connolly. Which one will it be?"

Bridget stood and shook her head in helpless horror.

"I'd advise you to make it quick, Miss Connolly, because if you haven't chosen in five seconds, Arthur will shoot them both. Now *choose!*"

Bridget gazed at Mick. Only days ago their love had seemed so strong, unbreakable. Eternal. And then everything had gone so wrong. He had struck her, called her horrible names. Perhaps somehow, in some dream-like subconscious way, she had done something to deserve those names. But if so, what little memory there was remained a jumbled, confused set of images and uncontrollable feelings, like a waking dream. But Mick's actions and her confused emotions had thrown up a wall between them. Could their love survive that?

The last memories that she'd had before waking in this strange room beneath the Skaket Inn, were of fighting and yelling. She had a vague memory of being hurt and knocked unconscious. For how long? And had Mick been there with her, by her side during that time when she must have been unconscious?

She seemed to recall a hospital room and a seemingly endless motorcycle ride spent clinging to the back of his jacket. Had Mick brought her here? And if so, why?

She glanced at the old man in front of her. His eyes gleamed with barely controlled malice. He would give the order to shoot and within the next few seconds, and if she didn't say anything, both men would be dead.

But how could she condemn one man to death?

She watched Mick. He was pale. The bruise on the side of his head was turning purple now, and a small gash had opened and was bleeding where something had struck his head. He gazed groggily back at her as if trying to focus. She could tell he was in pain. He was trying to speak, trying to form words, trying to tell her.... What? That he still loved her? But something told her that even if he didn't love her anymore, he would still do everything in his power to help her. Was that love? And if it was, was that enough to build a lifetime upon?

She looked at Westlake as another precious second ticked away. What about him? He'd told her that he loved her. That he wanted her. That he would do anything for her. But what did she feel for him? All she knew was that every time she saw him, her heart skipped and her loins tingled. She couldn't tear her eyes away. It was like some strange sort of drug. But was it love?

"Time's up, Miss Connolly."

Bridget jumped, startled out of her reverie by the harsh voice.

"Can't make up your mind, eh? Too bad. Then I guess I'll just have to make it up for you." He turned towards his youngest son. "Arthur, shoot them both."

Chief Arthur Frost cocked his .38 caliber service revolver and drew a bead on Mick for his first shot.

Without even thinking, Bridget screamed, "No!" and threw herself over his shoulders. "If you've got to shoot someone, then shoot me!" she screamed. "I don't want either of them to die, but if you're going to kill Mick, then kill me first."

"Bridget!" The cry broke from Westlake's throat like that of a wounded animal. "I would have done anything for you. Any power that I could gain would only mean something if it could be with you. And please believe me, I am so, so sorry for what I did. For how I used, or tried to use, the power of that evil talisman." He held up his handcuffed hands while trying to gesture with an imploring motion. "When I first read of the legend in my great, great grandfather's journal and what was supposed to be buried in back of the house, I laughed. But the more I read, the more a feeling of strangeness and unreality began to control my actions. Sometimes, I heard these voices in my mind." He glanced back at Bridget and, his eyes sought hers. "Yes, I know how this sounds. And maybe it's true. Maybe I am...crazy."

Bridget shook her head and said softly, "No, Edward, I don't think you are. I'm afraid that I understand just how real this can all be."

He nodded once and went on. "At first I just thought that I was becoming very intuitive. I seemed to have a way of knowing during a trial who was lying and who was telling the truth, and what the truth really was. But as time went on, the voices, or to be more precise, the voice...the voice of my great, great grandfather, Simon Westlake, began to tell me things. Things like what to do, where to go, and what I would find when I got there. That's why I just *happened* to be visiting Mick's brother, my old college roommate, that afternoon when you were attacked in the alley. And that's also why I just *happened* to open the door at the precise moment when you were in the greatest danger." He paused and turned to Bridget as if pleading with her to understand. "From the first time I saw you that afternoon, I knew there was something. Something about you, Bridget. Something that I just had to have, no matter what. And I knew then that I would do anything to get you."

He tore his eyes away and stared at the floor. "At first I thought that it was just lust. Your jet-black hair and green eyes that a man could drown in, and your body. That beautiful, perfect little body. I-I couldn't stop thinking about it. Couldn't stop fantasizing about you beside me. From that first moment I saw you in Franklin's office, I knew that somehow, someway, I needed to possess you. So when I got back to Tempest, I went straight to Simon's journal and carefully read his notes, observations, and speculations as to what the scrimshaw could do. The journal told me that although I could dig up the grave, I could not remove the scrimshaw from Zeke Tanner's remains. Only a woman who had known the true love of a man, both physically and spiritually, could do that. That was what my great, great grandfather was trying to do when his abortive attempt to coerce Fiona Dawes to remove the scrimshaw failed back in 1858. But what I did learn from the journal and from the things that Simon or someone or something, whispered into my ear, was that I could harness some of that power and use it like a form of hypnotism to gain what I wanted. And Bridget," he said in an anguished voice, "I wanted you so much."

Westlake took two halting steps forward, raising his hands still shackled by Chief Frost's handcuffs. "Bridget, I'm so sorry for what I did. For what I tried to do. I wish I could do it over again. I wish that we could meet like two normal people, just a guy and a girl, talking over a couple of drinks, and you could decide if you wanted to be with me or not, based on nothing more than just our real, natural chemistry."

Bridget watched him from where she knelt next to Mick. "Then what you're saying is that what I feel—what I have felt for you over the past week—is some sort of a spell?"

"I don't know, Bridget. I truly don't. I know what my great, great grandfather's journal said. I know what he believed and so many others. Like him!" Westlake whirled around and pointed at Samuel Frost. "You would love for this whole twisted fantasy tale of power and control to be true, wouldn't you? You would love to have an eternity to browbeat and dominate others. Yes, I can see it."

Samuel Frost appeared as though he was going to speak but changed his mind. His eyes narrowed as he watched Westlake intently.

"But despite all of your plans, your lying plot to get me here with promises of partnerships in wealth and power, it's all smoke and mirrors. Do you know what the really funny thing is?" He laughed. "You really didn't have to make up anything at all. My delusions and imaginary voices had already done your work before you'd even called me. It was they that persuaded me to come, not you. So I've delivered this worthless trinket to you and probably forfeited my life for absolutely nothing." He stared at the floor and whispered, "Except to be able to see Bridget one last time."

"What did you mean by smoke and mirrors?" Samuel asked.

Westlake laughed bitterly. "I mean, Frost, that it's bullshit, all of it. Is that plain enough for you?"

"So now you don't believe in what you've just admitted that you used to seduce this little black-haired piece of baggage?"

Westlake shook his head. "No, I don't believe it. Yes, I used something. I used what I found in Simon's journal and I think at the beginning he likewise knew that the scrimshaws had no real power. You see, during his travels in Europe and later the Orient, he had met many stage magicians and became a patron and devotee of the new art of mesmerism. Simon gleaned much from them and when he returned to this country he began to practice what he had learned. And because of the intense business rivalry that he had with your ancestor, Isaiah Frost, when his half-brother, Ezra Foster, told him about the scrimshaws, he somehow sculpted myth and science together into one package that used the scrimshaws as the focal point. The same way that I did after reading the journal."

"So you're saying then, that what you did, how you affected me, how you made me feel about you...it was all just hypnotism?" Bridget asked.

"I-I'm not sure, Bridget, but yes, I think so. I think that in some way by focusing on and accepting the story of the scrimshaws, I was basically able to hypnotize myself...and you too."

As Bridget stared back at Westlake in growing confusion, she felt Mick stir in her arms. He moaned and shook his head, struggled to sit up straight.

"Jesus, who the hell hit me?" He put his hand to the side of his head, gave a gasp of pain. His eyelids fluttered, and his eyeballs rolled back.

Bridget caught him and cradled his head before he could fall over. "Hush. Sshhh," she whispered. "It's all right, darlin'." She pulled his head down to her chest and, still kneeling, turned back to Westlake. "Please...Edward—or Ezra or...no, not Ezra, you are Edward. Then tell me, before Mick wakes up again, those feelings, those memories of...of me doing...things." She blushed but looked at him with a fierce determination. "Were they all just hypnotism, mesmerism as well? Just something planted into my memory. Something...that never really happened?"

* * * *

Westlake knew why she'd asked the question. It was because whatever Frost decided to do, she had made her choice. He drank in the soft lines of her high cheek bones and every curve of her body. God, how he still wanted her, but now not just physically. Now he would gladly give what might be the few remaining moments of his life to trade places with Mick and to have his head resting on her breast. And to have her voice whispering in his ear in her soft lilting tone, "Hush, darlin', it's all right."

"Daddy, it's midnight. What you want me to do?"

"Thank you, Arthur. I have to admit, that I myself was becoming... mesmerized by this little soap opera being played out in front of us."

His eyes hardened. "But now it's time to bring all of this guilty, self flagellating confession to a close. You can believe anything you want, Westlake, since you won't have very long to believe it. I understand the use of power and how to wield the tools that focus it."

He motioned to his oldest son, Tommy, and his grandson, Dougie. "Throw him down in that hole and toss that little vixen's boyfriend in on top of him."

"Are we gonna kill 'em, Grandpa?"

"Yes, that's the general idea, Dougie."

"Can I shoot 'em, Grandpa?"

"Mmmm, actually no. I think that in this case we should respect

291

tradition and take our cue from the origins of the scrimshaws. There is a passage in Ezra Foster's letters that speaks of a blood sacrifice. So in the spirit of trying to keep things authentic, why don't you grab that ax, Dougie."

"Samuel, are you sure about this?" Jonathan asked.

"Tish, tish, don't be such a worry wart, Jonathan. Dougie won't get any blood on your judicial robes. Will you, Dougie?"

"Ah, no, Grandpa, I'll be real careful. I promise."

"Good boy, Dougie. I often wish that the rest of my offspring could be as considerate as you. And don't you worry, boy, old Grandpa Frost will see that you're well rewarded for this."

Douglas Frost pushed Westlake towards the hole. "Thanks, Grandpa."

He thought for a moment, and then his eyes glistened with malicious glee. "Hey, Grandpa, I know what I want."

"What's that, Dougie?"

Douglas Frost spun around and pointed a dirty finger at Bridget. He licked his lips. "Her."

Samuel Frost broke to a bubbling, coughing laugh. "Dougie, you are a rascal. Certainly, she's yours."

Douglas Frost broke into a wide-toothed grin.

"And the best part of all, Dougie, is that this time you don't even have to be careful." He clucked his tongue. "Not that you ever have been—especially with that Randolph girl." The elder Frost shook his head. "You know, it's a lucky thing that your Uncle Arthur came up with the inspired plan to pin her death on our rather impulsive young friend here." He pointed to Mick while Bridget's frightened eyes showed her struggle to grasp the horror of that implication.

"Yes, it actually worked out perfectly as the final nail in the Dawes coffin and the long but ultimately successful quest to drive this inn into bankruptcy and disgrace or eliminate anyone who would be willing to help them." He bowed slightly in Mick's direction. "Yes, Dougie, your unfortunate late night tryst with the unwilling Randolph girl after our young friend here passed out, actually turned out to be a blessing in disguise. When news of the murder spread, thanks to our own dear Gladys," the dumpy middle-aged woman simpered, "all of the remaining reservations were cancelled, leaving the Skaket Creek Inn unable to meet yet another mortgage payment, which leads us up to tonight."

He turned back towards Dougie, who stared at Bridget's small, firm breasts under her sweater. "So yes, Dougie, you can have all the fun you want with your new little 'dolly' tonight—even if your 'fun' may leave your play-toy 'broken' in the morning." He laughed like some jovial, sadistic Santa Claus.

Dougie reached for Bridget.

"*After* you finish your job."

Westlake seethed.

A momentary frown crossed Dougie's face, but he reluctantly moved his hands away from Bridget and fastened them on Mick's T-shirt. He dragged Mick to his knees as Bridget screamed, "No!" He bent down to put his shoulder under Mick's chest.

* * * *

Suddenly, Mick lashed out with both hands, grabbed Dougie's right foot, and pulled. Dougie went down—hard.

Mick shook his head to clear the last of the fog that drifted through his throbbing head. He gritted his teeth, steadied his breathing, and rolled into a crouch, ready to launch himself at the stunned figure.

A deafening report echoed through the closed room, and a bullet burned across the top of his hand.

The smell of sulfur and cordite drifted through the room as Chief Frost cocked the gun and rotated the next chamber under the hammer.

"So you were playing possum all the time, eh, hot shot?" He walked over and pulled Dougie up off the floor. "Go get that ax and get to work. And you, bright boy, get down in that hole next to Westlake and get ready to make like a," he chuckled, "a Thanksgiving turkey."

"Fuck you, Frost," Mick snarled. "I'd rather take a bullet trying to kill you than sit here and let your idiot nephew chop my brains out with an ax." Mick stood up.

Frost swung the barrel of his gun until it pointed directly at Bridget's head less than four feet away.

"Your choice, tough guy. You can take what's coming to you, or watch your girlfriend take one in the head first."

Mick froze. "Bastard," he hissed.

Douglas Frost came up behind him and pushed him abruptly so that he stumbled into the hole. Westlake moved quickly to break Mick's fall with his shoulder.

"Now finish 'em, Dougie, so we can all go home and get some rest for Christ's sake."

Bridget screamed and tried to run to Mick, but Tommy Frost moved quickly and pinned her arms behind her back.

Dougie raised the ax.

A vibration swept through the room along with a background rumble that Mick realized he'd been hearing for the last few minutes.

Helen looked around to see where the strange noise was coming from.

"There, Father! It's her! That witch! She's up to something."

They all turned.

Polly Dawes stood beside the gaping hole in the middle of the room. She seemed somehow taller, much taller. She stared at the far wall—the wall facing the sea, both of her arms outstretched, her palms facing upward with her thumb and second finger forming a circle.

The sound grew louder. Soon it became like the rumbling of the sea, then like angry waves smashing against a rocky shoreline growing louder and louder all the time. Mick shot a glance up from the hole at everyone in the room growing uncomfortable. It started as a pressure in the ears, like diving too far under water. The pressure grew, becoming more and more painful. Mick felt as if his ear drums were going to burst.

Helen Dawes pushed her hands against her ears and screamed, "Stop! Someone stop her!"

Thomas Frost, Attorney at Law, took two steps towards Polly and doubled over, clutched his stomach, and vomited on the floor. He continued to vomit until there was nothing left and blood gushed from his mouth.

Jonathan Frost motioned to his son Matthew who, as usual, had been lurking back in the shadows. He pointed to the wall behind Polly. Matt nodded and began slowly working his way behind Polly. As he rubbed his sweaty palms on his pants, preparing for the lunge that would throw her into the hole, Kathy Dawes stepped from behind her mother and grabbed Matthew Frost by his shoulders with both hands.

It was as though he'd been hit with an electric cattle prod. He lost all control of his muscles and motor functions. He couldn't even scream. He crumpled to the floor; his bowels voided, and saliva poured from his mouth. He lay on the floor gasping for air like a dying fish as the motion of his lungs stuttered and then completely shut down.

Jonathan Frost gave a gasp of astonishment and ran towards his son. Halfway there, his legs crumbled underneath him. He stumbled and reached out his arms to break his fall, but the muscles refused to respond. He crashed face first onto the floor and lay still.

Visibly stunned, Samuel Frost tried to speak, but nothing came out. Finally, he managed to croak out, "Shoot, Arthur! For God's sake, shoot!"

Arthur Frost swung the barrel of the gun around towards Polly, but before he could even sight, he screamed in pain. His trigger finger spasmed, and the shot went wild.

However, although it missed the thin chest of Polly Dawes, the intended target, the .38 slug cut across her shoulder muscle. She gasped with pain, and her concentration wavered and broke.

Mick swallowed, feeling helpless inside the hole.

Arthur Frost straightened up. With shaking fingers he tried to re-sight the gun and screamed, "Now, Dougie! Get her! Use the ax!"

Douglas Frost scrambled out of the hole, raising the ax above Polly's head. Westlake scrabbled out of the hole and tackled him from behind. Westlake slammed his fist down on the back of Dougie's right arm, and the ax clattered to the floor. Mick scrambled out behind him as Westlake yelled, "Mick, make sure Bridget's okay."

Mick hesitated for a moment and then ran around the other side of the hole, grabbed Bridget, and held her tight. She hugged him back fiercely, and he said, "Get up the stairs, quick. Take Kathy with you. I'll deal with these bastards."

Bridget glanced over to where Kathy was supporting her mother. The blood ran freely from the long gash Polly had received from the bullet. Her already pallid complexion was a turning a deathly bone-white.

"Shoot again, Arthur!" Samuel Frost pointed a shaking a finger at Polly and screamed, "Shoot her, damn you!"

Polly Dawes straightened. She smiled at her daughter. "Kathy, go. It's time."

"No, Mom. I can't. You're hurt...your shoulder."

Polly just smiled. Kathy's eyes traveled to her mother's shoulder and then widened with amazement. The bleeding had stopped. She wiped her mother's blood away with her hand. The wound was gone.

"It's all right, Kathy. Do you remember how you always asked me when it would be your time? And what did I tell you?"

"You told me that I would know."

"And now you do. It's time. Goodbye, Kathy. I love you."

"Mom...!" She studied her mother's face, and realization showed on her own. Yes, she was right. It was time. She choked back tears and said hoarsely, "I love you too, Mom."

Kathy hugged her once, then turned and ran for the door. She stopped and took both Mick and Bridget by the hand. "C'mon, guys. Quick. Up the stairs. Now!"

"But what about your mother, Kathy?" Mick started to move towards Polly Dawes, but Kathy grabbed his arm and pulled him back. "No, Mick, it's time."

"Shoot them, Arthur!" Samuel Frost's smug, self-assured voice had become hysterical. "Shoot them all, damn you!"

Arthur Frost raised his gun once more, but the room shook violently. A floorboard sprang up as the nails holding it to the old, hand-hewn beams popped and gave way. It smacked into his leg, and he screamed, stumbling back against the wall.

All across the room the boards cracked and buckled. The dirt and the sand boiled and bubbled out of the hole like thick, popping oatmeal.

Dougie Frost lashed out with one hand, trying to grab Polly's ankle, but Westlake smashed the hand down and pinned it behind Dougie's back.

"Go on, Mick, get Bridget out of here. I'll hold on to this weasel."

Mick looked at the room shaking and buckling around them. He looked at Polly Dawes, her arms outstretched facing towards the wall nearest the sea, and for a moment it almost appeared as though the wall had dissolved and they were staring out at the ocean. He could feel the salt spray, and her hair...her hair flowed back as if blown by a strong ocean wind. She turned to them. She smiled. She said one word. "Go."

Mick pushed the door open and nudged Bridget into the stairwell and up the stairs as the sound of sea, breaking boards, screeching nails, and a very faint, far off sound of a great sperm whale echoed behind them.

* * * *

Douglas Frost, small town bully with a badge, screamed like a frightened schoolgirl. He twisted out of Westlake's grip and ran bellowing hysterically towards the door, shouldering aside his uncle and grandfather in his terrified need to escape.

Polly Dawes smiled after them then turned her gaze upon Samuel Frost. "And now, Samuel, it truly is...time."

Samuel Frost, head of the family that had dominated the small seaside town for five generations, for the first time in his smug, self-satisfied life, stood rooted with true helpless terror. His knees shook violently as he muttered, "No, no," over and over again.

The air in the room seemed to almost solidify with the overpowering smell of ocean and seaweed. He felt his internal organs being shaken into jelly. The flesh on his hands began to crack and peel back. He screamed and ran for the door, but someone got there before him—his son, Arthur Frost.

"Arthur, get out of my way. No, wait, you must help me. Yes, help me make it up the stairs. Quickly, you idiot, I'm dying. She...she does have the power. She's killing me!"

Arthur Frost looked into his father's eyes with a triumphant smile. "Go to Hell, Daddy." He stepped through the door and pulled it shut behind him.

Polly Dawes held out her hand to Ezra Foster Westlake. He got up and stood beside her. She leaned up and kissed him on the cheek. "Thank you," she said softly. "Now all is truly well. The evil that has been lurking for one-hundred-and-ten years, poisoning one family, corrupting another, and sentencing still another to generations of waiting and watching, will be finally ended. Now!"

She reached out both of her hands, and he took them in his. A brilliant white light glowed stronger and stronger until it infused them both and filled the room. There was a sound as if a thousand sea gales had converged upon one spot all at once.

Then a flash.

And then...silence.

Chapter Forty-Nine

In Front of the Skaket Creek Inn
August 23rd, 1968
12:21 a.m.

"Mickey, help her."

Mick looked to where Bridget was pointing. He slowly pulled his arm from her shoulders and took a deep breath. He swayed unsteadily and wasn't quite sure if he had been holding Bridget up, or if she had been propping him up. But he did see that the pale, auburn-haired girl in front of them was about to collapse.

He took two steps forward, and sure enough, just as he reached Kathy, her knees gave way. He widened his stance and braced himself as she collapsed in front of him. Before she could hit the ground, he swept up her legs with his right arm while supporting her thin back and shoulders with his left. He was almost thrown off balance, expecting more of a weight. She seemed to weigh no more than a child of ten. And although she wasn't a large girl, she felt insubstantial in his arms. More like a Will-o'-the-wisp or some phantom sprite.

He set her down on the weathered gray steps of the inn's front porch and moved back towards Bridget. She was looking at the moon. Silver drops of moonlight ran over her face and rippled across high cheekbones as a cloud passed quickly over the moon's reflection. God, he loved her so much. No matter what happened and no matter what ever would, he could never stop.

"Bridget." The last syllable caught in his throat.

She turned to him. Her eyes gleamed a dark sea green in the moonlight.

He wanted to throw himself on his knees, kiss each of her fingertips slowly, and tell her that the only thing that he wanted was to take back what he'd said. Take back the childish, jealous, insane act of striking her. Take out his folding buck knife and chop off the guilty right hand if she would just forgive him. She stood quietly watching him.

Her sweet little pixie features solemnly faced him, her round, innocent-old eyes that had tasted a thousand disappointments and yet held out the eternal hope for just one more chance.

That was all he wanted.

"Bridget. Those things I said, those things I did. I can never make up for them, but if you still love me or can even try to, I swear to God that I'll bust a gut doing everything I can to make it up to you."

She studied him, her face still somber and thoughtful. Finally, she answered. "The only way we can be hurt is if we love. But if there weren't any pain then your existence would be nothing but numbness."

She put her arms around him. "I'd rather feel the pain—and the love—with you."

"Jesus Christ, give it a rest! This is where I came the fuck in!"

They both turned in unison and saw in an instant, with sickening recognition, the disheveled, bloated figure of Chief Arthur Frost. His formerly ostentatious, self-designed uniform was filthy and torn with his purchased medals for marksmanship and "achievement" hanging askew from his ripped left-hand pocket. His shirttail dangled down the right side of his pants. His hair stuck out straight like a frightened hedgehog's spikes, and lines of dirt and sweat streaked his face. But his eyes still shone with vindictive malice.

He drew his gun.

"It's past midnight, McCarthy. Your week is up, and your skinny, punk ass is mine." He wiped the sweat out of his eyes. "You think you've won? You think you've beaten me, you little shit? You think the Frosts are through in this town? Guess again. I've got everything I want now. The family's land, houses, money, businesses—they're all mine. The whole frigging shooting match, and there's no grasping, controlling old man to tell me what to do anymore. So the first thing that I'm gonna do in my new capacity as Chief of Police, first selectman, judge, jury, and executioner in this crummy little town, will be to arrest you!"

He glared at Mick, and his lips pulled back from his teeth like a chimpanzee.

"And the more that I think about it, the longer I think it's gonna take your case to come to trial. And every time that sassy little girlfriend of yours wants to see you," he leered at Bridget, "it's gonna cost her. Hmmmm, let's see, I think ten—no make that twenty—minutes alone in the interrogation room with Dougie."

Mick lurched forward but froze at the sound of Frost's .38 being cocked as he swung at the barrel towards Bridget.

"That's right, hot shot, you don't want this pretty Miss to get her brains splattered all over the front porch now, do you?" He laughed. "I know that Dougie sure as hell doesn't. At least not until he's had a chance to put her through her paces." His laugh died away and slowly turned into a snarl. "And I'm also gonna enjoy calling your old man and telling that ball-kicking, sucker-punching son of a bitch just what I'm gonna be doing to his smart ass kid and bitch girlfriend. Yeah, I'm gonna enjoy telling him that he can take his two-bit detective badge and shove it up his—"

"Why wait? All you've gotta do is turn around, you fat, inbred, gutless piece of crap, and you can tell Michael Francis McCarthy to his face."

Frost spun around. Former Boston cop, Big Mike McCarthy, stepped out from the shadows.

Frost choked out, "You...!" and raised his revolver.

"Oh, good." Big Mike smiled. "It's been almost two months since I shot a guy and I'm due for a little practice."

The barrel of Frost's gun wavered.

"Come on, Frost. It's all nice and cocked. All you've gotta do is squeeze the trigger."

Sweat dripped in Arthur Frost's eyes, but he didn't dare wipe it away.

"Shall I turn my back?" Big Mike said mockingly. "From what I hear, shooting unarmed suspects in the back is one of your favorite ways of upholding the law in Skaket Harbor."

Chief Frost tried to look menacing, but his lower lip trembled. "Dougie!" He shouted hoarsely. "Take him, Dougie." There was no answer. "Goddamn it, Dougie," he shouted, "you better fuckin' answer me!"

"Well," said a voice emerging from the small growth of scrub pines to the left of the inn, "since you put it so nicely...Dougie, be a good boy and answer your uncle."

There was the noise of a scuffle and a sound like a walnut cracking, then, "Owww! Ah, shit! Ah, crap, you broke my fuckin' nose, you bastard!"

A tough-looking kid with wiry red hair wearing a faded black leather jacket pushed a moaning, sniveling Douglas Frost across the lawn towards the front porch.

"Kevin!" Mick said.

"Hey, Cuz, how's it hangin', man?"

Mick hooked his thumbs into his belt and shook his head in amazement. "Do I even want to ask the sixy-four-thousand dollar question?"

"What's that, Cuz?" Kevin McCarthy asked with amusement as he watched the blubbering figure slouched in front of him.

"What the hell are you doing here?"

"Well, at the moment, I'd say that me and yer old man are saving your sorry butt...again."

Mick walked over and slapped his cousin, Kevin, from the sprawling, brawling McCarthys of South Boston clan, on the back. And although Kevin, and Danny, his other McCarthy cousin, seemed somewhat like a pair of loose marbles, perpetually rolling with no apparent plan or concern from one side of the law to the other, they'd always been there to back him up in a bar fight or a game of life and death. Like tonight.

Mick grinned and slapped his cousin's leather-covered shoulder again. "Like I always said, Kevy, you are just one 'wicked pissa' kid."

Kevin laughed at Mick's deliberate slip back into the banter and Southie slang of their boyhood hangouts. "Hey, isn't that what I always told you?" He stretched his arms over his head, scratched his belly and yawned. "Anyway, when Uncle Mike told me he was thinking of taking a ride down the Cape 'cause these two jerk-offs were gonna try to hustle his kid into custody tonight...well, I just decided to tag along for the ride. And ya know, Mick, I'll tell ya one thing about Uncle Mike."

"Yeah, what's that, Kevy?"

Mick's car-stealing cousin from South Boston winked at him. "He sure does know how to show me a good time. Right, Dougie?"

Kevin prodded the still sobbing Dougie with his foot, but he just slumped to his knees and curled up in a ball, holding his bleeding nose and moaning.

"Well," Big Mike said, "as pleasant as all of this is, Frost, my gun hand is getting tired. So if you don't mind, please make your move so I can shoot you and go have a beer with Bridget and my son."

The Skaket Harbor Chief of Police looked at Michael McCarthy for a few moments, bent over, and laid his gun on the ground.

"Oh, well." Big Mike sighed. "You can't have everything."

Big Mike turned towards Mick and Bridget.

Frost began to straighten up and suddenly reached under his right pant leg and yanked out a small .25 caliber Beretta.

Mick had barely enough time to blurt out, "Pop!" before Big Mike glanced over his shoulder and shot Frost in the foot. He fell to the ground cursing and screaming.

Big Mike looked at him. "Stay down if you know what's good for you."

"Yeah, real tough guy with a gun, aren't you, McCarthy! But if your kid wasn't always hiding behind you, I'd have had his chicken-shit ass in my jail a week ago, and his slutty girlfriend would be banging Dougie every night just for the hell of it!"

Mick broke away from Bridget, took three running steps towards Frost, and leaned down, screaming, "Get up, you fat, perverted son of a bitch! You and me are gonna go at it here and now—knives, fist, guns—until one of us is dead!"

"Oh sure," Frost sneered. "I kill you, and then your old man puts one in my head."

"I think that's a fair assumption," Big Mike said softly. He walked over to Mick and put his hand on his shoulder. "C'mon, Mickey, let it go. He's not worth it."

"No, Pop, I can't let it go. And I can't let him go either—not with what he's done." And Mick told him.

Big Mike listened, staring at Frost as Mick related the events of the past few days, leading up to the nightmare of the last two hours.

Finished, Mick turned back towards Frost and said, "Now you know why I just can't leave it. It's not just about revenge. You know as well as I do, Pop, that the Frost name still holds a lot of power down here and that somehow this scumbag and his weasel nephew will manage to wiggle out of all of this."

Big Mike looked at his son, then at Frost. He rubbed the back of his hand over his cheek. "You might be right at that, Mickey."

"Thanks, Pop." Mick took a step towards Frost. "I knew you'd understand."

"Mickey! No!" Bridget ran up to him. "Please. Not now. Not after all we've gone through to find each other again."

"Bridge, I've gotta. After what he did I can't...I can't just let him go. I'd never be able to look at myself in the mirror again."

"And what would there be left for me to look at if you weren't there?"

Mick clenched his fists. "Bridge, I-I've gotta do something."

Big Mike held up his hand. "Maybe. But maybe there's a better way."

He glanced over at Frost. He'd struggled to his feet and now stared at his gun on the ground and muttered curses. Big Mike watched Dougie Frost rolling on the ground holding his nose and moaning.

"I tell you what, boyos, I'm gonna give you a better chance than you gave Bridget and my son tonight. Your family decided to play with them before killing them. You gave Bridget a choice of which man she would have to see being executed in front of her. But they wouldn't play your little game. They each offered up their life for the other. That's called love." Big Mike smiled coldly. "So let's find out if there's anything left in your twisted family that even approaches that concept."

Mike walked over and kicked Frost's service revolver into the middle of the lawn.

"Frost, you and your nephew are both about ten feet from your .38. When I count to three you can both go for it." Big Mike examined both of their faces as what he'd said began to register, and a feral, calculating gleam narrowed each pair of eyes.

"So there it is. One gun, six bullets. The winner goes to trial, the loser goes to the morgue."

Dougie scrambled to his feet as Mike began to count. "One, two...."

Both Frosts dove for the gun. They rolled in the sparse, sandy grass. Chief Frost reached out with both hands and pulled the gun by the barrel and butt towards him. Dougie Frost bit his uncle's arm, and when his right hand whipped back, Dougie squeezed the trigger and shot him in the stomach.

Arthur Frost screamed as the .38 caliber slug twisted and tumbled and buried itself in his large intestine. "You miserable little bastard," he choked out.

Douglas Frost struggled to pry his uncle's fingers away from the gun. "You're old, all used up. I'm young. I deserve to...."

A muffled report sounded as the gun went off and a bullet tore through Dougie Frost's groin. A high-pitched scream filled the night sky then slowly faded as the younger Frost's eyes glazed over and rolled upwards.

Arthur Frost briefly flashed a gritted-toothed grin until a searing pain ripped through his abdomen. He coughed up blood, shuddered, and was still.

Big Mike turned without looking back, walked up to the porch, and took both of Bridget's small hands in his own. "Are you all right then, darlin'? Has this knucklehead been treating you okay?"

Mick walked up to his father and punched him lightly on the shoulder. "No, Pop, the knuckle head has been making the usual jerk out of himself."

Big Mike grinned at Bridget. "Well, I hope you can forgive him, darlin', or if you'd like to think about it for a few minutes, Kevy and I can take him around back and beat some sense into him while you're making up your mind."

Bridget stood up on tiptoes, kissed Big Mike on his scarred, weathered cheek, and smiled. "No, Mr. McCarthy, I think I—no, I know—I love him too much for that."

Mick picked her up in his arms and crushed her lips with a kiss that he hoped would never end.

Epilogue

The sun was just beginning to take on an orange, reddish hue as it began its descent over the waters of Cape Cod Bay.

Mick and Bridget rested close to one another and watched. They didn't say anything, they just watched. Mick, with his right arm around Bridget's shoulders, her head on his chest, her left ear over his heart, where she could hear it beating. They lay in the slowly cooling sand— in the same place that they had been ever since they'd returned with Kathy in her sailboat from the middle of the bay.

Kathy had come to them in the late morning and asked if they would help carry out what she felt was the final thing that her mother wanted her to do.

In the small hours of the morning, after the vicious pair of Frosts, who ran the tiny Skaket Harbor Police Department like their own private Gestapo, had bled out their last drop of spite and malice, Big Mike had called some of his old buddies in the state police barracks down in Barnstable. By the time the ambulances had come and the forensic boys had picked up what little evidence there was, they'd all made their way back down to the room underneath the house.

Everything had been dark and cold. The lights didn't work. Every bulb had been shattered in its socket. All of the floorboards were warped and uneven, and loose nails made clattering sounds with every step they took across the floor. Once beside the hole in the center of the room, they found the sandy dirt underneath the splintered boards wet and soggy with seawater. In fact, the entire room was wet. The walls and ceiling still dripped with water as if everything had been at the bottom of the ocean.

The boys from the lab had wrapped up the Frost clan in body bags. The county medical examiner had conferred with Big Mike in a corner. There had been a lot of very intense conversation, shaking of heads, and gesturing of hands at the strange scene around them.

As they had exited the uncomfortable room, Big Mike shook his head and whispered, "Well, I guess we're gonna see how much juice I've still got with the Staties and the ME down in Barnstable. If he buys this whole thing he's gonna find a big bottle of Bushmills in his stockin' next Christmas morning."

But in the end, apparently Big Mike still did have plenty of juice left in Barnstable, because when they woke up late the next morning, he greeted them all with a big smile. "I just heard from the ME, and he says you're all in the clear. It seems that all of the Frosts died of massive internal hemorrhaging, causes unknown."

He turned to Kathy. "He also told me they were releasing the bodies of your mother and Westlake. They both seemed to have died quite naturally, as if in their sleep."

"Thank you," Kathy whispered. "I'm going to bury my mother in the little plot above the creek, facing the sea." She looked thoughtful. "And I think if no one objects, I will bury Mr. Westlake there as well. I think that he and my mother would have liked that."

After Big Mike and Mick's cousin, Kevin, left for the drive back up to Boston, Kathy had said, "I know that I have no right to ask you guys to do anything else, but if you could, I'd really appreciate it if you could help me with one last thing."

That's when she told them that her mother came to her in her sleep last night and told her that she must put the chest and the scrimshaws somewhere where they could never be used by anyone again. And she had told her where.

It had taken most of the afternoon, but the three of them had finally managed to tack Kathy's small seventeen-foot Day Sailor out into the middle of Cape Cod Bay.

"What do you think, Kathy?" Mick yelled over the sound of wind and waves. "Is this far enough?"

Kathy looked around. "Yes." She nodded to Mick, and he dropped the main sail and let go of the jib line, leaving it to flap in the wind.

Without speaking, the three of them pushed the chest up to the starboard gunwale. A bright sun popped from behind a cloud and illuminated the brand new, chromed steel chain that now bound the old chest. A quick nod from Kathy, and it splashed over the side. They watched until it was lost to sight and settled on the bottom some twenty-five feet below the sailboat's keel.

"It's finally finished," Kathy said, and Mick pulled the main sheet taut again, and the boat began to move.

As the little sailboat caught a puff of wind and moved away, the same wind set up white-capped waves, which in turn fanned the slow but steady bay current.

* * * *

Twenty-five feet below, an old chest with verdigris-covered brass straps and a brand new, chromed steel chain, began to move. The wave-fueled current only moved the heavy chest a few inches before it began to dissipate and the chest settled once again to the bottom. But no matter, the thing in the chest could wait.

The Scrimshaw

It was very good....
At waiting.

* * * *

    The two people sitting close together on the beach continued to stare out into the bay, locked momentarily in their own private thoughts.

    Finally, Bridget said without raising her head from Mick's chest, "I had a dream last night."

    Mick didn't say anything. He just kissed the top of her head.

    "And in the dream, there was a woman. She was a tiny bit of a thing, not even as tall as me. She was dressed up in an old fashioned dress with a high collar, something from the last century. In the dream she stood next to my bed, but I wasn't afraid. She looked at me, and her eyes were full of love. Then she leaned over, kissed my cheek, and said, 'Thank you, daughter, and bless you.'" Bridget raised her head slightly. "What do you think it means, Mickey?"

    Mick shook his head. "I don't know, babe. A week ago, I would've said it was just a dream. But now, well, I just don't know."

    "Maybe I can help."

    They both sat up and looked towards the ocean. Mick shaded his eyes with his hand and saw the silhouette of a trim figure outlined against the setting sun.

    "Kathy, sit down," Bridget said, patting a spot on the sand next to her.

    Kathy shook her head. "Uh-uh. Thanks anyway, but I think you guys could use a little quiet time, alone. Besides, I've got lots to do." She dug her toes into the warm sand and continued, "And I hope you know that I like, really...I mean, I can't thank you guys enough for everything that you did for me and...Mom."

    Mick shook his head. "I wish we could've done more."

    Kathy smiled. "Well, after we got back from taking care of that chest, I decided that I really didn't ever want to see a scrimshaw again as long as I live. So what with the lawyers gone and the only copy of old Jeptha's will along with them, I gave a call to those guys down at the Peabody Whaling Museum and told them I'd take their offer for the entire scrimshaw collection. With the money from that and the gold coins that we found in the chest...," she put her hand on one side of her mouth and said in a mock conspiratorial whisper, "and by the way, when you guys go back up to your room you'll find a little souvenir on the night table. Something to use to maybe have a little fun and take a real vacation!"

    "Kathy!" Bridget said.

Kathy held up her hand. "Hey, come on, it makes me feel good."

She put a finger alongside her cheek then snapped her fingers. "But wait, you haven't heard the best part of all! With the money from all of that, I'm gonna turn the Skaket Creek Inn into a youth hostel for backpackers and kids without much money. So they'll have a cool place to crash or even hang out and maybe even do things connected with the arts. Like writing and painting and...music!"

She grinned. "I'm gonna completely remodel the Scrimshaw Pub with an entire new sound system, lighting, and name!"

"I don't blame you." Mick smiled. "Personally, if I never hear the word scrimshaw again, it'll be too freaking soon!"

"So what are ya gonna call it then?" Bridget asked.

Kathy's smile became mischievous, and she giggled. "The M&B Music Cafe!"

"Huh?" Mick said.

"Oh!" Bridget clapped her hand over her mouth.

"What, I don't get it?"

"You seldom do, you bloody, sweet fool!" Bridget smiled, kissing him on the cheek. "M&B, it stands for...Mick and Bridget!"

"Whoa! That's too cool. Having a music club named after us. Wow. That is definitely, as my cousin Kevy would say, wicked awesome."

Kathy clapped her hands together with delight. "Glad you approve, guys, and of course, you realize that you're now obligated to come down here and play on opening night. Okay?"

"Hey, you got it, Kathy." Mick nodded, nudging Bridget. "Okay with you, babe?"

Bridget nodded back. "Definitely okay."

"Well good. And now that that's settled, I'll leave you guys to watch the sunset. And just in case you get bored or something," her smile became impish again, "here's something for you to read."

She handed Bridget a letter folded neatly in half and tied with a faded red ribbon.

"I found this while I was putting away some of Mom's things. I think this is why she knew that you would be the key to helping us in putting things right again."

"Is it...?"

"Yes, it's a letter from Fiona written shortly before her death in 1919."

She put her hands in the pockets of her faded, tan Levi cut-offs. "Well, I've still got lots to do, so I'll catch you guys later. Remember," she called as she ran back up to the inn, "opening night, and bring your guitar!"

"Well, at least there's one thing around here that won't be dominated by spooks and spirits—good old Rock 'n' Roll!" Mick laughed.

Bridget rolled over and looked at him. "So then, now do ya believe that there are other things that might exist beyond your hard-headed, rational world?"

Mick smiled. "Hey, I'll take the hard-headed, but no one ever accused me of being rational."

Bridget smiled too.

Silence reigned for a moment, and then Bridget grew serious and asked in a very soft voice, "All right then, and answer me true, do you think that...." She struggled to find the words. "Do you think there was something about those scrimshaws that could have put me and poor Fiona, back there in 1858, under some sort of a spell or something? A spell making us helpless and twisting our minds to do wicked things, betraying the ones we love most?"

Mick thought for a moment before he answered. "A spell? No, I don't believe in.... Well, anyway, at least I don't think there are any such things as spells."

"Then how do you explain it?"

"Like I said, I don't believe in spells, but I do know that mesmerism, what we now call hypnotism, was first used back in the mid 19th century. We know from Simon Westlake's own journals that he was a student of mesmerism. What I think, is that he mastered the process in Europe and used it on a simple good-hearted girl from Skaket Creek."

"And me?"

"The same thing. E.F. Westlake had already read and studied his great, great grandfather's diaries, so he knew all about the process. And I think it was helped along by something else I've seen used before, but I'm sorry to say I didn't recognize it back then and I was too stupid and jealous to pick up on it this time."

"What?"

"Drugs. I think that Westlake slipped something into your beer that night at the Crown & Anchor. Some sort of drug to make you open to hypnotism and suggestion. And for all I know, his great, great grandfather could have used the same sort of thing on Fiona back in 1858."

"And the scrimshaws?"

"I think that old Simon Westlake was smart, clever, and ruthless, but I also think that he might have been just a few bricks shy of a load. I don't know if he actually believed in the power that the scrimshaws were supposed to have or if he eventually wound up sort of hypnotizing himself. But either way he was convinced that the power was real and that by breaking poor little Fiona's will, he could combine the power of the scrimshaw that she had been unwittingly exposed to with his own and use them to control her and her descendants forever. Kinda like having the beginnings of his own personal zombie army."

"Mickey! That's.... Oh, that's horrible! Do you really think he could have done it?"

Mick shook his head. "No, like his great, great grandson said at the end, no matter how old Simon may have deluded himself, it was really all smoke and mirrors. The power of suggestion. And don't take this in a bad way, sweet thing, 'cause I'm just nuts about every little thing about you, but both women who the scrimshaws were used on came from the same country. A place where they'd both been raised on wonderful, imaginative stories—but stories of the supernatural that were accepted as a very real part of the culture."

Bridget twisted her head around and squinted at Mick out of one eye. "So are you sayin' that I'm a simple, gullible fool, then?"

Mick kissed her nose. "If so, then crown me King of the Morons, 'cause I guess I worship a fool."

She sighed and put her head back down on his chest. He sensed that she had something else to say.

Finally, she said without looking at him, "Supposing that all that is true, and it was something that was just implanted in my memory, and praise God I never did, or ever would do, then what...what about the bruises," she whispered the last words, "on my breast."

A thousand thoughts ran through Mick's mind. He discarded them all and concentrated on only one—the one that said he loved her.

"Well, you know, I've been thinking about that and pretty much figured out, after I stopped being a jerk, that you were right all along."

Bridget raised her head and rested her chin on his chest. "About...?"

"About when you said it was me."

"You?"

"Yeah, just like you said that morning. You said I must have done it. And when I really think about it, I've gotta say, you're right. I mean, it makes sense and all. Hell, you know that I can never keep my hands off you for more than five minutes at a stretch."

Bridget held him very tightly. "Thank you," she whispered. "I love you, Mickey."

They didn't speak for a long time.

"Hey," Mick said, wiping his eyes and clearing his throat. "You haven't read that letter Kathy gave you."

Mick and Bridget leaned towards one another again as Bridget carefully unfolded the old letter and looked at the faded writing in a spidery, but still careful, feminine hand.

Thank you, my dear distant daughter, for
proving once and for all, that everything that Simon

*Westlake said was all lies. And that while his foul
powers could invade my dreams, they could never
make my flesh betray the love I bore my husband.
For that, I thank you, and always remember that
my blessing and love will be with you for all time.*

*My love and affection will follow you down
through the years.*

Your Devoted Fiona

Bridget looked up at Mick. "Daughter? What do you suppose she meant? And how could she possibly know me?"

"Wait," Mick said, "there's another letter underneath that one."

Bridget removed a smaller page written on flowered notepaper. "It's from Kathy's mother."

"Mickey, look." She pushed the letter over towards him.

"It's some sort of genealogy chart," Mick said, tracing his finger along family branches and old-fashioned names written in small boxes.

Mick handed it back to Bridget, and she quickly scanned the contents of Polly's letter to her.

"Kathy's mother says that she traced the family back to Fiona and discovered that Fiona gave birth to a daughter seven months after they returned from Nantucket. She says that Fiona was frantic with worry over Simon Westlake's prediction that he would control both her and the child. But when the child was born, it was a healthy, happy baby girl with a proud independent spirit and a sweet temperament. She grew up in a loving household and later got a job as a ladies' maid in a Newport mansion. While in Newport, she met a handsome young man, the captain of a schooner out of Belfast, Ireland. On his return voyage to Newport, they were married, and she moved with him to Ireland. The child's name was...Bridget."

Bridget sat bolt upright. "Bridget! And that man she married was Captain Brian McMahon, my mother's grandfather. And that means that the very same Bridget as whom I'm named after was actually...!"

"Fiona's daughter," Mick said in amazement "Phew!" He whistled and flopped back down into the sand. "Talk about coincidences."

Bridget looked at him and smiled. "So, you still don't believe in spirits then?"

Mick shrugged. "I don't know, Bridge. Maybe it's like you're always telling me: 'There's a lot more of what you don't know, McCarthy, than what you think you do.' Or maybe I should just leave it at what we read in Fiona's diary that old Jeptha told her when she asked him what he believed: If you say it's true, then it is."

Bridget squeezed his hand.

She put both arms around him and settled her head back onto his chest. He leaned back on the soft warm sand as she snuggled close to him.

"But there's one thing I do know," he whispered as his lips touched her soft, smooth cheek. "I know that come hell, high water, spooks or spirits...I'll always love you."

Her lips rose to his, and there was nothing left to say.

Author Bio

Ric Wasley grew up in the Boston area. As a college student he played music and was involved in the vibrant world of social change that was Harvard Square in the late sixties.

This later became the inspiration for his "McCarthy Family" series.

Ric has been writing for over 30 years. He has been published in several literary magazines in L.A. and San Francisco while living in California. He currently lives outside of Boston with his wife and three children, works for a major media company, and retains his love of music and writing.

Excerpt from

At My Window with a Broken Wing

by

Ric Wasley

I looked up. The sad little blonde was back holding out two large paper cups with pale thin beer.

"Come on, sugar, drink up, you'll feel better." The long legged brunette standing beside me reached for the cup in the girl's hand.

The tiny blonde held out the cup to me.

"Thank you, Debbie, I'll take care of that." Sherry snatched the cup away, and some sloshed over my shirt.

"Nice going, pea-brain!" She turned back to blonde pledge. Her mouth set in a hard line. "Tell you what, Debbie, since you can't seem to hold on to a beer, why don't you just drink the other one."

Debbie looked around. There was no one there for her. She slowly nodded and raised the paper cup to her lips.

"Wait! Every good chug-a-lug queen needs an audience. Hey everyone! Little Debbie here is going to chug a twenty ounce!"

A crowd gather around—just like at a car accident.

"Well?" Sherry arched her eyebrows. "What are you waiting for? Chug it!"

For a moment, I saw a spark of anger in Debbie's eyes, and then it was gone, like someone had blown it out. She looked at me and then closed her eyes and started to drink.

"Drink, drink, drink." Everyone chanted and hooted.

Sherry tickled me in the ribs and said, "Oh, don't take it so seriously, it's just a little hazing."

Yup, that's what it was. Just a little more hazing. One more night to get through after nine weeks of crap. Just a little more of the lighters and ice cubes and water to take and then it would all be over and cool and a big welcome with open arms to the brotherhood.

Until I stood up and smashed the guy holding the water bucket in the mouth, breaking one of his front teeth and cutting my knuckles. And *then* it was over.

"Drink, drink."

She was only halfway through. She was such a tiny little thing, there was no way she was gonna get twenty ounces down—or keep it down. I looked at Sherry. I looked at her eyes. Yeah, that was the point, wasn't it. The grand finale to this little show. Debbie puking her sad little guts out in front of everybody. Welcome to the sisterhood.

One tiny tear nestled in the corner of each of Debbie's eye as she struggled to keep the yellow liquid from running out of the corners of her mouth.

I reached out, lifted the cup out of her hands, and drank.

I finished it in a few seconds. All except for the last ounce. That I slowly poured over Sherry's expensive Bass penny loafers. I smiled and handed her the cup. She crumpled it and threw it my face, then stormed off to brighten someone else's life.

Huff looked over from where his girl *du jour* was staring at me in disbelief and shook his head. All he said was: "Wazy, Wazy."

I smiled and turned back to..."Debbie, right?"

She nodded. I think she was afraid that if she opened her mouth, all that beer was going to come rushing out.

"Feeling a little shaky?"

She nodded.

"Come on. Night air and moonlight's the best cure for that."

We sat on the back steps of the SAE house while she took deep breaths and I lit a cigarette. By the time I'd flicked the end of the cigarette into the night, she'd stopped looking green around the gills and had settled back, leaning her head against my chest. I smelled the perfume in her hair. Not dead flowers strong, but more like an open window in springtime.

After a while, she lifted her head up and smiled at me. "Thank you."

So I kissed her.